Your Feet Take You to Where Your Heart Is

Your Feet Take You to Where Your Heart Is

Cilka Zagar

Strategic Book Publishing and Rights Co.

Strategic Book Publishing & Rights Co., LLC
USA | Singapore
www.sbpra.net

For information about special discounts for bulk purchases, please contact Strategic Book Publishing and Rights Co. Special Sales, at bookorder@sbpra.net.

ISBN: 978-1-950015-75-7

Lightning Ridge opal fields

Most of my stories relate to opal mining, migrants and Aborigines.

Lightning Ridge, the world's opal capital, has miners from over fifty countries; they brought with them political and religious beliefs, traditions and memories. Gradually they blended into a unique society with a new culture, new character, new morals and ideals.

You never know who is who in Lightning Ridge, says Bill, an old opal miner. Aborigines and Europeans, doctors and illiterates, policemen and criminals camp next to each other and look for the same rainbow in the clay beneath the sandstone.

Prospectors come to Lightning Ridge in search of the elusive rainbow gem that would make them instantly rich, loved, and respected. A hope to find a Red on black opal, that is the dream Lightning Ridge opal miners live on.

Ratters are gem thieves who masquerade as prospectors, wait until a miner hits opal and then loot his mine. Ratting is the worst crime possible in the eyes of Lightning Ridge opal mining community.

Your feet take you to where your heart is

These seven stories are based on real people and events. Each story can be read separately or as one book.

The stories tell about women, who followed their adventurous men.

They also tell about opal miners who came from many countries and found their rainbow in the heart of Australian wilderness.

They tell about Aborigines integrating into the mix of nationalities.

Martina is a young Slovenian woman who came to Sydney with her Austrian husband and their children. She is one of the first Slovenian migrants.

Tina is Martina's granddaughter. For Tina's high school graduation her grandmother buys her a bus ticket to Lightning Ridge where Aborigines and opal miners of many nationalities live in apparent harmony. Tina soon learns that things are not as they seem.

Jana marries Vince, an Australian Slovenian holidaying in Slovenia. Vince promises to return to Slovenia with Jana every year but so much happens in their lives that Jana never sees her parents again. Jana becomes a Migrant-Aboriginal Liaison officer in Lightning Ridge. She enjoys solving community problems but when she retires she realises that she became powerless to solve her own.

My father is a story about Mira who does not know who her father is but she needs him during her divorce crisis. Mira finds him living with his large Aboriginal family in Lightning Ridge. Mira grew up as an only child of an English couple until her mother told her that her husband is not her real father.

Odd socks tells about Emma, a postal worker in Lightning Ridge, who lives in an abusive marriage. Michael is new in town and meets Emma when he comes to open a post office box. Emma and Michael fall in love. Emma finds comfort in this platonic relationship and writes poems about it at the back of her recipe file on the computer.

Daydreams is a story about three generations of one family going through the divorce

My Beautiful Sister is Maria's story. Maria remembers Hana as her beautiful sister. Toni, Maria's first love, married Hana. Maria married Stan and they escaped to Australia. Thirty-five years later Hana and Toni meet Maria and Stan again in dramatic circumstances.

I wish to dedicate this book to my sons Marko and Marjan. I brought them to the wilderness of Lightning Ridge and we travelled the same strange, unknown road amongst the world's adventurers.

I thank Lightning Ridge community for letting me know them and learn from and about them.

Contents

Martina 1
Tina 26
Going home 63
It is all in my head 145
Jana 155
My father 288
Odd socks 339
Daydreams 359
My beautiful sister 375

Breathes there the man, with soul so dead,
Who never to himself hath said,
This is my own, my native land!
Whose heart hath ne'er within him burn'd
As home his footsteps he hath turn'd
From wandering on a foreign strand!

—Sir Walter Scott

Martina

'We are here to celebrate the life of a man who has done great things, a man of integrity, who never wavered in his beliefs, a man who returned to his maker,' says the priest. They are trained to say nice words about the dead.

Our children and our friends also tell the funeral assembly that my husband Franc was a well-respected and dearly loved man. Well-chosen words inspire the mourners to sniff into their white handkerchiefs. The beauty of the words from the Bible makes crying almost enjoyable.

It is the fifteenth of June 1988, the beginning of winter in Australia. The afternoon is pleasantly crisp and sunny although we had the first frost in the morning.

I remember my wedding day in June 1938. It was the beginning of summer in Slovenia and the day was just as bright. I remember being overwhelmed with flowers everywhere.

'We lay his body to rest but everything that Franc was, he still is. Although he is with God now, he lives on in our hearts and in our memories. Franc made peace with his maker and received his last sacraments; he died a good death,' says the priest.

The main thing is to make your peace with God. As a child I regularly confessed that I was sincerely sorry for not praying more and for being distracted in church and sometimes being angry with my brothers and sisters. I didn't have wicked thoughts to confess yet then.

Franc and I confessed and received Holly Communion before we got married. We wanted to have a clean start to our new life. During our wedding ceremony the priest reminded us that almighty God sees our every thought and deed. During the fifty years of our marriage I often prayed to God to save me from evil thoughts. After my wedding I heard a woman say to her friend that the little bitch got her claws into Franc's money. I was the little bitch. I didn't know why people became unfriendly towards me after I married Franc. Mum said that I did the right thing.

'Here,' Teresa passes a clean tissue into my hand. In her capacity as a wife of a funeral director she often has to deal with bereavements with the same kindness and solemnity as her husband. Teresa was also a trusted employee of my husband.

I always loved the exquisite beauty of the funeral ritual. The intensity of life and death coming together, the grief and the relief washed with tears and the people joined in a web of tenderness. We are humble and pure and forgiving as we face death. God is watching.

Even as a child I was awed by death. I walked alone on the narrow paths between the graves in the local cemetery thinking of God and angels and life and ghosts. Only children can experience the wholeness of things so thoroughly.

Death is the fulfilment of everything life was. I am next in line. That's all there is. I hope to die a peaceful death. I made many novenas for that purpose. As a little girl I prayed for a happy last hour as directed by our parish priest and my mother. I confessed every Friday and received Holy Communion every day for months and months to make sure that my last hour on Earth would be happy. That is all one needs to pray for really.

Franc's friends stand close to me in their black funeral suits, their faces shining after the morning shave. The coolness of the day makes them cough occasionally and they wipe their glasses from time to time because the warm moisture of their bodies obscures the view. We are all next in line and that unites us. The invisible thread of life is leading us towards the grave.

'I will always remember his face glowing with happiness on the day he died,' whispers Teresa.

The awesome finality of death excites people. There is a rebirth in the hearts of the mourners. Smooth loveliness is spread over the funeral assembly like a veil over the bride.

'Mum and Dad had fifty happy years together,' says my daughter Martina as part of her eulogy. I drop a handful of dirt into the grave. There are fifty red roses on the coffin, one for each year of our marriage.

Franc was 86 and I am 66. In their speeches people praise Franc and express sympathy for me, the poor widow. It would be abhorrent to say that Franc's death came as a relief. Nobody would dream of admitting even in their own hearts that Franc's death was overdue because he became a cantankerous and contemptuous old man who enjoyed causing misery to people around him.

'People will always remember his generosity,' says the priest who barely knew Franc. Funeral is a celebration of person's divinity not his frailty. Nobody would dare say that Franc's greatest joy in life was to squeeze another dollar out of the person he did business with. People understand that you have to be prudent in business. Franc wasn't mean, he was prudent. To the last day of his life. Franc kept telling me that whatever he did was for the family. That was supposed to make everything right. He made me an accomplice in squeezing money out of those that were weaker than him. We learned to be grateful to Franc for keeping us wealthy despite difficult circumstances. Money helps you survive and make something out of your life. People take notice of those that made something of their lives.

'Poor people dream of being rich,' said Franc. 'They believe that all their dreams will come true if and when they win the lottery. They wait for that winning numbers all their lives. They don't know how to make their dreams come true, so they are jealous of those that do. Even God will not help you if you don't help yourself. It says in the Bible that one has to use his talents.'

Everybody seems to have moments of happiness. I wonder if all the poor really dream about the day when their bank account will be sufficiently sound. Maybe the desired winning ticket, like God himself, moves a step every step we make.

I remember Franc reciting the words he must have read somewhere:

'It's the same the whole world over
Ain't it all a blooming shame
It's the rich wot gets the pleasure
It's the poor wot gets the blame'

'I believe that people should live by the golden rule: Do unto others as you would have them do to you,' I reminded Franc.

'The real golden rule says: 'Those who have gold write the rules,' laughed Franc.

I thank God that nobody sees the thoughts that pass behind my grieving exterior.

'Whenever someone says: I don't care, they really care. When they say: Not that I am jealous, they are jealous. When people say that money means nothing to them I know that all they think about is money,' said Franc. Franc was probably right; he was an educated, experienced, older man.

'Some people dedicate their lives to the poor,' I said once trying to outsmart Franc.

'One way or another we all gather the riches. Some of us enjoy them now while others hope to get their rewards after death,' said Franc. I always believed that Franc was deeply religious although we never really talked about God. We never talked much about anything, come to think of it.

I forgot about sex long ago but these days every film announces right at the beginning that there will be explicit sex scenes, violence and coarse language. The government warns us that these ingredients may be disturbing and offensive to some and that they might choose to abstain from watching. When I am alone I enjoy crying as I watch unhappy love stories.

'Turn off that trash,' said Franc. He never liked me watching love stories or sex. He chose sport or news or war or politics or crime. He read stories about Hitler and Stalin and Napoleon. They are probably less dangerous to our moral well being than sex.

I don't mind watching sex. Occasionally one gets a knot in the stomach and a sort of a dizzy fit of desire while watching sexual activities on television. Sometimes I even have a pleasant dream after watching sexual scenes. I would never admit that to the closest of friends, of course. But then I do not have really close friends.

My doctor asked me about my sex life after my menopause. I told him that there was very little sex in our marriage for the last twenty years. He suggested that I take Valium. During the first years of our marriage Franc liked to have sex every day and I willingly participated. I was too scared to refuse Franc anything. I had my three babies to think of. I also considered myself lucky that Franc found me desirable and that he came home every day.

Recently I overheard Franc talking about sex with his friend Jack. They were drinking red wine while I cleared the dishes after dinner. The door was ajar and I heard snippets of what they said.

'It's not fair that one still thinks about it when the body can no longer respond,' said Jack.

'Sex is not everything,' said Franc.

'Actually it is,' said Jack. 'You grow up to have sex. You get married so you can have a steady supply and then you want some extra. When you can no longer have sex you think about it. I believe that you die when you stop thinking about sex.'

I thought that Jack was joking but I did not hear them laugh. Old men probably understand each other even when nobody else does. Maybe they were joking but did not bother to laugh. I was rather relieved that I still sometimes thought about sex.

Jack and Franc turned to television.

'Look at that skirt,' said Jack.

I glanced at television. It could barely be called a skirt. If it was any shorter it should be called a belt. You could see where the legs started as the girl's bottom wriggled on top of her high-heeled legs. Long strong legs, almost fat.

'I like big girls,' said Jack.

'Women,' said Franc. 'A necessary evil.' I wonder if he meant women generally or a particular woman like myself. Sometimes I felt that I was a necessary evil. I brought it all down upon our family.

'It is for the best,' mum said when I married Franc.

'The world needs another Hitler to bring back order,' said Franc to Jack.

'War and crime and violence fascinate people,' said Jack.

'The media glorifies murder. If criminals were presented as hopeless vulgar creatures they would cease to be popular,' said Franc.

'Media competes in vulgarity to escalate publicity and sales,' said Jack.

'They are too lazy to use proper language so they say fuck again and again,' agreed Franc.

'I am not going to be here long,' Franc kept saying to me. 'Everything will be yours when I am gone.'

Nobody dared upset daddy because he accumulated all this wealth which he was going to leave to us so we could live happily ever after.

If only Franc was willing to be pleased.

'Franc lived a good life and reached a good age,' says Teresa's husband.

My son Damian and my daughters Vera and Martina are happy that they reconciled with their father and that we celebrated the fiftieth anniversary of our wedding as one big happy family.

With the funeral prayers done, close friends hug me, kiss the air near my ear and tell me how very sorry they are for me. Some kisses touch my neck and others land on all sorts of places by accident in the awkward rush of sympathy and etiquette. People avoid my face because it is stained with tears. I taste the tears as I move my face this way and that to give people a chance to kiss something rather than the saltiness of my face and the bitterness of my lips. My face is respectfully left to mourn the loss of my husband. Acquaintances shake my hand and whisper their sympathies.

I last cried like this at the Christmas concert where my granddaughter Tina played an angel. She looked angelic in her wings and she reminded me of when I was young. My other grandchildren also had eyes on me as they sang and danced. I felt an intense pain of pure pleasure. There is life after death.

'How great you are, God,' I sing behind the mask of a crying face.

I don't remember ever crying because I was sad. Maybe people cry because they are sad, maybe they don't. What is sadness really? Or happiness? Or love? People make words and spend lifetimes searching for their meaning.

'Happy marriages like yours are rare these days,' says Teresa. She barely knows me. Only Franc knew me. He knew my place in the scheme of things. I was his servant and he was there to point out my mistakes. I feel alone without Franc; maybe loneliness is sadness. Maybe I am crying for Franc, maybe I am crying for myself, maybe I am crying because I am overwhelmed with the beauty of the funeral service. I am overwhelmed by emotion like I was before I met Franc. I want to frolic among the flowers like I used to when my father was alive. I want to shed my old skin. I don't want to hide under the old skin any more. Why is it that only snakes can shed the old skin? The old skin is hiding my young skin. People probably wouldn't recognise me in my young skin; they came to the funeral to comfort the poor, sad, widow in her old skin.

I got used to hiding in my old skin. Perhaps it isn't wise to let people know what is underneath. Maybe they would not like who I am. I am grateful that we all loved each other as we celebrated our 50th wedding anniversary before Franc slumped in the chair and died. We parted as a happy family. There is nothing to feel sad or guilty about. We have done the right thing and everybody can now rest in peace. RIP. To rest in peace must be the ultimate blessing. The dead seem to be under an obligation to rest in peace. That is all there is. RIP is an order. I hope Franc will rest in peace.

I was fifteen when I met Franc. I was singing through the woods on my way from school one day when my little sister rushed to tell me that our father died in a logging accident. I was the oldest of six children and I had to grow up fast. My father was working for Franc; everybody in our village more or less worked for him. Franc came to see us after my father's funeral. He had shoes made for all the children, he sent a pig, and a sack of potatoes and wheat and beans. He also brought a bag of clothes his daughters grew out of. Those clothes were much better than any new clothes we ever had. Mum told me that Franc was the most generous man. Mum often cleaned Franc's home to earn some extra for our family. Mum kissed Franc's hand when he gave her money to buy things for us children.

In the spring Franc offered to take me into service as a maid in his big house so I could help mum provide for my brothers and sisters.

'You are almost sixteen,' said mum. 'You will have a good life in the big house.'

Franc's wife was dying of tuberculosis; she has been bedridden for over a year. His three daughters were about the same age as me. I shined their shoes, washed their clothes and prepared their meals. I ironed girls' dresses, plaited their hair and cut their lunches before they left for school. Sometimes we chatted about clothes and boys and toys like we were friends. In the end, though, I was always made to understand that I was there to serve them. I felt lucky, really, because on Thursday afternoons I was free to go home and show off my new clothes and my white hands. My people worked on the land and their hands were cracked and callused and red.

There was an inside water tap in the big house and Franc had bought a big bath. Most people in the village have never seen a bath like that and the running water inside the house. I felt very lucky. I washed the bath every morning after girls left for school. Just before my sixteenth birthday Franc followed me into the bathroom. He put the finger on his lips telling me to be quiet, as his wife rested in a room next door. He grabbed for my breasts and kept squeezing them. I remember the smell of his breath as he kissed me. He pulled my pants down and pushed my legs apart. I leaned on the bath and nearly tipped over but he held my bottom to himself firmly. I only felt a little pain but the fear paralysed me. It didn't last long but Franc was breathing real hard and seemed exhausted.

'You drive me mad,' Franc smiled as he heaved himself away and buttoned his fly. He smacked my bottom in a friendly gesture before he left the bathroom.

I saw blood stains on my panties and I quickly washed the stains and myself. I stood there leaning on the wall. My stomach turned and twisted me into a knot. I retched into the bath. It was no use running away from it. The damage was done.

Franc came after me every time I was in the bathroom and the girls were at school.

Franc's wife died a month later and he married me before my pregnancy became obvious. I didn't understand why Franc's daughters began to hate me after our marriage. I served them as well as I did before but they wanted nothing to do with me. Franc sent them to the boarding school and we saw little of them.

Mum was grateful that Franc married me after I disgraced him by becoming pregnant.

Franc employed most of the local people on his fields and on his sawmill. I heard the village women sniggering close enough for me to hear. They blamed me for seducing a decent family man.

'They talk about me,' I complained to Franc.

'They are jealous, they hate those they are afraid of,' he said.

'They respect you but they are nasty to me.'

'Fear is the best reason for respect,' said Franc.

Franc told me that people, like dogs, know when you are afraid; they attack frightened people. I couldn't help being afraid.

Maybe being afraid comes from being poor or young or weak but there it is and you can't do much about it. People sniff your fear and they peck at it like fowls peck at other bleeding fowls. The memory of fear follows you your whole life.

Hitler invaded Slovenia. Our daughters Martina and Vera and their brother Damian were born during the war. I began haemorrhaging when I was pregnant with Damien. Franc sent for the doctor from Ljubljana. I asked why he didn't call our old family doctor. He said that he didn't want dirty Yiddish hands touching me. I never heard the word Yiddish before and I didn't understand Franc's sudden concern about the doctor's hygiene but later I heard that Austrians did not like Jews. Maybe Franc expressed his dislike of our doctor to show solidarity with Austrians, that he was Austrian.

During the war people forgot about our family. I suppose they had more important things to think about. They talked about their children being killed and about their families being transported to the concentration camps. Some talked about the victory against the rich and powerful. A lot of older people wore black. There was excitement, fear and adoration, hope and horror.

Nothing much changed for our family. I was too young and too busy with my children to know what it was all about.

'Hitler knows what people need,' said Franc.

'Christians have to unite against Godless communists,' said mum. I only knew what mum and Franc told me.

After the war I read the words unity, equality and democracy painted on the shire building. I had no idea what the words meant but they must have been important because they appeared on many buildings.

'You won yourself a dictatorship,' I heard Franc argue with the man from the shire.

'We are all equal now,' argued the official.

'Nobody will ever be equal because everybody wants to be a bit better. You order people to be equal because you don't want them to be free and run faster, be smarter, and become richer. Equal people are not allowed to improve their position. They are not allowed to think for themselves. You can compensate the poor and the stupid and the lazy for being born what they are but they will never be equal.'

'We will change all that,' said the man. 'We will get rid of your bourgeois mentality.'

It's funny how some words stick in your mind.

The man from the shire used to work for Franc before the war and revolution. In 1946 he brought a paper telling Franc that they nationalised his property. His accounts were closed. People called Franc a traitor and Hitler's collaborator.

'Jews won in the end,' said Franc to mum. 'They planned the whole war. They created communist revolution to get the poor on their side. The poor are the easiest to manipulate. Mark my word; they will soon dictate how we live,' continued Franc.

I could never work out who was who, let alone who to blame for our misfortunes. People became openly hostile towards us after we lost our property. I heard a woman say that God punished my family because Franc and I had sex while Franc's wife was dying. God apparently never sleeps and he saw that I took advantage of a desperately sad man who was grieving for his dying wife. 'There is God,' the woman concluded.

I wondered how God would have anything to do with communists since mum called them Godless but then I knew nothing about these things. Maybe God was always on the side of winners.

'She brought a curse on the family,' said an old woman.

'The poor woman dying in the same house,' said her friend.

I saw women actually pointing fingers at me.

'God will see to it. He is a jealous God; he will punish into third and fourth generation. She brought a curse on herself and her children.'

Apparently it wasn't enough that we lost our property.

'Communists never produced anything; they are just distributing what was once mine. That is the easiest way to convert masses,' said Franc.

'People spy and report on each other to get privileges,' mum agreed. 'They would sell their souls for coupons. A metre of cloth or a litre of oil means more than God.' Mum always agreed with Franc.

'It's a whole new religion. It's always religion,' said Franc.

'They had to get rid of God so they can be God,' said mum.

'I have no time for politics,' said Franc. 'The nations changed the leaders and the borders have to be re-drawn and all these things take time. Nobody is willing to give anything away without a fight. In the meantime I intend to look after my family.'

'People on the land will be happier because they will work for themselves,' mum tried to understand the way of the poor. Since I married Franc mum almost forgot that she was the poor.

'They believe that they will suddenly be rich. They were working for me, now they will work for those who have stolen my property,' said Franc.

A feeling of hope was in the air. There was a promise of better life. I couldn't understand it then, of course, but there was much excitement and enthusiasm. Even those who didn't believe in communism seemed hopeful. Children learned the songs of praise for their leaders. Someone wrote a song saying how nice it was to be young in our homeland. The tune carried a hope and longing for something better.

'The cream always comes to the top and the poor will always be poor,' said Franc.

There was a five-year plan to rebuild the country and people were ready for the sacrifice. We were told to be generous, brave, and patriotic and to trust our leaders. The hope for the future filled the air.

'Factory workers are given rewards if they exceed their work norms. They achieve record norms because they can't survive without them. They work harder than they ever did,' said mum.

Mum and Franc often talked about the new government. They agreed on everything. I never saw things as clearly as they did. Maybe they saw things the same way because they were the same age. Or maybe mum just wanted to be like Franc, to please Franc, because she was grateful to him for marrying me.

'Communists gave the land to the poor to work on, but the poor are allowed to keep very little of what they produce. They have to sell the surplus to the co-op for almost nothing. They are beginning to realise that however hard they work they will always remain poor. The surplus they produce does not pay the cost of producing it. It is simple mathematics but our communist leaders are not good on mathematics,' said Franc.

'You are not allowed to buy milk from your neighbour. You can go to jail if you sell a litre of wine outside the Co-op. When you buy from the Co-op you pay three times as much,' explained mum.

'People only work more if they can keep more and sell more on the free market,' explained Franc.

'They are taking back the land they gave to the poor,' said mum.

'It's all a learning process for them. I could have told them, but then they would not have a reason to take my land.'

'They treat landowners as criminals,' said mum.

'Communists take private property to make people dependent on the government. Working ever harder stops them from thinking,' said Franc.

People gradually realised that working hard won't save them. Some escaped, some gave up, and some tried to get into management. But the poor remained poor. The heart has gone out of their victory, their work suffered and the production was poor. Nobody dared criticise the government or complain. They heard of arrests and disappearances. Anyone, who wasn't happy, was a traitor and had to be converted or eliminated.

I never said anything political, because I didn't know what is the right thing to say. I also didn't quite know which group of people I belonged to.

'The beggar is always more greedy than the person who was born rich,' said Franc who knew about those things.

'They became the law and the judges,' says mum.

'The winners are always right. The losers remain losers until they change things for themselves and become winners again. I will never allow my children to grow up as losers. If you can't prosper in one system choose another.'

Franc told me to pack our belongings because we were moving to Austria. Luckily Franc took his money to Austria before they closed his accounts.

'Pays to be prepared,' he explained.

'We can't carry everything with us,' I said.

'I sold the house. Take what you want and give the rest to your family,' said Franc.

The day we moved my whole family came to pick up what we left behind. I remember them carting our beds and wardrobes and tools on the big bull wagon. Ours were the only proper mattresses in that part of the world and people came out of their houses to see the treasures my family inherited. Most villagers slept on bags of husks they peeled off corncobs or simply on straw. During winter they made soft doonas out of feathers.

We moved to the farm where Franc was born near Graz in Austria. The caretaker was using the old house so Franc bought a house and the property next to it. When we moved to Austria I tried to forget about communists and especially about Franc's daughters. I tried. Luckily I had much to do and little time to think.

The border between Slovenia and Austria was tightly guarded. Although we only moved one hundred kilometres north into Austria we never returned to Slovenia. In Austria we lived much like we lived before in Slovenia. It was like moving to another village really. Half of the people spoke Slovenian; the shopkeepers and the priest were Slovenian. Franc hired Austrian workers and I quickly learned enough German to deal with any help we had on the land or in the house. Most spoke the sort of German we spoke before the war, half German half Slovenian, I thought, but Franc said that it was corrupted, deformed, Slovenianised German.

Before I left for Austria mum told me most solemnly: 'Wherever you may go, you will find our people. There are invisible ties between you and your people. When you need them, they will be there for you.' I think mum felt that she had to give me something for my journey, so she gave me all Slovenian people as my people. There must be an umbilical cord holding us together. Franc believed that people are a genetic mixture and one has to decide for himself what one wants to be. He didn't like me mixing with Slovenians in Austria but I was happy to hear them speak in the shops. It made life easier for me, knowing that they were there.

The reasons for Slovenians living in Austria, as a minority, were as many as there were people. The borders between Austria and Slovenia were never very clear until communists agreed on them and fiercely guarded them ever since. Most Slovenians in

Austria felt discriminated against and were making demands from Austrian government.

'I don't want to waste time with your useless nationalism. Austrian Slovenians chose to stay in Austria,' said Franc to a man who invited him to join in Slovenian demands.

'We chose to be in Austria rather than under Serbs but if we had a choice to be independent we would all want to be Slovenians,' the man argued.

'You hope,' laughed Franc. 'It is easy to be patriotic if it does not cost you. If Slovenians had to choose between a good pay packet and a poor pay packet they would choose money. Why come to Austria if you want to be something else? Anyway, I don't understand what all the fuss is about.' Franc explained that most Europeans have at some time been under Roman Empire or under Germanic rule and under Napoleon.

Franc was a powerful man in Slovenia but I think he himself felt like a foreigner in Austria. Of course he refused to be treated as a foreigner; he was Austrian by birth after all. The fact that he used to own a part of Slovenia was the only reason why he lived in Slovenia.

I could tell that Franc wasn't happy in Austria. He once said that he needed to get away and start again. Whatever that meant. I heard some Slovenians say that he wanted to be more Austrian than Austrians. I think that he didn't feel important enough in Austria. I also heard people say that Franc wasn't Austrian at all. I don't know if that was good or bad. Apparently his mother was Slovenian.

'Austrians were all for Hitler but now they are scared to admit it,' said Franc.

Franc's daughters were doing really well in Slovenia. They finished universities and worked in the management. One of them said that I was dragging Franc down. I wonder what she meant. I followed Franc.

Mum eventually came to live with us. Gradually most of my family moved to Austria. We all received Austrian citizenship and our children went to school as Austrians. They never considered themselves foreigners. I believed that everything was as it was meant to be.

'Just count your blessings,' advised mum. 'Think of poor people who suffer under communists.'

When Franc gradually lost his desire for sex, he became grumpy and criticised me for little things I said and did. I tried harder and harder to please him but he just withdrew into himself and ignored me. We were getting older, of course. I felt a little bit sad that he didn't want to sleep in the same bed with me but I got used to it. I can't expect to have everything my way.

Franc sometimes said that I had no idea what I was talking about. People become bored with each other, I suppose. We did not want to have more children anyway so why bother with sex.

In 1951 Franc applied for us to go to Australia. He never explained his decision and I didn't dare ask because I could see that he wasn't happy where we were.

In Sydney I took care of the family while Franc organised his business. I never knew exactly what his business was, but he gradually became happier. Our new house is overlooking the ocean and from the balcony we can see the hotel Franc bought. He never worked in a hotel but we looked down at it perched, shiny white, near the ocean. Franc was happy as we stood on the balcony and admired the evening view and the lights of his hotel.

Franc also bought a king-size bed and we started to sleep together again for a while. Franc actually decided to have sex every Saturday. He bought a bottle of wine for those occasions and our dinners were brought in. I was relieved that Franc found me desirable again.

Franc had an office at home and Teresa came twice a week to take care of his paper work. She is German but she came to Australia as a child.

Franc began losing his memory somewhere in the seventies. I suppose people do that after a certain age. He constantly blamed me for misplacing things, losing things and forgetting things. He also accused our children of stealing things from his office.

In 1987 I talked about it with our daughter Martina. I thought she would understand but she didn't.

'Don't be melodramatic mum, you are both old enough to be able to talk things over,' advised my daughter. She is as practical as her father.

'I can't take it anymore,' I said.

'Of course you can take it, mum. Don't be selfish, think of your children and grandchildren. We all want to see you together. Anyway, what could our old daddy have done this time, my daughter asked?' I am sixteen years older yet she treats me as a child.

'He is convinced that I am hiding and misplacing things. Most of the time the things he is looking for are there right in front of him. If I point that out to him he says that I want to make him look stupid.'

'Poor daddy,' said Martina patting my hand. 'You promised to be there for each other in sickness and in health.'

'I am sick of him.' My rebellion frightened Martina.

'Be patient, mum. We all have bad days.'

'I am not going back.'

'Where will you go? What will you do? He is eighty-five. Mum, he hasn't got long. We'll organise a big party for Christmas.'

'If we last that long,' I said feeling suddenly foolish and guilty and unreasonable. We shouldn't be good just because we are waiting for someone to die.

'Mum, you could never manage on your own. Dad has always done everything for you. You have never done a day's work in your life,' said my daughter.

Funny how one can deceive oneself. I thought I did everything for Franc. He never opened a cupboard door to find his shirt or a drawer where the spoons were. His shoes were always shiny and his clothes always ironed, his meals fresh and his garden immaculately weeded. His children were always presented to daddy respectful and clean. But I let everybody believe that Franc did everything for me, because he knew everything and was able to do everything. Franc was happy when I pointed out to others that I could not manage without him so I often pointed this out to others. I suppose if you hear something often enough you begin to believe it.

'Mum, just be happy while you still have daddy,' said Martina.

'Nothing makes him happy.'

'Humour him; he is an old man after all. I'll talk to him, if you like,' promised Martina, my smart counsellor daughter.

'I bought a bag of apples and one was a bit rotten. He told me how careless I always was with his money and how I never check things out. He went on and on all evening about me throwing his money away. In the morning I had to take the apple back to the shop.'

'Did you?'

'I threw it in the bin inside the shop and bought a new shiny apple while he waited in the car.'

'You bad woman, you cheating on daddy,' teased my daughter.

'He gets angry if his every wish is not granted.'

'Men are like that,' said Martina. I wonder what she knows about men. She worked all her life and so did her husband. They never seemed to have had time or reason to argue. They couldn't do without each other. I really don't know my daughter or her husband well. Franc was greatly disappointed when Martina married Joe, his mechanic. A hired help. I think it was then that he chose to sleep in his own room again.

'He is cruel and mean and he always was,' I muttered under my breath. I don't know what came over me. Maybe I watched something on television that made me behave recklessly. No wonder Franc did not like me watching television.

'Dad didn't change as much as you did,' said Martina, shocked by the change in me.

'I had to change all my life. I don't know who I am anymore,' I said.

'You are confused,' diagnosed Martina. She is smart; she knows the law and all, working in the law office all these years. Vince, her boss, relies on her. They must be helping lots of confused people.

'You fool yourself that you will change somebody but you can't even change yourself. If you are born poor you will be apologising for it all your life. Poverty is in your blood. People smell the poverty in you,' I told Martina. She probably does not know what I am talking about. She was always better off than those around her.

'Dad is not going to last long,' said Martina.

I didn't like her implying that we were all waiting for him to die. It is not nice or Christian. Especially with Christmas coming.

'He is forgetting things, I suppose. He is saying that you kids only come to steal from him,' I smile to justify my anger.

'Poor daddy does not know what he is saying. Senility is normal at his age.'

'He follows me all the time and demands to know what I am doing and why and how. He insists I peel potatoes the way he would do it. He never peeled a potato in his life but he saw it peeled on television and he wants to change the way I peeled potatoes all my life.'

'He is old and bored.'

'He is obsessed by waste. He tells me over and over what I could do with stale bread. He spends thousands of dollars lavishly on his associates and pretends that he never considers the cost yet he checks if I threw a slice of old bread or a worn out rag in the bin. He tells me that people who never learned to save on little things will never own anything.'

Our whole family arrived for Christmas 1987. Our grandchildren invaded every room. Franc followed their every movement. Martina's boys wrestled on the bed and Franc told them to stop. They fell off the bed laughing. The excitement proved too much for Franc. 'Get out of here,' he growled. Damian's girls came then and used the bed as a trampoline.

'You let them get away with murder,' said Franc to Damian.

'Oh, stop barking about it,' laughed Damian. 'Relax, it's Christmas.'

I knew at that moment that the festive mood ended. You don't say that your father barks. Your father is not a dog. Of course I know that Franc used to say to anybody who complained or raised his voice, to stop barking. Damian picked the phrase and used it without thinking.

Franc stopped talking.

Vera's little toddler lay on her back and kicked the wall. The brown polish of her shoes made a mark on the white wallpaper.

'You let the bastards wreck my home,' said Franc.

'We'd better go,' said Damian.

'And don't come back. Goes for all of you.'

'What did we do?'

'You called me a dog for Christmas,' growled Franc. He locked himself in his office.

'It's all your fault,' he growled after they left. I suppose I should have reprimanded Damian but he is almost fifty and anyway he is Franc's son and not easily corrected.

A week later, on the New Year's Eve, Franc called his daughters in Slovenia. He talked to them like they were still his little girls. He laughed and joked and promised to come and see them. He also invited them over and they promised to come. I became frightened of them like I was frightened of them as a little girl. Nobody here knows about Franc's daughters; even our children forgot about them. I realised that I was afraid of his daughters all my life. I never knew what they could do to me.

'Christmas is a stressful time. Everybody tries to be on best behaviour but people get tired of smiling and kissing and wishing. Too much togetherness,' smiled Teresa. She probably knew that our Christmas didn't turn out well.

Franc began to talk about his daughters' visit. He became more agreeable. I think he wanted them to see how happy he is and how well he has done.

'We'd better kiss and make up,' advised Martina. 'Your 50th wedding anniversary is coming up in June and we should make a big get together. I will hire the restaurant so the kids don't wreck dad's place,' she laughed.

Martina doesn't know about her stepsisters coming. She never related to them and she always considered herself to be the oldest in the family. For our wedding anniversary Martina invited Franc and I out for lunch and as we entered the restaurant everybody was there singing and congratulating us. Franc was pleasantly surprised. He drank the toasts and loved everybody. After lunch he slumped in the chair and his gargling breathing sound made me aware that something was wrong. Damian called the ambulance and Franc died on the way to hospital.

I phoned Franc's daughters that Franc died but they couldn't make it for the funeral. They arrived from Slovenia when they received a letter from the solicitor saying that Franc left them most of his assets. Franc changed his will after Christmas argument and then forgot to change it back again.

Franc's three daughters look older, wiser and more confident than I could ever manage to look. I am a child again and they are the mistresses of my home. My children do not want to meet them and the old women have nothing much to say to me. They book into the hotel while directing Franc's solicitor about their inheritance. It came as a shock to all of us to learn that everything but the house we lived in went to Franc's daughters from his first marriage. They haven't even kept in touch for years and years.

'We'll let the solicitors take care of that,' said Damian. 'We will contest the will.'

'We have to prove that dad wasn't in the right mind at the time he changed the will,' said Martina.

Franc told us over and over that everything he had would be ours one day and we put up with things to show gratitude. I depended on the life we had and on the money Franc had invested. One gets trapped like that.

'Don't worry mum,' says Martina. 'We never expected anything from you, anyway,' she adds.

I am disappointed that my children expected nothing from me. Why did I try so hard? Why did I follow Franc and his money? Nobody will ever depend on me like we all depended on him.

I wish I could be fifteen again. I hate the old skin my life is wrapped in.

Martina's daughter, my granddaughter Tina, reminds me of me, when I was fifteen. I am especially fond of Tina. I wonder if she knows how radiant her fresh young skin is and how her eyes sparkle. It is rather unfortunate that only the old can properly appreciate the fresh, young skin. For Tina's high school graduation I bought her a ticket for a tour to Lightning Ridge. Franc and I were there once; someone told Franc about the Lightning Ridge healing hot water springs. We both loved the place

My heart leaps up when I behold
A rainbow in the sky.

Wordsworth

Tina

I was named Martina after my mother and grandmother but my dad shortened my name to Tina. My grandfather said that Tina sounds cheap. He also made it known that Joe, his mechanic, who became my father, wasn't good enough for mum, his daughter.

My grandfather was a tall broad shouldered man with a face half-hidden in a shiny white beard. People took notice of him.

My parents are migrants; they were brought to Australia as children so they grew up as Australians but I suppose they are still migrants. I wonder when a person stops being a migrant. I was born in Australia; although I understand some Slovenian and German I do not speak anything but English. I could hardly be called a migrant. But then everybody is a migrant in Australia. Even Australian Aborigines came from Asia or some other continent thousands of years ago. I wonder sometimes what was there before the first humans came.

'If you choose to live in a foreign country, you have to become one of them. You re-establish yourself faster if you forget about nationality and politics,' said my grandfather. He also said that no particular nation or social order is better than the other. People take for themselves what they can get away with. First they fight for power and wealth and then they fight for peace so they can keep what they took.'

I sometimes wonder what nationality really means because migrants clutch to it, some even dig into their origins to establish their identity. I suppose they have to, cutting themselves away as they did; they have to attach themselves to something. It is different for me, of course; I have my family here.

After my grandfather died Nan sold her big house and moved into the granny flat next to us. I have no idea why Nan likes me better than her other grandchildren but she does. Maybe she wants me to live her life for her. I finished high school and was accepted to Teachers College. As a graduation present Nan paid for me to go by bus to Lightning Ridge.

'Tina, darling,' said Nan, 'find out what the rest of the world is doing. Don't grow old and sorry for not doing the things you could have done.' Nan gave me a brochure about Lighting Ridge and I read about this largely undiscovered and mysterious town that lures adventurers hungry for excitement, riches, love, and change. I read that the name Lightning Ridge came long before opal played any role in the lives of Lightning Ridge people. The red iron stones on the lonely ridge-hill apparently attracted electric storms that once killed some 600 sheep and some shepherds at the turn of the twentieth century so they started calling the place Lightning Ridge. There are different stories about who first saw the rainbow in the dust of Lightning Ridge.

Says Roy Barker: 'Aborigines always had eyes to the ground foraging for food as they were, so they surely noticed pretty stones on the surface of Lightning Ridge ground. Some opals would have surfaced after the rain eroded the ground. They must have been delighted by the beautiful colours but they never considered them as having commercial value. They were not food and they did not provide shelter.'

Nobody is quite certain which white settler first spotted a flash of lightning in the stone. Maybe it was the first white shepherd in the middle of the nineteenth century wandering around the mound of raised dirt in the middle of the flat outback. Maybe grazier's wife, Mrs Parker from Bangate station, became intrigued by the shiny stones Aborigines brought to her; maybe it was Mrs Ryan strolling near the government tank at the beginning of the twentieth century that saw something shiny in the dirt; maybe it was Jack Murray who first took a serious notice of the sighting and began to look for opal.

Lightning Ridge blossomed as the black opal town when European migrants came during the sixties and seventies. The population fluctuates from three to twenty thousand depending on the latest opal rush. So here I am in Lightning Ridge with the bus load of tourists for the Easter weekend. My school friend Jessica came with me.

My first memorable impression of Lightning Ridge comes from the paintings on the walls of Diggers Rest hotel. The pictures tell a story of a hopeful city sleeker with big dreams and a flash car coming to town. The artist followed the man's riches to rags story for six months of sweat and toil. After six months the man walks away with his head down and the bundle of rags over his shoulder.

'Diggers Rest hotel in the middle of Lightning Ridge is the main meeting place for opal miners. It is a meeting place for all the misplaced adventurers,' the bus driver warned us. 'Drinking singing and storytelling is how they spend their free time.'

We order drinks and move into the corner to have a better view of the boys at the bar.

'Tall, tanned, broad shoulders, olive skin,' Jessica points to the man at the bar.

'He has an incredible smile.'

'He is adorable.'

'He's got the nicest butt I've ever seen.'

We meet Anthony and his friend Jim. After a few drinks we arrange to meet again in the morning for a tour of the opal fields. Anthony shows us his mine and his camp and his opal cutting gear. We are fascinated by his primitive bush existence. We are transported into the Stone Age. No running water, no electricity, no gadgets. The boys are in their twenties. Anthony chiselled the white sandstone into brick like blocks and made four walls on the slab of cement. He covered them with corrugated iron and moved in.

'I don't need doors and windows yet. I have nothing worth stealing. When I find some opal I will put the locks on,' he laughs. 'I sleep outside under a mosquito net anyway.'

Jim lives in a caravan right next to Anthony's camp. He tied a large piece of canvass to a tree and he lives under this annexe most of the time.

The boys suggest that we come on a sightseeing tour to Glengarry. Anthony drives an old army jeep and we are thrown towards each other on the bumpy dirt track. Mobs of wild pigs, kangaroos and emus are escaping into the bush. It seems like the bush track is disappearing into the stunted growth of pale green grey shrubbery. After an hour we spot the diggings and miners busy making campsites and setting their hoists and generators to begin their quest for riches. A group of barefooted kids have eyes glued to opal dirt brought up from the mines. They squeal with delight as they lick the dirt off little pieces of silica to spot bits of colour. Everybody in Lightning Ridge seems to have traces of opal dirt around their mouths from licking the stones to make them shine. Anthony tells us that this rich new opal field was found by some farmers from Gilgandra so there is opal fever on opal fields. Almost overnight most of the Ridge moved fifty kilometres west into the virgin mulga bush. Gilgandra mob hid their diggings and their campsite under the tree branches but the news trickled into town and it could not be contained for long. Bushay, an opal buyer, chartered the plane and cruised over the bush until he spotted the mining machinery. He told his friend and his friend told his friend and the news spread like a wild bushfire. Down in the gully were about half a dozen men madly digging and the word got around that they were getting millions so the place became named Millionaires Gully forever.

The world is young; everybody seems young, excited, and hopeful. I listen to snippets of conversation and realise that mysterious Lighting Ridge is a lure for vagabonds who hope to dig the rainbow fire hidden in the clay. A trace of opal means the realisation of young dreams. Ridge is a place made for dreamers. Maybe all the people in the world are dreamers but opal miners took that extra step; most of them are migrants from all over the world speaking a mixture of languages but everybody understands the common opal language. They left their country, their family and their jobs to scratch in the dirt for the elusive colour; for red on black; for orange green; for harlequin pattern; for rolling pattern; for the most mysterious mixture of colours with the hint of violet under the green and blue with the fire over it that brings tears to men's eyes. Gouging and specking and fossicking, shin cracker and silicate, puddling and agitating are words quickly added to my vocabulary.

At the end of the day miners gather around the fire and barbecue lamb chops. The nearby grazier killed a lamb and chopped it only an hour ago. The evening lights the sky with millions of stars as we sit on the mounds of dirt. The bush is alive with chatter as miners exchange information about the traces they found during the day. The bits of silicate called potch are passed around from person to person and everybody licks it to find the colour hidden in it. Seam opal is new for most that were mining in the Ridge where opal is mainly found as individual stones called nobbies. Some nobbies are found as solitary stones but when a few of them are found in proximity they call it a patch and the lucky ones who find a good number of stones nesting together call that a pocket which means cash.

I am on cloud nine. The calls of the big native birds tremble into the enormous silence of the outback. Wide clear skies and the scents of gum trees are overwhelming. There is fire in the eyes of the men going down the ladders into the shafts to uncover the mystery of the land. Men tell amazing stories about the opal they found and the fun they had finding it. It is years since the currency changed from pounds to dollars but on the opal fields nobody talks in dollars yet. Anthony recounts how he went to the buyer asking 900 and meant 900 dollars for his stone and the buyer said that he can only give him 800 pounds; Anthony quickly collected his 1600 dollars without saying anything.

Jim adds his story of how he went to Chaplain, a Japanese buyer, asking 400 for his stone. The buyer said that he can only pay 300 per carat for it. The stone weighed eleven carats and Jim only wanted 400 for the whole stone so he quickly pocketed 3300 pounds.

'Chaplain knows what he is getting. He has been around longer than I. That's how you learn on the job,' says Jim. Jim has a crop of curly red hair and eyes so green that they dazzle you.

'I read in the Sunday paper that a man found an opal down in the Millionaire's Gully as big as your fist, red on black. He sold it for three thousand and the buyer then named it Oriental Queen and sold it for one hundred and fifty thousand pounds,' says Bill who is the only old miner I met. The rest are my generation or a bit older.

'You could buy the Ridge for that money,' says Jim.

'Bill must be close to sixty but he still goes up and down the ladder every morning,' explains Anthony.

'It seems unreal to find that kind of money just by scratching in the dirt,' says Jessica.

'There is much dirt between opals,' smiles Bill.

'What made the farmers come here in the first place away from everywhere?'

'Keith is an old prospector. He bought a farm in Gilgandra but he could never forget the thrill of finding a new rush,' tells Bill.

'Opal is the romantic stone that grabs you and never lets you rest again. That's why we escaped from real life,' says Jim.

'We are in love with opal,' laughs Anthony and squeezes my hand.

'What real life?' says Bill. 'In the city you watch TV and you think like TV and talk like TV. You begin repeating the opinions of the journalists who repeat the opinions of the politicians who repeat the directions given to them by their party leaders paid by the multinationals who are building their global markets.'

'We can think for ourselves,' I protest.

'Of course you can. You can cook as well but it is cheaper to buy take away. They teach you that it is more sensible to do nothing.'

'I can cook,' I say. 'Mum made sure of that.'

'Of course you know how to cook but will you cook? Will your children know how to?'

'Here you work like mad somewhere between sunrise and sundown to find a bit of colour. The rest of the time you spend as you like and anyway you like to spend your time is fine,' says Jim. 'There is always hope that opal will be in the next load of dirt.'

'When you join the system you put yourself in line for promotion and then you wait for promotion and pay rise. You are constantly afraid that you will fail because you may not be good enough. When there is no more chance for promotion, you slip away and die,' says Bill.

'Bill lives in a tin shed near a dam about hundred metres from here,' explains Anthony.

'Here you believe anything you like and live in anything you like,' says Bill. Perhaps he wants to explain that he lives in a dusty hot tin shed because he chooses to.

'I could never get used to this,' says Jessica.

'In Lightning Ridge you are either high with excitement or tired from digging,' says Bill. 'You pay cash and don't have to explain where you come from or where you are heading. Think about that. Opal miners are the only people moving incognito. You only stay on the opal fields if you value your freedom highly enough. No sane person would stay in the dust and heat if freedom wasn't their highest priority.'

'I am surprised that taxation allows cash industry,' says Jessica.

'The government is happy that mining keeps the men out of mischief,' says Bill. They know that we are a rare breed still willing to break our backs for less money than the social security offers you for watching videos. They allow us to sell opal for cash, because they have it on computers how much opal is sold. They know that this amount could not keep ten thousand people either in prison or in a mental hospital.'

'People say that opal miners want to get rich fast,' says Jessica.

'Getting rich is only a dream. Miners know how unrealistic this dream is but you have to have a dream,' says Bill.

'As long as you have hope, you are rich,' says Jim.

'Here you live in an unspoiled future. It does not matter what mistakes and wrongs were in the past because the past is gone and finished with. The only important time is the time ahead and only in the future can we achieve anything remotely like perfection. To dream about the future is the only happiness,' says Bill.

'You are telling fairy tales,' laughs Jessica.

'Fairy tales promise that sometime in the future the prince charming will kiss you and you will live happily ever after. It is only a dream. Like opals,' says Bill. 'Fairy tales make you believe that there is actually someone who will make you happy. Nobody makes you happy. You are happy or you are not.'

'When I came to Lightning Ridge an old miner told me: When you get a feeling that you have to do something, lay down until the feeling passes,' laughs Jim.

'Here you lean on people who do nothing; you wait for each other to do nothing together,' smiles Bill.

'Maybe we are wrong in thinking that being smart, active and creative means being better,' I turn to Jessica.

'Maybe whatever makes you happy is better,' says Anthony.

'Helen, the Swiss mental health nurse, observed that Lightning Ridge is much like her mental hospital only people here cook for themselves,' says Bill.

'Someone told her that they took mental patients from Bloomfield mental hospital for an excursion and the bus broke down in Lightning Ridge so they stayed here,' adds Jim.

'Don't frighten the girls; they will think that we are all mad,' says Anthony.

'There are more philosophers and politicians in Lightning Ridge than anywhere else looking at life and doing nothing about it,' laughs Jim.

'You go to the club to hear voices. Everybody talks but nobody listens,' says Bill.

'You hear who made it on opal and who didn't. What else is there,' says Jim.

'Perhaps everybody needs to do something and does something. Maybe this is the reason people paint more pictures and write more poetry in Lightning Ridge than anywhere else,' says Bill.

'Anthony built his castle out of the sandstone, says Jim. 'Some miners build castles in the clouds. We are all waiting for the fairy princess to illuminate our lives.'

'I'll show you a real castle my friend Amigo is building. He is bringing iron stone boulders home on his pushbike and builds a huge beautiful structure,' says Anthony.

'He said that when he finishes the castle he will start looking for a princess to live with him,' adds Jim.

'We build monuments when we can't find opal,' says Bill.

The boys want to impress us and we are totally impressionable after a stubby of beer. Our eighteen years old innocence is making it possible for us to fall in love with anything. We are in love with life, our future seems promising and the excitement of being a grown up is totally intoxicating. We feel safe in men's company.

'Ridge is a place where you can become a nobody,' says Bill.

'Who would want to be a nobody?' says Jessica.

'Sometimes you will want to escape from being who you are,' says Bill.

'I suppose when you get old,' says Jessica.

'Age has nothing to do with it. I came here twenty years old to do whatever I fancied, when I fancied it and however I liked to do it. Nobody is watching you here. You can call yourself Red or Blue or Charlie or Mary. You live outside the calendar and business hours and identity papers,' explains Bill.

'Since social security came to the Ridge miners only pretend that they are self-sufficient,' laughs Jim.

'I have never been on social security, I would not put my name on a computer,' says Bill. 'Nobody knows that I exist.

Social services began searching for our weaknesses and needs. The system takes your strength and makes you dependent. Every time you help the chick out of the shell you deprive the bird of the strength that hatching is meant to provide.'

I will never forget the magic of this sunset. The sky is unbelievable. The deep purple changes into green and red and pink and violet as the sun is setting. You can see pictures of anything you want to imagine in the sky. It is easy for us, eighteen years old girls, to imagine. When you are in love you see the colours around you and remember them forever. Jim brings out an old guitar and begins strumming popular tunes. We end up singing Abba songs and these romantic tunes vibrate into the night. Anthony holds my hand in the privacy of darkness.

We are leaving a few days later and Anthony gives me an opal ring before I board the bus. We kiss passionately.

I return to Lightning Ridge a month later. Mum and dad are horrified, they threaten to disown me and they tell me never to return if I go. They even call the police but they can do nothing about it. I am old enough and free to do as I like.

I am eighteen and in love for the first time. This love is the greatest thing that ever happened to me and no reasoning enters into it. I could climb Rocky Mountains on my knees barefoot.

I help Anthony build the camp. My hands become rough, my fingernails are chipped and dirty, my hair is straggly, and my clothes are impregnated with clay dust. My eyes shine.

Anthony is always surrounded with friends. They bring him opal to cut and they talk opal and mining as they drink in the shade of the gum trees. After six months I become sick of the dirt and grime and poverty. There is nothing for me at the Ridge. I need my parents and my friends and the buzz of the city. I need a long shower and a hairdresser. For Christmas I move back to Sydney.

'I want to go to uni and finish my degree. Maybe I will do teaching. Maybe I will come back,' I tell Anthony.

'You'll do as your heart tells you,' says Anthony. We kiss good bye.

Anthony isn't ambitious, he isn't going anywhere. He likes the lifestyle and the bush but that isn't enough for me. It isn't enough for my parents either. Back in Sydney we celebrate the New Year's Eve in the Slovenian club. I dance with Mark. His mum Mojca and my mum look at us approvingly as we dance cheek to cheek. At midnight Mark and I walk out and kiss next to a huge Christmas tree. Everybody is kissing for New Year.

Next morning I have my first morning sickness. I try to fool myself that it is just a hangover but I know that I am pregnant. The knowledge comes from within. I miss Anthony and I want to tell him that we are going to have a baby. I want my child to have a father. I love Anthony. I return to Lightning Ridge and marry Anthony in the Lyons Park. Mum and dad refuse to come and witness my vows to the man who ruined my life. They don't know about the pregnancy.

Jim is Anthony's best man and Marilyn is my witness. I met Marilyn in the courthouse, where she works as a clerk. I inquired about the marriage licence and we became instant friends. When you are alone and new in a place it is easy to attach yourself instantly like that.

In March I go down the shaft to surprise Anthony. I slip on the ladder and fall down a couple of metres. I don't worry about it but in the morning I lose our baby. Anthony and I comfort each other. There will be another baby. We settle down and I learn to cut opals while Anthony mines. I am too ashamed to run back home. I am married.

Mark arrives in April for the Easter weekend.

'I wanted to see the famous goat races you told me about,' says Mark. I am on the verge of tears most days since I lost the baby. Mark seems to be there whenever I need a sympathetic friend. In Sydney our families meet at dances, funerals, weddings and protest marches. Migrants are like that.

'Anthony's people come from Italy,' I explain to Mark.

'The three of us were born in Australia to parents who came from places only a few kilometres apart,' says Mark.

'We grew up with our parents' nostalgia for Europe and the good old days they escaped from,' I say.

'Italians, Austrians and Slovenian are Catholic and as good Catholics they interbred through centuries,' says Anthony.

'I don't really care where we came from. We are Australians,' I say.

'I was actually born in Italy but I don't know anyone there because my parents came here when I was a baby,' says Anthony.

'We really don't know much about our ancestors,' Mark agrees. Anthony and Mark like each other from the start. Mark decides to stay.

'I have finished a lapidary course and would like to try cutting and buying,' says Mark. He buys a big house on the main street of Lightning Ridge. It is covered by a jungle of old grapevines, which he carefully prunes and cultivates. It produces a bumper crop of delicious grapes. Mark and Anthony decide to make wine. Anthony makes a winepress.

'If the grapevines produced as well in Slovenia, I bet my father would never have come to Australia. His family had a winery,' explains Mark.

'The wine will keep best in the mine, because the temperature is even underground,' says Jim.

'We could lower the drum into the shaft near my camp,' says Anthony.

'You will come to visit regularly then,' I smile at Mark.

'There will always be an excuse to come over,' Mark winks at me.

Mark is a link to my other life in Sydney. We are just friends, of course, but he is the reminder that there is life outside Lightning Ridge. I haven't been anywhere for ages and I am becoming restless for that other life. Anthony and Mark spend more time with each other than with me.

'A couple of friends from Sydney are coming for Easter. I bought a pig and you can help with the spit,' says Anthony.

'I wish you would get a phone connected,' says Mark.

'If I put the phone on, people will stop coming to see me.' Anthony shuns modern conveniences.

'But you are never home,' says Mark.

'But when I am home there is always someone coming.'

'We have no rain for a year and then for Easter it rains every time,' says Bill as he comes to say hello to our visitors Gino and Mario.

Mark and Anthony prepare the spit. Jim gets the fire going. They taste the new homemade wine.

'It has great bouquet,' says Gino after his second glass.

'It's dynamite,' says Mario.

'Come I'll show you the traces,' says Anthony and they follow him underground.

I seem surrounded with men who barely notice me. They come to get drinks and food and to be told where the towels and the socks and the glasses are. I miss the intimacy Anthony and I used to have. Mark and I flirt in an unintentional, obscure way that makes me even less contented. I am homesick. I want to escape. I remember my family, our traditional Easter breakfasts, our going to church and our remembering. I want to be part of all the traditions Nan brought to Australia and which mum so carefully preserved. Everything in our home was as it should be; the right crockery the right tablecloth, the right dress and the right food for the occasion. Propriety was the most important thing in mum's life.

Mark sits in the shade of a gum tree turning the spit. I prepare the salads and the tables.

'You miss your family,' Bill senses my unhappiness.

'They probably miss me more.'

'It takes time to accept solitude but it can be a great substitute for people. You realise how big you are, when you become a part of everything,' says Bill.

'I feel small,' I smile holding back tears.

'You have to disappear into smallness before you become a part of greatness,' smiles Bill.

'They must be finding opal,' calls Mark.

'Wine more likely.'

'The pig is ready,' Mark calls down the shaft.

'Be right up,' yells Anthony.

'We can't wait,' calls Mark.

'Come down for a minute,' calls Gino.

'I'll be right back,' says Mark going down the shaft. Bill follows.

'To Lightning Ridge,' toasts Anthony.

'To Mark and Anthony, our winery experts,' toasts Bill pouring a second glass for Mark.

'Viticulture, man,' says Anthony.

'It's too strong for me on an empty stomach. I am out,' says Mark.

'Let me go first,' says Mario. He tries to lift himself up the ladder.

'What's wrong with you,' says Gino. 'Let me.' His hands don't hold him and he settles back on the opal dirt roaring with laughter.

'You bastards are drunk. How much did you have?' Says Mark.

'Two glasses,' insists Mario.

'Yeah, right, the first and the last,' laughs Mark. 'Go up in front of me and I'll push you up.'

'I don't think I can make it,' says Mario.

'What's the matter with you, you can't get drunk on a couple of glasses.'

'Of course not,' says Anthony as he lies next to Gino.

'If you don't get up the flies will eat the spit,' I call down the shaft but there is only laughter coming back.

'Throw down some rugs and pillows, the bastards are drunk,' answers Mark.

'Where is the opal you promised to show them,' asks Mark but Anthony is half asleep next to Jim, Mario and Gino. I drop old blankets in the mine and Mark and Bill put them under the men. Everyone knows that damp dirt is dangerous for your joints. Bill and Mark help me pack the food in the small kerosene fridge before they go home.

'The grapes were overripe and the wine is as strong as spirits,' says Bill.

I try to forget about the stupid drunks. I feel painfully alone. Fay, a pregnant Aboriginal girl is staying next door in a tent with Jim but she is too shy to join the party. She doesn't even come out of the caravan to see what the men are doing. I call her for coffee but she doesn't feel like it. I need someone to share my misery with. I go to her tent and she offers me a smoke. I have my first cigarette. I feel silly trying to make friends with this native girl. Fay wouldn't understand how I feel but she is all I have. At this moment I would tell a cat how I feel. I want to go home and start again; I want to go out and have fun with my school friends. I want to forget that I have ever been to Lightning Ridge. I cry myself to sleep for the first time.

The men come up after midnight. They sleep late. For lunch we eat cold pork and they laugh about their attempts to get up the ladder.

'At least you don't have to cook lunch,' says Anthony.

I am only here to cook and serve and listen to their crude yarns. My resentment grows like Mark's grapevines.

'Where are you mining now,' asks Mario.

'Here and there,' says Jim. 'I found some traces at Three mile.' The deep Three-mile is a proven field but it is mostly worked out. Anthony and Jim pegged three claims at the edge of an open cut where others found a lot of opal. They found promising traces. Jim began to build his camp on one of the claims.

'What about you,' Mario turns to Mark.

'Mark is on opal, big time,' explains Anthony.

'I found some colour on Coocrain but the road is bad after the rain. I might register a claim next to Anthony on Three mile,' says Mark.

'Mark is lucky wherever he starts,' says Jim.

'You might all be on millions,' says Gino.

'Jim and I have three claims there,' says Anthony.

'You can't miss, then,' says Gino.

'There will be plenty for all of us,' says Anthony.

'Don't count your chickens before the hens start laying eggs,' I warn.

'Don't count on your milk until it is spilt,' corrects Anthony.

'Watch your milk if you are going to buy chickens for it,' Mark tries to put the old fable right.

'You can't buy yourself ribbons before the eggs are hatched,' says Anthony.

'One thing at the time,' says Bill. 'This old fable teaches you to be patient. You put a pail of milk on your head to take it to the market. On your way you dream about selling the milk to buy some eggs to hatch some chickens, to sell the chickens and buy a ribbon for your hair.'

There come other versions of Aesop's milkmaid fable. 'The moral is not to toss your head prematurely,' concludes Mark.

'You only toss your head when the ribbon is firmly in your hair,' says Jim.

'And spill the milk.'

'No use crying over spilled milk,' Gino sums it up.

'You will toss your heads when you become millionaires,' warns Mario.

'Never,' laughs Anthony.

'It is sad how money changes people,' says Bill. 'Only it does every time. Most Glengarry millionaires got divorced when they found opal. A wife with two children left her husband to live with a man whose wife left him with their two children. There is a whole chain reaction. I know of up to a dozen couples who split when they came on opal. Money got to their heads.'

'My Tina doesn't believe in opal,' says Anthony. He knows that I am upset and he tries to include me in the conversation. His arm is over my chair and his eyes are begging to be forgiven. I love Anthony.

'Money would never change my Anthony. He is not greedy, he gives it away,' I try to joke.

'Tina wouldn't be here if she didn't believe in opal,' says Jim.

'She believes in me,' says Anthony.

'I'll get some coffee,' I say.

'I love Anthony, I keep convincing myself but first doubts appear. I don't believe in the way we live. There is nothing for me in it. The aroma of freshly ground coffee beans fills the air. The bubbles on the surface tremble as I place the cups on the table.

'You know how I like the smell of real coffee,' says Mark. He brought me a big bag of best coffee from Sydney.

'Have a nip of whisky with it,' suggests Anthony.

'Thanks, I am right.'

'Mark bought the best place in town right next to the post office,' Anthony tells our visitors. I think he is boasting about his rich friend.

'I am buying and cutting so it is easier for miners to find me,' explains Mark.

'It is safer as well so close to the police station,' says Jim.

'Camp life is not good enough for the likes of Mark,' smiles Anthony. It is obvious that Anthony and Mark like each other.

'I wouldn't mind to live in a romantic hideaway like yours,' says Mark.

When Mark first came to the Ridge Anthony let him cut opal on his machines but Mark soon bought his own gear.

'I really knew nothing about opal or cutting until Anthony showed me,' Mark readily admits.

Mark is lucky like that, whatever he touches turns into gold. He started mining with Jim and Anthony but they never found much. He then found a new field at Coocrain and struck it rich. All the miners tried to peg around him. After the Easter rain the road to Coocrain is closed. The slippery clay mud makes it impossible to get through. Mark registers the claim next to Anthony's claim at the Three-Mile field.

'Only until the road to Coocrain dries up,' says Mark. 'I have to wait for the grader.'

The drill brings up colour in Mark's claim. Red on black. The word spreads through town like wild fire. Everybody looks for free ground around Mark. Anthony and Jim find only purple and blue-green traces. Other miners want to buy their claims but they are not selling.

'It's only a matter of time. We have three claims all around Mark, we can't miss,' says Jim. They pay the drilling rig to drill new shafts and it brings out promising traces, but the red on black is not among them. Jim and Anthony work every day, they buy the agitator to wash their dirt, they find crumbs of red and green in the dirt but the good stone eludes them.

In their spare time Anthony helps Jim build his camp. Fay is going to have a baby and it would be hard for her in a tent. The memory of my lost baby haunts me. I envy Fay. It is obvious how much Jim loves this exotically beautiful pregnant native girl. Everybody is talking about the opal Mark finds at Three mile.

'It looks promising,' is all Mark says.

Jim and Anthony spend most of their savings on drilling but they are barely covering expenses.

'There must be opal in one of our claims. We couldn't be so unlucky,' Anthony keeps reassuring himself.

'We shouldn't have followed Mark,' says Jim.

'Mark followed us,' Anthony corrects him.

'How can Mark be so lucky?'

'Some miners tried all their lives, some worked on and off for years and never found anything worthwhile,' says Anthony.

'Mark is lucky with anything he touches,' says Jim as they rub bits of dirt from the opal they find.

'Everybody talks about Mark and his luck,' says Anthony when we are alone.

'He takes risks,' I say.

'You can pick and choose if you have money,' says Anthony.

Money and Mark are creeping between Anthony and me. We try to ignore both and remain optimistic but I know that Mark's millions are on both our minds. In Lightning Ridge anyone finding a bit better stone is called a millionaire.

'I have to cut for miners to get the money for mining,' says Anthony.

'It's not Mark's fault if he is lucky,' I side with Mark.

'I bet he found millions right next to our claim,' says Anthony.

'Our turn will come,' I say.

'Money brings luck,' says Anthony.

'Mark wasn't always rich. His father had a little green grocer shop where Mark started his first job. In Sydney people still remember Mark as his father's delivery boy,' I tell Anthony. 'When his father died a big company wanted to build a hotel where his shop and home were. Mark sold the lot for a couple of millions, which he invested.'

'What about his mother?' Asks Anthony.

'Mark's mum, Mojca, is well provided for. She is a bit snobbish. His dad was hard working but his mum was always the boss,' I tell.

'Mark turned after his mother then,' says Anthony. I realise that Anthony doesn't like Mark any more.

'Mark became interested in lapidary only after he sold the shop.'

'You can afford a hobby, when you don't have to worry where your next dollar is coming from,' says Anthony.

'His father left the little country cottage and the farm near Cooma to Mark's sister,' I tell.

'How much did she get for it?'

'Her German husband planted a vineyard and an orchard. Tourists come and pick their own fruit. They also have a winery, wine tasting and a restaurant. It became a major tourist attraction. I suppose wine growing really is in their blood.'

'Money speaks all languages,' says Anthony.

'Bob Dylan once said that money doesn't talk, it swears,' I try to dismiss the issue.

'It changes people.'

'Money never changed Mark,' I say.

Is Anthony jealous of Mark's luck or of his friendship with me? Maybe he thinks that I am attracted to Mark's money.

Everybody is attracted to money. Everybody pegs around someone who is on money to be close to the person who is a success. No hopers bring you bad luck. Maybe nobody can help being jealous. Of course, Anthony is not like that, he is easygoing and not worried about money. He has never been ambitious and he says that he has everything he wants. But, is anybody really like that? Can anybody not be jealous and insecure? How well do I know Anthony? He is my husband, I should know him. Yet I know nothing about his background or his family.

'Money does not buy happiness,' I hug Anthony. Everybody likes Anthony. He helps out and he shares his home with those that have no home. People confide in Anthony, they ask his advice and they ask for money and for the credit with opal cutting. Sometimes Anthony's cheerful helpfulness gets slightly on my nerves. Why can't he look after our interests first like everybody else? Like Mark. Why don't people ask Mark for a loan and for help? They are grateful that Mark talks to them. It's an honour to be friends with someone who is a winner. Money makes people respectable and everybody likes to be with respectable people.

Maybe I returned to Anthony because he gave me a beautiful opal ring the first time I came to the Ridge. He did not even know if he will ever see me again. We only kissed a couple of times and parted like friends.

'To bring you luck,' he said as he saw me off. His dark eyes ignited fire in me. I felt there at the bus stop that we would share much of our life although we never made any promises. I had the ring valued and was shocked when the certificate stated that it is worth $8000. I never admitted it to anyone that I had the ring valued. Maybe I am ashamed of checking out on Anthony's gift.

Mark often comes with us to the club for a drink. Anthony and Jim got mobile phones. It is cheaper than the land connection to the camp.

'Tina and I are with Mark in the Bowling club,' says Anthony into a mobile.

'Where is Jim mining,' asks Mark.

'Three mile. Next to you,' says Anthony.

'I am thinking about open cutting my claim,' says Mark. 'It is faster than working underground.'

'You can afford it,' says Anthony.

'Any luck yet in your claim yet,' asks Mark.

'We had a couple of stones but nothing to crow about,' says Anthony.

Ratters use mobiles these days, Arthur calls from across the bar.

'What do you mean?' Asks Mark. Arthur comes around and leans on Mark's chair. He lowers his voice into a conspiring whisper.

'Miro has one of those to warn his partners. There are four of them ratters. One sits on top of the mine while the other two dig out other people's opal while one partner is in town keeping watch on the owner of the claim. They are cunning bastards. They keep in touch by mobile phones.'

'You mean this is going on and everybody knows about it,' says Mark. 'Why not go to the police?'

'You need evidence. You can never prove what was taken from a claim. There is no proper legislation covering ratters. Miro got two hundred dollars fine for trespassing but I heard that he stole a couple of hundred thousand worth of opal. Someone put a stick of gelignite into his bed last week. All the windows were blown out with the explosion.'

'Was Miro injured,' asks Mark.

'He was probably out ratting when it happened. Maybe next time,' says Arthur. 'I hate the bloody bastards. They are openly boasting about it in the club.'

'Miners should do something about it,' says Mark.

'Who are you spying for?' Arthur menacingly looks at Anthony's mobile.

'You are sick. Everybody has one of these now,' says Anthony.

'So everybody is ratting,' laughs Arthur.

'You know all about it; you have experience, I bet,' says Anthony. Arthur and Anthony are becoming aggressive. I don't know why they hate each other but one could cut the tension with a knife.

'Some people are lucky like that, they know who is on opal and they go into his claim and dig it out at night,' snarls Arthur. Is Arthur making an accusation? Is he warning Mark? Everybody wants to be close to Mark since he found opal. They elected Mark on a committee of Mining Association. He knows the mining Registrar. People come to Mark for advice on mining. I feel an invisible barrier come between us.

'I hope you can trust your partner to rat for you,' laughs Arthur. 'Everybody for himself first. He is there on his own; you never know what he is up to.'

'I trust my partner, but nobody trusts you,' snarls Anthony.

'You don't have to trust me. I am not ratting for you,' laughs Arthur with an evil twinkle in his eyes.

'You are jealous,' you bastard, you have it in for Jim because Fay escaped from you and came to him. Everybody knows that you are an impotent jerk,' spits Anthony.

'Watch your tongue, boy, or you might lose it. Anybody can have that black cunt. I can have her any day I want,' laughs Arthur.

'Try it,' says Anthony.

'I don't have to, I know what the slut needs,' says Arthur with a snarl that looks as ugly as it is evil.

'Just keep away,' warns Anthony.

'And what will you do if I don't?' Laughs Arthur.

'You trust Jim,' Mark turns to Anthony.

'Once a thief always a thief,' says Arthur.

'Watch who you are calling a thief?' Anthony gets up. I am becoming uncomfortable. Arthur orders a new round of drinks.

'When did you get the mobile?' Asks Mark. I hope Mark does not suspect Anthony? Anthony would never steal. He found some nice stones lately himself. Or did he? A tiny voice in me says that he could easily have gone next door into Mark's claim.

'Why?'

'Oh, I might get one myself,' says Mark.

'Technology is the gun in the hands of crooks,' says Arthur placing the beers in front of us. 'Ratters will always be one step ahead of us honest miners.'

'You wouldn't know what honest is,' says Anthony.

'Leave it,' says Mark.

'The bastard is looking for trouble. Let's move to the table,' says Anthony.

'Can you reach all the fields with the mobile?' Asks Mark.

'Only about twenty kilometres around town for now.'

'So it would be no good for Coocrain or Glengarry?'

'Not from town. Not clear enough anyway. They are working on it.'

'Good enough to send a message. You are not likely to chat on it with everyone listening in,' says Arthur.

'He is a rotten bastard,' says Anthony as we move to the corner of the club.

'Arthur has his ears to the ground. I'd like to get the ratting bastards myself,' says Mark.

'Arthur has his ear to the ground for an easy dollar. He is trouble,' says Anthony.

'What has he done to you,' Mark wants to know.

'He is picking on Jim because of Fay.'

'What about Fay?'

'Fay used to be Arthur's woman. He bashed her in the bush one night so she ran away to Jim's caravan and stopped with him. Some Aborigines heard Fay crying so they chased Arthur away. His surname is Dunn. The story goes that someone yelled after him Run, Dunny Bunny. The new nick name stuck. Arthur is paranoid about it because since then people refer to him as Dunny Bunny.

'Arthur offered to open cut my Three-mile claim,' says Mark.

'I wouldn't want anything to do with the bastard,' says Anthony.

'He only wants thirty percent. He will do all the processing.'

'He knows what he wants,' says Anthony. 'He is into everything. Miners work for him when they don't find opal to pay for the fuel and repairs of the machinery. Nobody likes to work for Arthur but he provides work and it is better to earn a bit right where you are than going away to find accommodation and work. Arthur has people doing farm work and mining and road work, open cutting and restoration of the mines.'

Arthur follows us to the table. He is smiling now and slaps Anthony on the shoulder: 'No hard feelings, ah.' Anthony does not respond; there is not much he can do.

Arthur tells a story about the tourist he found in his open cut. We all pretend that we are just having a friendly yarn.

'I saw a car parked on top of my open cut and the tourist digging in it,' Arthur begins his story. 'I started to empty the tourist's car. Hey you up there, yelled the tourist from the open cut. I kept on throwing out his belongings. He came up. What do you think you are doing, he said. Same thing you are doing, I said. Why are you looking through my belongings, asks the tourist. Why are you looking through my mine?But that's my car. That's my open cut. I didn't see the sign, says the tourist. Fair enough, I didn't see one either. I am going to call the police, says the tourist. You'll save me the trouble, I said. Put my staff back in the car, you bastard, the tourist runs up towards me threateningly. I grab him for the collar, turn him around and kick him in the backside. The man rolls down into the open cut head over heels. Next time I'll run a bulldozer over you, I tell him. The tourist stutters that he found no opal. He empties his pockets, takes off all his clothes to be checked out. He stands there in his undies terrified. Never try anything like that again, I say. He shivers all over as he drives away. I bet he'll think twice before he goes on the field again. I won't let any bastard get away with it. They won't even try while I am around.' Arthur is telling the story to Mark. He turns his back on Anthony and me, like we don't exist. The story sounds as a warning to us not to mess with Arthur.

'I just want to make sure nothing happens to your opal,' Arthur slaps Mark on the shoulder and leaves.

The tension scares me. Arthur wants to get to Mark so he has to discredit Anthony.

'Mark is getting millions. Everybody wants to be friends with him,' says Anthony as we return home. 'Every man wants to stand next to the rich man,' I remember Bill's words.

'Trinity said that two things get to the man's heart: gold and bullet,' Anthony quotes the line from the film. He is a fan of spaghetti Westerns.

Mark's Ratters

'I don't trust the shifty bastards,' says Arthur to Mark when they next meet in the club.

'Which bastards?'

'The ratters,' says Arthur. 'We should be allowed to shoot them.'

Mark didn't tell anybody that someone dug in his claim.

'What are you saying,' asks Mark.

'I know nothing, I told you nothing,' says Arthur mysteriously. 'But watch out for Jim and Anthony.'

'Maybe Arthur saw Anthony or Jim or both going down my claim,' the thought enters Mark's mind for the first time. Arthur has been on the field for years. He knows what is going on.

'Anthony and Jim are friends,' says Mark.

'There are no friends where money is concerned,' says Arthur.

'We spend most of our free time together,' says Mark.

'So they know at all times where you are,' laughs Arthur.

The suspicion casts a strange coolness on Mark. He remembers the words of his mother: Friendship is like a flower, once trampled on, it never recovers completely. Mark has ratters on his mind. Ever since he found opal on the Three mile, someone is digging it out at night. He was going to tell Anthony about it but since Arthur warned him, he changed his mind. Mark goes to Anthony's place determined to find the answers. Everybody feels a bit awkward since that time in the club. Maybe it's all in my mind, maybe I am the only one that feels awkward because I don't trust them anymore, thinks Mark. He doesn't tell anyone about the ratter digging in his mine at night. He is determined to find out who the ratter is before he complicates his friendships. Mark learned quickly that you cannot trust anyone with opal. He would like to trust Tina but she is Anthony's wife. Her loyalties are to Anthony and his partner.

Mark sat in his car hidden behind the trees near his claim many nights waiting for the thief but he never saw him coming. This night-miner was like a Father Christmas of long ago. However long Mark was waiting for the old man laden with gifts, he never saw him coming. Mark tried to convince himself that he was imagining things. He marked his diggings and the next morning the markings were moved and the hole got bigger. But there was no lose dirt. He put grease on his ladders, he put the alarm bells on his hoist but nothing was ever disturbed. Yet every night some of his opal dirt was dug out. Not much but enough to let him know that someone was there.

Mark inspects every corner of his underground diggings. Finally he finds a carelessly covered hole at the far end of the mine. He clears the dirt away and finds that the hole is an underground passage from the claim next door. Anthony's claim. Mark goes through it and there is another hole like that leading into Anthony's neighbour's mine. Jim's claim. Mark travels from claim to claim and almost loses his way in the underground labyrinth. He could be found in anybody's claim and accused of ratting himself. The trench leads to the edge of Arthur's open cut. So anybody could dig in Mark's claim. The ratter could come underground from a kilometre away. It could be anybody, of course, but Anthony and Jim are the closest and they know that Mark is on opal. Then again everybody knows when anybody is on opal. No wonder Mark did not see anyone go into the mine from the top; they came from underground. There are hundreds of dug out claims on the Three mile field and any one of them could be connected to Mark's claim. And there is the open cut.

Mark heard of another miner who caught his ratters by burying a plastic bag of paint into the dirt. When the ratter broke the bag with his pick he got splattered by paint. It worked because the ratters had to go out the same way they came. Here, however, they can hide in anybody's claim until it is safe for them to wash the paint away.

Mark goes home and smashes a box of old bulbs. He brings the broken glass into his mine. He carefully takes out the dirt covering the passage into Anthony's claim and mixes the broken glass into the dirt. With the mixture of dirt and glass he blocks the passage in the same way he found it. Next day the dirt is still in place, the passage is carefully covered just as Mark left it but Mark knows that it was moved. He marked a stone on his side of the passage. The stone disappeared. Mark finds it in the middle of the dirt covering the passage. There is no digging in his claim overnight. The ratter must have cut himself and left.

Mark goes to see Anthony. He wants to know once and for all. He has no evidence, he cannot go to the police; he only wants to know for himself.

'Not working today?' Asks Mark.

'Jim took off somewhere so we are having a late start. I have to see the wrecker just now to get a part for the Ute,' says Anthony.

Anthony feels that there is something very wrong. He senses a change in the mood more than other people. Pieces have this intuitive ability. Anthony read that somewhere and people told him often enough that it is impossible to fool him. He spots a fake a mile away.

'What is Jim driving?' Asks Mark.

'His Ute.'

'I saw his Ute parked in front of his caravan.'

'Must have gone with someone.'

'What happened to your hand,' asks Mark.

'Caught it in the hoist,' says Anthony.

'Let me have a look.'

'It's fine.'

'No, no, I really want to see it.' Mark tries to lift a bandage. Looks like there is a bit of glass sticking out there,' says Mark. He wants to see Anthony's reaction.

'The nurse said that I better keep it bandaged,' says Anthony pulling his hand away.

'You have scratches on your face as well,' says Mark.

'Have I?' Anthony goes to the mirror.

'Where? '

'Were you in a hotel fight?' Laughs Mark but there is hollowness in his laughter.

'What are you saying; there are no cuts on my face?' Says Anthony.

'What's that on your nose then,' says Mark.

'That's from last week when I was starting the generator and the handle hit me.'

'Look at him,' says Mark as Jim walks in. 'So you two had a fight.'

'No, why,' says Jim.

'You have cuts to your face. The bits of glass are still sticking out.'

'You must be joking,' says Jim heading for the mirror. 'It's not the April's fool day. What's going on?'

'Mark is having a joke,' says Anthony. He knows that something is wrong.

'I am off,' says Jim. 'I just took the batteries to charge.'

'Have some coffee,' says Tina.

'I have to go as well,' says Mark. He wants to know if Tina knows. Of course, if there is anything to know, wives know everything. Maybe it is not Anthony at all. Maybe even Jim knows nothing. There is no glass or cuts on his face. There was nothing unusual about the way they reacted. 'If Jim and Anthony are guilty they will know that I know if they are not they will take it as a joke,' reasons Mark.

'Stay for lunch,' says Anthony.

'You like my stuffed capsicums,' invites Tina.

'Nobody suspects anything, maybe there really is nothing to suspect. It would be wrong to suspect them if they are innocent,' reasons Mark.

'Thanks all the same,' says Mark. 'Anthony's band aide could cover any kind of a cut, reasons Mark. I have no evidence, not yet. But I will know soon.'

'If you'll excuse me,' says Anthony. 'You stay and finish your coffee. I won't be long.'

Mark brushes past Tina on his way to the window. The scent of her body envelops him. Tina is the reason he came to the Ridge. They look across the table at each other. The unspoken question is written in their eyes: 'What do we mean to each other? Where do we go from here?'

It would be so right and so easy. But it wouldn't be fair and it would complicate things. They never said a word about that New Year's Eve since Mark returned. A week later Mark announces that he is going to Japan.

'There is a gem exhibition in Tokyo and I have stones to sell as well,' says Mark casually. 'Would you keep an eye on my claim for me? I covered it up. I don't want anyone to fall in but just keep an eye on it.'

'Sure, but ratters won't come while I am there. They come at night,' says Anthony.

'So Anthony knows about ratters being in my claim,' reasons Mark. I never mentioned ratters to anybody. Then again everybody talks about ratters and Arthur almost accused Anthony.'

It's nothing unusual about Mark going to Japan. He is buying opal for the Japanese market. He will only be away for a week.

'What is the ground like in your claim,' asks Mark.

'Come and have a look. It looks promising but so far, nothing to write home about,' says Anthony.

'I'll see you before I go,' says Mark.

Anthony and Jim are at work when Mark comes to say good bye.

'Come to the back,' yells Tina when Mark knocks on the front door. 'I am hanging the washing.'

'What can I bring you from Tokyo?' Smiles Mark passing clothes pegs to Tina.

'I have no money to order anything. Anyway I don't need anything. Come in for awhile,' Tina holds the laundry door open for Mark. He takes a quick sweep of the cutting corner. A tray of dob-sticks with about twenty fair sized opals are carelessly covered with a plastic apron.

Mark sits at the kitchen table while Tina puts the kettle on. The silence is growing.

'Is something wrong,' asks Tina.

'I am not sure.'

'What do you mean? I know something is wrong.'

'I'll tell you when I come back from Japan.'

'Why not now?'

'Maybe you already know. Maybe you know more than I do.'

'About what?'

'When I return I will know if you know,' says Mark. 'If you don't know I will tell you.'

'You sound mysterious. I thought we were friends. Don't you trust me?'

'I thought we were friends and I trusted you,' says Mark.

'I don't like the tone of your voice. Why the past tense, what have I done?'

'You haven't done anything and I trust you.' Take care, says Mark.

'The stones in Anthony's cutting room could belong to any of Anthony's customers; Anthony is a cutter after all. It's not fair to suspect him,' reasons Mark.

Tina wonders if Mark ever remembers that New Year's eve in Sydney; does he ever think about the well wishing that sounded so promising. Maybe it was only an illusion; maybe they had just enough to drink for their imagination to run wild. They both like Anthony and want to behave honourably. That makes the attraction tantalising.

'I'll see you when you come back,' says Tina. They do not kiss like friends do because they know that there is a spark that may ignite.

Mark returns from Japan.

'Anthony is in hospital, he might not walk again,' Tina sobs on Mark's shoulder. He heard someone digging in your claim and went to investigate. He slipped and fell in.'

'How bad is he?'

'It's his spine, they don't know if he will fully recover.'

'I am going to see him,' says Mark.

'I'll come with you.'

'You better not. I have some business in Dubbo as well and don't know when I will be back. I have to be alone to sort some things out.'

Mark looks at Anthony through the window of his hospital ward. Anthony's head is bandaged and only his eyes can be seen. His wrists are connected to tubes. He has a metal frame like a halo around his head. 'Only he is no saint,' thinks Mark as he stares at Anthony. 'I am almost sorry for the bastard. I thought I knew him. You never get to know anyone; you can't afford to trust anyone. Especially where money is concerned. We are both after the same thing. And there is Tina. I can't trust her either. Maybe she is on it with Anthony. Maybe she was watching while he was stealing. Maybe Jim does not know anything about it. Maybe Anthony does not trust Jim. Nobody trusts anybody on opal. Everybody for himself.' The betrayal leaves a bitter taste in Mark's mouth. 'If he asked me for money I would have given him. I'd even give him a chance to mine with me. Anthony introduced me to mining; we pegged claims together and even worked together at one stage. Of course, Anthony would not have charity. He would rather steal.'

Anthony opens his eyes and closes them again. After a while he opens them again and the two men stare at each other.

'You bastard, you'll pay for this,' says Anthony.

'What were you doing down my mine,' asks Mark.

'You told me to watch it.'

'I never told you to go down. It was covered.'

'I heard someone from my claim; I looked down your shaft and saw someone move.'

'Probably your partner.'

'It was Arthur peering out.'

'Don't try to shift the blame on Arthur.'

'One day you will find out for yourself,' says Anthony.

'Arthur warned me about you,' says Mark.

'I want half a million. Or it will be an attempted murder. Claim it on insurance, if you like,' says Anthony.

'You know I have no insurance on the claim, you bastard. Nobody has insurance,' says Mark. 'The shaft was covered.'

'You should have insurance with all your millions.'

'You had no business down my claim.'

'You asked me to watch it. Tina was there. She will be my witness.'

'She knows I didn't ask you to go down.'

'She will stick with me and tell the truth. I will take opal as a payment.'

'I will kill you first. You were stealing from my claim all along. I know how you cut your hand.'

'So you admit that you wanted to kill me, it was premeditated murder attempt.'

'I will kill you if you don't drop this nonsense.' Mark's voice is steely. 'You will die as a rat and make no mistake about it.'

'You cut the step loose on the ladder to trap the ratter going down. But Arthur was already down when I stepped on the ladder. You will pay for this.'

'Next time you mention money I will tell everybody that you were ratting,' says Mark leaving the hospital. Mark doesn't want to hear about Arthur.

'How is Anthony?' Asks Tina when Mark returns. She knows something happened. Something was dreadfully wrong. Maybe Anthony died. Maybe he is paralysed.

'I need a drink,' says Mark. He seems older and changed; he slumps in the chair with a false smile on his lips.

'Anthony is quite cheerful. He will recover all right.'

'Thank God,' Tina hugs Mark. They hold each other and a feeling of freedom and relief sweeps over them. Tina's tension and the anxiety is over. Anthony will be all right. Mark is caressing Tina's hair. His lips are on her neck. The anger in him turns into desire. There is an irresistible sweetness; this is how things were meant to be. Slowly, without hesitation they begin kissing like they did when they first danced for New Year's Eve in Sydney years ago. Everybody was kissing everybody. Anthony does not know about it. There is nothing to know. They just wished each other a happy new year.

'We are meant for each other,' Mark keeps saying as they move into the bedroom.

'We can't, not now, not with Anthony in hospital,' Tina resists mildly.

'What he doesn't know won't hurt him,' whispers Mark.

'I never slept with anyone but Anthony.'

'We owe it to ourselves.' The urgency is greater than the reason.

'When I lost the baby I wanted to come to you,' says Tina as they hold onto each other spent and stunned and guilty.

'Move in with me,' says Mark.

'We can't, not now. We are all Anthony has. He would never forgive us.' The enormity of what happened frightens Tina.

'What happened had to happen. Pack your things. I will pick you up in the morning,' says Mark.

'I have to think. Give me time,' says Tina.

Going home

I feel enormously guilty; a sense of total liberation and horror overwhelms me. I walk into the bush and sit on a log just as the sky turns all colourful before the sunset. I sat on this log with Anthony when I first came to the Ridge, when we fell in love. I love Anthony, I want to go to Anthony and be forgiven for what I have done. I cannot undo what I have done. I could never tell Anthony but he would know. I try to think about Mark but the memory is tainted. We did not make love; the hungry, rushed sex was something else. I want to forget it. I see Marilyn coming but I don't want to talk to her so I remain hidden behind the bushes. During the night the images of Mark and Anthony come and go in my dreams. I am running after Anthony but he is disappearing in the distance. Mark is laughing, I am crying.

Marilyn comes again in the morning.

'Tina I am so sorry about Anthony,' says Marilyn.

'So am I. Mark said that he is going to be all right.'

'Are you going somewhere?' Marilyn looks at my packed boxes and suitcases.

'I just packed winter clothes away,' I say.

'Tina, is something wrong?'

'No,' I say evenly. 'I am just not certain what I will do.'

'Anthony rang last night. He wants you to ring him straight away. He said it's urgent. I couldn't find you last night. You can come and ring from my place,' says Marilyn.

When Marilyn leaves I load my belongings in the car and drive towards Dubbo. I pretend that I have never been in Lightning Ridge; that I only woke up from a nightmare. A five-hour drive will give me time to think. Maybe I will stop and see Anthony in Dubbo hospital or maybe I will just drive past towards Sydney and my real life. The tension of the last two years is shaken off my shoulders. I put a tape of Bob Dylan on and hum along: like a bridge over troubled waters.... Everything feels unreal.

I know I should cry. I should worry. I should be there for Anthony. Maybe I should have moved in with Mark. Possibilities and musts are floating in front of me but there is freedom out there and no one to tell me what to do. I am on my own. I am free. I want to sing. Maybe the last two years never happened. I am going to Sydney to finish uni and start my career. I know I should cry but I can't. I know I will cry one day.

The grass is tall and green, big splashes of yellow flowering canola look like sunshine spread over the countryside. There are splashes of purple Paterson curse flowering on the paddocks in front of me. Lightning Ridge was a curse for me. Beautiful from the distance and prickly to touch.

'Every silver lining has a cloud,' Anthony once laughed when another of his stones turned into nothing.

'Every cloud has a silver lining,' I corrected him.

'Goes both ways,' said Anthony.

In a couple of hours I will have to decide to either stop in Dubbo hospital and see Anthony or drive on. A sense of shame and fear is creeping after me but I drive on and hum the tune. I have to get away, I can't make a decision now; everything will be out in the open soon.

I look at Anthony through the glass of the hospital door. He lies on his back, pale and still. I wish I could go and kiss his pain away. He needs me and I love him but deceit is written on my face. Anthony would know. He senses things that are not spoken. I shudder. I could not lie and I could not tell the truth. I can't face Anthony. His eyes are closed and his hands are connected to tubes. I love Anthony, I can't hurt him.

I write a letter. 'Anthony, I am going away. Please forgive me for leaving you at this time. I need time to think. I may come back one day. I wish you happiness and health. I love you.'

I want a new start, a lily-white page, to write the rest of my story on. When Anthony and I first moved together we had that brilliant future right in front of us. We were going to find opal and then we would do all the fun things and be happy ever after. We wanted children and travel and clean bush adventure. Only the dream took too long to come true. Everybody else was finding opal except us. I haven't bought a single item of clothing while in Lightning Ridge. I haven't been to hairdressers or on holidays. We built our camp. Every cent was lovingly devoted to our idyllic home. I became restless. I try desperately to rub out everything that happened. I want to start again. I have to finish my studies and make something out of my life. I have things to do and places to go. I couldn't be happy in a little town where nothing ever happens.

'Men are thrilled by discovery of a gem in the clay but most women need more,' said Marilyn when I moved in with Anthony for the first time. I wonder what does one need to be happy?

I begin teaching in Redfern

Come mothers and fathers throughout the land and don't criticise what you can't understand, I hum along the song as I prepare the lessons for my class. I finally made it, I became a teacher. Anthony never came looking for me. Lightning Ridge and Anthony's accident are not part of my life any more. I wonder if Anthony knows that we have a son.

'I wish you started at a better school,' says mum. She has been looking after my son Toni since he was born. She knows that we couldn't manage without her. Nan died a couple of years ago. Dad died last year so mum needs Toni and me to do good things for. She also goes to work part time because Vince, her boss, couldn't do without her.

Toni is a cheerful, contented boy. I think he inherited his father's sunny temperament.

'I only want to see you in a secure, permanent job,' mum apologises for whatever she remembers.

'Now I have what you wanted me to have.'

'If you have a secure job, you have a secure life. You can go a long way,' mum rambles on as she irons Toni's clothes. She always had her life ironed out.

Mum would have stayed in the same job all her life, cherish her security and glow with the air of importance. She has made herself indispensable wherever she worked. Lifelong job means lifelong life for mum.

'In your time people lived to work, but these days we work to live. I provide for today not for some distant future. We might not have the future,' I backchat my mum.

'You are never with your son,' says mum. Her words echo in my subconscious.

'I give him quality time,' I say. 'Everybody is talking about quality time these days.'

'Once a week,' says mum. 'If you are not out with your boyfriend.'

'Toni is the only important person in my life right now,' I say.

'Men come and men go, but your son will always be your son,' mum echoes my thoughts. She considers it her duty to impart pearls of wisdom onto her unwise daughter. I will probably do the same to Toni. My boyfriend, Jack, is a teacher at my school. He has a daughter Debbie from his previous relationship. For Christmas Debbie stays with Jack and he wants to take her to the zoo and would I come along. I never met Debbie. 'Bring Toni,' says Jack as an afterthought. We meet at the entrance to the zoo. Toni says hello to Jack as instructed but he looks at Debbie. People communicate at their own level. Toni is still at an age when he is not threatened by the thought that I may love a man. Men are not a part of his world. He follows Debbie and soon they run ahead of us like old friends. Jack is as casual with his daughter as he is with me or my son. Jack is like that.

'Fatherless kids become a statistic. Toni does not even have one parent. Half of his mother is out looking for a man,' mutters mum.

'I have to have some life. We don't live in the dark ages,' I argue.

'Look at statistics; you don't want your son to become a statistic. You'll only have yourself to blame.'

'Being a single parent is not a big deal these days, I say. 'People don't marry for life any more, if they marry at all. Who would want to be stuck with the same person for life?'

'Nothing is a big deal anymore. See where that will get you.' Mum's quiet words thunder into my consciousness. If you are told often enough that you are guilty, you begin to feel guilty.

'I am not the only one,' I ward off her predictions.

'Maybe it is time for you to settle down,' mum ignores my reasoning.

'Whatever that means,' I snap. Sometimes I play with memories of Anthony. Sometimes I even dream of visiting him. Mum does not know about Anthony's accident. I rang the hospital and they told me that he would never walk again. It is not my fault that he fell into Mark's mine. A tiny voice in me says that maybe it is. Maybe Anthony did it for me, because I am greedy. I admired Mark for his luck. I argue that I never asked Anthony to do it, he never told me that he did it, I don't know if he did it. Anthony does not know that I had sex with Mark while he was in hospital. It doesn't matter as long as Anthony does not know. It meant nothing.

Anthony and I are not the same innocent young people that fell in love a few years ago but we have a memory of those two people. We also have a son. Maybe Anthony should share in my guilt.

'The society is breaking down, nags mum.' She will next tell me how I contribute to the breakdown, of course. I know she means well but she makes me feel inadequate.

Since I got my periods at the age of twelve mum prepared me for womanhood. Whatever you do, don't let a man make you pregnant before you finish your studies, mum used to say. Becoming pregnant before I finished my studies seemed to be the greatest disaster that could befall me. Mum refused to come to my wedding because I defied her orders to finish my studies.

'I am really afraid of the future,' says mum.

'Life was never as free and easy as it is now. People are healthier and live longer,' I assure her.

'But are they really happy,' says mum.

'Nobody was ever really happy all of the time, mum. We wouldn't know it if we were. People want more out of life. They want to know more, they aspire to be more.'

'More you know, more you want to know, more you have, more you want,' says mum.

'You have to have dreams,' I argue.

'As long as you have a clear road ahead, you can dream all you like.' Mum always manages to dampen my spirits.

'What do you dream about, mum,' I ask. Mum never reveals anything about herself. What would she know about dreams?

'I dream of your future and Toni's future,' says mum sensibly. We are an extension of her; she wants to be happy in that extension, she wants to be what she was meant to be; what her father wanted her to be. I will never escape mum's words. I can deny them, I can dispute them, but they will follow me like mothers follow their wandering children.

'I am just telling you how things are,' says mum self-righteously. 'It's my duty to tell you. There is a place for everything and when everything is in its place there is harmony,' concludes mum and I can't argue against the ancient reasoning.

'In my days,' mum starts reminiscing, 'children learned manners and respect. You are a teacher and you have a duty to teach them how to behave.'

'Blame the teachers, why don't you. Everybody else does. Parents think that they are less guilty if they place their guilt on teachers.'

'You are qualified,' says mum.

'I am not allowed to chastise a child while a child is allowed to swear at me and threaten me. Nobody is appalled if the students bash a teacher but if a teacher smacks a student, all the newspapers scream about child abuse. Police are in the same boat. They turn the blind eye when they see kids doing things they shouldn't. Kids are protected but our jobs are not. Change the government, mum. There are lots of old people in the government. If you are right how come they don't see it your way?'

'They have no time for their kids so they blame teachers,' admits mum. 'I wonder what we pay the government for if they can't keep the country orderly. Some people don't deserve to have a vote.'

'What people, mum? Are they women, Aborigines or poor or sick or uneducated or disabled? Which group of people?'

'Those, who work hard, and behave well, always pay the price,' says mum.

A mother of my student said the same. Her daughter never received a golden award for good behaviour. I never even noticed the woman's daughter. The girl quietly plodded on with her work, was friendly and polite but she was not outstanding. The boy who annoyed kids and teachers spent one whole day without getting in trouble so he got a golden award for improvement. Was the award only a bribe to stop the boy annoying teachers?

'I don't dare walk on the street. Young thugs snatch your bag and trample you to the ground. In my day we learned to believe that God would strike us dead if we were disrespectful to our elders,' says mum.

'You believed that God would strike you dead but you knew that it wasn't true,' I back chat.

'It is more important what you believe than what is true,' says mum mysteriously.

'You believe that big bully parents can smack their children but the little powerless child cannot hit a parent,' I say to mum. 'A policeman can strike you but you cannot hit him.'

'I don't know where you get these ideas from,' says mum exasperated. 'Even a sparrow knows where he stands in the scheme of things. There is a chief sparrow and the soldier sparrow. One thinks the other does. Everybody should know his place. Parents and teacher are there to be obeyed.'

'My generation was forced to line up and swear the allegiance to the queen and God and parents and teachers, the scoutmaster, the Girl Guide, and the law of the country,' I remember.

'Our streets, our schools and our homes used to be safe,' argues mum.

'Gender, religion, colour and culture no longer determine our lives.'

'Don't bet on it.' I enjoy baiting mum and making fun of her outdated ideas. 'This is my life,' I say.

'Life is not something you own. Life is a link in a chain. You are put in place to join the past with the future. You are as much my life as Toni is yours. We work and save to give a better chance to the next generation.'

'You built a better future for us and we are left with nothing more to build unless we break up what you built.'

'Don't be so ungrateful,' says mum in her perfect martyr voice. 'We went through hard times so you can enjoy a better life.'

'You try to make me feel guilty about enjoying this better life.' Mum was always the most important person in the lives of people around her. Our family couldn't do without mum, her boss couldn't do without her and neither could our neighbours. Mum organised the fund raising and the church cleaning and the running of a school canteen. I am totally useless compared to mum. Mum is a secretary to a solicitor Vince, who is also her Slovenian friend; she knows that her place is to make her boss's life smooth and easy. She never complains about doing the man's chores in her spare time on the way to work or on the way home. She carries his dry-cleaning and the flowers for his mistresses and the gifts for his children. She keeps his diary neat and uncomplicated, so his life events would never clash. She knows when he needs a cup of coffee and what brand he prefers.

'Men are hopeless,' mum warned me in preparation for my womanhood. Maybe mum's domestic life is just an extension of her business life and she feels contented with the job well done. Dad had his responsibilities around the home; he repaired the car and mowed the lawn. He also had to punish us children when we misbehaved. He would never notice our naughtiness if mum didn't remind him of his responsibility. My brothers went to a boarding school so they could concentrate on getting the best education available. Mum and dad felt that it was their duty to provide the best.

'Were you happy with dad,' I ask. Mum married for love and her father made sure that we all remembered what a mistake she made.

'Neither of us ever looked out of our marriage and we never argued. This should speak for itself,' says mum. I want mum to tell me how they made each other happy or unhappy but you can't ask a mother that, at least not my mother. Mum was always careful not to spoil any of dad's enjoyment. Dad was our king. Mum ordered dad to be our king. That's how things were supposed to be. She was meant to have a king so she made dad a king. I don't think that dad had any say in who he was. I am sorry that dad did not see me starting my teaching career. I finally achieved what they planned for me. I have a suspicion that dad didn't worry as much about me being a teacher as mum did. Mum used to say: 'I wonder if dad will like it or approve of it or allow it.' Dad was called our breadwinner although mum earned more money than he did. I suppose mum wanted to have a man who is bigger than she is. It seems that mum's sole mission in life is to guide me towards perfection. Maybe all the loved ones are like that. They promise to love you more perfectly if you could manage to be a bit more perfect. There is always room for improvement. It is no longer enough that I am a teacher; I have to be at the best school. It isn't enough that I am a mother but I have to be the best mother, best daughter, and best friend. There is no one as perfect as people want their loved ones to be.

'One generation builds and the next destroys and the third one begs,' says mum without directly blaming me for this sequence of events.

'Don't worry mum, there are still millions of people starving this very minute. There are little children making baskets and shoes and clothes from morning till night so they can eat and we can buy these things cheaply.'

'It's better for kids to work than to starve.'

'Mum explains things by saying that she wasn't born yesterday. My parents always provided me with the best of everything a Blacktown girl could wish for. I was better off than most of the kids in my neighbourhood. People used to say that it's a wonder I didn't behave like a spoiled brat.

Dad never asked mum what she wanted. It was his responsibility to decide what they will buy and where we will live. It was his responsibility to decide where we will go for a holiday. I suppose he lacked imagination so it was always the same, we went fishing and mum cleaned his fish and cooked it and tidied our tent.

'If you can't choose the neighbourhood you live in, at least make your neighbourhood respectable,' maintains mum in her conventional wisdom. Mum has always been the heart of our family; a heart so steady and even and constant that we forgot about it. All the vital organs work like that, I suppose, and only when this vital action ceases, its absence becomes visible and recognised. Mum never seemed without direction or unhappy about her life.

While we lived at Parramatta dad lost his job and he found another in Blacktown so mum had to find herself a new job in Blacktown. It was a natural thing to do and she did it without complaining. Every morning mum packed our lunches before she prepared breakfast. After we slurped our juice and ate the toast she fussed over the crumbs and the jam and butter smudged on the bench, she wiped all the stains and vacuumed the floor, picked the towels off the floor and socks from under the beds and empty food packets from our bedside tables. She wiped the toilet bowl and the hand basin, swept the hair off the hairbrush and replaced the lid on the toothpaste before she had a quick shower and tidied her hair for work. On the way out she emptied the garbage into the bin away from the house and left the small kitchen bin inside the front door to put in the kitchen on the way home in the afternoon. In the afternoon mum placed the shopping bag on the kitchen bench and went into the bedroom to change from her work clothes into her home clothes before she started dinner. She hung her good clothes straight away and that saved her ironing it next time. By the time dad returned she had dinner cooking and dad's stubby waiting cold and open. A plate of cheese and biscuits was in front of him. Dad needed to unwind with the beer and the paper. He didn't like talking while he relaxed. Mum is a thread that holds our family like a ribbon holds a bunch of flowers. We are nothing like flowers of course but she gathers us around her every so often and we have no heart to disappoint her. We used to be on our best loving behaviour, my brothers and I, while dad presided over the meal mum lovingly prepared for their wedding anniversary every year. Maybe our getting together was the proof mum needed, that she was indeed successfully married and that she raised a good family. We knew that she earned her celebrations by being totally devoted to what she calls my family. Since dad died we gather less frequently but mum makes sure that we come together and visit dad's grave on all saints day. No other Australian family would do that. We would have nothing to tie us together if mum did not instil in us that we owe her to remember each other's birthday and that we eat Christmas dinner at her place.

Maybe mum knows how essential she is and how hopelessly lost we would all be without her. It is clearly up to her to keep us respectable and functioning. Mum probably never had to search in the mirror to find out who she was and what she wanted. Everything in her life is running like a clock, her clock. She is in charge. Maybe mum does not expect praise, because she knows that what she is doing is for her own satisfaction. She was careful with every family dollar. She grew all our fruit and vegetables and mended and sewed our clothes. Dad told her often enough that it is a waste of time to do all these things but she did them anyway. Maybe she was afraid of poverty or dirt or disorder. Maybe she realised that she made a mistake marrying the poor man but couldn't do anything about that after three kids. As a sensible person she made the best of what she had. Maybe she dreamed of having some other life but she knew deep down that no other life was possible. Who else could love her untidy, unruly children?

Dad was always dirty. It was his job as a mechanic probably, but it seemed to me that he enjoyed being covered in grease. It was the greatest chore for him to get dressed for Sunday mass but he did. That was his contribution to orderliness. We also observed the Sunday dinner rule. We had to be there, rain or shine, we had to wash and put the respectable clothes on.

I want more than mum had. I want money and love and sex and success. But all I really care about is my son Toni. I love Toni. Maybe I love that part of myself that lives in Toni, maybe it is just self-preservation and a selfish self-love but the love for Toni is all I feel. I love all of Toni and I adore the part of Toni that is part of his father and part of our loving. Mum and dad believed that Anthony was just an unwelcome intrusion into my life and I will come to my senses and get over him. When I returned from Lightning Ridge pregnant, they were both there for me so I could finish the college.

Mum was so proud when I decided to buy a flat in Darling Harbour. She gave me her savings as a loan for the deposit on a unit that has the ocean view she always wanted. Mum is disappointed because I took a job at Redfern, which is quite a few notches below the working class Blacktown. In my part of Redfern I am right where dirt and grime of the society lives, where few people work and fewer still aspire to do better.

'Redfern is no environment for young Toni,' declares mum.

'Toni goes to a good private school in a good suburb where all the nice children have learned nice manners from their nice families. Toni is safe in Darling Harbour where we live, mum.' I tell mum that there are many kids, just as beautiful and clever as Toni, who live in Redfern and don't know anything better. These kids graduate from meat pie and coke to beer and plonk and drugs. They end up injecting anything that can be injected and swallow whatever can be swallowed to get rid of boredom and despair.

'I don't like you getting mixed up with that lot,' warns mum.

Jack is also a teacher at Redfern, he comes from the good address as well but he likes it down in the pits. Jack and I clicked instantly.

'What brings you down into our prestigious school?' He greeted me as we met on the playground duty. Jack has a curly smile dancing around his lips and you never know if he is serious or not.

'I am new,' I say like a proverbial ugly duckling. 'I have to start somewhere, so I thought I'd start at the bottom.'

'Some people look self-righteously down at kids who scratch tattoos on themselves with pins during silent reading session. How could they, why doesn't someone do something about it, they say,' Jack mimics righteous people.

'I am surprised that kids are not scared of punishment or of poisoning or of the future or of the shame,' I say.

'Their mums and dads carry same self-created pieces of art on their bodies. If mum and dad have tattoos, the tattoos must be good. They see no shame, no punishment, and no consequences.'

'Mum and dad are the only people who really matter,' I agree.

'Parents have the strings of the Welfare purse. The government has their parents on the string as well. Teachers only push education that nobody here wants.'

'We are their role models,' I say.

'Can you realistically believe that any of the kids here aspire to become a teacher? They live in a different world. They don't know how to use education, they never lived with an educated person; there is no literature in their homes. They expect everything from the government who has this magic purse. Education and teachers are a kind of punishment government imposes on them; they have to go to school to repay to the government for giving them money for good things like pies and coke.'

I try to talk to April, a beautiful dark girl just being enrolled in kindergarten. She is too shy to tell me her name. Her eyes are covered with a fringe of heavy black hair. I put my arm around her shoulder and tell her my name but she remains silent. A little girl bumps into her and my little shy April yells at her: 'Fuck me dead.' Her voice is strong and clear and confident. I ignore April's outburst. This is a whole new world for both of us.

April's father Scott later comes to school to apologise for April missing school. I think he wants to talk to someone. He is divorced. His two years old twins live with their mother and April lives with him. She hates being away from mum and her brothers. April scratched Scott's car and threw stones at him. He threatened to smack her but she said that he is not allowed to touch her. She will tell her mother. Scott does not want to lose April. He receives a single parent pension because he has April. 'I'll go to the police then,' said Scott to April. 'They won't do anything to me because I am too young to know what I am doing,' said April. You learn what you live. Scott is looking at me for help. What can I say? Welfare agencies are in and out of school. They are watching out for signs of child abuse. Parents leave the kids on the street. We ignore what kids do, so nobody can accuse us of abuse. As long as we do nothing we don't do anything wrong. Parents are scared that Welfare will take their children if they discipline them.

'A good smack on the bottom would save us all a lot of grief,' says Jack. Jack is just as old fashioned as my mum.

'Pamela told me that her dad hit her sister Suzy with a wooden spoon,' says Cathy, our kindergarten teacher. Suzy is in my class.

'It is mandatory to report the abuse to the Welfare,' Cathy reminds me. I check Suzy's legs and find a bruise hidden under the longish school uniform. I ask Suzy what happened and she says that she fell over. Cathy reports the bruise to the Welfare. Suzy's dad Amos comes to school.

'You bastards, you let Welfare destroy my family,' he yells at the principal. 'You can feed and clothe my kids as well from now on. I am not going to work for them.'

Suzy's mother Alice comes to see me. 'I hope you are happy now. Amos left, he quit his job,' she yells at me. She is embarrassing her daughter in front of the class. She accuses me of reporting her husband to the Welfare.

'Please talk to the principal,' I say calmly. I cannot even explain that Cathy felt duty bound to report the bruises. I am not allowed to say anything on the matter because it is in the hands of the Welfare.

'Why don't you look at what the kids are up to on the street? They drink, sniff petrol and glue; they smoke dope instead of going to school. At least my kids had a home until you wrecked it for them.'

Amos is a hard working man who provided for his family. He is much like my father was; only in my day my father had a duty not to spare the rod. I would like to tell Alice that Redfern is not a proper environment for raising good children. My mum is adamant about that. I was going to take Anthony with me to Redfern School so he could see what a real life looks like but mum literally raised hell about it.

The Welfare advised Alice to see a marriage counsellor. Alice tells me about it. The elegant young woman counsellor asked if Alice is happy in a relationship. Alice broke down and told her that she puts up with things for the sake of the children. Kids need their father.

'Never stay in an unhappy relationship for the sake of the kids. If the marriage does not allow you to grow as a person than you are better off out of it. Children suffer permanent damage if they grow in a dysfunctional family,' says Ms Right marriage counsellor. 'Criminals and drug users are the result of dysfunctional families.' she warns.

Alice wants her family to function; kids are crying for daddy and her bed is empty. Alice doesn't dare tell her counsellor that she wants Amos back. The Welfare might take her children from her if she defends a child abuser.

Alice tells me that Amos loves his children. 'If I find another man I will never know if he will love my children or abuse them? Amos is the only man I trust with my kids,' she says.

Noelene is in my class. Her father, Pete, yelled that he'll beat the living daylights out of Noelene if she didn't do as he told her. The neighbour heard him and she called the Welfare.

'Poor Noelene must have been terrified,' said the neighbour. I could have told her that unless Noelene is terrified she never does as she is told. Pete comes to pick Noelene after school. He is upset. The Welfare did not even inform him before they took Noelene away. Pete blames me for the Welfare. He has to blame somebody in authority.

Pete got custody of Noelene after his ex de-facto wife Tammy was taken into rehabilitation. She was in horrors most of the time. In the morning she used to take Noelene and her younger four children into town. She bought potato chips and a coke each. They didn't want to go to school so she found excuses for them because she loves them. Sometimes the men Tammy was drinking with brought coke and pies to the children. It was fun sitting on the sidewalk bench learning about real life. The children missed a lot of school so Welfare took them and eventually gave them to their father, Pete. They hated staying with Pete because he made them go to school; he also made them eat those green things and wear school uniforms. The principal implored Pete to do something about kids' abominable behaviour and language. There is little a school can do since the corporal punishment was abolished and nobody is allowed to touch a child.

Pete realises that he is responsible for his kids' behaviour but he is scared to hit them because they are under the surveillance of the Welfare. He is also scared that the principal will report kids' uncontrollable behaviour. His children swear at Pete in the fluent language they learned on the street. He begs and bargains and negotiates and, exasperated, he yells and threatens but the kids just laugh at him. Pete tries to hide the tears. He blows hard into his dirty handkerchief and looks away to compose himself and I look away not to embarrass him.

'Fuck you, you dog,' Noelene snarls at Pete and runs away. 'You can't make me do anything I don't want to do. I'll get the Welfare on you,' she threatens.

Noelene's ten years old sister runs after Noelene down the road and yells at Pete: 'Mother fucker. Fuck me dead motherfucker.'

The word motherfucker still frightens me. I never heard language like that before. The fucker is aggressive and powerful, the fucked up is powerless. Fucked up means bad and beyond repair. The fucked is a woman. Preferably a mother. In most languages. And all the time these fuckers revere their mothers. She is a defeated fucked up martyr and she has to be protected by a powerful male who is really a fucker.

Maybe the only difference between humans and animals is the shame of fucking. Animal males court the females they want to mate with but women are meant to be degraded by being fucked. Men rape. Soldiers poke their dicks into the dying, terrified women like they poke their knives into the terrified dying men. The poor human monkeys snatch the bananas from under the noses of other poor monkeys. Women defend men. Men are women's children.

Pete seems powerless. His eyes are red and his lips tremble as we stand at the school gate powerless to change the world.

'Now the kids are gone again,' he says with tears in his eyes. 'What can I do?'

'I'll talk to the Welfare,' I promise. I know that Welfare people don't like anyone to interfere.

After a thorough investigation the Welfare returns the children to Pete on probation to see how things will work out. They don't want to relinquish their power over Pete, they hold him in fear but they hold him alive. He hopes that one day his children will forget what they learned on the street.

I call a mothers' meeting to discuss discipline. I present a situation: Your twelve year old is fighting with another twelve year old. How can I stop them hurting each other?

The mothers look at me for the solution.

'I have to grab and hold your child to protect him,' I venture.

'If you touch my child I will sue you,' says a young girl bravely.

'What else should I do?'

'You are a teacher. You should teach them not to fight,' she advises confidently.

As a year six teacher I feel that personal development is important for many of my girls who would soon become women and mothers.

'You will soon get married and have babies,' I introduce my simple lesson.

'I am not getting married,' says Rebecca. 'Men spend your Welfare money on grog and marijuana.'

'I am going to have a baby and live on my own,' says Noelene.

'You have to think very carefully whom you choose to be a father of your baby,' I moralise.

'When you have a baby you go on the social and get lots of money every fortnight. You get rent money and you can live on your own,' she informs me.

'When you run out of food you go to the neighbourhood centre and they give you a food voucher,' Rebecca informs us.

'You get a baby bonus and you can buy anything you want when the baby is born,' says Noelene. I realise that 5000 dollars baby bonus represents a fortune to a girl who never had more than ten dollars in her pocket.

'Every baby deserves to have a father and mother,' I preach. I am glad that the girls do not know that somewhere in a nice neighbourhood my son doesn't even know his father.

The kids are sitting in front of me but their minds and hearts are far away in real life dealing with real life. I am no longer sure about things I do and say. I teach children to be kind and not to swear and they go home where people swear like they hear people on television and video swear.

Toni starts kindergarten.

'Samantha has two daddies,' Toni tells me. 'One daddy lives with her and one she goes for holidays with. Can I go on holidays with my daddy? Where is my daddy?'

'Your daddy lives in Lightning Ridge,' I tell.

'Can we go for a holiday with him?'

'If you like.'

'I am going for a holiday with daddy;' Toni breaks the news to mum.

Life keeps reproducing itself and wants to be lived. Toni's hands are as beautiful as his father's. I remember playing with Anthony's long fingers long time ago.

Toni wants his father so we are going to Lightning Ridge.

This is the first Christmas mum will spend alone with her memories. Mum loves her memories like she loves her old useless family heirlooms. She is hoping to pass the faded embroidery and chipped pottery to me to love. She doesn't realise that these days people don't pass things down. Things get converted into few dollars at Garage sales or taken to the tip.

Grandmothers and grandfathers don't even pass down stories to their grandchildren any more. Old people are put away in a home to wait for death that will put them away permanently. Real life is work and shopping and lovemaking and orgasm and take away fast food, television and computers. We solve problems by pressing buttons. Nothing is worth passing on, or polishing. I am careful to buy things that need no care and can be replaced once they are not exciting any more. What will Anthony remember of his childhood? What will I pass on to him? People live together until it suits them, if it suits them. Maybe we only ever get one chance to believe in love and all the rest is a repetition.

'Most women can't enjoy themselves without having a wedding ring in their sights,' said Jack. He is happy that I am not possessive.

'Marriage means little to me,' I insist. I know that something is missing, something that would make marriage necessary.

Jack and I didn't worry about the pill. We were prepared for a family if it happened. One night a terrible pain wakes me and

I vomit until my whole body is twisted over the basin. I know something is wrong. Mum calls an ambulance.

You had an ectopic pregnancy. There were complications and you lost one of the ovaries and your uterus, says the doctor. You will have no more children.

Jack is really kind to me; he is not terribly concerned about not having children. After all we have a child each from previous partners.

'We are going to travel and do all the fun things we always wanted to do. The world is getting overpopulated anyway,' he says. His parents are disappointed, my mum is devastated.

I read about fertility as I convalesce. A man can impregnate hundreds of women while a woman can only carry one man's child at one time. A man can impregnate a woman even when he can no longer provide for a child but a woman has to be of a fertile age. Fertility creates sexiness. Hormones help you fall in love.

'Men father children in one glorious mating moment but women mother men and children for the rest of their lives,' says mum.

Mum says that I am over-protective towards Toni but Toni is all I will ever have. Toni will never have a brother or a sister so he must at least know his father. I can't deny him that.

> 'If you have built castles in the air, your work need not be lost; that is where they should be. Now put foundations under them.' ~Henry David Thoreau~

After the school year ends in December I take Toni to Lightning Ridge to meet his daddy.

I imagined that everybody would stare at me and that vicious gossip would run through town but people don't even notice or recognise me. They just went on living and mining while I was in Sydney. People come and go and they are quickly forgotten in Lightning Ridge. They touch and celebrate, get drunk and mate and part and go on. It's not a big deal. Nobody is concerned about my role in all this.

I pushed my Lightning Ridge episode into my subconscious but I always knew that beside Lightning Ridge there is nothing.

I arranged to stay with Merlyn's family for a few days. Toni and I sleep in a caravan at the back of the house. Everybody seems to have a caravan at the back in Lightning Ridge. Friends and family come and stay in this tourist town.

'It must have come as a shock, when Anthony became paralysed,' says Marilyn.

'How is Anthony?'

'His usual cheerful self. He has a reputation as the best and most honest cutter,' Marilyn tells me.

'Honesty comes first with opal. There are so many temptations. Miners often bring buckets of uncut opal and leave it with Anthony to cut. Nobody can say what comes out on a cutting wheel. Similar stones may differ in price, sometimes a thousand dollars stone is much like another of ten thousand in the uncut state.'

'Anthony broke up with Mark after you left,' tells Marilyn. I leave Toni with Marilyn when I go to see Anthony. I stand in the open doorway and watch Anthony at the grinding wheel. The steps were changed into a ramp so he can move in and out of the house on his wheelchair. Anthony does not hear me coming because of the noise of the cutting machine. The strong light is illuminating his face, which is as handsome as it always was. He moves with ease, he seems delighted wheeling himself around.

Anthony once said that your feet will take you to where your heart is. You either love someone or you don't. If you do, you will stay if you don't, you will go. I came back but I don't know if I want to stay. I don't want to give Anthony and his son false hopes. I am also afraid that Anthony may reject his son. And me. I always knew that one-day I will have to introduce Anthony to his son. For awhile I wondered if Toni is Mark's son but he isn't, everybody can see that. He couldn't look more like Anthony. I am glad about it.

I knock.

'Come in,' Anthony responds without turning around.

I am there behind him waiting silently and after a few moments he turns.

'What are you doing here?' The curtain falls over his face and it takes him an eternity to recover.

'I wanted to see you.'

'Why.'

'Someone has been asking for you.'

'Who?'

'Someone who needs you.'

'Nobody needs me.' Anthony starts rubbing the stone on the wheel.

'Can you switch the machine off, I want to talk.'

'It's a bit late for that.'

'Better late than never.'

'You better talk to your friend Mark.'

I wonder what Anthony knows about Mark. And what Mark knows about Anthony.

'I am still your wife.'

'I have no use for a wife,' says Anthony.

'Maybe I have no use for a husband either. I just brought up someone to see you. Can we come later on?'

'Maybe never is better than late.' Anthony switches off the machine and we look to the floor in silence. The buzzing noise of cutting wheels separated us but now we face each other.

'Will you see us?'

'I am not going anywhere.'

We look at each other and I feel tears in my eyes. His lips are pressed together; maybe he is trying to quieten the trembling. We must not become emotional. We have to be sensible for our son. He depends on us to know best.

I get Toni. He is clutching my hand. He has no idea what daddies are like or what daddies should be like. I know that he is not expecting anything in particular; children his age get used to the newness of people they meet. Samantha must have painted daddies as something to be desired. We only judge childhoods from the one childhood we experience. Toni has a happy childhood.

Anthony and Toni look at each other; they stand apart to admire the picture in front of them. Toni's head leans on me but he wants to move to daddy.

'Say hello to daddy,' I urge Toni. You can always tell a child what to do.

'Hello daddy,' he whispers. Toni is not shy; he just deals with this new experience in a cautious way. He is still too young to know resentment and fear and guilt.

'Hello,' whispers his father and the emotion in his voice scares me. He doesn't move his eyes from the boy. I see tears in Anthony's eyes, his lip trembles, and his hands are shaking.

'Come to me son,' Anthony smiles after an eternity. Toni hugs daddy. There is no hesitation, both know who they are. I want to hug them and cry the tears I never cried.

'Can I come to you for holidays,' Toni breaks the silence.

'Anytime, you come whenever you want to,' says Anthony.

'Samantha has two daddies but I only have you,' says Toni.

'I only have you,' says Anthony.

I want to say that all I have is these two boys and that I love them, but I have to take one step at the time.

'What are you doing,' asks Toni. He got into a habit of asking everybody what they are doing. Anthony does not know that, he does not know anything about little boys or about Toni. He forgets about me as he shows the stones to Toni and explains to him every part of the cutting process. He pulls his son on his lap and even let Toni hold the stone on a cutting wheel.

'How old are you?'

'I am six. My birthday will be on 20th June,' says Toni with six fingers up in the air.

I know that Anthony is calculating.

'And so clever. Did you know?' Anthony looks at me.

'No.' What is he asking? Did I know about Mark or the pregnancy or the opal?

'Why did you leave?'

'I wanted to finish my degree and find a job.'

'Did you?'

'I am teaching in Sydney.'

Does he want to know about Mark, does he want to know if I know about the stolen opal? I suspected even then, of course, and the suspicion made it impossible for me to stay. I was as much to blame as Anthony; opal was there and Mark had enough of it. Why should he have all the luck? I didn't want Mark to know that I knew. I didn't even want Anthony to know that I knew. I suppose Anthony did not want me to know. Perhaps we were all a little ashamed of who we were. Being a ratter is the lowest sort of being in Lighting Ridge. Only being a ratter in your best mate's claim is lower. But I don't know if Anthony is a ratter. I don't know for sure if Anthony ever did anything wrong. Nobody ever openly accused Anthony of ratting. We never talked about it.

'It is always your family that make your life either happy or miserable,' smiles Anthony.

'Probably both.' I wonder how Anthony lives as a cripple and a ratter. Nobody knows about him ratting, of course. Except Mark. Do they have an agreement not to tell what each did to the other? Did I try to make up to Mark for what Anthony has done? For what I suspected Anthony has done? Did I somehow pay for the stolen opal?The only thing for me to do was to go away.

'Can we stay for Christmas,' asks Toni.

'Of course, son.'

Toni and I put our Christmas presents in a car to surprise daddy on Christmas Eve. It is a hot summer evening and the crickets are making their mating noises all over the place. I turn the radio on. It doesn't matter how many times the old Silent Night has been sung it still carries the magic of love. Peace and goodwill to all. Maybe that is why Jesus was born in the first place. Maybe people needed Jesus so they invented him and the carols. Toni and I sing along as I drive to Anthony's place. Christmas on Lightning Ridge opal fields is like a beautiful melody played somewhere far away. You can barely hear it but it stirs your whole being.

I knock on Anthony's door.

'Go away,' he growls.

Toni rushes in. Anthony holds his son and I see tears in his eyes. He is looking away from me. Anthony is angry. Maybe he is always angry but hides his anger behind a smile. Tonight he is drunk and he is not worried about hiding. Maybe Christmas Eve does that to people. Toni has no way of knowing that Anthony is drunk. He has never seen a drunk person.

'Merry Christmas,' I say bending down to Anthony's level to give him a hug. This is the first contact we had in years. I can feel him shudder.

'What are you doing for Christmas?'

'Not much, I hope. Have a beer.'

'We can have lunch together?'

'Where?'

'I'll cook it here if you don't mind.'

'What would you like to do for Christmas,' Anthony asks his son.

'Can we go yabbying?'

'It'll be too hot,' I say.

'It's never too hot for yabbying,' says Anthony.

We are creating Christmas memories for our son.

'You can go for a swim in the bore to cool off,' says Anthony.

'Wouldn't you rather watch a nice video,' I try.

'I want to go yabbying with dad,' says Anthony,

'Yabbying it is,' says Anthony. 'You can stay home and watch a video,' says Anthony to me.

'It's been awhile since I have been yabbying. I'll come.'

I have never been yabbying but Toni does not need to know that. Toni and I watched Marilyn and her children catch Cray fish-yabbies in the bore drain yesterday. I didn't let Toni get dirty and catch the burrs on his clothes but obviously he also wanted to catch yabbies.

I brought some fruit punch and ice cream and chocolate cake in the esky.

'Can we stay with daddy tonight,' begs Toni. I look at Anthony.

'If you like.'

'All right.'

'I love you mum,' says Toni. 'And you dad.'

Anthony puts a tape on and Christmas carols tremble among the gum trees as we look at the starry night. Anthony spots a satellite and we follow its path. I smile but all the time tears are trying to come to wash away everything that has ever been wrong.

The smell of coffee wakes me up the next morning and I hear Anthony and Toni whispering in the kitchen.

'Surprise, surprise,' calls Toni. 'We made a Christmas tree, mum.' There is a little native bush covered with cotton wool and strips of shredded coloured foil from the chocolates we had last night; there are presents under it.

'It's going to be a scorcher. The snow will melt,' I laugh.

'It's only a pretend snow,' explains Toni.

Anthony opens his present. His son gave him a silk shirt. Anthony made a didgeridoo for Toni. They try to blow a tune into it but they can barely make a hollow sound.

'Let me try the didge,' I grab the long instrument.

'Aboriginal legend says that women become pregnant if they play it,' warns Anthony.

I am not likely to get pregnant ever again but Anthony does not know that. Maybe he is thinking of Toni growing up all alone. Would he want me to be the mother of his child again? Would he like to father another child? Would he be able to? Anthony missed out on his fathering with Toni, maybe he would like to be a real father to a baby.

'I wish I had a baby brother,' says Toni.

'Maybe one day,' I say. No need to spoil the moment.

'This is my bestest Christmas ever,' says Toni.

I give Toni a book we made together. It is called My family. There are mementoes and pictures and letters. There is nanny and poppy and daddy and mummy and everybody is smiling. There is a picture of Anthony and myself as we were when we were very much in love. There are our wedding photos. Our heads touch as we lean over the pictures. We are the only people in the whole world that want to see every snapshot of Toni's growing up. Nobody else could possibly be so delighted about these most sacred images.

'I'll never lose this didge,' says Tony. This is my best present ever. 'And the book,' he quickly corrects himself. I wish I could surrender my dreams and settle here where Toni found home.

'What did you get for your last Christmas,' asks Anthony.

'I forget. We went to the zoo with Debbie,' remembers Toni. He doesn't even remember Jack or the presents or the party. We only remember things that touch our hearts.

'Are we yabbying today or what?' Says Anthony. Toni squeals with delight and hangs onto his dad.

'We need some cotton and meat and a net,' says Anthony.

Anthony wheels himself on the side of the road and we follow along the bore drain. Soon my fingernails are filled with mud and my feet are full of burrs and I am sweaty and sunburnt. The flies cover the smelly mess that used to be chuck steak I brought for bait. Fortunately the meat smells worse than I do.

'We are going to have a party,' Toni chirps.

'How many did we get?' Father and son count the dangerous looking crayfish in the bucket. I don't tell Anthony that the long crayfish tentacles remind me of cockroaches. I will have to eat yabbies for the first time in my life.

'We got eighteen, dad;' Toni is beaming with excitement. I am aware that neither of us will ever forget this Christmas. There were other Christmases I will never forget but this may be the first memorable Christmas for our son. I remember how mum used to help me create Christmas presents for everybody. We grew little punnets of flowers, we dried rose petals and sewed little sachets for them, and we made cards. Mum made a pretty new dress for me every Christmas. She made ribbons for my plats of the same material. Sometimes she made a little handbag I took to church on Christmas Eve. Mum put coins in my bag so I could give a gift to Jesus for his birthday. The silent night and the baby in a manger enchanted me and I was grateful to the kings for the gifts they brought for Jesus and to the angel for giving good news and to the shepherds for keeping watch over the holy family. I hope yabbying will brings the same magic of Christmas to Toni and Anthony. We return to the camp.

'There is nothing as beautiful as the sunset in Lightning Ridge,' says Anthony to his son pointing at the crimson, blue and violet in the west sky. 'If you look at the sky before the sun disappears you can see anything you want to see. There are angels and Father Christmas and opals.' My two boys gaze at the ever-changing evening sky. It is easy to believe in heaven and Jesus on the evening like this. 'Remember this picture because God created it especially for your Christmas. It will be gone when the stars come to cover the sky,' Anthony tells his son. 'Can you boil a big pot of water and drop a handful of salt in it,' says Anthony to me. 'There is a lemon to go with it.'

'This is the best Christmas party ever,' says Toni.

Next day I bring Toni and let him look for colourful chips in front of the camp. Anthony and I are close to the window watching our son who gets bored with opal and begins to build castles out of the opal dirt. He creates a little footpath and people walking on it. Toni is used to solitary games and he talks to imaginary people. He looks at his magnificent white sand stone castle from every side. Suddenly he levels the ground again. The dust rises and settles; it is easier to shape it the second time around.

'Where creation ends, destruction begins,' smiles Anthony.

'The need to create is stronger than the wish to have.' We are discovering life through our son. I hand Anthony a drink and our fingers touch. Anthony holds my hand and I lean over so our heads touch. I don't dare speak.

'That was nice,' he says.

'We shouldn't be afraid of each other,' I say.

'But we can hurt each other.'

'We probably will.'

'Don't be a pessimist.'

'Someone once said that a pessimist is a husband of an optimist.'

Toni wanders in.

'Can we stay with you forever, daddy,' he asks looking at Anthony. Daddy became his favourite word. Novelty, I suppose.

'You'll have to ask mum,' smiles Anthony looking at me. I want to ask if he would like us to stay but I don't want to know. Not yet. I have no right to play with their emotions until I decide what I want to do.

'Do you like it here,' I divert Toni's question. He knows that daddy and I love him. There is an unmistakable feeling of closeness. We belong together.

'Children make things look simple,' I say to Anthony.

'How come Toni does not go to school with you,' asks Anthony.

'It isn't good for parents and children to be at the same school.' It would take too long to explain that mum would never allow Anthony to mix with the children from the slum school where I work.

'Can we stay with dad? I like it here,' says Anthony again.

'We'll see.'

Anthony explains to his son how the colours are made in the opal. Toni does not move from his dad. Maybe I should not let him get so close to his father. He will miss him even more. I am afraid of closeness and afraid to destroy it. Without Anthony

Toni will never have a family. I try to reason that family is not what it used to be. Any loving group of people can be a family. How do I explain this to Toni? Maybe Toni will accept whatever comes, but children still like mummy and daddy family.

'How long are you staying?' Asks Anthony casually.

'School starts in February.'

'Can I go to school here, dad,' asks Toni.

'Have to ask mum.'

Toni doesn't even look at me.

Next morning I leave Toni with Merlyn's children and drive towards Anthony's place. I have to think, we have to talk.

'Can I do anything for you,' I ask.

'Like what?'

'Anything.'

'I am all right. I have a phone now and shops deliver,' says Anthony. He shows no emotion. No anger, no love, no guilt, nothing. Christmas is over. Maybe I do not mean anything to him. I wish he would accuse me of something, I wish to talk.

'Why is Toni not with you?'

'I didn't plan to come here.'

'Why did you?'

I wish to cry in his lap to bring back the closeness we once shared. The memory of our love overwhelms me.

'I was just passing by. I'll bring Toni tomorrow.'

'That's good.'

'Everything changed while I was away,' I say. I remember how we planted the flowers under the tree there.

'You can depend on things changing.'

'You have all the modern conveniences.'

'I have solar panels. I don't need much,' smiles Anthony.

'The things you buy don't mean the same.'

'I accept life as it is. I can't run away from it.'

'You are lucky to be able to settle down like that.'

'I had to stop running and start living.'

Maybe Anthony really came to terms with his wheel chair. Doesn't he want to go down the mine?

'What makes you happy?'

'I can cut opal, hear the birds, watch television, read, I can cook for myself.'

'I am sure you can do everything you put your mind to.'

'Nobody can do everything. I'd like to play soccer with Toni,' says Anthony. 'What do you wish for?'

'I have everything I want,' I say.

'Life goes on,' says Anthony.

'What is life?'

'It's what makes the blood flow and put fire in your eyes.'

'What puts the fire in your eyes,' I ask.

'Look at this,' Anthony points to the opal he was shaping. 'There is fire in the stone but right in the middle is the sand, the stone is flawed.'

'You like cutting.'

'Keeps me out of mischief.'

'Are miners still getting rich?'

'What is rich? One car or ten? One house or a hundred, one lover or ten. No person is ever rich enough. Being rich or poor is a state of mind,' says Anthony.

'What is your state of mind,' I quiz.

'I am all right,' he backs away.

'Are you angry with me?'

'No.'

Anthony and I never talked this much when we lived together. We were too busy making love and building a home.

'Technically we are still married.'

'Why didn't you divorce me? Didn't you want to get married again?'

'No. Did you?'

'What would I want with a wife?'I want to ask if he still wants me or if he still needs sex but I have no right to know.

Next morning I see Mark at the supermarket. He carries a baby and his wife wheels a trolley with a little girl hanging on. The children seem happy and their mother vibrantly contented. She is a very ordinary, rather fat girl with masses of reddish curls over her shoulders. Mark hasn't changed, he still has the boyish slender body and his hair is cropped even shorter. He looks like most Australian boys his age.

'Mark's wife, Kim, is a community nurse,' Marilyn tells me. 'She works part time visiting elderly and disabled.

'How come she is working? She is supposed to be rich and she has two little children. Surely she can afford to stay home. I am surprised that Mark lets her work. '

'Mark's mother Mojca looks after the children.'

I would like to say hello to my mum's friend Mojca but I am not ready yet to bring Mark's people into my life.

'Kim probably likes a bit of space from her pedantic mother in law,' says Marilyn. 'She once said that she could never hold her hand out for spending money and then report to her husband what she spent it on.'

'Maybe Mark isn't as generous with money as one would believe.'

'If you begin being generous you soon stop being rich. I think Mark was born to be rich,' says Marilyn.

'You think he is tight?'

'Money attracts money. Bees go for honey, flies go for shit.'

I have to forget Mark. I have forgotten Mark. I was bored with Anthony that's all. I was in shock. I wanted out; I wanted to see what the world had to offer. I am looking for excuses. I am all right now, I have a good job; mum is happy. Only Toni wants to stay with his daddy. I owe it to Toni to stay in Lightning Ridge. I have to give it a go. I gave him life. He asked for his daddy and he will have him, pain or no pain; at least for awhile. Everybody loves Toni. I love this little boy more than I ever imagined loving anybody.

I have to forget the past. People go to a therapist to help them overcome childhood traumas but there is nothing painful in my childhood. Everybody liked me; everybody was proud of me. The teachers praised me; the kids wanted me for a best friend; my hair was shiny and manageable; my skin never had freckles or pimples. Mum made the best lunches for me; boys liked me; my shoes were polished; my breath did not smell; my fingernails were always clean. There is nothing to overcome; there is no pain in my past. I have never been so beautiful or so ugly that people would hate me for it. I was never particularly clever although I am not dumb. I was never the richest or the poorest; I never stood out in any way. I am proportionally built in a healthy symmetry and mum often told me that I am pretty. People say that I have a pleasant voice and this is a real asset when one is a teacher.

I don't think about the brief sexual encounter Mark and I had. I don't agonise about it or lose sleep. Mark was there when I wanted to forget about the events around me. Next morning I walk past Mark's place and he calls over the fence.

'You are back?'

'Just for a holiday.' I lean on Mark's fence.

'Staying with Anthony?'

'I am staying with Marilyn.'

'How are things?'

'I am all right.'

'Married?'

'Yes, to Anthony.'

'I am married.'

'I saw your family.'

'Kim sees Anthony once a week.'

'What does she do for him?'

'Physio.'

'That's great,' I say.

'Come in for a drink,' Mark invites.

Inside we hug as friends do. You look good. You haven't changed; we echo each other's words. We embrace and kiss. We kissed before so holding back would be unnatural. The second time seems easier, only it means less. The pleasant sensation is still there.

'We've been through a lot together,' says Mark.

'Do you have regrets?'

'Maybe it's best to let the sleeping dogs sleep.'

'Does Kim know?'

'Nobody knows.'

We don't mention what nobody knows. We don't know what each one of us regrets.

'You can't undo what was,' says Mark. His seriousness indicates that we have Anthony's condition in our thoughts.

'Everything happens for a reason, I suppose. The water once muddied is never clean again.'

'Unless you filter it through rocks and sand.'

'Are you happy?' I ask. The silence frighten us, it has to be filled.

'As happy as one can be.' Do I want him to say that he still loves me? He never actually said that. We have to heal the pain we cannot talk about.

'Come with me to Dubbo tomorrow,' says Mark. 'We'll talk.'

'I'll see,' I say a bit breathless. It would be so easy to go, it might be enjoyable, nobody needs to know, nobody needs to be hurt, it would bring us closer. I could leave Toni with his father.

At the thought of Anthony I stand up. On the way home I change my mind about Dubbo. I don't need to be closer to Mark. I came to give Toni a chance to be with his father. I drive to the Three mile.

I leave the car away from Anthony's camp. I pretend that I am a tourist specking for opal but it doesn't really matter to anybody what I do. I don't matter. I want to find out about Anthony's life before I make a decision about my own.

I peer through the bushes into the distance where Anthony's camp is. I see Kim go to Anthony's place. I get up and brush the sharp stones from my knees. I move closer and look through the window hiding like a thief. I see Kim giving Anthony a glass and a pill. She makes coffee and they sit facing each other. She laughs at something he says. She puts her cup down and massages his shoulders. Her hand comes to the front and he covers it with his hand and guides her towards the neck. Maybe he is showing her where it hurts. Kim takes his cup and puts it in the sink. She draws the curtain casually. Maybe the sun is blinding her, maybe it is too hot.

Through the curtain I see the shape of their bodies close together. Of course, they would be together if she is giving him physiotherapy. Maybe she has to change his underwear. Maybe she has to wash him. Maybe she gave him a Viagra; the thought makes me smile. I am scared. Maybe she has some other pills to make Anthony happy. I see Kim leaving. Soon Anthony wheels himself out to sit on the veranda. I am amazed at how well he manages. Maybe he doesn't need me at all. I once left everything behind to be with Anthony. The things one gives up are always more attractive than those one keeps. I remember the day I first returned from Sydney to be with Anthony. We sat on the banks of Narran Lake in the middle of the wilderness and watched the reflection of the sky in the water. Brolgas danced their love dances; they had no eyes for us. Anthony spread the blanket over the young flowery grass. Millions of white daisies just opened their little button head flowers. We lay there until slowly our fingers met and our hands and our whole bodies merged silently while brolgas danced. Ageless white bodies of the tree trunks echoed with the mating calls of the birds. Hundreds of the water birds frolicked around us as we lay naked under the sky in the vastness of the continent.

I went mining underground with Anthony. At night as I closed my eyes I saw the colours sparkling. Anthony told me that this happens to every new miner. We talked about things we will do when we find opal. We worked for months without actually seeing any colour. In our spare time we finished our camp. Anthony made most of the furniture and I sanded and varnished it and made curtains. We never found opal. I became impatient, I wanted more. I regretted my decision to come to the Ridge. My hands became chafed; my face lost its glow.

'Welcome to the real world,' said Jessica, as I returned to Sydney.

I often go to the Three mile. I hide behind the bushes to look at the camp my son would like to live in. I feel reluctant to go in. Once I see Kim walk straight in. She takes off Anthony's shirt and runs her fingers down his spine before she begins massaging his shoulders and neck. She stands behind him and his head is cradled in her chest. She moves to the front then and plants a casual kiss on top of Anthony's head. She unscrews a tube and spreads something on the palms of her hands. Anthony pulls her closer, his hands are on Kim's big buttocks and his head is buried now in her bosom. What are they doing? Her legs are spread wide on each side of Anthony's legs so her skirt covers both of them. She is massaging his back, bent over him she is reaching down to his hips. Suddenly I want to be where Kim is and do to Anthony what she is doing, what they are doing to each other. I feel sexual sensations I never knew existed, I want to go in and beg them to include me into the magic of their union. Kim's fleshy body is bouncing over my husband. How come they did not draw the curtains this time? What would Mark say? Maybe Kim is doing something medical to Anthony but I can only see their closeness. They wouldn't have sex like that almost in the open. Anybody could be watching. After an eternity Kim steps back; she spreads her legs and puts her arms out for Anthony to put his arms on top of hers and they both get up and stand like that without moving. After a few moments they step to the side, Anthony is out of the chair; he stretches to full height while leaning on Kim. With his arms on her shoulders she pushes his buttocks this way and that. They dance for a few moments on the spot like that before they disappear into the bathroom. When they come back Anthony's hair is wet and he smiles at Kim as she helps him back into a chair.

'Love is what you do, not what you dream,' I remember mum's words. She wasn't talking about sex but about all the little things one does for another. Maybe love is what Kim does for Anthony. I want to do all these things for Anthony. A cold sober emptiness envelops me. Life goes on as if I never existed. Time is all we have, we walk a little way, we play, we mate and preserve life and then we die. The simplicity of it is all there is.

If I choose to stay here, I will forever dream about the rest of the world and the life I could have had. If I go to Sydney I will long to be back and be a family with Anthony and Toni. I sit on the fence and all the time Toni is growing up without knowing where his home is. I will have to give up something to get something else. I will have to do it before Toni grows up and goes away. Maybe Anthony doesn't want me to stay. Maybe he would never have me live with him again. He has his freedom and Kim looks after him.

'Life is seeking the answers,' said mum. There are no answers; there is only an eternal seeking. My parents excluded all others from their lives and maybe the pain of that exclusion made their union precious. They gained a sense of commitment and goodness and righteousness. They must have been tempted but resisting the temptation strengthened their commitment.

I did not resist Mark, I surrendered for the moment but the quick passionate, hungry sex only made me feel empty and uncertain and unworthy. I could do it again but I know that I will not find what I am looking for.

What is Kim sharing with Anthony? He is a handsome man and maybe being a helpless paraplegic adds to the excitement like danger does. Is there nothing sacred and perfect?

Kim takes her bag, goes into the car and drives away. Anthony looks after her through the window for a moment and then wheels himself to the cutting machine. Thank God nobody knows that I am hiding in the bushes. My knees hurt from kneeling on the rough opal dirt. My body is stiff so I straighten and walk to my car.

My loneliness turns into despair. My mind cannot reach Jack. He went bush walking with his mates. He doesn't know that Lightning Ridge holds the essence of my existence. I want Toni to have a father; I want us to have a home. I want to be loved. I need a man to love me and make love to me; the man who loves my son.

'When you find a good man who will father your children, cherish him. Praise your man for the good things and he will do good things. Children come and go but the man will grow old with you and you will remember together,' said mum.

The starry nights of Lightning Ridge are calling me home, there are the glorious sunsets, the enormous sky and the crickets chirping all night. The primeval vastness of the unspoiled land is promising pain and joy. I need this intensity; I need to feel essential to life.

I leave Toni with his father as I go to Sydney for the weekend to bring up my belongings and to find tenants for my apartment. I tell Jack that Toni would like to live with his father.

'What about you,' says Jack.

'I want to be where Toni wants to be.'

'It's your life,' says Jack. We both like the freedom we offer each other.

'Toni wants to stay with his dad,' I explain to mum.

I apply for a job in Lightning Ridge School and enrol my son. The Department of Education offers me a house as well as a job. I am set. Toni will have his father.

'Without sacrifice you will never know what real love is,' mum's words echo from the past. Toni is the only person I would make sacrifices for. I want Toni to have a sense of a family like I had. Maybe we only know one way to live and that is the way our parents lived. Maybe the whole reason for a family is to perpetuate it. I don't know if it is possible to give Toni a sense of exclusive intimacy I had with my family. Anthony and I are not yet willing to admit our sins even to ourselves. Maybe perfection remains the light on the hill.

'You can only take from the family what you put into it,' said mum. 'Family is not given to you, you make it.'

Everybody keeps telling me that these days women don't have to put up with things our mothers did but deep down most girls want to live the life their mothers lived with their fathers even when the girls know that their parents did not have the ideal life. The memory of one's growing up is a magic time. We measure the childhoods by the only childhood we ever had.

Maybe children have no right to expect the same kind of life their parents had. We live by different rules; we are not willing to put as much into the family as they did. Their kind of life does not exist anymore; maybe that kind of life was wrong; maybe our parents were not as loyal and faithful as they would have us believe.

'Marriage is like a cake,' said mum. 'Good ingredients and good timing will make sure that you will enjoy it.'

I want to start again but the ingredients of my life are tainted. Maybe it is too late for me to fall in love or to love or be loved as I want to be loved. It is too late to choose the man to father my children because Toni is the only child I will ever have. There is a chaotic disorder inside me. Maybe Toni doesn't have to have everything he wants, other children live without daddies quite happily, I try to convince myself but the years of mum's teaching follow me and I know that I will never be happy if Toni is not happy. Maybe fidelity offers its own rewards; maybe the uniqueness of experience makes the experience unique. Maybe one rose is more special than a paddock of roses.

'I worry about mum. She is a lonely old woman,' I say to Anthony when I return from Sydney.

'Why don't you bring her with you?'

'Mum is attached to her routine. She washes on Thursdays and irons on Fridays; she cleans the house on Saturdays and potters in the garden on Sunday. On Monday, Tuesday and Wednesday she goes to the office and has the same conversations with the old lawyer who does the same mundane office work she does. Mum knows the butcher and the baker and the milkman, they all know that she is alive as long as she pays her bills.'

'We need someone like that here,' smiles Anthony.

I can hear mum complain that I am risking my boy's future by bringing him to live in Lightning Ridge with all the ratbags coming from all over the world? It's not healthy for the boy.

'Come here Nan. It is good here,' Toni chirps excited on the phone.

'When are you coming home,' asks mum.

'I want to stay with dad. Please come,' insists Toni.

'How are you?' I ask mum on the phone.

'I sorted the photos of our family,' says mum bravely.

'That's good but how are you?/

'I tidied the house; I emptied all the drawers and cleaned all the cupboards.'

'I know you did, but how is your life?'

'My house is my life now,' says mum.

'This is her first Christmas without us,' I tell Anthony. 'She tries to sound cheerful but I know that she is swallowing tears as she tries not to beg me to come home. Our family and her work meant the whole life for her. Her boss retired and her office has closed. She can't escape the loneliness of our home where the memories are. Life is as sacred as you make it, mum used to say. Traditions die if you become too lazy to observe them.'

'I would like to meet your mum,' says Anthony.

'Mum goes to the cemetery every Sunday to change the flowers and cry on dad's grave. She organised a prayer group that visits our departed every November for the All Saints Day. Mum would miss that in Lightning Ridge,' I tell Anthony. 'Australians don't even remember their dead on All Saints day.'

'Melbourne cup makes November special for Australians. People dress in their finery to bet on a horse. It's an Australian tradition. It's almost like thanksgiving in America or like all Saints day,' says Anthony.

'Thanksgiving sounds better than betting. We don't cook a turkey and the family does not say grace together on the Melbourne cup day. We meet on the racecourse and eat pies, hot dogs and hamburgers made by the fund-raisers.'

'We raise funds for the Catholic Church, so maybe there is some good in getting together,' smiles Anthony.

'Come and stay with us for awhile,' I say to mum.

'Maybe I will.'

'Why didn't your parents come to our wedding?'

'They hoped that I will come to my senses. They didn't know about pregnancy. Their plan for me was to rise above and be extraordinary. I suppose I ran away from this great responsibility.'

'It must have been hard to leave them,' says Anthony.

'I was in love, we were in love, we believed in love, we were enormously happy,' I say.

'Until you left.'

'There was the road and everything told me to go for it and finish what I was meant to do. I crave ordinariness like some people crave excitement.'

'Why did you marry me?' Anthony changes the subject.

'I was pregnant.'

'That's an honest answer.'

'Did you expect me to lie?'

'Why did you stay with me after you lost the baby?'

'You were my first love and my husband.'

'How long did you love me?'

'Are we making an inventory?'

'It would be nice if we could be honest with each other.'

'Why did you marry me?' I ask.

'Because you were pregnant,' he smiles.

It would be so easy to put my arms around Anthony and wrap my body into his to make us both bigger and stronger and happier and more lovable. If only life could be a simple addition, if more bodies would mean more strength, more heart, more love, more happiness. I wish Anthony would say that he loves me but neither of us seems able to surrender yet. Anthony never asked me about my sex life or love life or life at all.

'Why did you stay with me after you lost the baby?' Asks Anthony again.

'I believed that you will find me a big opal.'

'And you left when I didn't.'

'Yes.'

I want to ask if he still loves me but I don't know if I still love him. One is never as sure of love as in the first moments of loving.

'Tell me about Kim,' I say.

'I know Kim from Sydney,' Anthony cheers up at the mention of Kim. 'Her mum used to look after me. We lived on the same block until we were twelve. Kim and I played together and told tales about each other. We were in the same class.'

'What happened then?'

'They moved from Blacktown to Coogee. I haven't seen her for almost twenty years. Kim is really very nice.'

Should I tell Anthony that Mark is really nice and that he invited me to come with him to Dubbo?Marilyn told me that Mark is a mining association president. He is a friend of the Mining Warden and the Mining Registrar. People look up to Mark and try to please him.

'Jim came back,' says Anthony.

'I didn't know that he was away.'

'We go a long way back, Jim and I,' says Anthony.

'How long?'

'His mum took me in when my mum died. He was my best friend; my only friend.'

'Is Jim mining again?'

'Arthur hunted Jim out of town after you left. Now Jim returned to get Arthur and Mark. '

'Why?'

'It's a long story.'

'Tell me.' I am glad Anthony brings things out in the open; we have to deal with it sooner or later.

'You remember when Mark, Jim and I registered claims at the Three mile.'

'I was there.

'Arthur told Mark that ratters were stealing his opal and that he should open cut.'

'Arthur accused you of ratting.'

'Arthur registered a claim down the road and he came into Mark's claim underground. He checked all our claims at night. Most of the ground on the Three mile is worked out; there are underground ballrooms and corridors connecting claims. Mark's claim and our claims were on the edge of what was a very prosperous ground. They were the only solid claims left. Arthur found opal in Mark's claim so he wanted to convince Mark to let him open cut it on percentage.'

'But why pick on you?'

'Arthur had his eye on our claims right from the start. He had the only bulldozer in town. Jim and I had three claims next to Mark's open cut. He also wanted to get even with Jim.'

'I don't think Mark really liked Arthur. Nobody liked Arthur,' I say.

'People know that Arthur is a crook. He wanted to turn Mark against us so he told him that we were ratting in his claim. He needed Mark who seemed to be a respectable opal buyer. When Mark went to Japan I heard someone picking in his claim. The shaft was on the border of my claim. I have been down before with Mark and he came into my claim whenever he wanted. I didn't go down to steal,' says Anthony.

Could Anthony walk away if he came down the shaft and saw opal traces in the wall? I will never know. Neither will Anthony. He wasn't tested. If I went down that claim and saw a stone in the clay wall, would I be tempted? Nobody would know if I took it. I deserve a share of Mark's opal. If it wasn't for me, Mark would never be in Lightning Ridge. How could Anthony not be jealous of Mark who found opal wherever he started digging?

I remember Mum saying that you can't unscramble an egg. You can eat it scrambled or throw it away.

'Jim and I looked down Mark's shaft,' continues Anthony. 'We saw a face look up. We were both sure it was Arthur. I went down to investigate. The ladder was greased, one step was cut loose, I slipped and fell about fifteen metres. Jim called for rescue. They had to lift me out on a stretcher. I would have died, if it wasn't for Jim.'

'Mark never said to anyone that you were ratting.'

'Maybe he felt sorry for me, maybe he believed that I wasn't ratting in his claim; maybe he thought that I suffered enough. He came to see me in the hospital and I threatened to sue him for compensation. He promised not to tell anyone about me being in his claim if I never mention compensation again. I knew that suing Mark would not do me any good. He was a golden rich boy and I was a broke cripple without a soul in the world.'

'What did Mark say when you told him about Arthur digging in his claim?'

'Arthur told Mark that he had witnesses who saw him in Dubbo that day. He also told Mark that Jim and I were ratting every night while he was away. 'Anyway Arthur open cut Mark's claim and they became millionaires while I was in hospital. You left and I did not care anymore.'

'I would not let Arthur get away with it.'

'What goes around comes around. You have to believe that to stay sane. Arthur is a snake but someone will step on him one day. While I was in rehab he told Jim how sorry he was for me. He offered to open-cut Jim's claim. Jim did not want to open on percentage but he agreed to pay ten thousand to Arthur because Arthur had the only bulldozer in town. Jim and I scraped our last dollars to pay for the open cut. We were going to share the profits. Arthur opened the claim but the opal we found barely paid expenses.

A year later the Mineral Resources office issued a letter saying that Jim had to restore the claim within six months. Arthur pushed for the restoration through Mineral Resources office. He knew that we had no money for restoration.'

'You paid the bond for restoration? You could have forfeited the bond,' I reason.

'The Mineral resources office informed Jim that any future bond would be much higher if we did not fulfil our obligation and restore the claim ourselves.'

'Arthur offered Jim to restore our open cut if I would transfer to him my claim, which was next to Jim's. Since we found no opal in Jim's open cut I transferred my claim to cover restoration costs.'

'How much does it cost to restore a claim?'

'We never talked about money. It took Arthur two days to push the overburden into the hole with the bulldozer.'

'How much do they charge for a bulldozer hour?'

'About one hundred dollars.'

'It would cost two thousand dollars at the most to restore the claim. How much was the bond?'

'Two thousand dollars.'

'You could have given Arthur the bond.'

'Everything was settled until Jim received a Statement of Liquidated Claim from the local court for thirty two thousand dollars. Arthur charged that for the restoration of Jim's claim. He claimed that he had to bring the dirt from a dump a couple of kilometres away. Jim explained to the Mining Warden that I transferred my claim to Arthur as a payment. I was in hospital and I didn't think straight. The Mining Warden asked the Mining Registrar what was the deal for the transfer of my claim. The transfer was made for one hundred dollars which is the value of the bond for underground mining. Everybody knows that this figure is put on the paper every time the claim is transferred. In Lightning Ridge people deal with cash and they never state the real value of the claim.'

'It's rather silly not to get something in writing.'

'We were stupid. We also had no idea what sort of crook Arthur really is. He can be awfully friendly when it suits him. He didn't have anything in writing either.'

'Did he itemise the bill?'

'Arthur stated that there was no dirt nearby and he had to bring 18000 m3 of dirt from 2000 metres away which alone cost him $27 000.The witnesses who carted the dirt for Arthur told the court that they worked for three weeks to restore the open cuts on the Three mile.'

'What happened to the dirt taken out of Jim's open cut?'

'It was pushed on the edge of Jim's claim only months earlier. It should more than cover up our open cut. The loose dirt bulks up to twice the amount of dirt needed for restoration.'

'What happened to this dirt?'

'There were five old open cuts in the area, which Arthur promised to restore at the same time as a favour to the Mineral

Resources. He said that he wanted to be in good books with the Mineral Resources Department so he restored these old open cuts for free.'

'He stole your dirt to cover other people's open cuts. Did those old open cuts have bonds over them? What happened to those bonds?'

'Jeff, the Mineral Resources officer, said that he had no record of any bonds paid on those open cuts. It was done before his time.'

'The bank must have records; there must also be some expert opinion on how much dirt is needed to restore the claim.'

'Jim told the court that all the dirt needed was on the edge of the open cut and that it only took a couple of days for the bulldozer to push it back into the cut. Jim did not even engage a solicitor; he believed that justice will be done when he told the Mining Warden in the Local court what really happened. Mark was called as an expert witness for Arthur. He told the court how much dirt would be needed for restoration and how much the transportation would cost. Jeff from the Mineral Resources office witnessed that there was not enough dirt to cover the open cut. Jim argued that there was not enough dirt for five old open cuts but there was more than enough for his. The Mining Warden said that in his experience there is never enough dirt for restoration. He pointed out that Jim has no evidence to show that he paid for the restoration; he summed up the case saying that it looks to him that Jim tried to avoid his responsibilities. He directed Jim to pay the costs of the court and lawyers on top of what Arthur wanted. Jim saw Jeff and the Mining Warden having lunch with Mark in the Bowing club. They were all against us. We had no hope beating the big guys.'

'Did Mark know that Arthur stole your dirt for old open cuts he restored?'

'Of course he knew. He wanted to punish me for something I haven't done. He punished me enough when he took my legs from under me. To think that I taught Mark everything he knows about opal.'

'I can't imagine Mark and Arthur being friends.'

'Respectable people need crooks to do dirty jobs for them and crooks need people who have connections.'

'Did Jim pay?'

'He transferred the claim with the camp and the machinery over to Arthur who bulldozed the camp and open cut Jim's claim. He always wanted that claim but Jim would not sell the claim on which he built his home.'

'It isn't fair.'

'Life isn't.'

'No wonder Jim is looking for justice.'

'He accused Jeff, Mark and the Mining Warden of assisting Arthur. He was there day after day. In the end they banned him from attending the local office of Mineral Resources.'

'Why didn't he appeal?'

'Jim only had a right of appeal to the Supreme Court on the point of law; that means that the Supreme Court judge had to decide whether the Mining Warden had a jurisdiction to decide on the case. We found out later that the Supreme Court judge almost never overturns the decision of the Local Court. He decided that the Mining Warden had the jurisdiction to decide on the case. That sealed the case. We were doomed; we were broke. The Mineral Resources officers are all the law and order as far as mining goes. They are the first to know where opal is found and they have the final say who is going to register and mine what.'

'You could apply to the Freedom of Information Office to obtain the evidence on the bonds paid on those old open cuts. With the new evidence you could reopen the case.'

'When we received the evidence that the old miners forfeited the bonds, it was too late. The Mineral Resources office held this money for twenty years. In twenty years it accumulated with interests to over eighty thousand dollars. Arthur and Jeff from the Mineral Resources office probably split this money after Arthur restored the old open cuts. No wonder Jeff supported Arthur. Nobody supported Jim. I feel sorry for Jim, but I am tired of him hitting the brick wall,' says Anthony. 'He lost his sense of humour; he is quoting the Mining Act like Jehovah Witnesses quote the Bible; he knows the law and the lawyers and general attorneys and politicians. The trouble is nobody wants to know the bloke who has nothing. I accept that, but Jim does not. Everybody here is somehow dependent on opal so miners like to stay on the side of the Mineral Resources office.'

'Surely there is a way to prove that the local mining court decision was wrong.'

'Apparently not.'

'You should have gone to the member of the parliament or ombudsman.'

'We should have hired a good lawyer to start with but we believed in the justice system. We were also broke. No lawyer likes to work against the government unless he is well paid.'

'You should have talked to your Member of Parliament.'

'Marilyn wrote letters to the local Member of Parliament. The MP conferred with his colleague who is the minister of Mineral Resources. The minister made inquiries through the local Mineral Resources office. Jeff reported to the Minister that Jim is a suspected ratter, a known troublemaker and a nuisance. They refused to intervene on Jim's behalf. We came the full circle. The Mineral resources office produced a diary of all Jim's movements for their Minister. Jim went to the Premier's office in Sydney. He wanted to make an appointment to see the Premier. He was waiting there until Premier's secretary contacted Minister for Mineral Resources. The Minister explained that he knows about the case and dismissed Jim's complaint. Jim stood there and insisted to see the Premier. He was desperate by then, exhausted and almost suicidal. Two armed security officers escorted him out of the Premier's Department. He asked the Attorney General and Ombudsman to intervene but they all refereed the case back to the local Mineral Resources office, which dismissed Jim as a madman. Jim made a complaint to the Opposition leader who also referred him to the Mineral Resources Minister who referred him to the local Mineral Resources office. In the end Jim wrote to the ICAC, Independent Commission Against Corruption. He waited months until they wrote that they did not have enough resources to investigate every case and they did not have to give reasons why they would not take his case. Jim always believed that somewhere higher up he would find justice. In the end he wrote to the Premier. It was during the election campaign so the Premier ordered the minister for Mineral Resources to open an independent inquiry. Jim was elated. Two men in black suits came from Sydney and inquired. The government paid these independent men; they inquired and reported to the Minister for Mineral Resources. The minister ordered ICAC to investigate. They have all done what they could. The government paid tax payers' money to the independent men who told Jim that the government was innocent. What more do you want? Little crooks are on the ground but the big crooks are higher up holding the umbrella for little crooks,' said Jim.

'Why did they come to investigate in the first place?'

'To satisfy the electorate and show that THEY are innocent. Jim became obsessed. He begged people to help him write letters of complaints; he hitch hiked to Sydney and Canberra to talk to media, lawyers and politicians but they all dismissed him. In the end he forgot who he was complaining against, he attacked the whole system and the system kicked him back. Jim became a nuisance. Jeff asked for a transfer and was never heard of again. Most of the staff in the Mineral Resources Office was replaced. The new Mining Registrar refused to be involved in the old disputes.

I will die fighting for justice, said Jim before he left. Here is a letter Jim wrote to ICAC,' says Anthony and I read about the things Anthony already told me.

'The persecution against me began when I brought to the Department's attention that local Mineral Resources officers and the Chief Mining Warden favour some miners at the expense of others. I have paid an enormous price for making a complaint. The obstruction, slander, and persecution on every level have been directed against me. I became an example to other miners not to rock the boat. Miners know that Mineral Resources officers can and will destroy your mining ventures with little or no recourse available, if you are not in good books with them. My complaints are always refereed back to the Lightning Ridge Mineral Resources officers who appear to have succeeded to discredit the validity of my complaints. I have been stalked wherever I go. I feel powerless and have nowhere to turn. They created for me a feeling of desperation and fear for my safety. They destroyed me.'

'You don't have to read the lot, he repeats himself a lot, says Anthony. 'In the end Jim forgot who his real enemy was.'

'People could witness that Jim is an honest person,' I say.

'In a small mining town people don't like to witness against sharks like Mining inspector and the big boys like Mark and Arthur. A miner never knows when he will need one of them.'

Jim comes in without knocking. I knew a happy ginger haired guitar strumming Jim who lived next to Anthony's camp with his Aboriginal girlfriend Fay.

'Hello stranger, long time no see,' I extend my hands to Jim as he comes through the door.

'I saw you going to Mark's place,' Jim ignores my hands. I see that he wants to cause trouble between me and Anthony. I didn't tell Anthony about my visit to Mark.

'I just told Tina about Arthur and Mark,' Anthony explains.

'You can tell Mark that Jim is back,' Jim turns to me.

'I don't carry messages,' I snap.

'I'll come when you are alone,' says Jim to Anthony.

'He is upset,' says Anthony when we are alone.

'I don't owe anything to him.'

'Jim is like a brother to me. I'll invite him and Fay for a drink if you don't mind. I'll explain everything,' says Anthony.

'Explain what?'

'Jim thinks that you and Mark conspired against us.'

'Why would I do that?'

'Jim saw Mark here before he went to Japan and while I was in hospital after my accident.'

'Of course Mark was here, he was here when you were home and sometimes when you weren't. He always complained because we didn't have a phone so he could call us.'

'We have to reassure Jim that you are on our side. You are, aren't you?'

'I need someone to help me write to the newspapers,' says Jim as we sit on Anthony's veranda.

'Give it a rest,' says Anthony.

'Never. I want to expose Arthur and Mark and Mineral Resources and chief Mining Warden and the Mining Association and the members of the parliament and judiciary.'

'Most of the time they are the same people or friends of the same people,' says Anthony. Nobody wants to admit that they made a mistake. If one of them admits it, the whole case can collapse. People have reputations to look after. Miners want to be in the good books with the powers to be and the only power that matters here is the local Mineral Resources office. Arthur put himself in the good books with them by restoring old open cuts on our account.'

'If some influential journalist gets interested in the case he may be able to help,' I say. I can write letters. I have a computer,' I promise. 'Journalists are always searching for some interesting story.'

'You live in Sydney.'

'I took a job at school here.' I believe that since I am not a miner, Mineral Resources officers can't touch me. Nothing can happen to me if I help Jim.

'What happened to Arthur?'

'He sold the farm for two millions to Aborigines, tells Jim. He built his palace in town. '

'He bought the property ten years ago for one hundred thousand dollars,' adds Anthony. Aborigines bought it with government money. Their experts found sacred sites on the farm.'

'I wonder who Aboriginal experts were and how much they were paid. Money talks all languages,' I say. 'Some of mum's money wisdom was passed down to me.'

'Aborigines have their own Mafia. Black culture brokers distribute the government money. The rest of Aborigines have no say. Everybody is careful not to criticise Aboriginal Mafia because they could be called racists,' warns Anthony.

'Not if Aborigines make a complaint,' I say.

'Fay's uncle Brian told me that Aborigines cannot claim legal aid if they complain against other Aborigines or against Aboriginal organisations, says Jim. Arthur promised Aborigines sacred sites and artefacts but when the government paid for the property they only got an old farmhouse full of rats and cockroaches,' says Jim.

'Be careful. They might sue us. The artefacts and the sacred sites can easily be recreated,' says Anthony.

'I don't know what I am getting myself into,' I confess to Anthony after Jim and Fay leave.

'Fay worked for Arthur on the property, says Anthony. Jim and I never heard of Arthur before this black pregnant girl knocked on Jim's door.'

'Is Arthur the boy's father?'

'As far as I know Fay got pregnant with someone else. When Arthur found out he tried to kill her. She refused to go to the hospital because she was scared of Arthur. Jim put her into his bed and she never left. Arthur swore to hunt Jim out of town. I was Jim's partner so I was hunted as well.'

Jim's family lives in a caravan under the tree next to Anthony's camp again. We are where we first started. It is forty degrees in summer and in the caravan it comes to fifty. Jim made an annexe and they sleep outside. They cook on the grid iron and eat around the stump under the tree. They have a drum of water nearby and they wet themselves to cool down.

Anthony is better off, he is on the invalid pension and he earns some extra from cutting opal. He has solar panels, generator and even runs an air-conditioner.

The whole truth is never a truth until all people who ever lived have seen and accepted it.

The law of the boomerang

Fay and I sit in the shade with cups of coffee in our hands. Fay does not drink alcohol. She occasionally offers me a cigarette and I take a few puffs. Smoking together creates intimacy. In a small town like Lightning Ridge, you have to open yourself to friendships with people you have little in common with. The cigarette has a strong rather offensively bitter smell. I am not a real smoker; I can take it or leave it.

'They are home grown,' says Fay. Her movements remind me of ballet dancers, her eyes are quick but her words are barely audible.

Fay's two children are like chalk and cheese. The older boy Jack is very dark while her daughter Emma has Jim's fair skin and green eyes. Toni plays with them happily. Children are just children. Fay's uncle Brian brings some fish he caught.

'Where did you catch them?' I ask.

'My family always lived along the Barwon river, we know every water hole, says Brian. 'Aborigines bought that part of the land now from that bastard Arthur.'

'You know Arthur?'

'I wish I never laid eyes on the bastard. I knew his father and he was evil.'

'How did you catch them,' asks Toni pointing to the fish.

'I caught some big fish in my life but the biggest was a cod I caught in the weir, Brian turns to Anthony. My brother and I couldn't carry it to the camp so we had to pull it on the ground with two gaffs.'

'How big was it?' Toni wants to know.

'About as big as your mum,' says Brian. 'Crop spraying polluted the river and the big cod has gone now but I still catch a few, over ten kilos some of them,' Brian turns to me.

'How do you catch them,' asks Toni again.

'You go at night as they come feeding towards the riverbank in a shallow and you throw a spinner and drag it across the water. Cod will bite on anything that acts like a spinner; even a red rag on a hook will get them. Some people use shrimp or worms.'

'Can I come fishing with you, Uncle Brian?' Asks Toni. It is easy for children to adopt new family members.

'Course you can. Cod gives you a good fight so you have to keep it strained all the time. If you let them loose, they play and snap off. You can catch cod by hand close to the riverbank.'

'How,' asks Toni.

'If you ever had a pet pig, you'll know how it lays on the side if you tickle his belly. Well, cod is much the same, they just flip over.'

'Can we get a pet pig,' asks Toni.

'I can catch you a sucker in the bush if you like,' says Brian.

'What would we do with a piglet,' I laugh.

'Same as you do with the dog. They are very affectionate. You throw some scraps and it grows fat and then you can roast it for Christmas.'

Toni is fascinated with tales of fishing and hunting but I want to hear about Arthur.

'It was during the fifties when I was shearing around Walgett that I had a bit of bother with the police. Arthur's father was a policeman then; he was also a jailer and a grazier. He took his prisoners home to do his shearing and other work on the property at weekends for free. All of us shearers had to be union members at the time and rules of the union prohibited us shearing at the weekend. One day, as we were to move to a certain shearing sheds, a white sheerer said to me: Brian, one of the shearers there will be a chap that shore for that policeman at the weekend. As we commenced shearing the following Monday I said to this chap: You cannot shear with us because you shore for the policeman at the weekend. Sometimes later, Dunny's father pulled me up in town and said: It would suit yourself better to keep your tongue between your teeth. I reported him to The Australian Workers Union. One early morning a jeep pulled in front of my home and Arthur's father,-the policeman, accompanied with a detective called me out. He said: You reported me to the union. I said: That's correct. He said to the detective: Hand me that jack from the back of the truck and I will bash the black bastard's brains out. By that time my wife woke up and came out. Before he took off, he said: I'll get you, if it is the last thing I do, I'll get you.

I was a member of the Buffalo Lodge at the time. We had a meeting a few months after the policeman's visit. After I went home an argument broke out on the footpath in front of the Buffalo lodge. I was told that one man was in hospital as a result of that argument and had later died from injuries sustained. Dunny's father stated that this old man died from a brain haemorrhage caused by my punch to his head. I was summonsed to court. I engaged the barrister and explained what happened. In court the barrister summoned the local doctor, who attended the dead man, and asked him: Isn't it true that the deceased went home after the meeting, had a row with his wife and subsequently died of a heart attack. The doctor then admitted in court that there was no haemorrhage of the brain. The judge told the jury, that he wanted them to find me not guilty or he would have to overrule the verdict. I went free and went out shearing again, but I was weary of the police from then on. Dunny used to hassle drovers on their routes and demanded that they give him poddy calves (the calves without a mother), from which he made his own herd. Later I heard a rumour that some drovers stripped him, bashed him, and thrown him into the lagoon naked.

Two months later I was fishing on the Barwon when Dunny's father came and hit me on the neck with an iron bar. Another man was with him and they kicked me and urinated on me before they left me covered in blood. I promised then that I will get the bastard if it is the last thing I do.'

'What did you do?'

'Nothing. Some weeks later old Dunny chased a wild pig and fell over the log and his gun went off. He shot himself in the groin. He was never right after that and he died about a year later.'

'The law of the boomerang,' I say.

'Arthur is the same bastard as his father. He is God as long as he provides dope. He got them all hooked on marijuana,' says Brian. 'Grog, marijuana, tobacco and needle are Aboriginal killers.'

Is Fay getting her home grown tobacco from Arthur? The thought frightens me. I keep Brian talking.

'Tell me about Aboriginal history.'

'Aboriginal people were dispossessed and dispersed. Those that weren't killed outright were moved from their traditional ground and resettled on other people's traditional ground. Now the government tries to put things right. Aboriginal organisations get the funds from the government for special projects. They bought the property from Arthur for over two millions from this fund. Arthur invited the local Aboriginal Land Council to inspect the sacred sites on the property. The local Aboriginal legends are supposed to originate there. Arthur provided lots of grog and a barbecue. Everybody was impressed by alcohol and they forgot to check the sacred sites. I heard that Arthur would have settled for half a million. Aborigines never had a thousand dollars on their bank account so million dollars has no realistic sound for them. It's government money. Aborigines never felt the weight of it in their pockets.'

'Who applied for funds?'

'Barry, I think it was Barry, he is clever like that,' says Brian.

'Who is Barry?'

'He works for the government. He collects the money government pays for Aborigines. He is a smart man. Everybody wants to be Barry's friend.'

'If he is so smart why would he pay so much for something that he could get so much cheaper?'

'Much of Aboriginal money goes this way.'

'How come Barry did not negotiate the price?'

'Someone must have been lucky,' says Brian.

'You think he was paid a commission.'

'I did not say that,' Brian cuts me off. I went too far.

'My daughter has been on a waiting list for Aboriginal housing for years. Those related to Barry, come first. His friends come second,' says Brian after a long silence.

'Closer to the trough,' I agree.

'White people talk about prejudice now but I reckon that we had a much better arrangement when we negotiated with the farmers directly. They needed us we needed them and nobody worried what the other thought of them. Government can give you all the rights and all the money but if people around you don't like you and respect you, you have nothing.'

'Times are improving,' I say.

'We don't have to be put down any more, we feel worthless,' says Brian.

I begin teaching in Lightning Ridge Central school. It is an exciting busy time for all of us. There are children of many nationalities and colours. It seems that every child comes from a different background. After a few months the principal calls me into his office.

'A complaint was made that you behaved inappropriately towards an Aboriginal student.'

'Which student,' I ask.

'The incident with Philip's lunch was reported to the Director of Education, Health inspector and Aboriginal Advisory council. They are all coming to talk to you on Friday,' says the principal.

'I have done nothing wrong.'

'You will have to explain it to them.'

'There is nothing to explain. I told him to put his lunch in his bag that's all.'

'It's out of my hands now,' says the principal. I don't know how the principal feels about Aborigines but I know that everybody is especially careful not to put a foot wrong in inter-racial relations.

'You know exactly what happened with Philip,' I plead with the principal.

'I read your report.'

'Do you believe me?'

'It doesn't matter what I believe.'

'It matters to me.'

'It is a delicate situation. It always is with Aborigines.'

'I have done nothing wrong.'

'Barry and his wife are coming and you can explain it to them.'

'They know what happened.'

'People seem to believe Phillip's version of events. Aboriginal parents are saying that you are picking on their children.'

The principal is new in town, how could he understand. Did he ever have an Aboriginal friend? I realise that I am just as new, only I have been thrown into the deep end of the Lightning Ridge politics. Barry is in charge of Lightning Ridge Aboriginal purse and people will do as he tells them. He is one of them and he can make things happen. Aborigines know who is cutting their bread. It is only human nature, I try to console myself.

I remember Redfern. Aboriginal children always supported each other. White kids said that they saw an Aboriginal kid take something that belonged to the white kid and Aboriginal kids testified that they all saw him not taking it. How can you see someone not doing something? Aborigines got away with it because we were scared that someone will call us racist. I have seen it often enough. When there is a dispute Aborigines gang up against the enemy. Barry, Fay and Brian are Aborigines. They may tolerate me but I have nothing to offer them. I am not their mob.

Fay heard Brian say that Arthur paid two hundred thousand dollars commission to Barry because he made it possible for Arthur to sell his property to Aborigines. Maybe Fay told Arthur and Arthur warned Barry. I should not trust Brian or Fay. I am too naive.

'Aborigines are gullible, they will do as Barry tells them,' I try to make my principal understand.

'You have to take them as they are. You better take a leave until this blows over. Maybe you should consider a transfer. Once Aborigines feel wronged they will never forgive you,' says the principal.

Philip's father, Barry, wants me out of town. Maybe Barry believes that I know more than I really do. A small town can't keep secrets. Aborigines who don't get privileges from Barry's office, are grumbling; they are asking questions. Those in the office, their relations and friends, are getting scared.

'I know who is behind this and I will not leave until I tell Barry's story. I have done nothing wrong,' I tell the principal.

'I'd rather avoid publicity,' says the principal.

'He can't get away with it. I will have taxation office investigate him,' I try desperately.

'You should not mix your private life with the school.'

I did what I hoped every teacher would do to my child. I was on a lunchtime duty at school. Philip had a nicely packed lunch. He also had a packet of lollies. He threw his lunch in the bin and started distributing lollies to his friends.

'Where is your lunch,' I asked.

'He chucked it in the bin,' said a little girl.

'The plastic bag with Philip's lunch sat on top of the paper in the bin.'

'Pick it up and eat it,' I said to Philip.

'I am not eating from the bin,' said Philip.

'Your lunch is perfectly all right. It is wrapped in the paper and it is packed in the plastic bag. It is on top of the paper in the bin.'

'I am not going to have it,' said Philip. 'You can't make me.'

'Pick it up.'

'You eat it, miss.'

I became angry. I know teachers must not become angry but I like children and become angry if they refuse to do the right thing. I picked the plastic bag and pushed it into Philip's hands. When Philip started to cry I calmed down. Maybe I should have ignored his lunch.

'I want you to take your lunch home to your mother so she will know that you did not eat it. She went into a lot of trouble preparing it.'

I opened the bag then and unwrapped a neatly made ham and salad sandwich to demonstrate to the children how good Philip's mum was and that she was entitled to know that Philip did not eat his sandwich.

The children took no notice of my demonstration, they crooned over crying Philip and they whispered as their eyes shot glances in my direction. I wrapped the sandwich again and placed it into Philip's bag.

The bell rang, the children scattered to play and I tried to forget the incident. At the end of the day I still didn't feel right. It bothered me that the children ganged against me. Aboriginal children always stick together, I tried to console myself. Aboriginal children like me. But that changed. I am not their mob. I sat down and wrote the report about the incident and showed it to the principal. He did not comment on it.

Sally, the Aboriginal Liaison officer, warns me that Aboriginal parents are mad at me for making Aboriginal children eat from the rubbish bin. They used to scavenge for food in the past when they were hungry and they are shamed by it now. They are really angry. Specially Barry's family. Aborigines are particular about food, they spend all their money on food, explains Sally.

'And on grog and drugs,' I say before I could stop myself. I must not have an argument with Sally but I can't take the words back. I know every Aboriginal family will hear them. They will crucify me. Sally wasn't with me in Redfern where many Aboriginal kids had no lunch because their parents spent their social security money on grog and drugs and gambling. Sally comes from a good Aboriginal family and she is offended by my comment. Most Aboriginal families in Lightning Ridge are nice hard working families. I am prejudiced because I knew Aborigines that weren't so nice.

'Aboriginal people are suffering from prejudice and discrimination,' says Sally. She has been to many in-service courses where they told her that she has to watch out for signs of prejudice and discrimination at school. It is her duty to protect Aboriginal children against the racist teachers. Sally's opportunity came now. I wrongly assumed that Aborigines would stick with me simply because they liked me and I liked them. I forgot that I will never be one of them. The loyalty to their own people comes first. I should have known that.

Toni comes crying into the staff room.

'Black kids don't like me. They hit me,' he cries.

'Toni said that he doesn't want to play with blacks,' Aboriginal kids tell the principal.

My son is six and I know that he cannot deal with the situation. I know it is time for me to go. I came here so Toni would have his daddy. I always knew that there is nothing in Lightning Ridge for me. I wish I could cry. I never felt as helpless and powerless. I got mixed up into something that is bigger than me. Did Barry convince Aborigines that I am prejudiced?

About twenty Aboriginal people come into the schoolyard during lunchtime.

There is a television camera and people writing notes. An Aboriginal mother tells reporters that I forced an Aboriginal child to eat from the garbage bin. Either I go or they will take their children out. I can hear them from the staff room, I feel the hatred. Barry stands aloof in the background like all this had nothing to do with him. He is just one of innocent parents protesting against the racist teacher. The principal promises an inquiry. He will have me stand aside while the inquiry is going on. Aboriginal parents call their children and they testify that I upset Philip and that I pick on Aboriginal children. They say that their children are not going back to school if I am there. All Aboriginal children, even Fay's children, are accusing me. Their strength is in unity. Don't they know that Aborigines are my only friends in Lightning Ridge? Or so I hoped.

Barry won. I have to stand aside and wait for an inquiry. I feel vulnerable; I am stunned. People welcome the excitement of the scandal; they whisper about it; some blame me, some blame

Aborigines. Nobody blames Arthur or Barry. Nobody in Lightning Ridge knows me or cares about me. The town seems rejuvenated with gossip. Little groups gather on street's corners to exchange the bits of news. Anthony and Jim are angry but they are powerless. Both have been chastised and have lost in the town's battle.

I am too proud to ask Mark for help. I feel alone and out of place. I am afraid to send Toni to school where kids hate him. I don't want to worry mum unnecessarily. What can she do? I don't think that she ever saw an Aborigine, let alone spoke to one. Toni could not tell the difference between Aborigines and non Aborigines until now. I am thinking about a transfer. Maybe they will take me back at Redfern. There is a large Aboriginal population in Redfern; the word might get around to them, that I am a racist. Aboriginal grapevine is much like migrant grapevine. When the word gets around it has a habit of getting bigger and more damaging.

Toni would be upset without his dad. If I could at least convince Fay that I am innocent. If one person believes me maybe I have a chance to convince others. Fay's family is probably scared of Barry. And of Arthur.

There is a terrific storm. Dust covers the town before the storm moves towards Three mile. After it is all over I go to Anthony's place to see if he is alright. Anthony is not home. Fay is sitting in front of their caravan. Her arms are bruised, her cheek is angry red and her mouth is bleeding. I instantly forget my problems.

'What happened? Where is Jim?'

'Jim went to pick the kids from school. Arthur came. Look what the bastard did.' I do not ask which bastard, Jim or Arthur. I try to comfort Fay.

'There was this horrific storm around here. It lasted only a few minutes but it blew the roofs of the camps. It broke a tree and it hit the roof of the caravan and smashed the window. The wind lifted the opal dirt off the ground and covered the caravan with it. Jim and I were terrified,' Fay tells in between the sobs.

'Our dunny was blown away. Jim wanted to move the dunny on top of another shaft only yesterday. It was too close to the caravan and started to smell,' explains Fay. The swelling on her face is getting dark red and purple in places but she does not seem concerned with it.

Dunny is a name for an outside toilet placed some distance from the house. In the olden days it used to be just a toilet seat placed over the sanitary can. It smelled. Jim's dunny is a thirty metres deep shaft drop with the tin shed on top of it. Inside the shed was the toilet seat on a can.

'Jim went to get the kids from school while I tried to clean the place,' says Fay. 'Arthur drove by and asked if he could help. I told him that Jim will be home soon and that he will be mad if he finds him here. He said that he will take care of Jim. Arthur tried to shift the branch off the caravan and then moved into the caravan after me. He pressed me to the wall. I yelled so he punched me and pressed his hand on my mouth. Jim returned because he forgot an umbrella. He found Arthur on top of me on the floor of the caravan. They struggled in front of the caravan and moved to where the toilet used to be. Arthur tripped and fell into the shaft.'

'Did Arthur try to rape you? '

'Yes,' says Fay like an idea was just planted into her mind.

'Where is Jim now?'

'The ambulance took Arthur. Police took Jim.'

'Did you tell the police what happened?'

'I was too upset. They said that I will be called to make a statement and to testify in court. I should go and help Jim,' says Fay suddenly alert and ready to go.

Did Arthur ever come to see you while you were with Jim?' I ask as I drive Fay into town.

'Not since we came back.' Fay looks down; she knows that I don't believe her.

'He was drunk,' says Fay trembling. Her eyes are red but there is a little smile on her face. Maybe she remembers something or maybe she just has an idea. Fay and Arthur must have had tender moments when they lived together. Something is just not right here. There is something in the way she tells things and looks up sideways to see if I believe what she says. Did Arthur supply Fay with marijuana? The thought was there in the background for a long time but I denied the idea that Fay and I smoked marijuana. I didn't want to know. Did I become a drug user? I only had a couple of homemade cigarettes and I didn't know what they were, I try to minimise my guilt. Can I really plead ignorance? I have to. I am a teacher. I lost my job because I told an Aboriginal kid to eat his lunch. What if they find that I am a drug user? I will never smoke again. Fay is not smoking now. Maybe she ran out. Maybe without Arthur Fay can't get it. Maybe he brought her dope. Maybe Arthur and Fay had an ongoing affair and it has nothing to do with dope.

It would be easy to condemn Fay but I remember how easy it is to kiss a man you used to kiss before. Mark and I kissed. We remembered that first kiss and it was natural to kiss again. It was just a kiss for the old time sake. It is natural to touch something you once touched with pleasure. There is a sense of déjà vu; it is nostalgia for something lost and the opportunity to have it again.

When I first loved Anthony, I believed that I will never want anybody else as long as Anthony will sleep next to me. I adored Anthony.

'Did Arthur hit you before?'

'He used to bash me and lock me out at night when he was drunk.'

'Why did you stay with him?'

'He told me that he will kill me before he lets another man touch me.'

'You were scared,' I say.

'Just as well Jim wasn't home when Arthur came. He would have killed him. I tried to escape from him but Arthur ran after me and fell into the shaft, Fay changes the story and looks up at me to see if I believe her. How could I? How can she hope that I forgot her first version of events.

'What did Arthur want?'

'He found out that I went to the police.' Fay's voice becomes a whisper.

'Why?'

'He threatened to take my son. I told the police that he supplies marijuana to Aborigines.'

'Why did you tell the police?'

'I was scared that Jim would find out,' she says before she goes out of the car and into the police station. It seems natural to Fay that I accept this new version of her story.

I drive back to Three mile and find Anthony at home.

'Arthur is dead,' says Anthony. 'They charged Jim with murder. I could never understand what hold Fay has over Jim. She brought him so much grief. She brought so much grief to all of us.'

'It was so unfortunate that the storm blew the toilet shed away,' I say.

'God's justice,' Anthony tries to be solemnly serious.

'I don't know if God would appreciate you attributing this to him.'

'He created the storm that blew away the toilet and left the shaft unprotected.'

'Dunny bunny in a dunny,' I smile.

'He had a soft landing.'

'In Jim's shit,' I add.

'The law of the boomerang.'

'What goes around comes around.'

'It was one hell of a storm. Most camps are damaged but mine is intact,' says Anthony. Our hands meet and we look at each other for a long moment.

'We have to help Jim,' I suggest.

'Depends on Fay's statement,' says Anthony.

'She reported Arthur to the police. That's why he bashed her.'

'I hope she sticks with the story.'

'I think she loves Jim.'

'Why did you return to Lightning Ridge?' Says Anthony very softly. It isn't a question really.

'I don't fancy the idea of you living here. Why don't you move into town with us?' I change the subject.

'Are you sure?'

'There are three bedrooms, one for each of us. Toni will be happy.' I make it clear that none of us has to surrender our independence. We are doing it for our son. We will only share the house.

'I'll put this place for sale,' promises Anthony.

'Jim might want to buy it.'

'Who knows what Jim will do if he ever comes out of prison.'

'Did he tell you what happened?'

'He probably pushed Arthur into the shaft. Who knows?'

Fay returns with Jim. She made a statement that Arthur wanted her to sell marijuana to Aborigines. He threatened to tell Jim that she was smoking it. She complained to the police. When Arthur found out that she went to the police he threatened to kill her son. Fay told him that she will go to police again. He hit her; she escaped and ran out of the caravan. Arthur ran after her. He tripped and fell into the shaft. Police write it off as an unfortunate accident.

'Jim was in town with the kids when it happened. He has nothing to do with it,' Fay insisted. Arthur was already in the shaft when Jim returned. Jim called the rescue service, the ambulance and the police. He didn't do anything wrong. It was an accident. Jim is in the clear.

Aborigines come to comfort Fay. They are all happy that Arthur is dead. They hated the bastard. Barry is especially pleased and he offers Fay a house in town. 'It is the Aboriginal Land Council's decision,' he says. She wouldn't want to live next to the dunny where Arthur drowned. It isn't right for the children.

'Barry is a really nice bloke,' Fay tells me.

Barry and his wife come to school to withdraw the complaint against me. The principal calls me in. It was a misunderstanding about Philip's lunch and everybody is satisfied now. Barry's wife says that I did the right thing telling her son Philip that he should take his lunch home and tell his mum that he did not eat it.

'Maybe you should ring us if anything like that happens again,' says Barry's wife.

Why do they send kids to school if they don't trust their teachers to solve little problems for their children? They have to, of course, school is compulsory and trust is not. I am not a monster. I haven't yet met a teacher that did not like kids. They wouldn't be in this job if they didn't. Most teachers do more for the kids than their parents. And they are less biased and more qualified and all together better people.

I try to put the incident out of my mind. I have to rise above the prejudices of a small town. It has nothing to do with the town being small, of course. In a bigger place there are different problems; that's all. It has nothing to do with the prejudices either. It has to do with money; love and money and power.

Why should I care if the kid eats his lunch? I am not here to change the world. I am here to do my job. Maybe it was my job to tell Philip to eat his lunch. Maybe it wasn't. Why didn't I look the other way? Everybody seems to look the other way. People live differently. Why should I care?

I see Toni sharing his sultanas with Aboriginal kids. It is easy for him to make friends. Just as well children instantly forgive and forget.

Anthony and Jim are drinking under the annexe. The breeze is cooling their brown bodies. They never wear shirts in summer. They refuse to wear sun screen yet their skins glow with health.

'The bitch was dealing dope for the bastard. I will never trust her again,' says Jim. He does not know that I can hear him in the kitchen.

'Calm down,' says Anthony. 'You are free. You got even.'

'Arthur screwed my life and she helped him. I'll kill the lazy, fucking bitch.'

'No, you won't. You will go to jail and your kids will have no parents. Forget and forgive.'

'Never.'

'Never is a long time.'

I don't want to know, if Jim found Fay with Arthur, gave her a black eye and pushed Arthur down the shaft. As far as I know it was an accidental death. I am not protecting a killer. It's up to them and the police and the court. Why should it bother me? I will look away. I hope Fay will forget what she told me before she had a better idea. I don't want to know if Arthur brought her marijuana in exchange for sex either. She told me that she is not using anymore. I must ignore things that have nothing to do with me. With Arthur out of the way there is no reason for me to leave town. We need a new start. We have to do a lot of forgetting and forgiving. Life wasn't meant to be perfect. Nobody is perfect, I remind myself.

'It takes a murder to make people forget their little problems,' says Anthony.

'It was an accident.'

My problems are forgotten, people have bigger fish to fry. They gather on street corners to exchange bits of information mixed with a lot of speculation and imagination. People in a small town thrive on gossip.

Anthony finally reluctantly moves out of the camp, that was our first home. He moves in with us into a new Department of Education three-bedroom brick house in the centre of the town only a stone's throw away from Mark's place. We became a fragile family and treat each other with careful gentleness like one treats a sick child. Jim and Fay's family are only a street away.

It is our eighth wedding anniversary. Anthony prepares a dinner celebration. He arranged for Toni to spend the night at Jim's place. After dinner Anthony opens a bottle of champagne. We sit on the back veranda hand in hand to admire the sunset over the horizon.

'To us,' says Anthony.

'I love you,' I say. I realise that he is too proud to say it first. I left, so I must come back.

'I always loved you,' says Anthony.

It is the most beautiful night of my life. The tenderness of our total surrender brings tears to my eyes. Our hands explore and caress each other for the first time since I left years ago. I savour every moment because I cannot expect the tenderness like that to last forever.

Our lovemaking is as gentle as a flower in the first bloom and we know how flowers are; they wither away and spread seeds and grow again and surprise us with newness. Perhaps one never appreciates the first love as much as the second chance.

Mum put the house in Sydney for sale. It is too big for her anyway. She moves to Lightning Ridge with all her crystal and fine china. She invites Mojca for coffee. Both are happy to have someone who can appreciate the Royal china and hold it properly.

Mum and Mojca believe that they are a notch higher on the civilisation ladder than the rest and that the world would be a better place if people would take notice of what they say. Their generation valued propriety and respect.

'I wonder how poor Vincent is doing,' says mum. She says the word Vincent with proud reverence. Her boss took her out a few times and I taught that there was something going on but apparently there wasn't.

'I am surprised that you didn't marry him,' smiles Mojca.

'We were just friends,' mum dismisses the suggestion.

'Mark is much like me,' says Mojca. 'He is into everything. Poor man is the president of almost everything in Lightning Ridge.'

'Some people are born leaders,' says mum, casting an eye into my direction indicating that I am not leadership material and I didn't marry one either.

'Men need to be in charge,' says Mojca.

Mum made dad feel in charge but she decided what clothes he wore and what food he ate. She decided for Vince, her boss, what presents to buy and what meetings to attend.

'And you never know if people appreciate everything you do for them,' says mum. She likes to begin sentences with And. I keep telling my students not to start sentences with And but maybe sentences, like thoughts, sometimes need to be connected like that.

Maybe mum doesn't realise that we were all made to appreciate everything she did. We were happy when she told us to be happy. We ate what she said was good for us; we lived by her rules.

I return from school one day to find mum in the bathroom brushing bits of reddish colour onto her cheeks; she smiles into the mirror and then rubs the blusher off again. She brushes it on again and rubs it off a little less. She holds her hair up, brushes it back off the face and holds it up again. Mum always had neat permed curls pinned back. It seems like she just discovered her face. I never noticed her face before either. It glows. She would be embarrassed if she knew that I am watching.

'I feel so relaxed in Lightning Ridge. It must be the pool; hot water pool suits me,' says mum. She holds the bottle of perfume to her nose and then sprays once onto her chest under her blouse.

'Would you think that I am mad if I said that I am in love?' Mum is blushing to her ears.

'Being in love does not necessarily mean being mad,' I say seriously.

'Would you approve of it,' says mum and the tears sparkle in her eyes.

'I would have to see if the boy is suitable,' I say.

'It might not be healthy for me but I feel so light-headed. You must know who he is,' she says.

'No idea,' I pretend.

'Have a guess. He makes me feel young and beautiful and special. Nobody ever made me feel like that.'

'It must be somebody in Sydney, I tease. Is it Vince?'

'No, it's somebody here.'

'Be careful mum, miners are hopeless adventurers. He could be after your money,' I say in mock seriousness.

'He doesn't even know if I have any.'

'I suppose you are old enough to know what you are doing,' I concede.

'He asked me to marry him. He warns me that I may regret it. If I don't do it, I know I will regret it. He makes me feel precious.'

'Why are you asking me then?'

'I want you to be happy for me.'

I' wish you every happiness with Bill, mum.'

'How did you know?'

'All the birds are chirping about you two. It's written on your faces.'

'Sometimes life turns dreams into reality,' says mum. 'What is meant to happen happens.'

Mum has never been free to adore a man. She had to look after her family and after her boss. Bill and mum are like two naughty children who know how naughty they are. Only very young hide their love like that because they are surprised by it and think that they should not be so happy and that life should not be so good. Maybe Bill and mum feel that they are too old to feel so young.

Bill wears socks these days. He shaves almost every day around his mouth and I had a whiff of the old spice after-shave. His grey beard is reaching to his chest but it shines. Like his eyes. He reminds me of my grandfather. He tries to make his clothes look worn but I know that he never wore them before.

'You turned into a proper city gentleman,' I try to embarrass Bill.

'A gentleman has a plastic card to remind him who he is,' laughs Bill. 'I pay cash.'

'I don't know what the world is coming to,' says mum.

I realise that only one's own generation can be amazed and shocked and appalled by the same things. Bill and mum are the same generation.

'Happiness comes to those who wait,' says Anthony.

Mojca invites us all for Easter lunch. She wants us to come together and taste her Easter delicacies. She knows that we had a falling out of some sort but she does not know the depth of history we have with her son.

'I might get some nice sea food,' says Mojca.

'Kids went fishing and got some fish and yabbies. Toni thinks yabbies are the only festive food,' says mum like I wasn't even there.

'Jesus has been squeezed out of Easter,' says Mojca.

'It's just a holiday and chocolate eggs,' agrees mum. She was never especially religious; I think old people feel that it is their duty to sound pious when talking to young people.

'I hope they all come to church for Easter,' says Mojca.

'Mojca would like us all to celebrate Easter together. What do you think,' I ask Anthony later.

'Do I really have a choice with all the women against me?'

'Toni would enjoy sharing the day with Mark's children,' says mum. Life is simple after all. We have to keep busy and not search for more. Maybe great things happen only in our minds. I watch Toni follow his daddy everywhere. He calls daddy with utmost reverence. I am so in love with my two boys that sometimes I feel that I will break into small pieces and weep.

'Girls laugh at you if you don't know what the word is,' Toni declares solemnly to his daddy as they read fairy tales together. Anthony is seven and already he feels threatened by girls. He wants to be their hero, but girls in his class are better readers.

'I love you, mum,' he snuggles into my lap. Perhaps he still does not make a connection between girls and mothers.

'We all love you.' I kiss the top of his curly head.

'Girls ask me to help them with computers,' says Toni proudly.

We put on our festive clothes for Easter Mass. Children love the magic of Alleluias and the preparation for Easter bunny and Easter eggs and big Easter party. Anthony and I simply have to do it for Toni. I suppose mum does it for our sake. Even Bill puts his white shirt on and stands at the back of the church. Every man in Lightning Ridge has a white shirt and dark pants just in case there is a funeral to go to.

'On Good Friday Jesus died so we can have a new life. We can leave the pain behind and start again,' says the priest

'This is the beginning of our new life,' I whisper to Anthony. He squeezes my hand. Mark wheels Anthony into his home. Toni is already playing with Mark's children. Mum is helping Mojca and Kim to prepare the festive table. We know that it is not natural to celebrate together; we are not best friends but then we are the only real friends. We have roots. We share history.

'I am so glad you could make it,' says Kim. 'Anthony is about the only friend I have in Lightning Ridge. It gets lonely here for women. Men have all the excitement.'

'You have known Anthony before,' asks mum.

'Anthony was the best looking boy in my class. He was always a good guy and always on my side.'

'I am only six months older than Kim. It was a great honour to be her knight in shiny armour,' explains Anthony. 'Now she is mine.'

'Isn't it a miracle how out of millions of people, you meet again the ones you like,' says Kim.

So it was Kim who persuaded Anthony to come.

'You all have relations, only Kim and I have nobody,' explains Anthony. Kim's an only child and her parents died in a car accident when she was still at high school.'

Kim and Anthony seem so innocently happy. Maybe they are innocent. Maybe each love serves its purpose. I am grateful that

I finally have my family all in one place. I am glad Anthony and Mark and Jim say good day to each other. Maybe in time we will all like each other again.

Mum and Bill are getting married. I don't know why they should but they are convinced that they would be a bad example for us if they just moved in together like young people do.

Toni is looking forward to his role as a pageboy at their wedding. Mark's daughter will be a flower girl and Mojca will be mum's Matron of Honour. Anthony will give mum away. I will be a bridesmaid. Everybody has a reason to buy new clothes and prepare the speeches. Mark and Kim are preparing a wedding feast in their beautiful garden. We all act as if we were best friends in the hope that we will be.

It is all in my head

To believe in God is to yearn for his existence and furthermore, it is to act as if He did exist.

Unamuno.

It is all in my head.

'I have this dreadful headache,' I tell Marilyn as I slump into a chair.

'Should take something for it,' says Marilyn.

'I can't stand the noise. I am restless and fatigued at the same time.'

'Things will improve when you settle down,' says Marilyn.

'I am not unhappy but something is nagging at me.'

'There are as many ways of being unhappy as there are ways of being poor,' Marilyn chatters on about unhappiness of others in an abstract way. She does not hear me saying that something is wrong in my life.

'I cannot sleep.'

'You have it all; a good job, a nice house and a loving family,' Marilyn reminds me. 'Think of those that have nothing to do and nowhere to live. Count your blessings.'

'I wake up in the middle of the night and can't go back to sleep. I have panic attacks.'

'You will eventually settle into the mundane life we all live.'

'I became impatient;' I try to make Marilyn register my complaint.

'Oh Lord, it is hard to be humble, laughs Marilyn. 'You really have the world at your feet.'

'I am humble,' I protest. 'I know how lucky I am.'

'There are lots of lucky people looking for happiness. Some drink, others take drugs, many pray. To me happiness is every morning as the light makes the sky turn blue and life begins again.'

Marilyn attends Bible studies with Jehovah Witnesses. Every Wednesday is her free day and she goes from house to house to teach the Word. She developed this annoying pious attitude to life. I carefully skirt around Merlyn's religion. Mum warned me about Jehovah Witnesses. Any version of the almighty is much the same to me. I have no wish to squeeze God within the walls of any particular church.

'I am scared,' I tell Marilyn.

'You ARE restless,' Marilyn finally takes notice.

'I have to remind myself why I am here. I know I would not swap for any other place and yet I don't feel right.'

'We all muddle on regardless. Life is what the day brings. The events distract us from thinking. You have to accept it. Maybe hormones are telling you that you are ready for the baby again,' tries Marilyn.

'I can't have another baby. I had hysterectomy after ectopic pregnancy.'

'Your ovaries are still ruling the way you feel. It'll pass. Procreation is a heady staff. It is not something one could reason about.'

'I could just pack my bags and go. But I love Toni and Anthony and mum and you, so I stay. Bill said that the only duty of a slave is to escape. If one had no shackles one would have no reason to escape,' I laugh.

'God programmed every living creature for a purpose. Your purpose will be revealed to you in time. When you realise why you are here, you will be happy.'

I wonder if Marilyn read that in her Bible.

'Anthony came to live with us because he wanted to be with Toni. We put a brave face on it but we are scared that one-day it will all explode into our faces.'

'He loves you.'

'Never believe in the power of love to create something in a person that wasn't there before,' said my grandad. 'Things hidden inside explode to the surface sooner or later.'

'If you let them,' says Marilyn.

'We are trying to make our marriage work but I can feel the irritation in Anthony's voice and I resent him for stopping me from going away. I feel guilty.'

'A little guilt is healthy; all good people feel a little guilty, but don't let the guilt rule your life,' says Marilyn. I wish she would stop preaching.

'I became snappy; I keep apologising. I think I am going to go on Prozac. Millions take Prozac to escape.'

'Drug manufacturers promote depression,' says Marilyn.

I tell my doctor that I feel anxious and restless. He prescribes Prozac. Prozac is a wonderful drug, nothing worries me anymore. I feel in control. I tell the hairdresser to lighten my hair because I want to lighten my mood. She tells me about the new makeup that stays as smooth as your own skin. I need something to make me look smooth and balanced, calm, and in charge. I wake up with a headache every morning and mum says that I am grumpy. I feel tension building in my head. I blame headaches on the stress of my situation. I cannot explain what is wrong with me. Or with my situation. I take aspros in the morning before the headache has the chance to irritate me. Aspros are supposed to be good for you anyway. I feel nauseous if I don't take a pain killer. I am going through an emotional trauma. Anthony and Toni are oblivious of my problems. I don't want to involve them;

they have nothing to do with the way I feel. Mum knows that something is wrong, she complains that I am not listening, that I am absent minded. She doesn't know about Prozac. I double my Prozac intake.

'You are becoming neurotic,' accuses mum.

'I have a splitting headache,' I snap.

'Oh, it's all in your head,' snaps mum.

'Headaches usually are, I try to crack a joke.'

'Your husband and your son feel bad because you behave strangely,' warns mum. 'Talk to them; tell them what is bugging you.' My headaches are progressively worse, my vision is blurry sometimes and I am losing balance. I don't want to bother Anthony so I lay down often and ask not to be disturbed. It is just a migraine. Nothing can cure a migraine.

Something really weird happened when I opened the fridge. I moved my hand but it didn't feel like my hand. My arm probably went to sleep as I sat at the table correcting students' homework. My headaches become worse. I lost my balance and fell on the street. I don't tell my family how clumsy I became. I tell the doctor and he sends me for a routine CAT scan and MRI.

The doctor is serious when I return. He explains that there is some abnormality. I am glad they found the course of my condition. So it wasn't all in my head; I wasn't going mad. I wasn't just nasty.

'It could be an infection,' says the doctor. An infection does not last long.

'I need more tests. Could you bring your husband along,' asks the doctor.

'My husband is away,' I lie. I don't want to worry Anthony. The doctor sends me to Sydney and the specialists do all the tests I need. The results will come to my doctor.

'There is a lesion on the brain,' explains my doctor. I have no way of knowing if it is malignant without examining the actual tissue.'

I listen with my mouth open as the doctor explains how a specialist surgeon would shave a small part of my hair and make a window in the skull to remove as much lesion as possible.

'Talk about it with your husband before you decide.' Somehow shaving a part of my head stuck in my memory. I didn't want to know about cancer or surgery. My life with my two boys just began.

The doctor shows me black sheets of film.

'At the back of your head is a large lesion. It might be more than one but one is huge, says the doctor. Take your time and think about it,' doctor offers me a way out.

'What is there to think about? If it has to come out it has to,' I say bravely.

'One good thing about glioma is that it does not spread to other organs.' Doctor is offering good news to comfort me.

I refuse to spoil things for my family. I don't want to scare them. Maybe it is only an infection and it will go away while I am thinking about it. If I don't let the doctor make a window in my skull I can keep it shut away.

'I will think about it,' I promise.

The pain is getting worse, the infection refuses to go away and I see my doctor again.

'I think you will have to take it out,' I blurt to the doctor.

'Glioma is a type of tumour that grows tentacles into the surrounding brain tissue. Some tumours grow rapidly and double in size every week,' says the doctor. He is talking about other people's tumours.

'What happens after you cut the window in the skull,' I ask.

'Radiation. Chemotherapy.'

'How long would it take to fix it?'I am planning to go to Sydney during school holidays and have this little window done. I don't allow glioma to interfere with my life.

'Whatever you do, you have to move fast,' says the doctor.

'How long will it take for me to recover?'

'Nobody knows.'

'I will be all right after radiation.'

'There's a small chance.'

'And if you don't open?'

'You might go like that for months but it could also worsen.'

'You cannot fix it permanently.'

'No.'

From the distance of my awareness I hear my doctor talking about this unpredictable, mischievous growth in my brain tissue. My symptoms are consistent with the condition. I don't need an operation or even medication and can expect a reasonable life. He could operate to confirm the diagnosis, he can also take out the growth to relieve the pain but it will grow again. Radiation treatment may help if the pain persists. The doctor sounds like an advertisement for the wonderful things doctors do. I am to think about what he said and see him again in a couple of days after I talk to my loved ones.

'How long,' I say and doctor understands what I don't know the words for.

'Nobody can predict,' he says.

'Can anybody help?'

'I promise to keep you as comfortable as I can but only He can make you well.' Doctor's finger is pointing up.

I sit down in the doctor's waiting room and cannot get up to go home. My legs don't hold me. The doctor had long forgotten about me and my little gliomas; he has another patient; he might be called to an emergency. He is no longer my doctor.

I need to lean on someone. I cannot tell Anthony, Toni, or mum; I cannot lean on them, they lean on me. I don't want to be a burden to them. I am the strong one, I must forget about the pain. I am so full of life and love, that pain has no room in me.

I have to do all those things with Toni that children want to do with their mothers. I have to tell him all the stories he wants to hear so he will be able to survive on the memory of me. I have to let them all know how much I love them and how precious they are to me. Toni will eventually grow up without his mother. Thank God he has a father. Bill and mum will take care of them.

I want to run away and cry and pray for a miracle. Maybe it is only an infection. I eat lots of vitamins. Glioma cannot be confirmed as long as I refuse to have a window in my skull. 'It's all in your head.' Mum was right. Now I have an explanation for my moods. It's normal to feel as I do. The explanation offers some relief. It's not my fault.

I was always lucky. I am lucky to get a reminder that I am alive and that every moment counts. Other people just live their lives until they die unprepared.

I haven't been to church since Easter. I am not a churchgoer. I never pray. I only need the silence of the church. I need a sanctuary. I sink into the pew, close my eyes and allow the images from the black negative of my x-ray to emerge before my eyes. 'Huge,' I remember doctor saying. 'A small chance.'

I remember my first visit to Lightning Ridge. I told my grandmother that I was in love. She hugged me and her eyes were shining with tears. I couldn't tell anybody else how overwhelmed I was with the enormity of feeling. I was walking on air. Nothing else mattered, nothing else was real. Life offers moments of absolute joy when one least expects it. The enormity of joy is so personal that the rest of the universe stops existing.

I tell God that I am not a believer. I apologise for not believing and for not coming to church. I apologise for not praying. I beg him to give me courage to be patient, accepting and strong. Help me show my three people how much I love them, I beg. In the silence of the church I hear God. Maybe all scared people hear God.

I remember the stories of people who found God and religion. I used to laugh at silly converts. 'I am not a convert,' I tell God. 'I will not join any gospel-preaching group; I just need strength not to become a nuisance to the ones I love.'

I don't believe in bothering God with little insignificant bits of my little gliomas. If He wants to, He will take them away. I intend to live happily for all the days that I still have. We all have to go sometimes, only my days may be numbered. Everybody's days are numbered.

My doctor tells me about Thalidomide tablets. After the disaster they caused to the unborn babies they returned as a cure for everything. Tumours and leprosy and lesions have been cured by thalidomide.

Thalidomide capsules caused much misery. Mum told me that she took thalidomide against morning sickness when she carried me. She shudders at the thought that I could have been born without legs or arms or both. But I was born perfect. The doctor tells me that a thalidomide may prove useful in my case. It is good that I cannot become pregnant because thalidomide is not to be taken by women who can become pregnant. Maybe I am again fortunate.

'Maybe a new drug will be found in time,' he promises.

There is nothing I can do but wait. I wanted something more in my life. Now I have more. I have gliomas. I have to hide this intruder. I ignore IT and pray that it dies of neglect. I call gliomas IT to minimise their importance. After all it's all in my head, it isn't real. IT made a nest within my brain, IT coiled itself like a snake around my thoughts. This uninvited, secret companion wants to delete everything that I am. I don't have to have surgery. Even with surgery there is no cure. I have to condense all my living into the days left to me.

'There is an infection,' I tell my family when the doctor puts me on sick leave.

I write a diary so Toni will be able to read about us one day when he will understand. I write about the precious moments we share, about the tears of joy and the tears of sadness.

'Dearest Toni,

I thank God every minute for having you. You are the best thing that happened to daddy and mummy. Nanna adores you. We are proud of you. Your friends like you. I love watching you on daddy's knees and singing with him. You both have beautiful voices. Uncle Jim is teaching you to play a guitar. He is a good man. Pete and Emma are waiting for you outside our house every morning so you can walk together to school. You never played with toys much but you made houses and roads and rivers out of dirt and water and sticks and stones.

Remember yabbies you and your daddy caught for Christmas? That was the best Christmas daddy and I ever had because we had you and you were happy.

When I will go to heaven daddy will stay with you. He will need you so you can remember me together. Nanna will also stay here and tell you stories and things I used to do when I was young. Uncle Mark's family loves you. You can always trust Uncle Bill because he is a good man and he knows a lot. All these people are your family and they all love you.

Your mouth and your eyes are like daddy's; you have the same long fingers, and you are as kind as he is. Your hair and the shape of your face you got from me and I got that from my grandmother.

My nanna told me to go to Lightning Ridge. I am grateful to her because here I met your daddy who is the most wonderful man on earth and we have a son we both adore.

I would not want to change anything in my life because I would not want to miss a moment that I had.'

Writing these love notes for Toni makes me forget that my brain tumour is growing rapidly. The tumour wasn't a surprise really. Deep down I knew that something was terribly wrong when my headaches refused to go away. I don't need to rush any more. I don't have to impress my superiors in order to get a promotion. I can stop and talk and listen and tell Toni all the stories I never had time to tell. I can look at all the butterflies with him and help him catch all the yabbies he wants.

I won't be there to meet Toni's girlfriends; I won't even be there to kiss him better when he falls off his bike or when someone's words hurt him. I want to stay around as long as possible but when God wants us back he takes us.

'I am afraid of pain,' I tell my doctor. 'I don't want my family to see my pain. Give me whatever it takes to control my pain. Don't worry about the safe dose since my life cannot be saved. I wish to die a dignified death. I would hate to frighten Toni with my pain.'

Doctor gives me patches of morphine that make me relax and sleep.

Maybe there are miracles. Maybe there is somebody somewhere who knows what he is doing. I am on my knees, perhaps I am a little closer to God.

In prosperity, our friends know us; in adversity we know our friends

J. C. Collins

Jana

'My name is Jana. I welcome you in the name of the organisers of today's festivities and in the name of all Slovenians. I hope that you will enjoy being with us and that you will return home every year.'

I was chosen to make this little speech for Slovenian emigrants who returned to Slovenia for holidays in 1968.

A tall blue-eyed sun-tanned young man comes on the stage.

'I am Andrew from Sydney in Australia, says the golden boy taking my hand. My Slovenian is not as polished as Jana's but my gratitude for your welcome is sincere and I hope that we will meet here every year from now on.'

Andrew envelops me in his arms to the cheers of the crowd. It is a glorious summer day and we feel an exhilarating sense of wellbeing. We are a bunch of exotic flowers in the valley lusciously green and buzzing with life. Andrew introduces me to his parents and friends. We are the chosen stars of the exquisite day.

'Jana promised to introduce me to Slovenia,' Andrew tells his parents.

'Andrew was only four when we left after the war,' says Andrew's mother.

'We called him Andrej then,' says his father.

Andrew and I drive all over Slovenia. We admire wild flowers, touch summer grass, climb the hills and splash in the river. There is not a single cloud in the sky. Andrew is teaching me to drive on the narrow country roads. I am nineteen and I believe that everybody is looking at me with awe and admiration. The world is my oyster and I am the biggest pearl ever. I want to fly over the oceans and live happily ever after with Andrew. The exotic Australian continent sounds as romantic as Andrew himself. I want to fly and cut all ties that hold me to the ground.

I bring Andrew to meet my family but my parents don't realise how fortunate I am.

'All that glitters is not gold,' says mum quietly when we are alone.

'He is only here for his holidays,' warns dad.

Mum and dad were proud when I enrolled at university. Nobody anticipated a hurricane like Andrew to destroy their plans for their only child.

Andrew asks me to marry him and his parents are overjoyed that their only son found a Slovenian bride. That was the plan, I learned later.

My parents are devastated. Dad begs me to give myself time and finish university. He hopes that given time I will fall from my cloud nine and land on the firm Slovenian ground.

'I will finish my studies in Australia,' I promise.

'You will miss us,' friends warn. I resent their gloomy predictions.

Mum is sobbing all through the wedding. 'You made your bed,' says Dad and turns away to wipe the tears. I hug my parents and promise to visit them next year, every year like Andrew promised in his speech. I could taste their tears.

'You will come to my graduation,' I promise. I need to see the world but I feel guilty leaving mum and dad behind. I turn twenty as we come to Sydney.

Andrew is a building supervisor with the Sydney construction firm where I become a receptionist, secretary, accountant and tea lady. I have to improve my English before I start university. We are saving so Andrew can build our dream home.

There is a Slovenian club in Sydney but we rarely go there. Andrew does not really consider himself Slovenian or a migrant. He does not remember the seasons and the countryside and the songs of my childhood. Sometimes I cry remembering.

Twenty-five years old Freddy comes to invite us to a Slovenian mass. Freddy's family were the first Slovenian family I met; they escaped from Slovenia because the communists persecuted Catholic Church. Andrew is not interested in the church and neither am I really. I was brought up in a communist system but I follow Freddy to mass so I can write to mum and dad about it, to make them happy. I like Freddy. In his altar boy vestments Freddy looks like a clean cut handsome saint. He kneels and his head is almost touching his praying hands. I watch him as he crosses himself and then he turns his eyes to me and smiles. It is an intimate, almost hypnotic smile that makes me want to stay close. I become a regular church goer. Slovenian mass and Freddy bring a bit of home into my life.

I realise that most Sydney Slovenian mothers want their daughters to marry Freddy. I suppose most of our women share fantasies about this holy man who has a knack of making us all feel desirable.

Andrew has Australian friends and we come to each other's homes for BBQ almost every weekend. There is beer and food and friendly people so I have no real reason to be unhappy. I have no time to be lonely. There are things to do and see and learn. There are millions of people to meet and get to know. 'Strangers are friends you haven't met yet,' says Andrew.

Andrew enjoys watching football and cricket on television with his friends. Sometimes we go to see a match and Andrew becomes very excited. I am happy to be with him although I can't see much sense in kicking the ball from one end of the oval to the other. I have never been to the football game at home.

Our children Ben and Ana are born within a year of each other. We saved enough to begin building our home. I work part time now. I like getting out of the house for a few hours a day. My neighbour takes care of the babies after lunch. They sleep most of that time anyway.

Andrew's parents lived a thousand kilometres away on the Gold Coast. Andrew's father has a heart attack while driving and both Andrew's parents die in a car accident. Andrew inherits their home and the block of land next to it. We move to Gold coast to sell his inheritance.

I fall in love with Gold Coast. Our whole family is enchanted with the white surf rising high over the glistening blue Pacific Ocean. The weather is glorious all year round in this tourist resort. There is no pollution. We love our evening walks on the sandy beaches. The salty fresh breeze is brushing against my skin. Ben and Ana love the beach. They are gorgeous, healthy toddlers. We decide to make Gold Coast our home. We move in a modest house where Andrew's parents lived. On the block next to us Andrew plans to build a block of apartments. Just as well we saved in Sydney. I am looking after our family while Andrew begins to organise his business. I write home how delightfully happy we are. At the end of each letter I promise to see them soon, really soon. What else is there to write? My parents could not be interested in the foreign countryside, unknown friends or my daily chores. The photos of our children in the surf should cheer them. We simply have no time to go home at the moment but I write that next year we will come for sure.

Andrew is a wonderful husband; he is not the rock to hold us down, he is more like a huge, soft cushion willing to bend and turn into anything we want. Our children have him wrapped around their little minds; he turns into a little boy as quickly as he turns into a successful businessman or a skilful lover. I am so proud of my husband. We are a successful, happy family.

Mum and dad are always at the back of my mind. They beg me to come home. I write and promise that next year we will come for sure. Andrew promised to take us home but every year there is something more important to do. I don't like to nag.

'Plans are man's odds are God's,' I remember mum's favourite saying. I suppose it is easier to make God responsible. As long as God is in charge he must be responsible.

I remember the story of A Little Red Riding Hood, mum used to tell me. The little girl was to walk straight to her grandmother with a basket of goodies. 'You must not look left or right because in the woods there are things that may lure you into danger,' her mother warned. But the little girl became distracted and enchanted by strawberries and flowers and wolves and hunters. Mum added new distractions as she told me the story over and over. There was a talking bird and a frightened rabbit and the lightning and the storm and the water spring and the deer and the trees and the squirrels storing nuts for winter.

Life is sprinkled with surprises. I am so distracted right now that I have little time to think about home. I write a chatty long letter for Christmas and promise to come home next summer. I send a lot of pictures of us smiling on the beach surrounded with deliciously fragrant frangipani blossoms. I write about the silly little things children do and say. We will go home very soon.

Andrew promised. We have it made on the Gold Coast. We are coming up in the world. Children settled at school and they bring their friends home.

Andrew likes to impress people. Sometimes he sounds like an advertisement for his building skills. I suppose one has to put the best foot forward to impress the potential customers. I feel slightly embarrassed by his exaggerating but perhaps we all exaggerate when we want to inspire confidence in others. It is rather funny how we all try to perform the hardest tasks not for the survival but to impress those we love and specially those we hate. I rather like to impress by being a clever shopper who finds bargains while Andrew is trying to impress with the money we can afford to pay. We are both bent on getting attention one way or the other, I suppose. Maybe we compensate for each other's extremes. We even teach children how important it is to impress the right people.

'Be nice to Ted,' Andrew tells our four year old daughter.

'Why,' asks Ana like children do.

'He is very rich and he is helping daddy,' explains Andrew. I think Andrew is really telling ME to be nice to his new friend who is coming for dinner.

'Ted is an investment something or other,' Andrew tells me. 'He is connected to business and politicians. He even talked to the Premier about his projects.' I can tell that Andrew is impressed. Andrew met Ted through his work. I still don't know exactly what sort of business Ted is in but he looks successful. He has a luxury car, a penthouse, and a smiling face. Andrew said that Ted made a lot of money on the stock exchange. He even helped Andrew make deals that he couldn't make otherwise. I really have no idea about the stock market.

Andrew tells Ted that I studied medicine and that I will go back to uni to become a doctor. It is true that one day I hope to resume my studies but not right now. I think Andrew is just proud of me and wants to impress his friends with my intelligence. I feel a little embarrassed.

Ted likes my cooking. He brings good wines and chocolates and flowers. He is a tall, casually elegant easy going man much like my Andrew. One would think that Ted fancies me but he doesn't. He likes to tell me stories about girls that fancy him. He treats me like a sister or a mother. He is older than I am, so perhaps like a sister.

There is a building boom on the Gold Coast and people are buying and selling like never before.

'People are like rats running for a mighty dollar. Everybody wants to be a millionaire overnight,' says Andrew.

'New millionaires are made every day. Life is a rat race. Some rats get there first, but in the end we are all just rats,' laughs Ted.

Andrew is making lots of money. He wants to begin building a beachside block of apartments on the land his parents left him. Andrew asks Ted to invest as a silent partner in his new project.

'Not at this moment,' says Ted. 'I am on a big investment offshore. Keep this between us. It is just too good to miss. I will double my money in a couple of years. '

'How,' asks Andrew.

'I make an investment. Tax-free. It's not a crime; it's a loophole that has not been discovered yet. No risk, as safe as houses.'

'There is always a risk,' smiles Andrew.

'Not if you know what you are doing. I would not recommend it to you but for me it is a golden opportunity.'

'Why not for me,' asks Andrew.

'You have a family to look after and you need cash for building. I have nobody and I enjoy a gamble. Anyway I am sure you can borrow from the bank to get started.'

'Everything you touch turns to gold,' says Andrew.

'There is a golden rule in business,' says Ted. 'If you want to sell something put a sticker on it saying SOLD. People want what others already chose for themselves. They up their offers when you tell them that others are waiting and that you are not interested.'

'You could start with the money we saved and then borrow from the bank,' I say to Andrew. I am the bookkeeper in our house. My feet are dragging us on the ground while Andrew wants to fly.

'Bank interest of eighteen percent would kill us,' says Andrew.

'The plans have been approved; why not start with the money we saved in Sydney? You can do foundations and the interest rates are likely to fall by then. They could not stay this high for long.' Andrew and I have always done things together; we earned and spend the money by agreement.

'Maybe you can even sell off the plan,' I add.

Andrew becomes withdrawn. I know he is worried about something. There are silences and absences and gazing through the window. I am worried that he is not well. I feel a brick wall growing between us. Maybe he is having an affair. I check for signs of another woman but there is nothing. He is very affectionate and we have good sex life.

After a month Andrew makes a confession. It comes like a bolt of lightning. Andrew lost the rat race. He is saying sorry over and over. He loves me more than his life, he says. He cries. My darling has skinned his knees. I am in shock.

I suppose Andrew was greedy. Maybe what he did was not right, maybe what happened was what was meant to happen. He feels guilty and desperately sad when he tells me about it. I just cannot see any sense in making him feel worse by blaming him. What good would it do to make him feel guilty? He played dangerously and I forgive him like mothers forgive their naughty children. One rat has to lose so the other can win. Andrew invested our savings with Ted.

'I cannot blame Ted; he urged me to think really hard before I decided,' tells Andrew. He paid me the interest for the first year up front in cash even before I invested the money,' says Andrew. He trusted me but he wanted me to keep it between the two of us. He didn't want to worry you.'

After I recover from the first shock, Andrew tells me that he also took a loan on the land.

'Ted disappeared,' says Andrew. 'I waited a week and then I went to the police. There are other investors. About nine million dollars disappeared with Ted. Before the liquidation of his investment firm Ted sold worthless shares to gullible people like me.'

I am speechless.

'I filed for the divorce before I file for bankruptcy,' says Andrew. 'You take whatever we still have as part of the divorce settlement. I arranged for the house and the land to be sold. You take the money and buy where you want. I am sorry. I was stupid.'

'What about the children?'

'They are too young to understand. Let's make it easy on them.'

'How?'

'My friend, Shane, suggested that I try opal mining. Shane and I went to school together. We were close. Opal is cash industry and you work on your own. You go ahead and I will join you later.'

'What about our family?'

'Let's say that daddy has to do some business and mummy has to move to Lightning Ridge. I will join you later. I will stay with you if you will have me and if not I will live in a camp on the field.' Andrew has it all worked out. I am stunned. I am angry and mad at Andrew and Ted. I cannot tell anyone. Who is there to tell? I wouldn't dream of upsetting my parents? I promised to come this summer for sure.

'What will you do?' I ask.

'I'll manage. I will get even one day,' says Andrew.

'Don't tell children about the divorce,' I say.

'Don't tell anyone about bankruptcy,' says Andrew.

I find Shane in Lightning Ridge Mineral Resources office. He recommends a cheap caravan park until I decide which house to buy. Andrew arranged it all on the phone.

In 1975 I buy a beautiful house right next to Lightning Ridge post office; I get a job at the post office and enrol our children at the local school.

I write to my parents that we moved to Lightning Ridge and that we will visit as soon as we settled down. I have no time for regrets. Getting settled in the new job and new home keeps me busy. Children settle in the local school. Andrew is ringing every day and he cheers me up. He is all I have. I am not close enough to anyone to cry with. I cannot cry talking to Andrew. I cannot let children see me cry. I cannot cry even when I am alone. I have to sound cheerful in my letters home. I have to keep busy. It is hard to be angry when I have no one to share my anger with.

'You made your bed;' dad said when I married Andrew. In the silence of the night I hear the snippets of my parent's wisdom. I need to return into the lush meadows of my youth. I never really knew mum and dad. I want to go home and talk to them. I saw them both cry for the first time when I bravely married Andrew. I am no longer brave. When my children are peacefully asleep I begin to question my decisions.

'Who dares, wins,' Ted used to say. Maybe Andrew wanted to become like Ted, who seemed bigger than the system that keeps people orderly. We all admire the rich and those that get away with whatever they dare do.

Andrew joins us after six months. I always loved Andrew. I still do. Everybody loves Andrew. I forgave him for investing with Ted. He learned from his mistake. He changed. I changed. I used to believe that nothing bad could happen but now both Andrew and I are prepared for anything. With Andrew's loving arms around me I feel safe again. I have to forget Gold Coast.

Since we moved to Lightning Ridge, Andrew insists that we have separate bank accounts just in case. Nobody knows that we are no longer married. In Lightning Ridge nobody really cares about you unless you happen to be on opal. People of all colours and nationalities live in this small mining town.

I met Louise and Joe, a simple, old Slovenian couple. In Slovenia I would probably never stop to talk to them but here they represent the whole of Slovenia to me. We speak the same words, remember the same rivers and songs and seasons. Sometimes we cry remembering. I love their strange tales of childhood and of their wanderings. They never became Australians; they never relaxed enough to melt in with people around them. They meant everything to each other and they died within months of each other. Now I have no one to remember with.

Dad writes that mum is sick and waiting for me. I am sad that we cannot go just yet. I write that we became opal miners and need some time before we can come.

Andrew became an opal buyer. He managed to salvage some money from his parents' property. He started buying cheap stones and took more expensive ones on consignment. Opal miners like him because he buys something from everybody. He is an easy man to like. Beautiful people have an advantage, I believe. I say hello to almost everybody in town. People know me from the post office and miners know Andrew.

I met Kathy at the local clinic.

'You are new here, says Kathy as she jabs a needle into Ben's arm.

'I feel quite at home already,' I try to look cheerful.

'Everybody feels at home in Lightning Ridge because we are all as different as each other,' laughs Kathy.

'United in diversity,' I agree.

Kathy is a huge nurse with a huge laugh. She is working mainly with Aborigines. I like Kathy. She tells me that her parents immigrated from England to Australia before she was born.

'Your husband is very popular,' she laughs. Other buyers tell you what's wrong with your opal but Andrew tells you that your opal is cheap and good and well cut and polished. It almost makes you want to give it to him for nothing.'

'He loves his work,' I say.

'I love my work too. Seeing babies being born into this misery brings tears to my eyes. But then I cry when a cat has kittens,' says Kathy and her whole body shakes with laughter.

'I think my tears dried up. Maybe it's the heat. I know there are tears but they just don't want to surface,' I try to make a joke of my predicament.

'Watching others muddle through life makes you forget your own blunders,' says Kathy. 'When I first arrived on the opal fields an old timer took me aside. I'll tell you a secret, he said. If you ever get an urge to do something in Lightning Ridge, lay down quietly until the feeling passes. Here people who do nothing meet with others who do nothing. They share their experiences while they are waiting to do nothing.' Kathy sometimes comes for a cup of coffee and a chat.

'Peter and I finally agreed to disagree on everything,' laughs Kathy. 'I even vote Labour to spite Peter.'

'As long as you agree,' I try to see a funny side of her arrangement. Kathy's husband Peter owns a petrol service station.

'We have a love-hate relationship. He loves me and I hate him. He believes that we would have a perfect marriage if only I loved him. I tell him that we would have a perfect marriage if only he was as lovable as I am,' laughs Kathy. 'I don't see much of him, thank God. He spends his time with his drinking buddies.'

'Men are like that,' I say. I don't really know much about men or drinking buddies. Andrew has no buddies. Except Shane. Neither of them drinks.

'I went to immunise Aborigines against hepatitis,' Kathy tells me. 'We don't have to have it, said a woman standing in the doorway. No, you don't have to have it, I said. All right, said the woman. I'll have it then.'

'Aborigines hate being told what to do.'

'Most people do. Dad told me not to marry Peter so I did it,' laughs Kathy.

'My parents didn't want me to marry Andrew either.'

I remember my parents' warnings but do not share them with Kathy.

We watch the television program about stem cell research and cloning. People are excited, indignant and amazed at new possibilities.

'Medicine and science became so exciting. I regret that I never became a doctor. One day I might go back to uni,' I tell Kathy. I shouldn't think about things like that right now. Universities are a thousand kilometres from here. I need my job. My children need me. Andrew needs me.

'They can bank embryos and DNA so we can reappear in the future. We can finally live forever,' says Kathy.

'They grow organs. They might resurrect Jesus from the DNA he left on the shroud of Tureen.'

Would anyone rejoice at the birth of another me? Would people love me more in my second coming? Would I be a better daughter? Who would be my parents? Would I have a family at all? Which tribe would I belong to? What kinship ties would I feel? Would I need the whole new generation of clones to call my people? If I reproduced myself would I be able to step back in time and see mum and dad. And apologise for my past lives.

'The clone would be a parent and the child,' I say.

'Who would love whom? Would anybody? I don't want to be my own parent,' says Kathy.

'When scientists select the good genes and destroy the bad, you are no longer who you were meant to be.'

'If they removed the gene that causes sadness, would we be perpetually cheerful?'

'I want to keep my own sadness and madness,' says Kathy.

Shane and Andrew spend a lot of time together. Shane is a tall, dark haired man with olive complexion.

'Here is an old timer who knows everything there is to know about opal,' Shane introduced Hainy to Andrew. Hainy is a few years older than Andrew. They become friends. Hainy lives in a camp on the Three-mile opal field. He is Austrian; his home is only fifty kilometres from my home in Slovenia. We remember the mountains that separated us. We remember the seasons. We both know the family from the village on the Austrian Slovenian border. We are almost like an extended family. There is really nothing special about Hainy. He is never in a hurry, he is never very angry or very excited or very happy. He wears work boots, shorts and tee shirts. Hainy often comes to sell opal to Andrew and while he waits we talk about home. I notice that Hainy's eyes sparkle when he tells yarns. Since Andrew began buying he rarely goes mining.

'Opal holds strangers together and splits the best of friends,' says Hainy.

'I am glad Andrew has you to show him how things are done here,' I say to Hainy.

'Andrew learns fast,' says Hainy. He laughs as he says it but I don't think it is meant as a compliment. I feel that Hainy doesn't really like Andrew.

'He likes to show off,' Hainy tries to repair his comment.

'Andrew is not modest but he is very generous,' I defend my husband. 'And honest,' I add.

'He is doing well, thanks to Shane,' says Hainy.

Is Hainy trying to tell me something?

'It is useful to know a man who knows everything that is going on in town,' I defend Andrew.

'I bet it is,' smiles Hainy.

Shane is the boss in the Mineral Resources Office. He tells Andrew where a new rush is and Andrew registers claims, drills holes and checks if there is colour. If it looks good he offers the claims to other miners to work on percentage. If there is nothing in the claim Andrew asks Joe, our neighbour, to sell it for him. Joe is always wheeling and dealing.

'Where would we be without entrepreneurs like Joe,' says Shane as the men examine the new traces Hainy found.

'Joe and his ex-wife Milena are the heart of opal business. He sells claims and she sells opal,' laughs Andrew.

Selling claims is just a game for Joe but watch out for Milena. She is poison,' says Shane.

'I was with Joe one day when he was going to buy Diggers Rest hotel. The deal was almost done when Joe changed his mind and put the money on a horse instead. And lost the lot. That's when Milena left him and began to build her empire,' explains Hainy.

'Joe would sell you his own grandmother,' says Shane. 'People say that they will never again buy from him but they do it again and again.'

'He is actually proud of Milena's success. She bought half the town,' adds Hainy.

'She says that she is Romanian, but I know she is a Jew,' says Shane. 'She acts like a Virgin Mary but we all know that she sleeps with ratters so they steal for her in other people's claims.'

'I actually admire Milena,' says Hainy. 'With her four years of irregular primary school education she is managing her multimillion dollar empire well. It all needs some management and she seems to be doing all right. Other people with her kind of disability live on social security.'

'It is easy to do it with ratter's money,' says Andrew.

'Milena cannot go down the mine with her crooked leg. In fact she has never been down the mine herself,' says Hainy.

'She got ratters stealing for her,' says Shane.

'No opal buyer asks where opals come from. They buy from anybody and sell it overseas. You are only jealous because you see properties Milena is buying. We don't know how much profit other buyers make overseas,' says Hainy.

'I can't understand why you are defending Milena. Everybody knows that she is a crook,' says Andrew.

'So she is buying opal from ratters. Do other buyers ever ask you where you found your opal? They buy if they see profit. How is a Japanese opal buyer to know who is a ratter and who is not. We all wait in line to compete with other miners to sell.'

'But we all know the miners and the ratters,' says Shane.

'If Milena invested her profits elsewhere we would never know that she is a crook,' persists Hainy.

'But she invested right under our noses in the middle of Lightning Ridge and it hurts to see her getting richer and richer. Nobody likes her,' says Shane.

'I just don't want to have anything to do with her,' says Andrew.

'She works ten hours a day in her shop and she finds time to do gardening and managing all her other investments,' says Hainy.

'She is obsessed with money making,' says Shane.

'Some people are on poker machines every day. They are also obsessed with making money,' says Hainy.

I am amused by the men's double standards. I know that Andrew and Shane are using Joe to sell their worthless claims to unsuspecting miners. Are we all hypocrites? Still I am surprised that Hainy defends Milena.

'I am buying a claim from Joe,' says Hainy as we meet in town a few days later.

'You are full of surprises. You said you would never buy from Joe.'

'I saw the specks of brilliant colour in the wall.'

'How much,' I ask.

'Five thousand. One good stone will pay for the claim.'

'Don't say that I did not warn you,' I smile.

Don't worry about me, says Hainy.

I feel uneasy. Why should I warn an old chum about opal mining? He knows that Joe is a crook. I wonder if he knows that Joe is selling for Andrew. I don't want to lose Hainy's friendship. Yes, I began to consider Hainy a friend. I don't dare betray Andrew. A few days later Hainy and I talk in the kitchen while Andrew is in his office buying opal.

'Joe changed his mind about selling the claim,' says Hainy.

'You are a lucky man,' I say.

'Joe said that he will work in it himself but I have to have this claim,' insists Hainy.

'Joe never works. He is a gambler,' I say.

'This time he wants to mine,' says Hainy.

'Hainy wants that claim at any cost. I told him that Joe is a crook,' I tell Andrew later.

'Don't interfere in other people's business,' says Andrew. 'You sell stamps at the post office and leave opal business to me.'

I am sure the claim Joe is selling belongs to Andrew and he wants to get more for it. Would he betray Hainy? Maybe he does not consider Hainy his friend.

'Business is business,' says Andrew.

I heard Shane once tell Andrew that Joe drills little holes on the surface of the wall in the mine. He glues bits of colour and black potch into the holes and seals it all with glue mixed with the opal dirt. Nobody can tell that the colour and potch are not there naturally. I wish I could tell Hainy about it but I don't dare. Hainy probably knows more about Joe than I do. I better stick to stamps.

'I offered Joe ten thousand for the claim but he is still not selling,' says Hainy.

'You must really want it. What if there is nothing in it,' I warn.

'I know this is the one,' says Hainy.

'What if it isn't?'

'I will take a gamble. I can smell good stones there.'

'You know how it is, lots of dirt between opal,' I say.

'Lots of water between fish but we still like to go fishing,' smiles Hainy.

'Poor bastard is going to be sorry,' says Shane when Andrew tells him that Hainy took the bait.

'I paid fifteen thousand,' Hainy tells me after a few days. I feel guilty; I become friendlier to Hainy to compensate for my guilt.

Andrew sells opal I sell stamps; we have separate bank accounts but we share the bedroom; I own the house we live in; he pays household bills. I do housework, he mows the lawn and keeps the cars in order. He became his own cheerful self again.

We don't see Hainy for a couple of weeks. I miss him.

'He only has himself to blame. He is as greedy as the rest of them,' says Shane.

'It's not like he does not know about mining,' says Andrew.

Hainy drops by when Andrew is away.

'I am not staying,' he says. 'I just wanted you to be the first to see what I found.' Hainy has a jar of stones. The beauty of the colour almost makes me cry. Red on black with violet and blue smoothing the sharpness of gold and orange and deep green. Hainy hugs me with excitement. We hold onto each other not knowing what to do with our closeness.

'You are actually crying,' he laughs.

'I am happy for you.'

'Here is one to remember my luck. Hainy gives me a lovely red nobby, a lump of dirt covered silica with the fire colour underneath.

'I can't take it, I really can't,' I say placing the stone with the rest of them.

'I'll keep it for you then. Maybe one day you will take it.' I am happy for Hainy. The burden of guilt evaporates. Andrew and Shane return and they are speechless as they pass the stones from hand to hand licking them and turning them around to find the best faces in the uncut nobbies.

'I pegged two more claims but there is more ground if you want to have a go,' says Hainy to Andrew. 'I wanted you to be the first to know. This is only a trace, there is more.'

'Don't tell anyone or you will have ratters overnight digging it out,' warns Andrew.

'They will get a surprise if they try,' says Hainy.

'I don't believe it,' says Andrew when Hainy leaves. 'There was no trace when I checked the claim.'

'That's opal. Nobody ever knows what is hiding behind the next inch of dirt,' says Shane.

Andrew pegs a claim close to Hainy. Everybody tries to peg and register around him.

Hainy names the best of his stones My princess. It is displayed at the international Expo. On a black velvet lies a flame of red that turns green and violet blue as it rotates on the pedestal. The price is one million.

'I knew there was opal,' says Hainy. 'I just knew the first time I was in that hole.' People want to know how Hainy knew; they want him to check their claims; he becomes a household name; he became an overnight expert.

'He will never sell it for that,' says Andrew.

'He does not want to sell his princess. He has lots of other stones to sell,' I say.

'Maybe you should have done a few truckloads before you sold,' says Shane to Andrew. The whole town is revitalised. Andrew has not found a decent stone for a long time so he gave up mining and started buying. Now he wants to have a go at mining.

'I'll get it one way or another,' says Andrew. I detect bitterness and sadness in his determination. There is something cold and unknown growing between us. My husband is no longer a sunny carefree golden boy I married.

'If someone else bought the claim you might never know what was in it,' I try to cheer Andrew.

'I don't want to know,' snaps Andrew.

'Hainy knows about opal,' I say.

'You are always on Hainy's side. Is he going to share the stones with you?' Just as well I didn't take the stone Hainy offered. I didn't even mention the offer to Andrew. The secret makes me feel guilty. Hainy snatched the opal right from under Andrew's nose, so to speak. I wonder if he knows that Andrew actually sold him the claim through Joe.

'I would rather Hainy found them than a stranger,' I say.

'At least I would not have to know about it,' says Andrew.

'You are buying from Hainy.'

'I am buying what is rightfully mine.'

'I went to see Milena,' says Hainy while he waits for Andrew. She told me that people accused her of buying stolen opal so she demands that everybody tells her exactly which claim their opal came from,' says Hainy.

'I wonder why?'

'Not only do ratters steal and sell to her, she wants to tell them exactly where opal is to be found. Some naive miners draw a map and her gang goes during the night and digs the opal out.'

'Did you draw a map?'

'I am too old to fall for her tricks. I know Joe's tricks as well. I bought the claim from him because I knew more than he did.'

'I am glad,' I say.

'I have been around the block a few times,' says Hainy.

'Ratters caught red handed, I read the headline in the local newspaper. 'The police catches a gang of ratters with blood on their hands,' says the title in the national paper.

Hainy comes and swears me to secrecy before he tells me how he caught Milena's group of ratters.

'Yes, I drew that map for Milena. I set the stage and hoped Milena would fall for it.'

'Why didn't you go to the police?'

The police are either scared of ratters or in partnership with them. Mostly they are lazy. They always complain that they have no evidence. I wanted the bastards caught red handed. I went down the shaft and dug a hole in the wall. I put in a plastic bag of red oil paint and covered it with opal dirt. I used Joe's method of mixing glue with dirt. I also glued bits of colour into the surface dirt covering the paint. The bait was set. I invited a couple of friends from Sydney. They waited in a mine next to mine from lunchtime until midnight. When they heard the ratters they rang the police and watched from the nearby bushes. The police shone a reflector down the shaft and called the ratters to come out. It's a new ground so they had nowhere to run and hide underground. Sure enough they came out red-handed. One of them tried to dig out the colour I glued into the wall and the other was holding the light and catching the opal in his hands. Behind the colour was the bag; the pick broke it and the red paint splashed over the ratters. My friends returned to Sydney as soon as they saw the ratters handcuffed. Nobody knows who informed the police. I'd rather you didn't tell anyone either.'

'They will know that you laid the bait.'

'I invited Milena and her friend for a drink in the club so they could keep an eye on my movements while the ratters were on the job,' says Hainy. 'Milena and I were together when the police came to tell me that they caught ratters in my claim.'

'Milena must know that you tricked her.'

'No doubt the stories will be made about it but you are the only one who knows the truth.'

The intimacy of a shared secret brings us close and we hug in the excitement. The town is rejoicing with Hainy. Everybody hates ratters.

'They were only charged with trespassing,' says Hainy. They have no proper legislation to cover ratting. Milena considers me her friend but she does not know that I know that the ratters work for her,' says Hainy.

Something is worrying Andrew. I find him lying on the couch sometimes staring into the ceiling and that frightens me. I hope he is not sick.

'I am fine,' he assures me in a flat, dull voice. There is nothing I could put a finger on but I feel that he is shutting me out.

'You don't want to know us now that you are rich,' Andrew is teasing Hainy.

'You didn't do too badly yourself,' says Hainy.

'Peanuts compared to you,' says Andrew.

'I don't really know if I am as happy as I should be,' says Hainy when we are alone. 'When I actually found it I almost felt let down. Maybe searching for opal was more exciting than finding it.'

'When are you going to buy yourself a big house in town?'

'I am too old to change my lifestyle. '

'What are you going to do with the opal?'

'Look at it. What else can you do with opal? I can look at something people would pay a million to own. I don't know what else I would want to do.'

'You are a millionaire.'

'Opal has been there before and it will remain when I die. I only take care of it for the time being. In a way it owns me; it demands my attention and care. I am its custodian. It does not do anything else. It's like a painting on the wall. It's a bit like having a baby. You love to take care of it. For free; because there is the beauty.'

I would like to ask Hainy about his family and any children he might have but people in Lightning Ridge don't talk about personal things like that.

Nobody really owns anything. Hainy's words follow me as I water my garden. The plants and weeds compete for my garden space. Some grow strong, others die in a perpetual struggle. There is an exquisite order and harmony in nature. So much life teeming and blossoming and ripening in a quiet unquestioning eternal reproduction. There is no guilt, no shame, no doubts in the scheme of things. Plants grow as they were meant to. They depend on my care so I become part of them and can call them mine. Perhaps they too rejoice and suffer in their struggle to survive. Animals show signs of distress but plants just wither and die silently. There must be a divine reason and purpose for all this. Everybody gets a moment of happiness. That is all we own, a moment. And a memory of the moment. And the gratitude for the time. Hainy had his big moment when he uncovered the rainbow in the clay. Now he does not know what to do with it.

Why doesn't Hainy go home? Would he come home with me? Of course not, this is just a fantasy. I often fantasise about going. I want my children to meet their grandparents. I never had time to tell my children all the stories my mum told me. I wish my mum would show them the places where I grew up.

Andrew does not even want to talk about going home any more. Not now, he cuts me off. Andrew is busy with opal. We were always busy. I haven't seen my parents in fifteen years.

Just as well children settled in their boarding school. They have everything. They are lucky because we can pay for the best school. I barely know my children. They changed since they left home.

The letters to my parents are rare. I am tired of lying.

Shane and his wife Debbie come every Saturday and we play cards. About ten years ago we each put the coins amounting to twenty dollars in a jar and we played for that same money ever since. At any given time we have approximately twenty dollars in each jar.

'Cards are like life,' says Shane. 'You are winning one day and losing the next. It does not matter what sort of cards you get, or how well you play, or how hard you try.'

'Win some, lose some,' agrees Andrew.

'If it isn't your day you can't push your luck,' says Shane. 'No use getting upset when you are losing because you know that soon it will be your day.'

'Gipsies laugh when it is raining because they know that sunny days will follow,' I add this home-grown wisdom.

Cards are just something we do while we exchange the news about opal mining and reveal bits of ourselves. Knowing each other makes it easier to like each other.

'Everybody is allocated a fair share of luck,' says Shane.

'Especially Hainy,' I say.

'The poor bastard does not know how to enjoy it,' says Shane.

'He will get his,' says Andrew.

'What do you mean?'

'Bad luck and good luck follow each other,' says Shane.

I have been lucky for a long time. I am afraid that my share of bad times is lurking around the corner.

'Deb here checks on the Internet every morning what she is supposed to do to fulfil the horoscope's prediction,' laughs Shane.

'If our story was written in advance then we are absolved of all responsibility,' says Andrew.

'Of course it was,' smiles Debbie. Andrew and Debbie are always teasing each other. I think they like each other.

'Some people just don't know how to enjoy life,' says Andrew. Andrew has Hainy's opals on his mind. Hainy is on all of our minds.

'When you have one million you want two. With every million you are more scared of the bad luck,' says Shane.

'You are on your way down as soon as you stop going up,' says Andrew.

'Hainy said that greed is a sickness no money can cure,' I remember Hainy's words.

'It's easy to be smart when you pick millions,' says Andrew. Andrew gets snappy when I mention Hainy.

Debbie is a natural blonde with huge blue green eyes courtesy of her Swedish father. Her skin shows olive traces of her Aboriginal ancestry. The combination is stunning and people can't stop looking at her. Her teeth shine and her skin glows. She is the only Aboriginal teacher here and she tries to be better than anybody else at whatever she does. Her house is immaculate, her clothes are fashionable, and her behaviour is casually appropriate. She almost looks aristocratic. She walks like a lioness. Her work and her house have been displayed on many occasions. Her picture was in the national newspaper. She has been promoted all her life as a role model for Aboriginal people.

'I am sick of being an Aboriginal role model,' says Debbie. 'My father is Swedish and my mother is half-Scottish, mum's grandfather was English yet I am only known as an Aborigine. I don't feel particularly Aboriginal.'

'Everybody wants to be on Aboriginal gravy train and claim benefits and compensation,' says Andrew.

'I can look after myself. It scares me being classed as a role model. One-day I might fail at something and fall from pedestal face down into some shit or other,' says Debbie.

'Not you,' says Andrew.

'An Aboriginal leader said that anyone with a drop of Aboriginal blood is an Aboriginal. How come anybody with a drop of Slovenian blood is not Slovenian,' says Andrew.

'During the slavery in America everybody with a drop of black ancestry was classed as black. Being black meant that one was a slave and less human,' says Debbie.

'Not anymore,' says Andrew.

'In the minds of many it still is. If you are black and you made something out of your life you are exhibited as a freak. Like I am. I would just like to be taken as an ordinary individual,' says Debbie.

'Aren't you proud of being Aboriginal?' I ask.

'I might be ten percent Aboriginal but nobody even mentions any of my ninety percent of other bits. It's not fair to my father and grandfather. Aborigines say: who does she think she is. She wants to be better than the rest of us. Well, I do. I am. I am better than Aboriginal drunks in the gutter. I am also better than most European no-hopers. I am working on being better. Mum tells me that she never felt prejudiced against until they told her that she should watch out for prejudice. She was brought up by her father in the Scottish home because her Aboriginal-English mum died in the childbirth. She never even considered herself Aboriginal or different. Let alone being prejudiced against.'

'There is a lot of bullshit written about stolen generation,' says Shane. Times were tough for everybody then. Sometimes the black mothers kept their children, sometimes their white fathers took them. Sometimes neither mother nor father could properly look after them so the Welfare took them.

'It was the same for white kids, I suppose. Before the family planning they had big families and many children died of neglect,' adds Debbie.

'They took the children of unmarried girls for adoption. Many ended in orphanages,' I add.

'They treat Aborigines like some fragile species,' says Shane. 'Aborigines survived in the desert for millenniums.'

I sometimes wonder if Shane is Aboriginal. With his black hair and olive complexion he certainly looks more Aboriginal than Debbie.

'Where do your people come from,' I ask.

'I am a fourth generation Australian,' says Shane. My great great Italian grandfather bought a lease in Walgett but the family moved to Sydney ages ago.'

John comes to Lightning Ridge before Christmas 1980. He wears a black suit and carries a briefcase to inspire the confidence of those that have neither a black suit nor a briefcase. In Lightning Ridge men own a white shirt and a tie to go to the funeral but miners have no use for a black suit.

We meet John at the Bowling club Christmas party. I am the last person he is introduced to so I get stuck with him. John is new in town and wants to make friends.

'Everybody wants to be friends with this fancy new man,' says Kathy.

'He is easy to like.' John is our friendly, handsome lawyer. People in a small town are still rather honoured to have a friend who knows the law. A lawman is much like a doctor who can kiss the problems better. Most miners and Aborigines are receiving social welfare and so are entitled to free legal aid when dealing with their sins or disputes. They need John.

John applies for a grant from the government and establishes an office to liaise between the government and migrants and Aborigines. He convinced the government that such Liaison centre is necessary in a place where migrants and Aborigines are the majority.

'You could do a lot for migrants and Aborigines; you can deliver what government offers,' John says to me casually a few weeks after his arrival.

'How?' I ask.

'Leave your post office job and become an Aboriginal and Migrant Liaison officer.'

'I have no idea how to do that.'

'I will teach you,' promises John.

'Jobs like that are created at the whim of the government and they last for the duration of the government. After the election you will be out of the job,' warns Andrew.

'You will learn new skills. The pay is better and the initial contract is for two years,' says John.

That's how I came to have an office next to John. Everybody knows me as Jana from Legal. When either migrants or Aborigines have a problem, I manage to do something about it; with John's help, of course. He provides the names of those who hold the moneybags for multicultural advancement. I describe to the government the severity of the problems faced by my protégés and write programs and submissions for money that would alleviate the situation.

John really made us aware of multi-culture in Lightning Ridge. People suddenly see their neighbours and friends as different; they also see them getting privileges because they belong to a particular group. Cracks appear in our community as envy and prejudices seep in every crevice of our lives.

'The rich always need an underdog to kick,' says John.

John is Italian and fiercely opposed to English monarchy. He blames England for all that is wrong with the world. His father died in England as a prisoner of war when John was a baby. His mum came to visit relations in Australia and married an Englishman. John hated his stepfather; John tells me little bits about himself occasionally but I do not dare ask him more; we are not that close.

John is teaching me to write submissions and I secure much money for the Lighting Ridge poor. He has a very convincing vocabulary and a legal know-how to back up my claims.

'There are ways to get money from the government if you knock on the right door and use the right words,' says John. He knows which buttons to press; he also knows the needs and wants of the poor. I enjoy organising people. Working for the poor and lonely puts me above the lonely and the poor. Being loved by all the poor and lonely makes me feel less lonely.

John secured a refugee status for many new migrants. He also helped with their citizenship applications. Some of these refugees became ratters. John represents them in court. He paints a picture of poor traumatised men who once were decent people and would again become that, given a chance.

'Miners hung the effigies of the ratter and his solicitor off the tree opposite the local courthouse,' says Andrew.

'The court adjourned to Coonamble; they have to protect John and his ratters,' says Shane.

John and I establish Aboriginal Education centre; we secure the government money to open Safe families office which provides employment and safety for women. We organise a refuge for sexually abused and victims of domestic violence. I realise that there is much domestic violence and all sorts of abuse hidden in our little peaceful country town. Wives sue their husbands for domestic violence and often wait with their same husbands for the court to solve their problems. They sit in the shade of the trees at the front of the court house and prepare the defence or prosecution as the case may be while they smoke, drink their cokes and eat their pies and chips. The liaison officers, social workers and the counsellors often sit with the accusers and the accused.

'Poor sods are encouraged to drag each other through courts,' says Kathy.

Kathy is looking after the community health so she refers to me the victims of abuse and violence. Kathy and I have a lot in common and we often talk about the problems we have to deal with. We are in the same trade so to speak.

'I am amazed how often the victims cover up for their abusers. They are made to feel guilty for what has been done to them,' I say to Kathy.

'The victim feels guilty until he or she stops being the victim. Only they rarely do. Stop being a victim, I mean,' says Kathy.

I cannot go home now; too many people depend on me. I write cheerful letters to mum and dad. I describe to them the important work both Andrew and I do. Andrew promised that next year we are going to take off and see the world. I begin to appreciate the fact that my children have done well and that we have never been victims of either abuse or violence.

I speak and write for migrants and Aborigines. The government is generous with money in order to keep the natives and migrants quiet and orderly. I spend a lot of time with John so Andrew is free to do his own thing; he does not really mind me spending time with John; he considers John a nuisance rather than a threat. 'You never know when you might need help with the law,' he says to Shane.

John drives a modest car and lives in a modest flat. He has no social life or sex life as far as I can see. He has no one to impress. Maybe he really is obsessed with the poor. Maybe he wants to look poor.

Dad sends a telegram in 1986. He is urging me to come home. Mum is sick, she might not last. I make travel plans when dad rings that mum died. She hung on, waiting for me. It's too late now. I want to go to the funeral but Andrew is urging me to wait a few months so we could go together. I cannot cry. I feel a terrible loss and guilt but I have no tears. My children will never know their grandmother. They never knew any of their relations so they are not upset. 'What you never had you never miss,' says Ben.

I write a long letter to dad. I beg him to forgive me for not coming home. It will only be a few more months.

'I am sorry,' says Andrew as an afterthought. What is Andrew sorry for? His words cannot reach me. Nobody here knew my mother; I barely knew her myself; I was a boarding school girl like my children. Much of me died with my mother; much of what I needed to be; much of where I came from; much of who I am; much of what I will never be able to pass on to the next generation. I cannot cry but I shiver from the cold of loss and aloneness. I have to go home and talk with dad about mum. Dad does not write since mum died. I ring but he is not there. I am afraid that he died. I discover that he is in a nursing home. I ring and the matron tells me that dad is well looked after. I write to him on his new address and promise that I will come to see him soon. I promised too often. He does not write back but the matron of the home assures me on the phone that he is cheerful and eats well. I ring dad often but only the matron answers. I tell her that I will send dad a ticket to come to Ana's wedding. The matron tells me that dad's hearing and eyesight are poor. He is not fit to travel or talk on the phone.

Ana cannot postpone her wedding. She is pregnant.

I walk into the garden; it reminds me of mum. She loved her garden. My garden knows me, the new leaves and the dying ones, the buds and the petals and the seeds. The first sadness I was aware of was in the garden as the autumn cold put everything to sleep. We knew that as soon as the snow would melt new life would return. We celebrated with the blooms and ate what we grew. We saved the seeds for new spring and new life. Life is a never-ending story. People live and then they die. The dust becomes animated and then it settles. Life is not perfect but it is everlasting and ever-changing. Perhaps God is life. Or love.

I see an eagle coming lower and lower until it catches a bird, a live bird, his dinner. We are each other's dinner.

I believe that mum is watching me from wherever she is. What else would she be doing? I pray without words. I am asking God to look after mum until I come. I hope mum hears me.

John and I are very busy. People depend on us. John is also a scoutmaster and kids adore him. Maybe John and I, as migrants, miss our tribes and try to attach ourselves to other tribes to feel at home.

'Your own tribe will always stand by you,' said Dudley, an old Aborigine. That's why Aborigines are looking for the members of their tribe that were dispersed after the white settlers took over. Your own people are the only ones that know you. You are lost without your tribe.

'The world is becoming a global village and everybody is one tribe,' I try to cheer Dudley and myself. Aborigines call each other uncle and auntie. Everybody is somebody's cousin. They call me cuss, short for cousin out of affection to show that they accept me into the tribe but all the time I am aware of my white skin and the history they know nothing about. I will never be their tribe.

There are anywhere from three to twenty thousand itinerants scattered in and around Lightning Ridge. When there is a new opal rush, people come, when it dries up many leave. In my last census I registered fifty-three nationalities, most racial groups and most professions. Migrants, who came to Australia in the fifties and sixties, became old, lonely, and frail. Some need interpreter services, meals on wheels, home help services, medical services and transport. I provide language services because I speak German and most Slavic languages. John speaks Italian, French and Spanish. I visit people that have no other visits. Except for Jehovah witnesses. Most never go to church; some don't even go to the hotel any more since drinking destroyed their liver and their brains. I have six migrants on my list suffering from dementia.

After ten in the morning there is a steady stream of people with problems in John's office. Some of them he refers to me. I am a sort of an assistant. I don't know if anyone is closer to John than I am. I often wonder why he is so nice to me. I am neither rich nor influential. I am sure he has no romantic or sexual interest in me. I sometimes wonder...

John is very affectionate; we hug sometimes when we succeed to make the world a bit nicer place. He says that we energise each other. John occasionally plants a kiss on top of my head as he comes into the office. We feel at ease. Perhaps this is what people call the meeting of the souls. John is a little younger and much more desirable than I am. Maybe he needs his mother and has taken me as a surrogate. He is protective towards me and I often feel like his little sister. Perhaps this is because he is stronger and more knowledgeable. He is a natural leader and I am essentially a follower. Our relationship is light and cheerful, we like each other and feel liked but we are not in love. At least I am not. Occasionally I play with a little fantasy about John, that's all. I pretend that he does not talk about love because he respects my marriage. This is nothing but a fantasy. I feel that John would never do anything dishonourable. This kind of thinking turns John into a real hero but only in my head. I cannot say that I know him intimately. Nobody really knows anybody that well, especially in a town of strangers. Maybe to John I am just another needy migrant.

John goes to church and there makes himself available to anyone who needs a sympathetic ear. People tell me that many mothers of unmarried daughters have designs on John. And many other women, single or not, fantasise about him...

John and I help Aborigines open their Medical centre. Aboriginal people who found employment there, are given the opportunity to learn modern health practices and can also use their native skills of healing.

'The holistic health approach is needed to repair the mental and physical health of Aborigines,' says John at the opening ceremony. Some people do not agree with what John and I are doing.

'I am not going anywhere near the Aboriginal medical centre,' says Dudley's daughter, Diane, who works as an assistant at school.

'Why not?' I ask.

'They know nothing about health. They only gossip and play computer games. When I want a doctor I am entitled to the same doctor whites go to, 'says Diane.

'Aboriginal Liaison officers help you bridge cultural barriers,' I offer; I quickly learned the appropriate jargon.

'I don't want the whole town to know my medical problems. Aborigines don't understand confidentiality, 'says Diane.

'Aboriginal health workers chat with Aboriginal patients and keep them away from the medical staff,' says Kathy.

'The learning process takes time,' says John. He makes every problem look like less of a problem.

Kathy's husband, Peter, is known for his community work and for his prejudices. He is a big loud gregarious well liked man. As I stop to fill my car at his service station, I notice that his shop window is smashed.

'Vandals get away with murder. With John's help. He keeps crooks out of jail,' says Peter so everyone can hear.

A group of people around Peter is growing. The impromptu gathering becomes a protest meeting and the issues of law and order are being addressed. Everybody knows that Peter has a vendetta against John. Most farmers and miners and business people agree with him.

'The town is not the same since John moved in,' says a farmer.

'I don't feel safe anymore. Crooks can rob you and bash you but you are not allowed to lay a hand on them. That's the law,' says a woman.

'If they cut themselves on the glass they smash they sue you for compensation,' says a shopkeeper.

'We pay taxes so the crooks get free legal aide,' says an old farmer.

'We always pay for those who never lifted a bloody finger,' says Peter.

'Something is wrong with the system that rewards laziness and crime,' says Andrew.

'The poor stay poor to qualify for handouts. If they find opal or win on the horses they have to dispose of the money fast,' says Peter.

'Australia is the only country in the world with means tested pension system. Those that never worked get the pension but if you saved a bit for the rainy day you don't get it,' says an old migrant.

'John is the curse of Lightning Ridge. People should hang him by his heels. Nothing is safe, nobody can sleep at night. Kids are allowed to run wild.'

'John knows which side of his toast is buttered,' says an old farmer. 'Aborigines and migrants provide lots of work for him.'

'The working person cannot afford a solicitor,' says Shane.

'You are up bright and early,' says Peter as John stops to fill the tank. The crowd lingers on.

'Work to do,' says John.

'Your clients are sleeping after the busy night,' says Peter pointing to the broken glass.

'They have nothing to get up for,' John laughs. He actually enjoys baiting the bigots.

'They have never done a day's work,' says Peter.

'They did not create unemployment,' says John.

'They pay black kids to produce black bastards. Every teenage black girl is pregnant,' says Peter.

'Be careful who you are calling black bastards,' warns Hainy, coming closer. I wonder which side he is on.

'What else should I call black children of unmarried mothers?'

'Have you ever offered an Aborigine a job,' asks John.

'I actually did,' says Peter. I offered Noel a job but he informed me that he can't afford to work. He would lose his rent assistance and family allowance or something. He is a smart man. He calculated that by working he would get thirty dollars less than his social entitlements. He can't afford to do that. He has five kids to think of.'

'Aborigines only want to be managers,' says Andrew.

'Most of them don't want to be tied down to any job. You lose your pension and your perks and your freedom. That's the government we elected,' says a farmer.

'Government jobs for Aborigines are funded for a year. As long as the government keeps them dangling on the purse string, they will vote for that government,' says John.

'Ben has been working for over thirty years as a garbage collector for the shire,' says Hainy looking at the man running after the rubbish that wind blew out of the rubbish bin.

'He is one of. I would have him any day,' says Peter.

'Most were like that thirty years ago. They would do any work for any money,' says Hainy.

'Until people like John here gave them the idea that the world owes them a living, says Peter.

'Migrants and Aborigines did all the hard work in the past but English got the credit for it,' says John. You could feel the crowd looking at each other. In Lightning Ridge everybody used to feel equal since everybody had an equal chance to find opal; they also felt the same in their differentness. Now they feel neatly slotted into their different categories.

'Migrant opal miners still live in tin sheds without water and electricity while Aborigines get new brick air-conditioned homes from the government,' says an old Hungarian.

'Aboriginal kids see that it pays not to work so they will never work,' says Peter.

'It's not Aborigines' fault. Government removed the incentive for work,' says Hainy.

'They did not make the system, they are just trying to fit in,' agrees John.

'They fit in all right with your help,' says Peter.

'White politicians have to be seen to be doing something to justify their fat salaries,' says John.

'The dregs of the nation are multiplying,' says Peter.

'If you believe that poverty creates criminals, why not eliminate poverty,' says John. 'Those at the bottom will always push towards the top.'

'Poor crooks take your spare change but rich crooks take your home,' says Hainy.

'I'll leave you to change the world; I have work to do,' says John.

Kathy and Hainy often visit and we talk about our community problems.

'Those on social security can never save enough to buy a house. They know that if they save enough they would no longer be eligible for social security,' says Kathy. 'They have to be flat broke so the government in its wisdom gives them enough money every fortnight for grog and drugs and poker machines and take-away food.'

'So they drink and gamble and take drugs to be eligible again for more money, laughs Andrew.

'Easy come easy go,' I say.

'Dole bludgers have nothing to lose since they have nothing and are nothing,' says Kathy.

'They have too much time to think about their misery and not enough money to do anything about it. It's a vicious cycle,' adds Hainy.

'At least we have work to distract us. Most of those I meet in the court are unemployed, frustrated, unhappy, young men.'

'With a permanent job you can plan and save to buy a car and a house. You get promoted and earn more and save more,' says Kathy.

'An Aboriginal leader said that Aborigines drink sweet water of idleness, which will render them useless,' says Hainy.

'We provide the sweet water of human kindness,' says Andrew.

John and I made submissions to the council for Aboriginal housing. Most Aboriginal teenaged single mothers are on social security. Whites don't want to rent to them. The council agreed to build a special complex for them but nobody wants these houses close to their homes because young people get drunk and disorderly on the pension day.

Dudley's daughter Diane is Aboriginal but her husband is white and their children are well behaved. Her home used to be in a respectable side of town. She complains bitterly when the shire built Aboriginal housing next to her.

'You don't want to build another Bronx with drugs and drink and domestic violence like Walgett,' says Diane. 'Even at school they make Aboriginal kids sit together so they learn nothing. They get into mischief and do not pay attention.'

Marta is a senior teacher. She is new to Lightning Ridge so I tell her what Diane said.

'Whatever I do is criticised,' says Marta. Aboriginal kids choose to sit next to their cousins. If I order them to sit next to whites they complain and their parents complain and they call me racist. I let them sit where they like.'

'Diane said that they distract each other,' I inform Marta.

'Parents should spend more time with their kids instead of complaining. Government provides tutoring for Aboriginal students. They have Education centre where they get all the help they want,' Marta tells me.

'Do Diane and other Aboriginal assistants help Aboriginal kids?'

'Nobody knows their job description. They are not trained so they may do more harm than good. They just hang around,' says Marta.

'It must be boring for them.'

'Teachers don't dare tell them what to do and how to do it. They don't want to be called racist. The present policy is that parents know best what their children need to learn,' says Marta.

'How could parents who never had a job know what their kids need to know to find a job?'

'The kids are waiting to qualify for social security like their parents,' says Marta. 'They are all after compensation, everybody is a stolen generation.'

I tell John. 'Marta is a racist,' he says.

Dudley often comes for a chat in my office.

'When we grew up we had to learn to do anything needed doing,' he tells me. I worked all my life on the station. All Aborigines had work to do and we never worried with stupid things like discrimination. Everybody liked and respected my family in the olden days. We knew our place and we learned respect. Government made our kids lazy and unruly. They are never happy and they don't know what they want.'

I report to John.

'It suited his English bosses to have a class of slaves,' says John. 'They brainwashed them into yes sir, no sir coexistence.'

'There will always be slaves and masters only the titles change,' agrees Marta. 'Pigs at the trough get fatter and those on the outside are kept busy so they don't squeal too loud.'

'I don't really understand Australian prejudices. Maybe I should talk to some old local whites,' I say to Kathy.

'Talk to Albert in a geriatric ward,' says Kathy. 'He can no longer remember the names of his children but he remembers his childhood well.' Albert is ninety something and only too willing to reminisce.

'I was born and bred in these parts,' says Albert. 'My great grandfather came from England and secured a lease along the Barwon River in 1848. When I was young we had lots of trouble with Aborigines stealing our stock. Aborigines were a nuisance in their wild state. Everybody was scared of the black savages. My dad said that dogs are like that, useful when tamed but dangerous while wild. We often had to disperse them.'

'What does that mean,' I asked.

'We went Abo shooting on a Sunday afternoon,' Albert dismisses my question. 'I went along with older men and we brought home rabbits for the dogs and talked about the other vermin we shot. Once we tamed them Aborigines became good workers.'

'Did you shoot any Aborigines,' I ask.

'They make good stockmen and shearers. The station would be lost without them,' continues Albert ignoring my questions. 'Next to Albert sits Norma,' an old widow from the sheep property.

'Aborigines were always a part of our lives. They were shy but not unruly like they are today,' says Norma.

John is encouraging Aborigines to claim Native title over opal fields and farms. He became a real threat to farmers and miners. Some became sick of it all and left. Houses and farms are for sale. I am glad John is in my life. We trust each other and share confidential information.

Sam comes to Lightning Ridge in 1995. Everything changes when this new preacher arrives. He introduces himself as Sam but people feel slightly sinful calling him by his first name.

There are four places in Lightning Ridge nominated as Safe houses; one of them is the preacher's home. Any child may at any time find a refuge in a safe house. While some parents drink in the hotel Sam cooks dinners for their neglected children, he gives them a bath and a bed. Parents know that their kids are safe with Sam.

Jason, an eleven years old boy was badly burned when his drunken father tipped a pot of boiling stew in his lap. Jason's mother is in hospital with a broken jaw and his father is in jail. Jason is in a safe house with the preacher until a place could be found for him or until mum returned from the hospital or his father served his sentence.

I enter John's office without knocking and I find Sam kneeling on the floor washing Jason's burns.

'Pardon me,' I say.

Sam is startled for a second but he quickly rearranges his pious smile. A knowing passes between us in that split second. We don't like each other, we are trespassing on each other's territory; we are a threat to each other.

I extend my hand saying: 'I am Jana.'

'Pass me that box, mother,' says Sam ignoring my hand. Jason quickly grabs the towel to cover himself. I pass Sam the first aide box and he begins dressing Jason's burns.

'Looks terrible,' I say referring to the burns.

Sam does not respond. I wander why I feel embarrassed.

'I am looking for John,' I try to compose myself.

'He won't be long. I can give him a message,' says Sam not lifting his eyes from what he is doing.

'Never mind, I will see him later,' I excuse myself.

I sit in my office shivering. I don't like Sam. He does not like me. Maybe I did not like him calling me mother. Did he imply that I am an old woman? A lesser being. The words old and woman add to insignificance. I feel put down. Maybe I did not like him being in my friend's office. Why would I give him, a stranger, a message for my closest friend? Why should I be jealous? I am not jealous. How dare he call me mother? The irritation lingers on. As I drive to town early next morning I see Sam on his knees weeding the school's football oval that is overgrown with clover which produces burrs. No wonder people call Sam a saint. I wonder why Sam does not suggest to the school's 400 students to pull a few clovers each. This enormous job could be done in minutes. Would Sam look less saintly if students looked after their sports oval? Why does he spend hours every morning on his knees on the damp lawn? Why doesn't he simply spray the weeds dead? Perhaps Sam, like me, needs to feel needed and loved. I never really thought of helping anyone in any tangible way like washing their sores or cooking their meals. I would not go on my knees to pull the weeds.

Dudley's wife Pauline tells me what happened to Jason. Maria, their daughter, got drunk and came home with a fellow. She didn't even notice Jason watching videos. Jason saw his father Scott coming. He knew that there will be trouble so he bolted the door to give his mum time to escape. The man who was with Maria pulled his trousers on and jumped out through the window but Scott caught Maria and hit her to the ground. He kept kicking her in the head so Jason grabbed the frying pan and hit Scott on the head. Scott turned around and grabbed the pot from the stove and swung it onto Jason. He didn't mean to hurt him. He didn't even know that the stew was boiling. Jason screamed all the way to Sam's house.

In the morning I knock on John's door. He comes to the door to see what he could do for me. Usually I just walk in and we have a cup of coffee while we plan our day and exchange news. I see Sam sitting at John's table drinking coffee.

'Oh, you are busy. I am sorry; I'll come later, it's nothing that can't wait.' I never had to apologise for going into John's office. Sam looks through the window while John is getting rid of me. He does not even invite me to meet Sam? There is an air of secrecy. I hate Sam. I have been abandoned and replaced.

Later in the day I see Sam and John talking in front of the court house. As I approach they stop talking and John says hello. Sam nods at me with his teeth smiling, before he lifts his head high again. He is a handsome middle aged man. Both of them are. Both are working for the poor, both probably want to be saints.

'You met Sam,' says John.

'We met,' says Sam.

An unpleasant feeling overwhelms me; I mention it to Kathy.

'Everybody admires Sam,' says Kathy.

'I don't,' I admit.

'Nobody is all good or all evil,' says Kathy.

'Except for saints like Sam,' I smile.

'There are no saints. I get suspicious if I can't see some bad in a person,' says Kathy. 'When you hide your badness so carefully it must be ugly.'

'He is patronising me,' I say. 'I feel like a dog people pat on the head so it won't bark at them or jump on them.'

'John likes him,' says Kathy.

Maybe I am jealous because Sam came between John and me. Maybe I am jealous because Sam stole people's affections from me. Maybe Sam is not who he would like us believe he is.

Kathy and Peter, Hainy, John and Martha gather in our backyard for a BBQ.

'I better retire before the kids have a chance to bash me,' laughs Marta.

'Why would they bash you,' I ask.

'Marcia, one of our teachers, told a teenager to pick up the paper he threw on the ground. Make me, you fucking white cunt, he said. Marcia told him to see the principal. Make me, the student stood defiantly. She bent down to pick the paper and he pushed her over. She fell to the ground and hit her head on the cement. Marcia sued the student for assault but the court decided that they couldn't move the boy from the local school because his extended family lives here. To resolve the conflict Marcia had to move. You know all about it, you represented the boy's family,' Marta turns to John.

'You protect criminals,' says Peter.

'That's my job,' laughs John.

'The case was hushed up because the boy was an Aboriginal. Marcia was new in town so nobody took much notice of her leaving. I decided then to retire,' says Marta.

'The world is getting scary,' says Kathy.

'When I first started teaching Aborigines were considered savages who had to be civilised and Christianised, says Marta. That was the reality at the time. Maybe we should have left them alone.'

'Every tribe in the world was taken over by other tribes sometimes in the history,' says Hainy.

'It seemed inconceivable until now that blacks would sell blacks into slavery but American Africans admit that Africans sold Africans to American traders into slavery,' adds Marta. 'They say that at the time they were just traders; the issue of race and prejudice came later.'

'The white traders did not dare venture into the African interior,' says Kathy.

'Serbs and Croatians would gladly sell each other into slavery,' says Andrew. The war between Serbs and Croats became the daily news during the nineties.

'Iraqis would sell Kurds or vice versa,' says Peter.

'How come you ended in Lightning Ridge,' Hainy turns to Martha.

'While I tried to change the world my husband took his girlfriend on a business trip. I applied for the transfer and they offered me Lightning Ridge,' laughs Marta.

'Everybody finds his place in a jungle,' says Kathy.

'Nothing lasts forever,' says John. 'I might just pack up and leave you all one day soon as well.' John's words scare me. The funding for my job will run out at the end of the year. Where has the time gone? What did I do, what did I achieve? I never finished my studies, I never returned home. There were simply too many distractions. Our children went to a boarding school and then they found work and married and had children. Ana lives in Melbourne and Ben lives in Sydney. Mum died waiting for me. The matron of the nursing home wrote that my father passed away peacefully in his sleep. I am grateful. Deep down I was always aware that he was waiting for me. I go to church and pray. Dad and mum must be very close to where God is. They are looking down on me. I stopped planning to go home long time ago. Lately Andrew and I spend little time together. He often travels to sell opal in Japan and America. When he is home he keeps busy.

'I am going to retire,' I say at the end of 2000.Andrew is neither happy nor unhappy about my decision. I do not need to work anymore. The term of my office expired. Cuts in expenditure hit many community services. I am not worried. I get my redundancy and superannuation money.

'Time to write your memoirs,' says John.

'I always wanted to write the stories Aborigines told me.'

'What about us Australian Europeans?' says John.

'You are right. I owe it to Ben and Ana to tell them why we ended up in this corner of the world. My children hardly know me. I looked after other tribes when they grew up.'

Lightning Ridge community organises a farewell dinner for me. They congratulate me on the work well done and Pauline presents me with an Aboriginal painting. I believe that everybody loves me. I tell them how very lucky I was this last twenty five years in Lightning Ridge. I enjoyed their company and the work I was doing. I don't tell anyone how I regret that I never had time to go home and that I never took time to be with my children. I never did what I promised mum and dad. I broke all the promises I made to myself.

I get almost two hundred thousand dollars in superannuation. I buy a house next door as an investment.

'At least I will be able to choose my neighbours,' I say to Andrew. It is a lovely house; the original owners kept it in a mint condition. The garden is full of flowers and it is spotless inside. It is very cheap because the market is down. It is easy to find tenants and I can collect rent myself. I hope that Andrew and I could finally take that trip around the world.

'Miners are leaving. Lightning Ridge is becoming a ghost town,' warns Marta.

I met Ian in John's office. He was suing a farmer's son Greg for racial vilification. Ian tripped Greg when they played football. Greg called out: Watch out you black bastard. Ian hit him and the fight started. Black against white. Police came and they arrested both. Ian was demanding fifty thousand dollars compensation for emotional hurt suffered because of the racist insult. He settled for twenty.

Ian's family lives in the camp on the field. He wants to rent my house. 'Money is no problem,' he says. He tells me that he gets three hundred a week playing in the band and singing on weekends in the club. They also get rent assistance and social security. He mines during the week. 'Money will never be a problem,' Ian assures me.

I barely know Ian's wife Edna but I know her parents Pauline and Dudley. Edna's sister Diane is a teacher's assistant. I have seen Diane's house and it is spotless.

'We are going to have new neighbours,' I tell Andrew. 'Ian is moving in.'

'It's your funeral,' says Andrew.

People tell me that I will be sorry renting to Aborigines but I was always on good terms with them. Finally I can prove it to everybody that I am fair dinkum no racist.

'I wish you luck,' says Marta. 'You will need it.'

I worked with Aborigines for almost twenty years but I never before lived next to them. I never before had Aborigines live in the house I owned. I have never been in Edna's camp. I didn't even bother to ask her family Pauline or Dudley or Diane for advice.

'I hope you like music,' says Ian. 'We practice a couple of times a week.'

'They like music,' I explain when Andrew complains about the noise.

'I don't like music at five o'clock in the morning,' says Andrew. I agonise about how to tell Ian and his family that we would like to sleep at night. I go to collect rent.

'I will pay as soon as the money gets through, love,' says Ian.

'When,' I ask. I do not ask through what.

'In a few days,' says Ian.

'Tell them that I haven't slept since they moved in,' says Andrew. His voice is becoming tense. Sleeplessness makes you irritable. I do not tell Andrew that the rent is not paid. It's my house, my problem.

'Kids are throwing rubbish on our side. Do something about it,' Andrew complains. I knock on Ian's door but he is not home. Edna has a black eye and the blood just congealed on her hairline.

'I need the rent,' I put my priorities first.

'Talk to Ian. I haven't got a slice of bread in the house,' says Edna.

'When is he coming home?'

'He is in jail. I got an AVO (Apprehended violence order) against him. I don't deserve to be beaten up like this.' The blood on her hairline made an ugly scab.

'How are you going to pay rent?'

'I have to feed the kids first,' says Edna.

'I'll get you a few things,' I promise. I buy the groceries for Edna without telling Andrew. Edna is used to charity. Only in the past it was government money. I can no longer issue food vouchers. I retired. It's not Edna's fault that I am no longer Jana from Legal holding a government purse.

'When will you get your social security money?' I ask Edna.

'I have to pay the telephone and electricity. They will cut me off,' she says.

'You don't need the phone,' I try to budget for poor Aborigine.

'What if the kids get sick? I have no car,' she reasons.

'What happened to Ian's compensation money?'

'He bought some drums and a guitar.'

'You better cook a big pot of vegetable soup,' I organise Edna. I bring the vegetables from my garden because I have to save her money so she can pay the rent. It is two weeks since they moved in and they still haven't paid anything.

'Maybe we could arrange for you to pay off the back rent by having it directly debited from your social security at thirty dollars a fortnight.'

'Thanks,' says Edna. I help her organise the payments to go to my bank account. Ian is away for four weeks. The rent is not paid for the second two weeks.

'I was in jail, I have no money, you will have to give me time,' he says when he returns. Thursday is a pension day and I go over for the rent money but they spent it on food. I tell Pauline. She is Edna's mother and my friend.

'Edna never lived in a proper house before,' says Pauline. She never paid rent or learned to do house work. She has hardly ever been inside a proper house to see how things are done. In the olden days when I was young the government apprenticed young Aboriginal girls to learn housework in a big house where the farmer lived. I learned to do everything that needs doing in a house. When I married Dudley we lived on a riverbank in a little shack we built. Edna grew up there and then she moved in with Ian and they lived on the opal fields in a camp. She never had a chance to learn. I knew that it would be hard on them to pay. You can't leave kids hungry. It's not the kids' fault if parents gamble and drink,' says Pauline.

'I can't let them stay without paying,' I plead. I realise that I never really listened to Aborigines before. They lived on the edge of the society but I let Edna into my house right next to me.

'Can you talk to Edna, please,' I beg Pauline.

'Trouble is, young ones don't listen to us anymore,' says Dudley.

'Who do they listen to?'

'No one,' says Pauline. 'We can do nothing.'

'We are powerless,' says Dudley. Powerless. I used the word powerless in my submissions for government money. I wanted to empower my Aboriginal friends with government money. John told me about powerless people but I never felt what powerless is. I faced problems and solved them. I was powerful. I had power to solve other people's problems. John thaught me how to get it from the government.

'The dogs are barking every night,' says Andrew. He still does not know about the unpaid rent.

'I'll ring the council about the dogs,' I promise.

'I have enough of this,' says Andrew at five o'clock in the morning as the singing next door continues. He moves into a spare room at the back. Kathy warned me that Thursday night is a pension night and the party goes on until the next day but this is not even Thursday or a pension day. I call the police and they turn the music off but I cannot go back to sleep. I worry about Andrew. He is never home. He is never happy. We don't talk. I am desperate. We are falling apart. It is my house and I rented it and it is my problem. My funeral.

'Someone has a birthday,' I plead with Andrew.

'Join them. Stay with them. They always come first.'

'I will talk to them tomorrow.'

'Do as you like. I don't care anymore.' I did not even notice when Andrew stopped caring. I go next door in the morning but they don't want to talk to me because I called the police.

'Fuck yourself you rich white bitch,' I hear from inside.

'I want you to move out in two weeks' time,' I call through the door. I know I have to give them proper notice.

'I will go when I am good and ready, you can't make me,' yells Edna.

Why is Edna hostile towards me? I bought her groceries; she lives in my house without paying. She is my friend's daughter.

'Edna, please,' I beg.

'You can eat your vegetable soup yourself, you fucking rich cunt. My kids need real food.'

'I gave you notice two weeks ago and I want you out now,' I say most seriously after another two weeks.

'You want my kids to live on the street. Why don't you go where you fucking came from, you stupid wog. This is my country, you fucking rich cunt,' says Edna.

'Get out. I couldn't care less where you go,' I say. I regret my anger, I should not get frustrated; I am used to dealing with Aborigines.

'Make me.'

'You pay the rent and you can stay,' I correct myself.

'Fuck off.' 'I understand that alcohol and frustration make you say things you would not say sober.

'We have to talk,' I insist.

'I will get a rental tribunal advocacy on you for harassing us.' Someone must have been couching Edna on her rights. Was it me?

'I want to inspect the house,' I try.

'If you step in the house I will have the police on you.'

'It's my house,' I say as I keep knocking on the door. I am desperate. The police arrive.

'She is harassing us,' says Edna.

'They don't pay rent,' I explain.

'You will have to go through the rental tribunal. I am asking you to leave, 'says the policeman to me.

I keep knocking on Edna's door every day. The police serve me summons to come to court. Edna applied for AVO. I am not to step on her block.

'Take a solicitor and argue in the court,' they tell me.

'I just want them out of my house.'

'The tribunal will hear your case and decide. We have no jurisdiction,' say the police. John went to Italy. I haven't seen him for over a month. I am lost without him. I don't know when he will return. How can he leave me when I need him? John would understand and do something about it. I want to tell him that I am powerless. He would know what to do, he would do it. He is the advocate for the powerless. Aborigines have been telling me for years that the government made them powerless. Now I know how it feels.

'And how is mother,' says Sam as he comes to collect John's belongings.

'Which mother,' I snap.

'Oh come, come,' he wriggles like a worm.

'When is John coming,' I pretend that I did not notice the sarcasm.

'He is setting a new practice in Sydney. 'John changed since Sam replaced me as the benefactor of the town's poor. I don't like Sam. There is something indescribably ugly about his toothy smile. John abandoned me. My world is caving in. I am alone and frightened and betrayed. Why didn't he tell me? We spent the last twenty five years together. We were partners and confidants. How could he do this to me? I was more attached to John than I realised. He warned me that one day he might go away but I didn't even ask where or when. Maybe John closed down because I retired. Maybe he just needed a change. No doubt he will ring and explain. I mean nothing to him since I closed my office. I mean nothing to anybody.

Andrew stopped talking to me. I beg him, I promise to do anything he wants but he does not care. 'Just leave me alone,' he says.

'I warned you not to try to change the world,' says Marta.

'It's not fair,' I say defeated.

'Don't talk about fair. This is a real world,' says Marta. 'Shit happens in a real world. Dog eats dog.'

I read a letter from the rental tribunal: The tenant made a complaint against you that you are harassing them. I ring the Tribunal but they tell me that they are acting for the tenant and cannot discuss the case with me.

'What am I to do?'

'You have to give them sixty-day notice in writing. If they don't pay in the two weeks after that, you give them termination notice and if they don't move out, you apply to the Tribunal to hear the case.'

'How long before the Tribunal will hear the case?

'Might take a month.'

'Who will pay the rent?'

'Get yourself some legal advice. You can sue the tenant in a civil court.' My legal advice abandoned me. I ask my doctor to write me a script for sleeping pills and antidepressants. I put antidepressants into Andrew's coffee as well.

In my dreams I try to climb the hill but my feet are bogged in the mud. I wake up tired and unhappy. I dream about guns and killing. In the morning my hands shake. I want to go home. I need mummy and daddy.

Edna's daughter Beccy moves in with Edna. She brings her three children and two dogs. Her boyfriend shot through after he bashed her and she has nowhere to stay. Aborigines are always there for each other. Edna cannot throw her daughter on the street.

I am waiting for the rental tribunal.

Beccy's boyfriend returns. He wants Beccy and the children to go with him. Beccy is shouting: 'Get fucked, you mother fucker.' I hear the window smash and children squeal. I hear the punches and slamming of the door. I call the police. Beccy's boyfriend is taken to jail. Beccy is taken to hospital.

'Help me, I beg the police.'

'We can't get involved in the renting matters. We have no jurisdiction.'

It has been two months. I got sixty dollars rent in that time. Edna stuck a beer box cardboard where the windowpane was. I write a long desperate letter to the local magistrate. He does not want to read it. The problem is outside his jurisdiction.

'Magistrates don't like to put Aborigines in goal,' says Marta. 'Some are scared of retaliation; others are scared of bad press. Some feel sorry for them. There is nothing in it for them.'

I give Edna one-week notice to inspect the house. The walls are covered in posters stuck over the holes in the walls. The oven is full of grease, the bathroom is filthy, and the toilet bowl is broken. The carpet stinks. Cockroaches march unperturbed from room to room, the door's unhinged. The flowers have long died in the garden covered in broken glass, dog bones and other indescribable litter.

'Help me,' I beg Andrew.

'I told you when you took them in. It's your problem. I am going to Japan. I hope you fix it before I return.'

Ian left. Beccy is in the hospital. There is just Edna and seven children in the house now. And the dogs. The rental tribunal gave them two weeks to find alternative accommodation. After two weeks they are still in. The Tribunal promises that the sheriff will move them out in a few days. Edna appealed. The kids are sick. She has nowhere to go. You can't throw sick kids on the street. Beccy is still in hospital. She might lose her eye.

I sit outside most nights. I pray; for the first time in my life. I sincerely pray. I talk to God because suddenly I realise that there is nobody else that would understand. I cannot call Ana or Ben. They live their lives and I have no right to disturb them. I was busy when they had problems. The sleeping pills have no effect. It isn't nice to think of murder. It is rather painful and futile because I simply don't dare commit murder. The next best thing is to kill myself. I need to cry but there is no one to cry with. Andrew is away.

'Move in and take possession,' says Kathy. 'It's your house, they can't throw you out."

I knock on the door but nobody answers. They are in but they don't let me in. I take my spare key and move in. Edna calls the police for trespassing. I sit on the floor and don't move. The young policeman does not know what to do with me. He tells everybody to go out so he can talk to me.

'I understand,' says the boy policeman. I become hopeful. 'But I can't help you,' he dumps me. 'By law I should arrest you for trespassing. If you move out now I will talk to them and try to get them to drop the charges against you. You really have to go to court and get a sheriff to get them out.'

I wonder if I am depressed or angry or going insane. I just want to sleep through the nightmare. I wish I could think about something other than Edna and my house. Nights are the worst. At night it is just me and my problem. What have I done to deserve this? I can't cope. It isn't fair. When I finally doze off I dream of Aborigines hurling abuse, about Sam pointing a finger at me and sneering, Andrew walking away, drums drumming, Edna calling me white cunt. Most of all I dream of wanting to run away but my feet are stuck in the mud. I wake up shuddering.

In the morning I look at my beautiful new house next door. I see Edna and her friend smoking and drinking in front of it.

'She needs a good fuck, the rich white cunt,' says Edna to her friend in a big aggressive voice for me to hear. I go to the fence to talk to Edna. She runs inside and locks the door.

'Please talk to me,' I beg.

'If you don't stop harassing me I will call the police. I have enough trouble with seven kids to look after.'

I go to Hainy. What could he do? I burst into tears and he hugs me.

'I wish I could help,' he says. 'When this is over you will know better. It can't last much longer. I'll help you to restore the house once you get rid of them.' Hainy is the only person feeling my pain. I go to Pauline and Dudley. They sympathise with me, but they told me before about their unruly children and grandchildren. They are surprised by my anger. I was always understanding, strong and helpful.

'Poor Edna doesn't have anyone to help her,' says Pauline. I remember that I was the one solving problems in Lightning Ridge. It was my job to solve their problems. They don't realise that I no longer have an office or a government purse. This is my life, my savings. I lived inside myself and translated outside life into my way of thinking. I realise that things are never as they seem but as one experiences them on their own skin at a particular time. I am powerless. The people with power have deserted me.

'I am sorry for Edna's children,' says Pauline. 'Beccy is not twenty yet and with three children she has no-where to go. Those in Aboriginal housing look after their own; our family always looked after itself. I was never begging for help.'

'The girls in the Aboriginal Housing office allocate government funds and accommodation to their friends and relations,' says Dudley.

'Couldn't you find something for them,' asks Pauline. Of course Pauline expects me to help. Edna and Beccy are family. They are powerless without me. I am powerless without the government money but they still believe that I have the magic wand.

'Couldn't Diane take them in,' I beg.

'Diane doesn't even like living next to Aborigines. Since she married a white man she thinks she is white,' says Pauline. 'She doesn't talk to her sister, because she is afraid that Edna would come to visit.

'Go to the government,' says Hainy. I feel like a lost Little Red Riding Hood running from the big bad wolf. I need my family. Andrew does not talk to me, my children are not even aware of my problems. I have no one to cry with. Crying is a sign of weakness and failure. I should rely on my knowledge and common sense. 'You know best,' people say. Nobody says: poor Jana.

'There must be something that you can do. You always know best,' Dudley repeats my thoughts.

'Government is looking after Aborigines, they should pay their rent,' says Hainy. 'You know better than anybody else how to find government assistance.'

'Landlord's insurance will pay for rent and the damage,' says Kathy.

'I did not know that you could insure against the loss of rent and wilful damage by tenants,' I say.

'I suppose we all learn by our own mistakes,' says Marta.

I miss John but maybe even he would sympathise with Edna's family. I am not as destitute as they are. Andrew seems distant and unfriendly. We haven't laughed or played cards for months. We no longer sleep together. I realise that work was a blessing for me. I was solving other people's problems and had no time to create my own.

'I warned you,' says Marta absolving herself.

'It's not the end of the world,' says Kathy. 'Look on the bright side. You have insurance in case they burn the house down.' Should I burn the house down? Maybe there is a bright side. If they burnt the house I would build a brand new one. I dream of the house burning. I am not used to being powerless and ignored; Not loved. Alone. Aloneness stares at me open eyed and cold. Nobody understands the urgency and desperation I feel. I can't deal with being a failure.

'You get rent assistance,' I reason with Edna.

'They cut my power,' yells Edna. There is a glimmer of hope that without power they can't stay. Edna goes to the Neighbourhood centre and cries that she can't warm the milk for her babies. Her daughter is still in hospital. The Neighbourhood pays for the power.

'I would never do this to anyone,' I say to Kathy.

'You were never in Edna's shoes so you have no idea what you would do if you were. Any mother would fight for her children.' So that's what it is. I am against the mother who is fighting for her children. I have two houses and she has none. I am capable and strong and well off. Edna is vulnerable and powerless.

I write to The Rental Tribunal, ombudsman, media. Nobody is impressed with my problem. It's only rent and children have to have a roof over their heads. Equity.

'You knew what they are like,' says Shane. 'You worked with them long enough.'

'Poor kids,' says Dudley.

'You must be able to do something for them,' Pauline repeats herself. I always did something.

'Can you take Edna,' I try.

'I have six grandchildren staying with us. It's only two bedrooms. Write to the government,' says Pauline. I wonder which part of the government is responsible for not knowing right from wrong. Maybe it is wrong that I have two houses when Edna has none. Government is to blame and I used to be a little part of that government. Dudley once said that in the past people knew their place but John said that there is no such thing as your place. In democracy people decide for themselves what is their right place and the right thing for them. Did white people destroy the basic morals of Aborigines? They banned Aboriginal parental teaching and took control. Perhaps there is no such thing as right and wrong. If there is no right and wrong, if people are allowed to decide for themselves what is moral and right, one always decides in his own favour. Edna knows what's best for her family. She doesn't care about me. I am a grown up woman; I will survive.

I write to our Member of Parliament. He tells me to go to the Rental tribunal. I tell him that I have been everywhere. He promises to look into the matter.

'When will you go out,' I plead with Edna.

'I have nowhere to go. Try to get me a house. Ian took my food money. He knows where I keep it,' says Edna.

Edna is not being funny. I always helped people like her to get houses. I had no right to retire after I made everyone dependent on the magic government purse. Andrew is rarely home. He does not eat at home and he sleeps in the room at the back of the house permanently because of the noise from Edna's home. I beg Andrew to talk to me but he wants to be left out of it. I didn't listen to his advice. We have not made love for months.

Andrew leaves to sell opals in Japan. He does not even say goodbye. He takes opal on consignment; he always sells well and people trust him. He takes their stones around the world and nothing was ever lost. Everybody knows how careful Andrew is and he is as honest as they come. Miners put their lowest price on their stones and what Andrew gets over is his. Very simple really. Sometimes he gets double the money sometimes he barely sells for the price people want but he sells it and miners like that. This is going to be a big trip for him. He will probably go to America as well. Hainy gave him a lot of opal this time. Andrew rings to say that he is sorry. We have both been under a lot of stress. He promises that when he returns we will talk and sort things out. He loves me.

'Please come back soon,' I say. 'I need you. I love you. I am sorry for causing all this.' I forget to ask where he is staying so I press for the number from which he phoned.

'Hilton hotel in Sydney,' says the man. So Andrew did not go to Japan yet. I check the number again and yes Andrew rang from Hilton. I get the room from which Andrew rang but the maid tells me that Mr. and Mrs Smith are out at the moment. I must have made a mistake. Andrew must have rung just before he left for Japan and before Mr and Mrs Smith took the apartment. Shane comes to see if Andrew rang. He took a few of his stones as well.

'Yes, he is fine,' I say.

'Debbie is doing a computer programming course in Sydney,' says Shane.

'Where is she staying?' I haven't seen Debbie for months. I forgot about my friends during the war with Edna.

'They put them into Hilton hotel, says Shane. Government is paying so why not.' I am in shock. Maybe the sleeping pills and the tranquillisers killed the feelings I should have. I tell myself not to jump to conclusions. There must be a simple explanation. I feel a sharp pain in my chest. I ring Hilton hotel again but they tell me that Mr and Mrs Smith booked out. I sit with arms wrapped around myself to escape from lovelessness. My heart feels like a rock but I cannot cry. Did my tears freeze into a rock? Did I forget how to cry?I need to go home. There is a bond that never fails to hold the children and the parents together against the world. There must be an eternity where my parents watch down on me. I remember an old saying:

Me and my clan against the world;
Me and my family against my clan;
Me and my brother against my family;
Me against my brother.

In the end we are all alone; I must not jump to conclusions. I must not make accusations. I can't tell anyone about it. Peter and

Hainy and Shane would be worried about the opal they gave to Andrew on consignment.

'Think three times before you speak,' mum warned. 'Count to ten and think three times.' As a child I wandered about the mystery of counting to ten while thinking three times. Mum must have known that the world is not a friendly place. I never had a reason to be jealous. Andrew boasted to his friends about his beautiful, clever wife; he was always demonstrative and affectionate towards me. He boasted about all his possessions. He is not a womaniser. He loves me. He tells everybody that I am the best thing that happened to him. Maybe he feels neglected. We lost the closeness we had. Maybe I took his love for granted. There must be an explanation. I cannot tell anyone about Andrew. The silence of the night speaks in angry voices. Is this the retribution for not being there when mum and dad needed me? I wasn't there for my children either. People are tired of my rent problem. I feel betrayed. Maybe I have blown it out of proportion; maybe I am overreacting; maybe it is only the full moon; I always have weird dreams during the full moon; maybe it has nothing to do with Edna or me or Andrew.

John rings from Sydney to say hello. He only has a minute before he goes to court with his client. I beg him to ring again but he doesn't.

I cannot tell Hainy or Kathy. They would worry about the opal they gave Andrew on consignment.

Edna's dogs howl more during the full moon. There must be an affinity between the moon, her dogs and me. I hear Edna yell at the children. Shouldn't they be asleep at midnight? They probably watch videos with her. It is refreshing to feel the breeze of the cool night after the hot day. I walk in circles on the front lawn. I heard that lions do that in the cage. And prisoners. Somewhere in the distance I visualise Andrew and Debbie but

I turn away from the picture in my mind. I can't deal with that now. I don't dare go back to bed. Nights are the worst. I want to go home. I want to see the familiar faces, walk on the roads of my childhood. I try to sleep; sleeping pills are making me feel numb but I cannot hold my eyes closed. It is three in the morning and the music is loud. I bang on Edna's door and yell: 'Turn down the bloody music.'

'Close your fucking windows,' screams Edna.

I storm into the house and smash her stereo.

'What about the rent? The house is wrecked.'

'Fuck the house,' snarls Edna. 'Why do you need two houses? This is Aboriginal land.' Edna pushes me out of the door. I return home and walk around with my hands over my ears. I want to shut the world and escape into the placenta. Dogs keep yapping. I get the rat poison and mix the whole packet with mincemeat. Like a thief I move along the fence and throw the poisoned meatballs over the fence. The big bulldog catches every ball. I throw two at the time in different direction so the smaller dogs can get some. The little dogs lick the ground and squeal pushing each other out of a way. I sit on the grass beside the fence. I watch the big dog vomit and groan. By five in the morning it stops squirming and it lays there probably dead. I go inside and make myself a cup of coffee before I nod off into my nightmare.

In the morning I see the police knock on Edna's door. I presume Edna called them to arrest me. Her dog lies motionless where I last saw it. The little dogs are nowhere to be seen. The policewoman is comforting Edna. She seems sick. Maybe she touched the poisoned food I threw over the fence. Maybe one of the children got poisoned.

My father used to say that people take their problems with them wherever they go. I had no problems until I met Edna.

Something must be wrong with me. They will lock me up. I might lose the house. I lost everything else. My mind included. I might as well kill myself.

I take more tranquillisers to stay in control. I just want to return to the world I used to know. I have to escape. I pack my bag and take a short cut to the highway. I walk through the bush on a dusty track. I am a child again; I am a little Red Riding Hood swallowed by a big bad wolf waiting for a kind hunter to rescue me. I have an intense desire to run only I can't because I carry a heavy bag. I am shaking. Maybe I really don't see things as they are but as I am. Most of my life I felt that everybody loved me and I could do no wrong. Why did this warm, fuzzy world suddenly turn against me? 'When God closes the window he opens the door,' mum used to say. I see no door. What have I done? How have I changed? Everybody and everything changed. 'Only perceptions change,' said Kathy once.

Other people's problems used to be a source of my salary, success and job satisfaction. Now they are a source of my sorrow and anger and anxiety. Why don't people take care of their own problems? I suppose I would never have had a nice job and power if people had no problems.

I stand on the highway waiting for a car to take me somewhere. One does not cry on the crossroads where strangers make choices about their directions. What good would crying do? Someone might tell me that things are not as bad as they look. That everything will be all right. I will ring my children to tell them that we are fine.

I would not dream of hitch hiking in my sensible life but now I am looking for a way out of the black hole that my life became. I am too tired to drive. If the driver, who picks me up, kills me, he will only save me the trouble.

I used to hitch hike in Slovenia as a student. It was safe because police were everywhere. In Australia the road stretches for hundreds of kilometres without seeing another person or a settlement, let alone the police. Anything can happen but at this moment anything is better than staying where I am. I hold my hand up as the car approaches.

'Where to,' a head pokes out of the white box of a car. All cars seem the same now, like all people. I look at the signpost pointing in the driver's direction and it says Angledool so I say Angledool. I place my bag between my legs but the man tells me that I will be more comfortable if it goes in the boot.

'You from Angledool?' He chats.

'Just visiting.'

'Who do you have there,' he wants to know before I have time to read his face and the make of the car. Finally things are happening outside of me again. I have to respond to questions. When you live outside yourself it is easier to shut away the pain that wants to choke you from inside. I have never been to Angledool, I hear it is a place with a few houses, I don't know anyone there.

'I will go to Queensland from there,' I think quickly.

'Lucky,' he says, 'I am going to Queensland myself. What town?'

'Gold Coast,' I make up the answer like it was my most considered plan. I know Gold coast; it is a place where I was blissfully happy once. And later totally devastated. Only Andrew and my family still loved and needed me then.

'I am going to Gold Coast. Have you friends there?' The questions demand answers. I have to remember the lies I make up as I go. I am scared that I will twist myself into the stories I tell. I am glad that I have no time to remember who I am and what I am doing.

'Yes.'

Finally I have time to look at the driver. He is a man, a very average man in very average greyish clothes. Probably insurance salesman trying to gain my trust before he insures me.

'Aren't you scared to hitchhike,' he smiles.

'Aren't you scared to pick hitchhikers,' I smile back. We both consider our situation and it does not seem dangerous.

'Staying in Queensland long?'It seems funny that he is interested in my travel plans but maybe he just needs to keep awake.

'I am not sure,' I try to squeeze out of the information.

'Are you married?' He continues.

'Not much, are you?' I try to be bold and untouchable.

'Not much is right,' he smiles.

'Where is home,' I ask.

'Dubbo.'

'Nice town. You travel much?'

'Yea.' I hope we won't have to chat until we come to Gold Coast. In ten hours we could know more about each other than we want or need to. I pretend to read a pamphlet from his dashboard. I know he can't read and drive at the same time so talking is next best thing for him. I need to think about the madness I entered into.

Tranquillisers gradually lull me into the world where everything is as it should be. One thing is as good as another so I lean back ready to chat.

'Are you selling insurance,' I ask to see how accurate my assessment was.

'I am with TAFE,' he says. Being with TAFE could mean being re-skilled, learning to read or build houses, being unemployed, being in charge or being a teacher. I want to find out what he is in TAFE (tertiary and further education).

'What do you do?' I ask. You can ask a stranger anything because it makes no difference what a stranger thinks of a stranger.

'I co-ordinate courses for the rural areas.'

'What sort of courses?'

'Literacy, numeracy, farming, building, opal cutting, machinery repair, computer skills, you name it. Whatever the needs are.'

'Interesting job.'

'Until the money runs out. We are funded from year to year.'

'It's like that everywhere these days; until the money runs out.'

'There used to be job security. You started your job and finished in the same job only higher up.'

'This government is cutting on welfare,' he says.

'Is your job welfare?'

'More or less. The courses empower underprivileged. People need to feel that they have something to contribute. Rich are getting richer and poor are pushed deeper and deeper into the gutter. About a quarter of Australians live below the poverty line.'

'There is no real poverty in Australia.'

'You might not have come in contact with it but there are still starving children,' he says. It is his job to write reports on poverty so the government will provide grants to alleviate it. By organising TAFE courses he will empower poor people. He will also keep his job. And the government car. He is a distant echo of my former self. I may actually be talking to myself.

'There is poverty and poverty. Some people feel rich if their rice bowl is full but others feel poor if there is no money for videos and drinks and smokes and dope. Some people feel rich if they have a roof over their head while others are unhappy without an air-conditioner.'

'People need education to become self-reliant, 'the man says. 'They should learn to make their own decisions and protect themselves against the ruling class.'

'The rich and the poor will always be among us. You either belong to the ruling class or to the exploited class. Nobody liberates you to rule,' I smile at the simplicity of it all. This man could be John incarnated. I don't tell the man that I was writing those same applications for grants for years and that I used the same jargon and the same reasoning. I made promises to the government that I will alleviate poverty and empower the powerless. I wrote out food vouchers for needy families. I made the powerless dependant on my power to get funds from the government. I don't want to dwell on my situation.

'Having a job empowers,' says the man convincingly. He has no idea how deep in the shit I am. Nobody is interested in my kind of poverty. Nobody wants to empower me. I have no vested power. I am nothing. I have no family. I have no tribe of my own to offer me sanctuary. There is no refuge for the likes of me.

'What do you do,' asks the man.

'I retired.' Retired people do nothing, are nothing.

'What does your husband do?'

'He is in export,' I say hoping that the field is big enough to hide in.

'Exporting what?'

'Opals, specimens, fossils, jewellery. He is an opal buyer.'

'Where does he operate?'

'Everybody deals with gemstones In Lightning Ridge. What did you do in Lightning Ridge,' I turn the focus on him.

'I organised literacy classes for Aborigines and migrants. There are so many poor migrants who never learned proper English. Now they have to attend classes in order to get their social security entitlements.' I am grateful that the man does not associate me with either poor Aborigines or poor migrants. The man needs a job so he is searching for needs like I used to. Other people's welfare is the source of his employment. How nice that old migrants finally have classes. They survived without classes all their working lives but now they have to be empowered. Or punished for becoming unemployed in their old age. Or becoming old and useless. The migrants will have to admit that after being self-reliant for decades in Australia they are still illiterate because they haven't learned to spell English words.

'What will you do on Gold coast?' I think he needs to chat to keep awake.

'I don't know yet.'

We turn the conversation to the weather and the trees and the sheep and the computers. Somewhat exhausted we stop and he asks if I like music. I don't mind so we listen to his tapes. I like John Denver singing: country road take me home. My tears are stuck behind my eyelids. I try to rub out Lightning Ridge but my life is there and I might as well try to rub out my life.

The police stop us. I know that they are looking for me because I poisoned the bloody dog. Maybe the bloody kids got poisoned as well. They check the man's driver's licence and tell him that his tyre needs replacing.

'What's your name,' if you don't mind me asking, the man says as we drive on.

I left my name and my home and my life in Lightning Ridge.

'Natasha,' I lie.

'I am Simon,' he gives me his hand like we were just formally introduced. We have a lot in common. We are about the same age and neither of us knows what we will do on Gold coast.

'I want to make a new start,' Simon says solemnly.

'I don't know what I want to start or finish.'

'My daughter died last year,' says Simon.

'I am sorry.'

'Someone spiked her drink. My daughter did not take drugs. She was only a child. Our only child.' I can't tell Simon that I just killed a dog next door or that maybe I killed my tenants. I wanted to kill my tenants. I feel ashamed. He has real problems while I only feel sorry for myself. I don't want to frighten Simon with my story. I haven't slept for ages so I try to sleep. I close my eyes and we travel in silence.

'I hit my wife;' Simon's voice enters my conscience. 'I hope she is OK,' he says calmly. She would not talk to me or let me near her. I am so depressed.'

'Aren't we all,' I say more to myself than to him. It is getting dark and more comfortable because we don't have to look at each other. He is nothing much to look at and neither am I.

'Where will we sleep,' he asks. I am glad he includes me in his plans since I have none.

'Motel,' I say.

He stops and the receptionist asks: 'Single or double?'

'How much are single rooms?'

'Single is eighty-five and for two is ninety-five.' In our practical way we calculate the saving if we take a twin. We worked for our money so we learned to save. We both taught people how to budget.

'What do you prefer?' He lets me decide.

'Whichever,' I return him the right to decide.

'Twin,' he says. 'I don't think he has much money. We know that we are both impotent. We have no energy to kill each other or make love. We both welcome company. Someone to say words to since we have no dog. I see flashbacks of the dog that died in agony; I see police comforting Edna. Maybe one of the children took the poisoned meat I have thrown over the fence. I complained about the barking bloody dogs bitterly and they know that I did it. I complained about everything. I complained about their garbage, their singing, their visitors and kids and language. I wanted them out of my life. I daydreamed of killing them all. People told me to take it easy and ignore them, Aborigines are like that; they like singing and music and dogs. It's their culture. Aborigines told me that I have no sense of fun. I nag. I must have lost fun.

'You take things too seriously,' said Kathy.

'I am going to kill Edna,' I said to Marta.

'You don't want to rot in jail for scum like that,' said Marta. No wonder John called Marta a racist. If only John came back. He would know what to do. I cannot bring myself to talk about it yet. Simon would not understand my frustration. It is only a temporary frustration compared to Simon's permanent loss. He lost his only child and his wife.

'I might ring my wife to see if she is all right,' he says.

I take a long shower.

'She is crying,' says Simon as I return.

I sit on my bed hoping to cry but the tears are like thorns behind the eyelids.

'Would you like to order some dinner or something,' asks Simon.

'I need a drink.'

'There is beer in the fridge.'

'I don't really want beer.'

'I'll get a bottle of whisky,' Simon offers. He knows that we need to be tranquillised. We sip our drinks lifelessly. I can't even decide why I am sad. If I am sad. I have only myself to blame. I wanted to help Edna and Ian and Pauline and Dudley. I forgot that I am no longer the government. I wanted to prove it to the society that I know how to deal with Aborigines. I wash down a couple of sleeping pills with a large whisky. Gradually everything is all right and I am at peace. I wake up at about three in the morning and hear Simon in the bathroom.

'I couldn't sleep so I went to read in the bathroom not to disturb you,' he says.

'We could watch a video.' Videos in the motel are erotic videos but Simon and I cannot even pretend erotic enjoyment. We want to erase the reality and go back to where everything was.

'Have a drink?'

'Just a small one,' I say. We sit; a generous glass of whisky in hand each in our own twin bed; one in each corner of the room respectfully separated watching people make love on the video.

'The psychologist suspects sexual abuse,' says Simon.

'Who?' I pull myself out of my murder plans.

'My wife accused me of molesting my own daughter. She called me a paedophile. That's when I hit her.'

'How would a psychologist know?'

'The school sent my daughter to the psychologist for assessment. She developed behaviour problems.'

Simon's problem is getting bigger and the room seems filled with sinister and morbid. Am I sharing a twin room with a man who sexually abused his own daughter? He seems a weak sad man. Maybe weak sad men search for love with those that are weaker than they are. Maybe his daughter provided love… It's absurd; it's horrible, dirty.

'Have another drink,' I pass the bottle. I have to get away before I get bogged into another mire of problems. I am no longer God or the Liaison. The whisky obscures the love making on the video and blurs the recollections of what Simon is saying. My poisoned neighbours are in another world. The pornographic scene on the video suddenly makes me laugh and we both begin to giggle uncontrollably. I see Simon wiping tears from his eyes.

We are drunk. Somewhere in the distance are sadness and the gravity of the situation. We finish half a bottle of scotch and fall asleep as the rising sun sends the first rays into the room. I dream about Aborigines calling me names and dogs are chasing me. People point at me. Andrew walks away and I can't catch up with him. The full moon pierces into me. I hear drums. We wake up at lunchtime hungry. Somewhere lurks the memory of unpleasant life.

'What would you like to do,' asks Simon.

'Sleep,' I say.

'Let's go for a swim while we are here.'

After eating fish and chips on the beach we go to our room to finish the rest of the whisky.

'I think I will go home tomorrow,' says Simon. 'Maybe we will start again. My conscience is clear. My wife is just depressed since our daughter died.'

'Of course. I am ready to go home too,' I say.

Simon and I hug and say goodbye where we first met only days earlier. Andrew is still away. The house is as empty as my heart. Everything is as I left it. Edna and her children and grandchildren are still next door. They are still my tenants. My problem. Pauline is there and Dudley and cousins and nephews. There is an ominous silence. Their heads are down; there is no sound, no music. I say hello to Pauline over the fence.

'Beccy died,' says Pauline. I go over to hug her and cry with her like there was never anything wrong between my neighbours and me.

'What happened?'

'Beccy's boyfriend picked her from hospital and wanted her to go with him. She would not go so he pushed her on the road and she hit her head. The police came in the morning to tell

Edna. You weren't home.' She wasn't poisoned; I feel a relief sweeping over me.

'Her funeral is tomorrow.'

'I am so sorry,' I say.

'I know,' says Pauline. Now is not the time to ask for the rent or to tell Edna to go out, get lost, and disappear. I have to go to her daughter's funeral.

'What will happen to Beccy's children?' I inquire from Pauline about this part of my problem.

'I suppose Edna will keep them.'

Edna sobs into my arms. I contact the Housing office and they give Edna a home they have for such emergencies. I speak to the appropriate people about her sad circumstances and about the loss of her daughter. I help Edna move into a new house. I let her have the furniture she used. The furniture is battered from the many wars Edna fought in my house. Edna is grateful. She hugs me and tells me that she is sorry for being rude. Giving Edna the furniture makes me feel free. It was only furniture. It was only a house. It was only the rent. It was only the words. Families are like that. I have no tribe of my own to fight with. Edna regrets the harsh words she said. She is respectfully mourning her daughter. Aborigines are reverent at the time of death. I have to understand that Edna is just trying to do the best for her children and grandchildren. I have to forgive and forget.

For the funeral I wear the expensive black silk outfit Andrew bought in Tokyo for my Christmas present. I never had a suitable occasion to wear it. I haven't even looked at it since I hung it in my wardrobe. Aborigines from near and far come in their black and white attire with roses pinned to their garments and smelling of soap and hope.

My heart and my bed are enormously big and empty.

Hainy organised the trade's people to renovate my house. Fresh paint covers the misery of the past. I claim for damages on my insurance. Forget about the rent. The Health Department built a new hospital and they need accommodation for nurses. No more problems with my investment. Nurses will stay in the house forever.

I get a letter from Andrew.

> 'Shane gave me a parcel to take to Debbie so I visited her in Sydney before going to Japan. I had opal with me. We decided to go for dinner in the restaurant downstairs. I left my case in Debbie's hotel room. Usually I put opals in the hotel safe but I didn't plan on staying so I thought it would be safe to leave them in a room while we had dinner. As we returned the opals were gone. Debbie was shocked. We could not face you and Shane and the miners. Especially Hainy. Tell the miners that one way or the other I will pay for their stolen opal. Please explain to our children. I love you all, Andrew.'

I paste a copy of Andrew's letter on my front door. We all know the same story and we can all make of it what we like. I am stunned. I ring our children and explain about opal. They have to hear it from me first. Andrew wasn't unfaithful to them so they don't need to know about Debbie. Maybe he is telling the truth. 'Daddy will be home as soon as he sorts things out,' I say cheerfully. I know Andrew will never return but children don't have to deal with that yet. I am left with the house and old memorabilia while he began his new life. Andrew has always been good to me; we were reasonably happy for over thirty years.

Sunday papers have Andrew on the front page. Just as well I told our children. There is no mention of Debbie.

'I want to get away from being a role model,' Debbie used to say.' I want to be myself. In a big city one can cut tribal ties. If you are Aboriginal role model you are responsible for the behaviour of your race. You are exposed and vulnerable.'

Perhaps it isn't easy to be a role model. Strong nation or races do not need role models. The pride comes naturally, collectively. A role model of a minority carries all the stigma of being small and different. You don't dare fail in the eyes of your tribe or in the eyes of the people that appointed you as their role model. You are meant to be a symbol of perfection. You stand on the pedestal. I always liked Debbie. I can't even blame Debbie for liking Andrew. If she does. If he does. If they do.

John appointed me a role model for migrants and Aborigines when I became their Liaison officer. I was given the power to solve problems other migrants and Aborigines could not. When I fell from my pedestal I shattered and became worthless. I did not even have my tribe to cry with.

Aborigines are grumbling that money from their grants disappeared. There are rumours that John took the money. A small town is always hungry for a scandal. People enjoy gossip.

'When it rains here, it pours,' says Marta. Lightning Ridge either has droughts or floods.

I have considered selling both houses, of course, but everything is for sale at the moment. Every so often Lightning Ridge miners become collectively disillusioned and want to leave. They simply lose hope. They mostly live on hope and when nobody finds opal and nobody buys it, the hope evaporates. I have seen it all before. As soon as a new field is discovered and some miner finds something spectacular, the miners return in droves. The fools and the dreamers again believe that it is their turn to become rich overnight.

Miners are asking how Andrew is doing and when he will be home but Andrew did not call since I returned.

'When is Debbie coming home?' I ask Shane.

'They extended her course. She wants me to join her. Maybe we will move to be closer to our children.'

I read the report about Aboriginal stolen generation. It is an agonising tale of ties breaking. Often the children were taken away for their own protection but the mothers and children do not reason about the benefits of separation; they just tell about the pain it caused.

I deprived my parents of their only child. Nobody forced me to break the ties with my people. It was my choice to go with Andrew. It was my fault that I never returned.

Miners are saying that Andrew took half a million worth of opal. 'You probably know how much he took,' I say to Shane.

'He took Hainy's opal and mine and a few stones from others,' says Shane.

'What are we going to do?'

'Easy come easy go, says Shane. 'I got opal from people who worked for me on percentage. Hainy won't miss his; others will have to forget about it.'

How could Shane shrug it off so easily? Is he involved in it? I always believed that people are who they say they are. Perhaps we all hide the darker, more sinister side.

Andrew writes from America. He is on a building project in Palm Springs. 'Do I want to join him?'

I lock the front door of my life. I don't dare feel anything but I need someone to hold me so I could cry the tears pressing behind my eyes. The dark cloud inside of me needs to spill into a flood. A couple of months later Shane is transferred to Sydney. That's how things are in Lightning Ridge. People come and then they go, never to be heard of again; only their sins and virtues are discussed for a while.

'Shane sold the lease,' says Kathy. 'His friend from Sydney drilled and found a fortune.' Miners call a meeting. When a new opal field is discovered, a prospecting lease is opened and miners put their names in a hat to see who will win it. The winner has a month to prospect and choose claims before the land opens to the rest of the miners. This time the ballot did not happen. Shane gave the opal-mining lease to his friend.

'John rang to apologise for his sudden departure,' I tell Kathy.

'The rats abandon the ship before it sinks,' says Kathy.

'Thank God for my women friends. Everything else changed,' I sigh.

'The rainbow and the stars are where they always were,' says Kathy.

'Yes, the full moon still drives me mad as it always did. Life is the shades of black. Or the shades of white.'

'Much the same.'

I am tired. This is not a place I want to be in. I never knew how precious love was until I lost it. All I want now is to fade away. Neither love nor lust inspire me.

'Jeff replaced Shane in the mining office. People are trying to become instant friends with the new untainted powers.'

'They come all fresh and innocent but the smell of money gets them,' says Kathy.

'Sam is leaving,' Kathy brings the good news. Town's people prepare a huge farewell for their saintly preacher. Sam tells us that he is leaving for health reasons. He looks like a skeleton. His going cheers me.

'Maybe he knew that he was dying and wanted to do penance for something, 'I say. I feel guilty for hating him. One shouldn't hate a dying person.

'You never really get to know anyone. Especially in this town. There is no family history,' says Kathy. The town just happened when a few people stopped a few years ago on their way across the planet.'

Mark comes for Easter and begins buying opal. I hear that Mark's parents came from Slovenia. I intend to get to know Mark one day to see what brought him to Lightning Ridge.

I weed my garden. The plants are my life now. I give them nourishment they give me joy. The car stops and I look up. Debbie smiles; I smile back. For a moment I forget that we are no longer friends. She keeps looking at me.

'Andrew is no longer here,' I snap.

'I came to see you. Can we talk?'

'What about?'

'Us.'

We sit in my kitchen facing each other as we did many times before.

'Have you split up already?'

'Shane and Andrew are in America. They have taken me for a long ride,' says Debbie.

'What are you saying?'

'Andrew brought a parcel from Shane while I was in Sydney. Only Shane knew where I was staying. Andrew invited me to dinner. He hid the opals inside a pillowcase in my room while we dined in a hotel's restaurant. I am sure Shane took the opals. Andrew pretended to be shocked. He told me that people will blame me. I couldn't face you or Hainy. I found a job in Sydney and stayed with our children. After it all died down Andrew left for America and Shane followed at a safe distance.'

'I blamed you for taking the opal and Andrew.'

'Women always blame other women.'

'Maybe they wanted to punish Hainy for finding opal in the claim they sold to him through Joe.'

'We will never know for sure,' says Debbie.

Hainy does not ask about Andrew and never mentions the opal he lost. He helped me restore the house next door. He would not take any money so I cook him a nice dinner. He brings a bag of apples from the farm and I promise to make apple strudel for him. He brings a bottle of wine.

'A smile beautifies your face and heals your soul,' says Hainy. I am slightly embarrassed by the intimacy of Hainy's words. Nobody bothered with my soul for ages.

'There is little to smile about these days,' I grin. I must be cheerful or Hainy may not want to look at my face.

'The world is as beautiful as it always was,' says Hainy looking directly into my world.

'I'll live,' I reassure him because we both feel a little uneasy. Everlasting happiness exists only in heaven, mum used to say. And in the fairy tales, said dad.

There are countless components of my life and when one of them is injured, the pain spreads to every corner of my being and the whole of me hurts. I carry the collective consciousness of my tribe, my religion, my nation, my political persuasion, my race, my family and my gender. It is hard to say which part of me is injured.

'Do you ever feel homesick,' I ask.

'It's no good dreaming about things you haven't, because other people dream about the things you have,' says Hainy. Hainy is still mining. He lives in the camp and drives an old utility. His hair and beard are getting whiter but his smile is as cheerful as ever. I wonder if there is anything that he agonises about.

'Looking at other people's problems makes it easier to forget your own,' John used to say.

What did John want to forget?I did not know John at all. Snippets of our conversations keep coming back but he is forever gone. The memories of his words are like stepping-stones into the past but we did not really share the past. I don't share anything with anybody. I need to attach myself to something, to become a part of somebody. People lie and cheat to make themselves lovable. Sam worked his fingers to the bone to make people love him. I invested my money and my life in the town that turned against me. I rented the house to Ian to show that I really trust and love Aborigines. I wonder if I changed or people changed. Maybe we are who we always were.

'You will forever be a stranger in a strange land,' said mum when I left. How did she know that?Warnings of my parents echo from the past. You can only pass down what you have. What you are. I expected Ian and Edna to be good tenants. They never lived in a house before. I was disappointed because my expectations were faulty. Ian and Edna trusted me to help them like I helped people who could not help themselves. I experienced success when I secured the government money to distribute among the poor like Santa distributes toys and sweets among children for Christmas. Everybody is excited about Santa for a few days but then he is forgotten until next Christmas. I turned Aborigines into my family and accepted their problems as my responsibility. I became Santa. I wish I still believed in Santa. Santa is more permanent than the government.

> No nation is fit to sit in judgement upon any other nation.
>
> Woodrow

'It would be a shame if everything people told you was forgotten; you should write it down,' says Hainy. He knows that I need a distraction. 'You should record Lightning Ridge history.' I begin listening to Aboriginal Australia. I need to understand why people loved me one day and dumped me the next.

'There were six Aboriginal families when I came to the Ridge but since then Walgett relations joined them,' says Hainy.

'There would be over a thousand now.'

'But every one of them is touched by some migrant ancestor,' says Hainy.

I wonder if any of these Aborigines are Hainy's children. Maybe even he does not know. Mums always know and sooner or later they tell their children so the children know who their fathers are.

I invited Aborigines to come and tell me about their history. They keep coming with their tales of hardship and pain. They also tell how their lives were sprinkled with joy and improvement and sometimes real happiness. Their stories merge with each other into a tapestry of Aboriginal Australia. The politicians first promoted and then banned assimilation policy but despite the policies Aborigines and Europeans became similar and in many ways the same. My old Aboriginal friends are disheartened with the way their young ones live.

'It is important to write down what we know of the past,' says Dudley. Once written it is remembered forever. Kids have to have something to remember their people by.' Dudley is a well-respected Aboriginal elder and he tells me his story.

'My grandfather was an American Red Indian from Cherokee clan who jumped ship in Batemans Bay. He met a local Aboriginal girl and stayed in Australia. Their daughter had sandy blight in the eye so they took her to Brewarrina mission where the doctors treated her. She met my father there and I was born in 1927 in a scrub cutter's camp near Dirranbandi. My father was in charge of the saw mill and he cut the timber for the Angledool mission which was built in 1934. My father was moved to Angledool as an overseer. The Angledool Mission didn't last long because there were health problems. The government moved Aborigines from Angledool area to Brewarrina, which was a huge mission station raising its own supplies of sheep and cattle. We also grew our own fruit and vegetables. We slaughtered our own meat and produced our own veggies. Once a week we received the rations of sugar, flour and tea. They also moved the houses from the Angledool mission to Brewarrina.

There were three lots of people in Brewarrina mission at that time. Brewarrina and Angledool Aborigines were much the same and mixed well but Tibooburra lot were still in their wild state. They didn't wear clothes and didn't speak English. We, Brewarrina kids, got a hiding if we mixed with Tibooburra kids, our people kept away from them. My father helped to move some Tibooburra people over in a truck while others came with their donkey teams. They didn't last long with us; they just drifted back to their traditional grounds back west where they continued to live their traditional life. Tibooburra lot still held their corroborates. I remember getting a hiding when I sneaked out to watch them. They danced naked around the fire. They smoked the kids to knock sense into them. They all had donkey teams and they soon moved back into the bush.

My family moved from Brewarrina to Pilliga where my father worked as an overseer. The saw mill produced all the timber for the missions in these parts. Dad had up to thirty people working under him. The only whites living at Pilliga at that time were the Mission manager's family.

The sawmill in Pilliga was dismantled in 1939 and sold to Dungalear, which was a huge station in them days. The mission at Pilliga closed. My whole family moved to Dungalear for a while and we all worked again on the sawmill there.

After the war sawmill closed and the station was split among the returned soldiers as a reward for their services. The younger people on the properties these days are mostly the children of those soldiers. It was a white man's war and Aborigines didn't have to go but some did. On their return Aborigines did not get a soldiers' block. There was Sigh Morgan, he came crippled from the war but he did not get the land. Aborigines were equal during the war but when the war ended they were the same as before.'

Other Aboriginal elders often join Dudley and his wife Pauline. They tell me what they remember and what they think and how things used to be. Old people like to reminisce about the olden days. I begin to write. I take their photos; because everybody looks for his face in the scheme of things. Everybody is the most interesting person to oneself.

Pauline tells me the legends that told them of how things came to be. Aborigines looked at the signs in the nature and in the sky to explain and predict God's plan for them. Did all people always try to explain God and creation? Mysteries of nature make people think.

'There were always good people and bad people, good times and bad times,' says Dudley. 'The trouble today is that people don't know right from wrong, nobody is teaching them right from wrong because nobody knows right from wrong any more.

We were not allowed to teach our children right from wrong and nobody else bothered to.'

'Now is too late. Our kids have no respect for anyone,' adds Pauline. Maybe she is trying to explain why her daughter wrecked my house.

'Grog got them all,' adds Dudley.

'Kids leave school to go on the street with their parents,' Pauline agrees.

'We never missed an opportunity to improve our lives,' says Dudley. 'We learned to use white people to learn from them but young people today abuse everybody and everything. It will get them nowhere.'

Where does the story begin and end. Every storyteller has a different view of their common history. Maybe I haven't met a typical Aboriginal family yet; maybe the typical Aboriginal family does not exist. Maybe they are all one people telling one story. Maybe all people are just people. I worked for Aborigines for over twenty years. They came to see me in my office but I have never been to their home. They have never been to my home. I was only an extension of the government.

'Tell me about your childhood,' I ask Dudley and Pauline.

'During depression the government brought us on a mission so we could get rations and go to school. I met Pauline and she became my girlfriend. We were fourteen so the manager decided that we were too young to be going together. They signed us both over to be apprenticed with different farmers. I learned the station and farm work and Pauline learned the housework. I got into fights a lot and ran away from the property but police took me back. They were very strict with me. I didn't like it much then but I give them credit now for what they taught me. I learned to shear, crutch and everything else that needed doing on the station. They taught me so well that I have never been out of work my whole life. I never needed social security. I rounded the sheep for sheering and cut their tails and balls. To do a calf you need two blokes, one to hold the head and the other to throw it on the ground from the back. I cut their horns with shear clippers or with a saw. I had to muster sheep and repair fences. When the floods filled the dam my whole family used to go fishing. We used to throw the nets from the boat and drag the yellow bellies out.

The boss took me wherever they went, like races or picnics with other farmers. They brought me home for Christmas and New Year dinner with my family and sometimes they took me shopping. They paid me two shillings and sixpence a week and they paid seven and sixpence a week into Aboriginal Protection Board's bank for me. I never worried about the money they paid into a bank because I got good wages when I finished my apprenticeship. While I was apprenticed I often wondered if at the end of my apprenticeship I would get a big box of seven and sixpences.

One day soon after the war, when I was about seventeen the Mission manager brought two welfare officers and they asked me if I got a girl in trouble. I asked if she told them that. He said that her family told them. They took me to the local courthouse where our families were waiting.

'So, young rooster, what is it going to be? Are you going to marry the girl?' They asked.

I told Pauline that they would send me to a boy's home if I didn't marry her. She said that they would send her to girls' home if she didn't marry me. We were still both under the legal age. She said that she would marry me but that she didn't want to live with me. So the justice of the peace married us in the presence of our families. We just went along with it so they wouldn't send us away. They had a party and a clay-pan dance but I never showed up. Pauline went home then and I got drunk. I never saw her for three months after that. One day I woke up and there she was in bed beside me. Who are you? I asked, and she told me that she was my wife.

We were drinking the day before and someone called the police because my uncle was fighting with his wife. Someone took me over to my wife's so the police wouldn't get me. From that day on we stayed together. Aboriginal Protection Board gave us a house at the mission and furnished it for us from the money Pauline and I earned when we were apprenticed. They bought furniture, bedding, pots and pans and even kerosene lights. I was glad they handled our money like that.

In the olden days Aborigines and whites lived their separate lives, there was prejudice on both sides, I suppose, but what white man thought meant nothing to Aborigines. White man lived his life and we lived ours. I didn't see it when I was young and it never bothered me before but looking back now I can see it. I worked for the same farmer for 13 years and he made me an overseer. He built a cottage for the white workers but I had to make my own tin shed because I was black.

Later I worked for another farmer for ten years. I saw his white employees go into the house for a smoko but he never invited me. While they had a cup of tea they would bring me a mug of water outside. The farmer was a good bloke; it's just that he was reared like that.'

'As kids we weren't allowed to listen in on the grownups talking, because parents told us what we needed to know when we were ready for it,' says Pauline.

'We had to obey and respect elders,' tells Dudley. 'If I was disrespectful I'd get a hiding of any older person. They'd take me home and I'd get another hiding from my parents. Kids need to be corrected to learn respect.'

'I remember my grandfather telling us kids stories to frighten us from wandering away,' says Pauline. He said that Yuri woman took naughty children away. I was always afraid of the Yuri woman with long red hair who was coaxing the children away if you were spiteful or swore or stole something. Older women used to show children the little footprints in the sand that were left by Yuri woman after the rain. They looked like baby footprints and they scared us a lot. When I grew up I learned how to make those same footprints to scare my children and grandchildren and make them behave. Wherever Aboriginal children were, the Yuri Woman wasn't far away.'

'Aborigines always believed that there was a Big fella in the sky, who created the land and put it in their keeping,' continues Dudley. 'My people also believe that they were emus in the Dreamtime and that after they die, their spirit returns to where it came from. Emu was our family totem. Totems identify people, tell them how to behave, whom to marry, where they came from and where they are going.'

'When we ran out of food and had no money somebody would always turn up with the money or food and my grandmother used to say: 'There is God,' Pauline continues her story.

'My people believed that if someone was bad they were punished. They pointed the bone at them and they got sick or died. There was God in Australia even before the white man came but my parents accepted a Christian way of life. The missionaries were kind to us and we had good times with them. Dad worked with AIM (Aboriginal Inland Mission) as a Native worker. We went everywhere with my father who preached the Gospel. My mother had a beautiful voice and she also played a steel guitar. We all sang and everybody joined in, because they all knew the hymns. It was the most exciting and happy time of my life. I can still remember the smell of fires and the meat grilling,' sighs Pauline. 'The mothers were sitting down flat on the ground raking the coals for the gridiron to cook the meat and damper. For us hungry children it was a beautiful smell and sight. We spent much of our time sitting around the fire talking and singing.' Pauline still like to sing hymns to her grandchildren.

'Welfare people broke our tribes and took us to different reserves with people who had different tribal ways and language,' explains Dudley. 'They herded us around like animals.'

'I remember as a kid being smacked if I spoke our lingo. We were government property, they kept us and owned us,' says Pauline. 'On the mission we were scared and if a white person came we just ran inside to hide.'

'I used to fight for Aboriginal rights along with Charlie Perkins' Freedom Riders. I suppose they learned from American Freedom riders who were fighting to end the segregation. Charlie told us to stand for ourselves and also demand free access to alcohol,' continues Dudley. 'Now liqueur became the greatest killer of Aboriginal people. I wonder sometimes whom Freedom Riders really helped.'

'Everybody is in it for himself, two for me and one for you kind of thing. Nobody is really interested in doing some good for others. They serve the government because the government serves them. In the meantime Aborigines are dying from grog. Greed, there is so much greed; our leaders only see dollar signs and the positions of power. Aboriginal leaders are implementing government policies on big salaries; they say: Bugger you Jack, I am all right. Somewhere down the track they'll come face to face with the grassroots because they are only someone's aunty Mary and Uncle Tom after all. Our masters forced us into the white man's competitive world; they wrote the rules of the competition. We used to be a sharing culture. We had to be to survive. Now our people became greedy for the things that are precious to whites. If they can't break through they find crooked ways that land them in jail. Or dead,' says Dudley.

'I want Aborigines to become owners of their homes,' adds Pauline. 'If you do not own the house you live in, you don't have to look after it.'

'The government says that they have to look after poor Aborigines but I reckon politicians need us more than we need them. They couldn't justify their positions, if they had no one to look after. If the government left us alone we would find solutions that would work for us. We always did. When the white man came we made arrangement with him and worked for him. The white man needed us and we needed jobs. Aborigines made a mistake in thinking that all the white people are enemies. The whites and Aborigines have the same enemy: the government. Politicians enjoy being our minders but throwing money at Aborigines won't solve our problems. The half casts learned the skills of their white fathers and the cunning of the Aborigines. They stood up to the white farmer and demanded a fair deal. They often settled their differences in a fistfight. Eight out of ten an Aborigine would dish the white man out. In other parts the white stockman would bash the black man but not here. There was more pride in an Aborigine during the 40s than there is today. Many of these Aborigines became good boxers. Some became national champions.'

'There were no luxuries for either white or Aboriginal in the olden days. Running water, electricity and fresh vegetables and fruit were rare,' says Pauline. 'New clothes and shoes were issued when the old wore out.'

Garry joins us; he is in charge of Aboriginal land council

'Dad's father was a Sri Lankan and came to Australia as an indented labourer; he was a dark man who married a local Aboriginal woman,' Garry begins his story.

'Dad was a horse breaker and he taught me to break horses. When I fell off the horse he hit me with a stock whip and I had to get up on a horse again. Mum rode the horses in the paddock once they were broken in. You had to tame wild horses so the women, jackaroos and farmer's kids could ride them. We used to go from property to property breaking horses. We packed everything and the family on the sulky and travelled. We pitched a tent for the night where we found work. There were no sheds then for black workers. My father owned a few horses. In those days if you owned a few horses you were considered a bit above the rest of Aborigines. My great grandfather on mum's side was an Englishman who came to Australia with the first explorers around 1850. He made a family with an Aboriginal girl who was a princess in these parts. My father was the only man here with three Aboriginal scar trademarks on the right shoulder and one on the jaw. He was a well-educated man who learned to read and write from his father and Aboriginal traditions from his mother's family. Mum's family lived on the Barwon riverbank. Mum remembered the Paddle steamers that stopped there coming from Brewarrina and Bourke. Locals loaded wool and other produce to send on the market. Black women and little naked black piccaninnies liked to watch the boat and the goings on but the sight of Aborigines offended farmers. Their wives with the feathers in their hats considered Aborigines savages. Aborigines used to work with whites and they fought in the war together but they weren't allowed to go to town hotel and have a drink with whites. I was there when Freedom Riders came and told us to stand for our rights and demand free access to likker. We received full citizen's rights in 1967 through the referendum and since then likker became the greatest killer of Aboriginal people. I used to go down the riverbank with my mates after work and drink heavy. We drank wine and metho. Wine, tobacco and needle are the greatest killers of our people. I gave drinking away and knocked off smoking. I used my will power but it almost killed me. I ate a lot until one day I just couldn't stand smoking any more. I had my lungs cleaned up in hospital. I couldn't believe what came out of my lungs. It was a horrible mixture of nicotine and soda ash. I used to treat water at the reserve with soda ash and chlorine and some of soda ash entered my mouth and settled on my lungs. They washed my lungs out three times.

Nobody can help you knock off drinking and smoking, you have to do it yourself.

In the olden days Aborigines used to have a drug called pitgery which they mixed with wild tobacco growing along the river and chewed that. It relaxed them. It must've had quite a kick in it because they also used to stun the fish with it. The older people know where to find the weed pitgery but they don't want to tell the children because it may be even stronger and more harmful than marijuana.'

'I was born on the mission,' Kim begins her story. Kim is a softly spoken gentle woman who likes to hold my hand while she tells about her sad life.

Brewarrina was a most beautiful mission in them days, says Kim. We had everything there, gardens for veggies and cows to milk and sheep to kill. People weren't allowed to go to town without permission but they could go walking in the bush. No grog was allowed on the mission but people used to sneak in metho or wine and they would drink down by the river and then they'd get into fights. Mission Aborigines got grog from town Aborigines and from some whites. They were searched for alcohol when they came to mission gates. Sometimes a taxi would bring Aborigines home and they would search it for alcohol. But Aborigines got real cunning. Sometimes they'd get a loaf of bread and take the insides out so they could put the bottle inside. Others unloaded grog in the bush outside the gate and went for it later. Grog caused so much sadness and trouble.'

Brenda joined us. 'My father was away from home most of the time droving. He was a real musical person. People liked him because he played a mouth organ in the open for clay pan dancers. He also liked to drink and that got him in a lot of trouble. He was thrown out of the Mission because he was drunk and got into a fight. He was a very nice person but grog turned him bad. Mum was terrified of him and she left us when I was only a baby. Dad's mother and father reared us. If parents neglected their kids a truck would come and the kids would be taken and put on the train to go to the boy's or girl's school where they looked after them until they were 18 or 20.

After I left school they sent me straight to the station into an apprenticeship to get experience in housework duties. I was really happy there and I could help myself to whatever I wanted. They liked me and took me to the pictures. I did housework and looked after the children. I had my own room and they gave me a gramophone and records to play. I was never lonely there.

I met Frankie when I was about 18. Frankie was a musician and an artist then. He played a guitar and taught me to play and we had a many happy sing alongs together. He carved beautiful emu eggs and he made boomerangs and spears. He taught our boys to play guitar and they also like to sing to it together.

Frankie and I got married at the registry office because I didn't know yet that I was a Catholic. I had a beautiful mauve dress with flowers on. A friend made a lovely cake and we had a party down on the riverbank. Later I met a nun, Sister Teresa, who taught me about Jesus and I became Catholic. I was baptised and confirmed by the bishop so Frankie and I got married again in the Catholic Church. I saw my mum for the first time after I married and had five children. She told me my date of birth and that I was baptised a Catholic. Mum and I held each other and cried. She told me that she left because she was terrified of dad who drank and bashed her.

Frankie was a clever, good man until grog got hold of him. He became an alcoholic and so are all of my children. Three of my children died because of grog and the others can't stop drinking. I think they should not sell grog to dark people. Frankie and I parted because of alcohol, he lost his leg because of it and still he couldn't stop drinking. He died with beer in his hand.

I used to have a lovely home and my garden was full of flowers until my children started coming home drunk.'

Donna and Garry join us. 'Garry and I don't drink and I told my children to keep away when they are drinking,' Donna turns to her husband Garry.

'Dad was a tracker,' says Garry. 'The station manager noticed that he was a good rider, who can handle horses, so he offered him a job as a tracker and station hand. I went with dad mustering sheep and cattle. I rode on a pony and dad taught me how to muster sheep and cattle. The manager would sometimes take me with him and teach me to drive a tractor when I was only a boy. Mum tried to teach me a bit by correspondence but I never went to school. Mum had a stroke and she found life very hard in the bush. Dad and I used to go to work and she stayed in our nice little weatherboard cottage on the station. Dad used to cook and put food for mum in our kerosene fridge so she would help herself. Mum couldn't cope; one day she took a can of kerosene and crawled a mile into the bush. She poured the kerosene over herself and burned herself. I used to go riding in the scrub looking for a spot where she died because I kept thinking about her.

Once dad and I drove to town and I got to know other youngsters; I soon got myself into trouble. The police caught me stealing cars. I was sent into a boys' home. That was home away from home for me. We had six groups in that home ranging from bad boys to good boys. You could earn points and get privileges and move into a higher house. Hunter was the top group and you got to play sports and even go to church on Sundays. You were even picked for the office work if you were really good. Office was considered a top dog job. We cleaned the carpet and the office windows and dusted the books and shelves. Sometimes you got to take important messages.

Lyons and Rotary clubs organised activities and games for good boys. I started in Allan house and had to work my way up. If you lost points for bad behaviour you lost privileges and didn't get sweets or other food you liked. You also had to do all the dirty unpleasant jobs like scrubbing and polishing the floor. They also took away your sport privileges and you went on detention instead. I think you deserved to be punished to be corrected. Each week they sent us out for training to do stock work, farming, dairy, maintenance, growing vegetables, Lucerne and hay. After about seven months I came out of there and went to see my aunt. She told me about the butcher who was looking for boys to help with his piggery. He gave me a job and I cleaned pigpens and fed pigs. I learned how to butcher and make sausages. I also did fruit picking. The butcher bought a rice farm and I began to plough the fields before they flooded it for cereal sowing. When they began to sow by tractor and combine, they had to wait for the ground to dry enough for the tractor to go over.

When the rice factory opened I started to work in it. I had to de-pollinate rice. The pollen comes away like powder and they use it in fodder. Then they tumble rice so the husks go one way and the rice goes the other. I saved enough money to buy myself an old car and I drove to Cowra where I met Donna who was just out of girls' detention home.'

'My father drank a lot and he bashed my mum,' Donna continues with her story. The welfare sent mum with her seven children to the mission. We went along really well until they sent me from the mission school to High school. I didn't want to go to school any more. They said that I became uncontrollable, so the court decided that I should be fostered out. I had everything with my foster family but I couldn't watch my brothers and sisters coming from the mission who had nothing. I asked the welfare officer to send me away in an orphanage. They sent me to a home for three months but I liked it there and stayed for three years. I helped the nuns with Aboriginal kids. At fifteen I got myself in trouble. When the nun hit one of the Aboriginal kids I hit the nun and they sent me away to a training centre. I stayed there washing and ironing for hotels and restaurants until I met Garry at seventeen, tells Donna. Garry was shy and he never went to ask the court about marrying us so I moved in with him and we had twelve children.'

Lucy joins us. 'It was good that the government took care of us when our parents could not,' says Lucy. She is well known by all the people who ever studied Aboriginal culture. She loves to tell about the olden days.

'I was brought up to be a lady. I don't swear and I go to church every Sunday. I go to school to teach the kids and the teachers right from wrong. If someone is disrespectful to me I put a curse on them and they are punished every time. They die,' says Lucy. She wears a hat and carries a handbag wherever she goes.

'My Dad was Irish and mum was part Aboriginal,' says Lucy. 'There was a lot of mixed breeding in those days. There were many single white men but no white women so these lonely men had children with Aboriginal girls.

I was born on the riverbank in Victoria in 1926. My mother died in childbirth from septicaemia when I was three, my brother was two and my sister was only a couple of weeks.

My father couldn't look after the family while he worked so he signed the children over to Aboriginal Protection Board. I was put in Cootamundra home. God only knows what would happen to me if they didn't take me. The ladies of the home were wonderful; they never knocked us about. If someone misbehaved they found out the person and punished her. When a girl tried to run away they wrapped a strap around her or if someone has done something wrong they put them into the cold bath.

When I was ten I was put into service to a doctor in Parkes. He was very nice to me but his wife was hitting me all the time. People told me that I was very pretty and I think now that maybe the doctor's wife was jealous of me. She was a very pretty woman herself so I don't know why she should be nasty to me. Anyway she was nice one day and nasty the next. I had to clean the silver, scrub the floors, sweep and dust and wash. While I was in the service, dad came and he told me about mum's family. My happiest memories are of meeting mum's family. Mum's father was a part Japanese, part Melanesian. Her mother was Aboriginal and her grandfather was English. When I was fourteen the matron took me to Brewarrina mission and left me there with the manager's family. I knew no one at Brewarrina. I knew nothing about men and life and nobody told me anything.

At the age of fourteen I met Terry who was forty-five at the time and I became pregnant to him. I had no idea why I was pregnant. The manager of the mission sent me into service nine miles out of Brewarrina to the wonderful people who took me with them shopping and they bought me a nice flowery dress and white shoes. I was there only a few months when I realised that I was pregnant. I had to marry Terry so that he would support the child. I had my first baby before I turned fifteen. Terry was a cruel man. He chased women around, drunk with metho he was, and he wasn't even good looking. I had three children by him. He bashed me up a lot.

I had a lot of bad luck with men. There is so much jealousy. Many Aboriginal men in those days drank metho and when they were in horrors they hit their wives. The metho made them mad, but they were not allowed to buy alcohol and they wanted to drink. I wouldn't see Terry for a week at the time and then he'd come and bash me up. I left Terry when I was about twenty.

I met Tommy in 1946 and he became a father of my five children. He wasn't too bad at the beginning but he was another metho king. He was a sheerer but he never gave any money to me for the kids. I went to the police a lot to complain. Sometimes he'd bring a bag of oranges from the farm but no money. One night he was in horrors when he returned home and hit me in the face as I slept in bed. I got mad and I took an axe. He blabbered that I wouldn't dare hit him with it but I put an axe to his neck and cut his jugular vein. He was taken to hospital and I packed my five kids and went to Goodooga. He never came after me.

There I met a nice white woman Miriam who let me move into her tin shed. I told her what happened and she helped me find clothes and food for the kids and a job for me in a hotel where she was working. I began to cook in a hotel. 'That was the first and only time I was in a hotel. Other neat and orderly Aborigines got a card from the government, they called it a dog collar, but this was just a card giving them the permission to drink in the hotel. I never had the card because I never needed it. I kept to myself and never worried about what other people were doing or thinking. I never had any trouble with police or white people. Women always have things to do. Even now I have my gardening and housework and my chooks. Aboriginal men have nothing to do so they drink and abuse their families. It is getting worse. Babies have babies and the kids are getting drunk these days as they wait for their parents in front of the pub.'

Ivy joins us; she is a ninety years old Aboriginal lady proud of the fact that she is one of the few people who still speaks tribal language.

'I was born in a humpy on the riverbank,' begins Ivy. 'Dad's father was white and his mother came from India. Mum's mother was a local Aborigine and her father came from China to work as a boundary rider. My father was a stockman at Dungalear cattle station; this brings back beautiful memories. We were real poor but we had fun and we were happy. Kids are happy when they are safe and with their loving parents and relations. The rest of the world doesn't matter to them. My Chinese grandfather wouldn't let us kids wander around into town and when he was cross he would throw his hat at us.

We had government stores and you could get your clothes and rations for nothing. They took it out of our wages for what we took. Dungalear used to be the biggest station around here and up to a hundred Aborigines lived there at times. Only the owner, the overseer, mechanic and some jackaroos were white. Everybody thought it was wonderful on the station. I used to wash and iron there in the wash room and the men went to get the orders to muster sheep and do other jobs. They had to get up early and they worked until night, then they went for their rations and tobacco. I smoked since I was ten.

A bloke came out with a truck selling clothes and shoes once every few months in them days. We had rain water tanks and everybody had water bags. Mum died when my brother was only a fortnight old. I was thirteen and had to look after eight younger children. The welfare man told dad that he is going to take the children and put them into a home. My father called a policeman who said to the Welfare people: 'What have you ever done for these people. They never got anything from you. Leave them alone.' We had to move to the mission though so the children could go to school.'

'My great grandfather on my father's side came from England and bought the first lease along the river in 1848,' tells

Elizabeth. He made friends with a nice Aboriginal girl who became my great grandmother. They had eleven children but he never married her. He was married to a white woman who lived in Sydney. Before he sold his lease he made arrangements for all his black children to have jobs on the property. His son, my grandfather managed the property for him. Most of us kids were put into service. Kids who did not want to go to school were sometimes taken away by Welfare. The authorities claimed that by educating Aboriginal children away from their families they would prepare them to live like whites.' 'Often the farmers had good-looking Aboriginal girls to sleep with them while their wives were away, says Garry. Many girls returned with boss's child to their family. Sometimes the respectable white man didn't want little black children saying: That there is my daddy when their white wives returned. So Daddy had these children taken away to be brought up in an institution.'

'The cattlemen made girls drunk to have sex with them,' Ted joins the story telling. 'The next day they wouldn't even look at them, they put them down and the kids they made. They gave sugar, tea, grog and tobacco to Aboriginal men so they wouldn't object to taking their women. When I was fourteen my father brought a mob of sheep to Walgett for the farmer,' remembers Ted. I asked the mission manager if I could visit my aunt. The manager told me that I must stay on the Mission and go to school there. I didn't want to stay and my father didn't want me to stay but we had no say in it. My father put up a fight but the manager called the police and the welfare people so they took me to school. I learned to read and write a bit. They made me a ward of state and apprenticed me to the station.'

'Missions were government run settlements outside town,' explains Elizabeth. 'Mission Aborigines lived under the control and supervision of the managers. They were classed the lowest because they had to obey the mission manager. Government built their homes and they had no say in anything. Fringe dwellers were classed a bit higher. They built their own dwellings closer to towns, on the Reserves and riverbanks. They worked on the properties. The people who rented homes in towns and those regularly employed were a notch higher than fringe dwellers. Town girls often intermarried with whites and considered themselves higher than those married to Aborigines,' says Elizabeth.

'Aboriginal tribal headquarters used to be where country towns are today. Aborigines living there first came into contact with whites and worked for them. Women became servants and soon learned the language and the white ways. They were the first town Aborigines. Women worked in the white households from the early days so they were better accepted than men,' explains Ted. 'Aborigines that resisted whites were culled out of the area and moved out and were later sent on to the reserves.'

'To stay on the mission during the depression was a privilege. If people did not obey the rules they were out,' says Garry. Until about the seventies Aborigines worked hard. They did most of the work on the land. Not working is new to Aborigines. Most Aborigines still haven't learned to handle money. Saving money to buy a house is new to them. Until 1940 they existed virtually without money. Traditionally Aborigines taught their young to survive on the land but long term planning and saving for the future is still foreign to most. Men used to be providers and teachers but since social security took up their role they lost authority and self-respect.'

'To survive today is still more important to most Aborigines than to become rich tomorrow,' adds Elizabeth.

'Things have improved for Aborigines when migrants from Europe came after the war. English people never married

Aboriginal girls but European migrants married them and made proper families with them,' says Pauline.

'European migrants were the first to show respect for Aborigines,' agrees Elizabeth.

'Most of our grandchildren believe nothing so they respect and obey nothing,' says Ted. 'They get all this free money from the government to keep quiet. They say that they are proud to be black but a man that does not provide for his family has no respect. So he gets drunk to forget. Australia never practised apartheid,' continues Ted. 'There were no signs keeping blacks out of town. Discrimination was decided on the spot. We just knew where the resentment was and we moved back as soon as we felt it.'

'Whites are often criticising us for sticking up for each other but family is all we have left,' says Elizabeth.

'It is obvious that all of you have white and black ancestors. How come you only say that you are Aborigines,' I ask.

'My white relations didn't want to know about me and I don't worry about them. Aborigines accepted all of us half-castes. If one of the family is sick, gets into trouble or dies, Aborigines often just quit what they are doing and come to be with the family. Aborigines are not worried about the trappings of the wealth and power. It does not matter to them what sort of house they live in as long as they feel safe. Our elders used to teach right and wrong way of living but the governments told our children that what we believed was a superstition, concludes Elizabeth.

'I think my father's father came from India but I don't know any of his family, Herbie begins his story. 'I lived with mum's people. Dad was a bit darker than I am; he was a quiet man and went along with everybody. He worked all his life. First he was a fencer and when droving started he was a drover and a station hand. He drank a lot. People liked him and offered him a drink. My family was moved to the Mission when I was very young but dad didn't like mission life and he just packed up and left. At the Mission they told you what to do and you weren't allowed to drink. Dad was used to looking after himself. We moved on a riverbank. As a boy I watched old men sitting on the wood heap making weapons. They explained what each weapon was used for.'

'Herbie is an artist. He makes artefacts and he paints pictures,' adds Elizabeth. 'He remembers some of the lingo and some of the songs.'

'At school we learned that white people's ways are better so kids became ashamed of their parents and their language and the way they lived,' continues Herb. 'I had to put my age up to join the army and went to the Islands and Japan for nearly three years. When I returned I still wasn't allowed into the RSL or a Hotel. It is estimated that up to one thousand Aborigines served in the Second World War. White Returned soldiers got land to work on but Aborigines got none. There were four or five of us returned Aboriginal soldiers here and we couldn't get into the ballot for Returned soldiers' Blocks in 1950s. Aborigines always lived off the land and they did all the jobs on the land for white settlers, yet they weren't considered experienced enough to hold their own piece of land. Six thousand Australians died during the last three wars and we remember them on ANZAC day. Australian soldiers fought around the world in other people's wars where other nations exploited each other. There are monuments for white dead soldiers but there are no monuments for Aborigines. Thirty thousand Aborigines were slaughtered before the federation and that war is not even mentioned in the history books. They died for Australia, they are our veterans, they died defending their culture and land; they spilt their blood for their homeland. If they were white, forested monuments would be erected for them. If we are to have a reconciliation we have to give our dead a decent burial. After the war I took up shearing. At the weekend I was searching for bush timber to make tools and weapons like I learned from the old men before the war. I felt that young Aborigines should learn how our ancestors managed to survive in this country for thousands of years.'

I realise that history is just one remembers.

> Laws are like cobwebs, where the small flies are caught, and the great break through.
>
> Bacon Francis

Muriel is a young single mother related to most local Aborigines. Her ancestors are American Indians, Aborigines, Japanese, Indonesian, German and Scottish. Bit by bit she tells me about her life.

'In primary school I had a very loving teacher Tina,' she says. When we were sick she would've come home to check on us and she still comes to check on our children. We have our own homes and boyfriends now but she still comes around and says good day. You don't see other teachers doing that. They stop teaching you and they move on and you never see them again. I loved my teacher and my children will be here for her to teach them and to love them and grow them up.

When I started high school boys were all I could see with my big brown eyes. Teenage boys and girls think that they are big men and women and that they learned enough in primary school so why should they prove themselves in high school. They put us with whites who were so up themselves. I couldn't handle that and I've done everything to get kicked out. I got the boot in year nine and got suspended for life.

I would like to see my children go right through to year 12 so they could get a job and make a name for themselves. Not like me, I didn't put my mind to anything educational. I was always on detention and got hit with the cane every day. I wouldn't co-operate with the teachers or other students; they put me in a special room until I was ready to behave. I got worse every minute of every day. It got to that stage where I just didn't want to listen, so one day I played up terrible on assembly. I got called off to the front so I walked up to the principal. He asked me to say out loud what I was saying on the line. I said no, he grabbed me and I told him to take his hands off me and he wouldn't so I hit him. He took me to his office and called my mum and dad and they turned up with the cops and the welfare. They had one and a half hour meeting to decide whether to kick me out of school for good or just for a couple of weeks. They decided to kick me out for good. I didn't mind. I hated school.

When I got in the door at home dad hit me real hard and sent me straight to the room. I stayed for a little while and then I jumped out the window and I never looked back. Mum and dad were worried for a little while but then they knew that I could look after myself.

I met Ricky and we made our beautiful chidden. They are doing so well at school; they must be taking after their father. I got told that he was a good student.

Now I am sorry I played up at school because now I don't know much about anything.

I met Ricky at the age of 15 and now I am twenty and broken hearted. I have three children, I love my children; they are all I live for. They haven't got the father anymore because Ricky killed himself. He came home from work and found Terry with me in bed so he went on a motor bike and smashed it into a tree. I am with Terry now. He loves me and my children just as much as we love him. He asked me to marry him but I said no because Ricky asked me to marry him a long time ago but I never answered him and now it's too late to do anything because of the sad tragedy. I loved Ricky. I was never out of money then, I had everything in life going for me but now I don't know if I am coming or going.

My grandmother passed away in 1983. I was so proud of Nan. She was one lady that never turned her back on anybody that needed help. If there was anyone who had nowhere to stay, well, she invited him or her in and gave them the bed and the food and she never asked for a cent off them. She was my pride and joy.

On a pension day she'd buy me a packet of lollies and a packet of chips with a lemon. We had so much fun and there was always food on the table at Nan's and you never went hungry. If we misbehaved she'd hit us with a jug cord or a hose because she wanted us to grow good.

Nan and my dad, her son, used to drink together. I used to hide beer under the bed for Nan because I knew that Nan would've passed out first and then dad would've had her share of the beer. I loved my Nan.

At night Nan used to make a fire at the back and grill all kinds of meat on a gridiron. She made a beautiful Johnny cake.

One-day Nan played cards. She was a long time coming home so I went to see if she was winning and she was too. I got ten dollars off her and went to the shop and bought a whole lot of lemons and chicken chips.

Nan got sick all of a sudden in the middle of playing cards. She had fallen off the chair and I rung for the ambulance. Nan died. She looked like she was asleep and having a funny dream because she had a beautiful smile on her face. Dad told me that it was natural for dead persons to have a smile on their faces. I have never seen a beautiful smile like that.

Nan had a very beautiful long service for her funeral. The good thing about it was that everybody had patience and they sat and listened the whole way through the service. Not like some funerals you go to where some people wait outside the church and walk in and out because the patience gets the better of them. Nan was well known and very respected too. She had many white friends too. Don't get me wrong, I am not prejudiced or anything like that but I just got a shock to see so many whites there.

My charming grandmother was one person that knew a lot about the Dreamtime and she tried to tell us all about it only I never took the time to sit and listen because I was only young and very curious of every other thing that was going on then. So now I know nothing about the Dreamtime.

What I know is how they run Aboriginal Land Council. They rip each other off for money. If there is some person not paying rent there is always some other person watching them. That person will go to the head boss and kick up a big fuzz by saying why didn't he or she pay her rent. We have to. Then they would call up a meeting and sit there for hours fighting and swearing at each other.

Most Aboriginal people drink and they can't get up in the morning to send their kids to school. That is wrong because children should get every bit of education to get the job.

Since I was 15 I was always in trouble with the police. I was in court every time there was court for a while.

I was locked up a few times; I had to cut my warrants. They locked me up at nights and I was scared because you hear all these little noises while you lay there real quiet and the base of the bed is only a slab of cement; the mattress is thin and the blanket is itchy and smelly, the toilets are right near the bed. You couldn't sleep because of the smell and the cold. The food is so bad like it was sitting there for days. They give you tea without milk or sugar, you have to ask for a shower otherwise they would let you lie in the cell and rot away. They never let you have your own smokes and drinks.

One day when my children grow up I might get out and look for a job. It doesn't have to be anything flash I just want to get a few dollars because I hate being on the pension. I like to get out and earn my money the hard way.

This used to be a good place to live in but now it is terrible. There has been a lot of cars stolen and burnt but the police can't find who's doing it. That's because they are smart but in the long run they will end up in jail.

It's terrible to see all the shops barred up and the town looks like a big Long Bay jail at night. There are kids on the streets at night because their parents are in the pub. The kids stand at the pub's door all night waiting for them. I know most parents and their children. I don't allow my children up the street after dark. It's bad enough with me being down there drinking.

My main problem is looking after my three children. My eldest knew her father; she is always crying and asking where her dad is. The younger two were only young when Ricky died.'

A few months later I meet with Muriel again as she is cheerfully buying clothes and toys for her children. The government paid fifty thousand dollars as compensation to her three children because their dad died in the motorbike accident. Muriel is pushing a pram with her fourth child. I invite her for a cup of coffee and a chat.

'I haven't got much going for me,' Muriel tells me. 'After this baby starts walking I am going into the shearing sheds to roustabout and make more money for my children to feed them and buy them some clothes. I have a nice little home for them now. What really gets to me is that Ricky died on Terry' birthday and I feel no good giving presents to Terry and sitting there thinking about the sad loss of Ricky.

I am on a pension now and get 510 dollars a fortnight. I pay my bills, I buy the food for the kids and what is left over I put aside for when I really need it.

Ricky was a good bloke who used to work in the sheds, he used to roustabout before he took up shearing. He worked very hard to keep us in food and clothes. I felt like I lost everything when he died but I looked up and started thinking about Nan when she died and how all the children hung on and couldn't let go. They had their children to look after but they just couldn't let go.

I sat there and thought about it and I decided that I am not going to drag myself down because now I have four children to look after. They never asked to come into this world. I had a rough time the first couple of months after Ricky's death but now I am coping all right. I'll never forget Ricky, I love him and I know deep down inside me that he's still with me and protecting me and my children. Terry can't cheer me up like Ricky used to but he loves me and I love him.

I hope all of my children find good jobs and get married and have children and settle down. I hope they don't get hooked up on drink like I did.

A month later Muriel tells me that she broke up with Terry and lives with Patrick.

Patrick and I were getting married this year, but I don't want to have one of them lucky dip weddings and I can't afford a proper one. So mum said if I can wait until after Christmas she would pay $3000 for a proper wedding.

Well, I like to go out and have a few drinks in moderation until somebody upsets me. That's when I fly off the handle and punch the living daylight out of everyone.

All in all I like to look after myself. All my friends from school, they all drink very heavy and they all look like old men and women. It's because they smoke and drink a lot of alcohol such as port and rum.

When my dad died I went to ruin for a while until my mum said to me that I was drinking a hell of a lot and if I didn't stop I would lose my kids and I didn't want that. If I wanted a life like that why did I make kids and go through the trouble of having them. So I just sat down and thought about it and within a week I was over it all.

The hard part is to see the rest of my Aboriginal friends are still going through with the same thing I was. I wish I could help them but I wouldn't make a good counsellor. I haven't got the brains or patience to help them. I'd get upset trying to help them and start snapping.

I have a good friend who is only a year older than me. He used to be good looking but to look at him today he is ugly and all through drinking moselle. I always say to him that he has gone to ruin. It hurts me to say that to my best friend. If only I could get him to spend more time with me so I could help him and talk to him. But who am I to judge people. He's going to hate me if I start to run his life.

Every time my sister comes home she drinks every day of the week. When she is in Sydney she doesn't go anywhere. That's why I reckon this town breaks you and makes you do things you don't want to do. It's people around you that start you off. Just seeing them having all the fun makes you want to get in there and enjoy yourself.

Muriel moved away and she writes to me about all her brushes with the law.

Patrick and I moved to Armidale but I hate it here. When I come back home people ask me if I like Armidale; I lie that I do. If I tell them the truth, they'd think that I am crazy living in the town that I hate.

I am glad that I have a boyfriend who thinks the sun shines out of you know what. Ha ha, only kidding, but he does love me and the children and we all love him too. I think he is the perfect match for me and I am going to spend the rest of my life with him. He is still working on the Shire Council and is doing well. I am living in a five-bedroom home now and I am loving it too. We have got a vegetable garden with the grape vine which is loaded with grapes, an apricot tree which is nearly ready to pick, three sheds at the back, two garages and a shed for birds, rabbits and horses, a big yard.

I miss my home. It broke my heart when I had to go back to Armidale where all I do is sit at home and watch videos. I wish I could move back home but Patrick won't, because he knows that I will get myself into trouble there.

I was home for the weekend and I got on the booze and stayed in the pub. I am still doing the community service hours. I've only got 22 hours left out of a 150. I'll be glad when I finish.

I don't want to meet anyone here because I am frightened of getting into trouble because I am not the sort of person to take jokes. I fly of the handle too quick. I'd go out one night with them to the pub and have a few drinks and then they'd have a joke with me that I don't like and I'd hit them. Next thing you know the pigs in their blue costumes will grab me and I'll go to jail, because I am on a two years good behaviour bond because of me bashing up three policemen. I went to court here in Armidale and, believe me, he isn't a really nice judge. He came down on me like a ton of bricks, because he said that I got away with too many offences and that I should have been sent to jail a long time ago. On my way out of the court I stuck my finger up at him but he didn't see me. Just as well, I'd be in looking out of jail now, ha ha.

I think I'll just pick up and come home for Christmas, like they say, there's no place like home. I hate myself for taking my kids away from home. They hate this place but they have no choice.

Look at me now, I am 26 and a mother of four beautiful children, which I love. They are my life and I will be there every step of the way for them through dust, hail, storm and wind. I'll be there.

I am on the program THINK to help me keep out of trouble.

I really think about everything I have done.

I got in trouble for the first time when I was fifteen. A bloke asked Ricky and I to do a job for him around his yard. We cleaned the yard and put the rubbish in the back of the Ute. I jumped in the Ute to take the rubbish to the tip. I just got out of the gate. I didn't see the cop car until they pulled me over. They had words with me and then asked me to get out of the Ute so I did. Then they put me in the police car and took me to the police station and charged me with driving without a licence. I was charged $350.

I got in trouble again when I got into a fight with a girl. I was standing at the front of the hotel when this girl started calling out to Patrick, saying that she liked him and wanted to go out with him. I got jealous, ran over and flogged her. She went to the police station and I got charged with assault occasioning actual bodily harm. This offence cost me $150.

The third time I got into trouble I was drunk in the hotel and had a fight. The publican couldn't break us apart. I picked up chairs, pool balls, and bottles and started throwing them. I damaged all the spirit bottles, cash registers behind the bar and then they rang the police. They grabbed me and escorted me to the police station. I got charged with malicious damage and fined $250.

One night I was at the RSL club with my friends having good time. When the band played I got up to dance and in the middle of the song two girls were dancing real close to us with wine glasses in their hands. I remember having a white top on and one of them spilled her drink on me. I asked her nicely to put the drink down while dancing but they didn't. I complained to the manager, then it happened again. I hit one of the girls. I got barred from the club. The police came and they took me to the police station and charged me with common assault. I was fined $50.

The fifth time I was in trouble when Terry' car got burned by a man that was jealous. This man was involved with me so he decided to get his revenge. I got charged with arson. I kept going to court for four years and ended up winning the case.

I got into trouble again when I was going with Terry to a pool competition at the hotel. He won the competition so he got the drinks and we all went home. We got into an argument so I walked out. He burned his car and he got a rope and threw it over a branch. I raced to the car because my bag was in the car. That's when Terry came behind me and forced me towards flames, my eyebrows got burnt, I screamed, then Terry let go off me and ran back towards the tree. He tried to hang himself. The police came because they saw the fire.

I tried to tell them what happened but they were too concerned about Terry so I started freaking out because I thought I would get the blame for everything. I got charged with three offences and they gave me three months in prison. I appealed.

Ever since then I've been seeing the probation and parole officer and drug and alcohol counsellor. This program Think is to help with my anger.

I don't intend to get into any more trouble because I've got children and Patrick and I want to be with them. Not only that, I am getting on in age now and I don't want my husband and children to see me in jail. I am trying my hardest to stop my firing temper.

I breached my probation so I had to go to jail. They tell me to think my life over and make it better. That's what I am doing. We learn art and craft-work and dancing. We play sports while we are thinking of a better life. Jail is lonely and scary for the person who has first been in prison because inside is very different than what outside is. We comfort new people to make them feel at home there so they don't get depressed. We make them a cup of tea and talk to them and make them laugh to make friends with them so they don't commit suicide.

I had my own room and television in goal. I like watching comedy that makes me laugh. It is good having my own room because I can do my artwork with no hassles. Sometimes you can share a room with a friend so you can talk. They are really good people here. I go to church sometimes.

I am out now and doing the Community Services Orders. I left my old ways behind because I have to look after my children. I hate being in jail all the time.

Terry used to gets me in trouble all the time because he is in court every time court comes up. I might leave him and stay with Patrick who keeps me out of jail. I am seeing a counsellor who is teaching me not to fly off the handle for every little thing.

When I was in jail Patrick came to see me. I was so ashamed because he found me washing the cop's cars. I think I went red that day. He only brought me lunch and had to race back to look after my children. Thank Christ he didn't have time to make a fool out of me. I had my lunch and then cleaned up the bull wagons. Every day I was in jail it made me think about being in trouble all the time so I promised myself I would keep out of trouble and look after my children. I stayed off the grog for a couple of days and I could see that it was working. I want to stay out of jail and see my children grow up. I have been with Patrick now for five years. He has never done anything wrong to my kids or me. I broke with him sometimes because he is older, he's got eleven years on me and he is not the type of person to go out. He hates parties, he doesn't take me to the clubs and pubs like Terry does. Patrick is the sort of person who likes to stay home and watch TV. He would not refuse any work. I don't mean to have two boyfriends but they both love me and my children and they treat us with respect. I would stay with Patrick in Armidale but I hate the town and I miss my family, I should be here where I belong.'

I like Muriel. Who knows how her story will end. Or mine.

> Friendship often ends in love; but love in friendship-never.
>
> Colton

'Aborigines hurt you pretty bad,' says Marta during the dinner gathering at her place.

'It was only one family. They messed me up because they were messed up,' I smile.

'I am glad you got over it.'

'Poor Edna lost her daughter; she had real problems while I almost went mad about the loss of a couple of thousand dollars. I had it all out of proportion. No wonder people dismissed my complaints. If I could only see it for what it was, I would have spared myself a sense of despair and failure.'

'Edna is drunk every day,' says Kathy.

'She probably needs to escape from her problems. None of it matters any more to me.'

'Australians know that Aborigines should get some compensation and will get something. Most whites would like to be seen as tolerant and compassionate but they realise that their own rights will be diminished if the rights of Aborigines were to increase,' says Hainy.

'People will always want more than they need and more than others have. Blacks and whites,' says Kathy.

'When the cake is cut most people believe that they deserve a bigger piece,' says Marta.

'Whites believe that Aborigines should finally thank them for the wonderful progress they brought to them. Only then would they concede that the colonisation of Australia could have been done in a more humane way,' says Kathy.

'Billions were spent on Aborigines,' says Peter. 'They have every imaginable service, and they have new homes and full bellies. That's more than the other half has. They should look at Africa or India or Brazil or Philippines to see what real poverty is.'

'They actually did not ask for any of it,' I venture.

In 1992 we all listen to Prime Minister's speech about Native Title. 'There is a difference between Land rights and Native Title,' he said. 'Land Rights would be a gift from white settlers to Aborigines but Native Title is the recognition that Aborigines always had the right to the land. The time has come to right the wrong. Native Title is the recognition of the very existence of Aborigines. We destroyed Aboriginal traditions and customs, we killed Aborigines, we brought the diseases that decimated them, we dispersed them and denied them the authority and respect of their very families; this was going on for 200 years.'

'Turn off this labour propaganda. What have Aborigines ever done with the land; have they produced one single tool; have they cultivated one square meter of the land,' says Peter.

'They lived on it and off it,' says Hainy. 'They had respect.'

'For as long as I remember, they lived off social security,' says Peter. 'White miners still live in their shacks while Aborigines on social security live in four bedrooms new brick air-conditioned homes.'

'The resentment started after Mabo decision gave recognition of native title to Aborigines. As soon as some people get privileges they become despised by the rest of the society,' says Hainy.

'I assumed that we have been equal until now. I haven't even noticed the colour of children's skin,' says Marta.

'They should have signed the treaty with Aborigines in the first place,' says Kathy.

'How can you sign anything with a bunch of savages scattered naked in the bush. They did not understand each other let alone had any idea of what writing or a treaty is,' says Peter.

'We will pay the price for all the wrongs now,' says Hainy.

'We cannot achieve reconciliation without the truth; however costly the search and the knowing of the truth may be,' says an eloquent politician.

'The historians are forever forming new views of the past, but there could never be one view in the multicultural society. The whole truth is only a sum of truths people perceive by their own senses,' says Marta.

'So much is achievable when it is desired by a passion,' says Hainy.

'Who is to say that this generation of Aborigines is not suffering the greatest injustice there is? Not being wanted or needed or respected or trusted or liked, is devastating,' I quote Dudley's words.

'We never worried about discrimination before, because white man needed us and we needed him. We knew our place,' said Dudley to me. I told John what Dudley said.

'Bullshit, there is no such thing as my place,' John got angry. 'We are all born free to become what we want to become.' I wonder if John really believed what he said.

'They let kids do as they like until they are old enough to go to jail and there maybe hang themselves,' says Peter.

'People chase equality all their lives but we are only equal six-foot under in our coffins,' says Kathy. As long as there are the criteria for a job, you have to discriminate. You have to pick the one most suited.'

'We were all wronged and damaged somewhere down the track,' says Marta.

'If bludgers don't get what they want, they call it discrimination and sue you for racial vilification,' argues Peter.

'Aborigines and whites eat the same pies and hamburgers and KFC's, we drink the same coke or beer, smoke the same cigarettes, watch the same soapies on television, swear with the same words, wear the same brand runners. We play the same ball games, same poker machines, same computer games, we curse the same law and politicians,' says Hainy.

'Everybody is forever looking for his tribe,' John once said. 'Your tribe is your refuge; it makes you strong and supports you, rain, hail or shine.' John was talking about dispersed Aborigines trying to find their extended family but now I am also looking for my tribe.

Andrew settled in America. I cannot hate Andrew. He is who he is. Maybe Andrew and Shane felt entitled to some of Hainy's opal. I will never really know. Perhaps they wanted to get out of the little town and spread their wings. Andrew rings sometimes; we exchange the news of our children and grandchildren. He never mentions Shane or Debbie.

Hainy and Marta and Kathy know my moments of joy and my depths of despair. I often wonder about John and Sam. Maybe they really were saints. Unfortunately people don't believe in saints any more. They have to push the saints from their pedestals to see if they will shatter. It is dangerous standing on the pedestal. It is hard to be a role model. There is safety in following the throng and the fashion. To be with one's tribe. It became a national sport to cut down tall poppies. Teachers, politicians and priests are favourite targets.

'Drought is crippling the country, the markets for primary produce are threatened, farmers and miners are leaving the area; many are broke. Small towns are dying,' says Peter.

'Muslims became the common enemy for the beginning of twenty first century. When new problems appear the old ones are soon forgotten. People are scared of terrorism and might venture into the bush again,' says Hainy.

'It's a disgrace how Moslem men force their women to cover their faces in Australian heat,' says Peter.

'You never know who is hiding under a black tent,' says Marta.

'They are not slaves to ever changing fashion,' laughs Hainy.

'If Muslims insist on keeping their traditions in Australia, why not ban schooling for their women as well,' says Peter.

'Why stop there,' says Marta. 'They might as well circumcise young girls.'

'And introduce honour killing. A man rapes a woman and then she has to be stoned or her father or brother must kill her,' says Peter.

'They want to ban Santa and Christmas in Australia,' says Kathy.

'This is a decade of apology,' says Marta. 'Everybody is sorry. The Pope apologised to Muslims for Crusades a millennium ago. Are Muslims going to apologise for pillaging Europe for half a millennium?'

'It amazes me how things go in and out of fashion,' I say.

'The master-slave relationship changed but the masters and the slaves are still here and always will be,' says Hainy.

'There is an international frenzy as people examine who we are and where we are heading,' concludes Kathy.

Be kind to others and to yourself, said mum a life time ago. Mum and dad never really died. Their words live in me. Now I am afraid to face my empty house, my empty heart, and my empty bed so I skirt on the surfaces of other people's lives. I deluded myself that Lightning Ridge poor needed me to solve their problems. As soon as I lost my office people forgot that I exist. I need to go home and connect the missing pieces of my life. I think of mum and dad hanging on, waiting for me to return. I hope they see me from heaven. I hope there is God and heaven. There must be someone in charge, someone who knows right from wrong and the reason and the purpose. Hainy does not agonise about the meaning of life. Andrew didn't either. John was fixing life rather than worry about it. Maybe men are different. Maybe they don't dare expose their fears.

'Opal mining keeps me out of mischief,' said Hainy. 'I am high with excitement when I find opal or so tired from digging that I do not worry what life is all about.'

Sometimes I wonder what happened to Simon. He took me to Gold coast when I ran away from home. Poor man. We might both laugh about our sad escape now. One cannot forget a person who shared that kind of despair but I doubt that either of us would want to remember.

'I want to live life to the full,' said my son Ben before he took his family to Africa to help develop Zimbabwe.

'Life half lived is not worth living, said my daughter when I told her that I am leaving Peter. I applied for a transfer, it might take a while but I will be going, says Kathy as we meet for coffee.

Everybody is leaving.

'You can come and visit,' Kathy offers me a lifeline.

'You are so strong.'

'It is only your perception because I laugh when I feel suicidal,' laughs Kathy.

'Why would you feel suicidal?'

'The same reasons most everybody at some time feels suicidal,' laughs Kathy. We are looking at television with cups of coffee warming our hands.

'I wonder if people dislike me because I don't like me or do I dislike me because others don't like me,' I say.

'Eternal questions. Are we good in order to be loved or are we good because we are loved,' says Kathy.

'It's the egg and the chicken story.'

'I intend to live life as it was meant to be,' says Kathy before she leaves.

I hear Kathy's neighbour talk about Kathy in the supermarket.

'Kathy prostrated herself on the driveway in front of Peter's car so he would not go to the pub but Peter swerved on the lawn and left.' The women laughed.

'She locked him out at night and when he returned, he took a bulldozer to get in, whispered the other woman.' Why didn't Kathy tell me? Maybe she told me and I did not hear her.

I should visit my children now that I am no longer busy. Perhaps they are too busy now. On a Sunday morning there is a knock on my door. 'Freddy,' I almost shout with joy. At this moment I would welcome a stray cat. Freddy brings back memories of the olden days when I was young in Sydney. We hug and kiss and travel our separate ways into the days when we believed that life was tailor made for us.

'This is Janez, the Slovenian ambassador,' Freddy introduces the important man standing next to him.

After refreshments I show the men to their rooms and the ambassador takes a rest while Freddy and I try to catch up on the missing years.

'How is your family?'

Freddy tells me that he married a beautiful Slovenian girl and that his grown up children are also happily married.

'My wife died two years ago,' says Freddy with an expression of great sadness. 'How is your family?'

'My husband also slipped away,' I try to laugh.

'I always knew that one-day we will meet again,' smiles Freddy. There still lingers a hint of mutual admiration. It almost feels like coming home.

'When we were in Sydney you were fighting Yugoslav ambassadors now you drive them around,' I change the subject.

'Janez is Slovenian ambassador.'

'His last post was as a Yugoslav ambassador.'

'He was always on our side.'

'People are born again.'

'We have to build bridges.'

'And ladders,' I tease.

'He can do a lot for us.'

'You used to do a lot for us.'

'You changed,' says Freddy.

'We both,' I agree.

'You live in isolation. Should keep up with changes,' says Freddy.

'I should not expect you to remain who I believed you were,' I say more to myself than to Freddy.

'One has to be realistic.'

'One can never be what one was.'

After a couple of sightseeing days Freddy and the ambassador leave. Freddy and I are disappointed because we changed. I realise that my people are no longer my people. You can never catch up the missing years. Freddy is no longer an innocent altar boy. I cannot return to Sydney because people in Sydney changed. Maybe I cannot return anywhere. The road of no return. Lightning Ridge became my home. I lived here all my life.

I invite Hainy and his friend Bill for dinner. Hainy and I need Bill to distract us from searching into what we mean to each other. Where does friendship end and love begins. Is Hainy the brother I never had or the lover I want?I am glad Hainy does not hold it against me that Andrew took his opals. Maybe Andrew felt cheated and entitled to his share. Maybe Shane also wanted a share because he told Andrew where to register the claims. Maybe greed is stronger than love.

'Greed always wins hands down,' Hainy once said.

'Have you started on migrant's stories yet?' says Hainy as I begin serving dinner.

'I barely know any migrant well enough.'

'There is a story behind every man in the bush,' says Bill.

'You can only write how YOU know someone. Nobody ever knows how that person knows himself,' says Hainy.

'Would you tell me your story?'

'My story is boring. What you see is what you get.'

'I would like to hear it.'

'One day,' says Hainy.

'You should go to the pub. Stories and beer go together,' says Bill.

'These days people have to be sober to drive home. You cannot talk about life if you are not properly drunk,' says Hainy.

'It's safer to drink at home,' I say and put three stubbies on the table.

I carve the roast and dish potatoes and salads. Thank God men like old-fashioned food. They love my cakes covered in cream.

'Nothing like a home-cooked meal,' Hainy compliments me.

'Cooking is my only excitement these days.'

'Like mine is finding opal, sitting all brilliant and shiny in the cool clay,' says Hainy.

'When gambling with opal one gets respectfully dirty and tired and broke,' laughs Bill.

'Or rich,' I say.

'I wouldn't be here if I worried about getting rich,' says Bill.

'Bill is getting married,' says Hainy. 'I am going to miss him.'

'Would you come to a BBQ on Sunday to meet my bride? '

'I'd love to. Who is the lucky lady,' I ask.

'Tina, our lovely teacher, brought her mother from Sydney and the miracle happened,' says Hainy.

'You are a lucky man,' I say.

'You never know when you will meet your soul mate,' says Hainy.

'Perhaps looking for the same thing makes us all soul mates,' says Bill. I wish I had a soul mate; I wish I could curl into someone's arms. I feel so vulnerable right now. On Sunday Hainy comes to take me to Bill's place. We sit in old rickety chairs on the gravel under the gum trees next to Bill's camp.

'This place is only suitable for cactus, drifters, gamblers and loners,' says Bill as we settle with a beer from the esky.

'This is Martina,' says Bill.

'Where are you from?'

'I lived in Sydney but my family comes from Austria. My mum was Slovenian,' adds Martina.

'I am Slovenian, I tell and feel happy to see this total stranger because she is connected to the same corner of the world.

'Where in Austria,' asks Hainy.

'Dad's people come from Carinthia, close to Austrian Slovenian boarder.'

I come from Carinthia close to Graz. We might have gone to school together, says Hainy.

'You never know who is who in Lightning Ridge, says Bill. Aborigines and Europeans, doctors and illiterates, policemen and criminals camp next to each other and look for the same rainbow in the clay beneath the sandstone.'

'People accept each other's anonymity and share of themselves what they want to share,' says Hainy.

'Tell me about opal mining,' says Martina sipping her wine. The rest of us drink beer from the stubbies. You don't pour beer into glasses on the field. Too hot. You have to retain every bit of coolness.

'At the turn of the twentieth century shepherds found colourful silica flushed out by erosion and washed by floods. They weren't looking for it, it surprised them shiny and colourful in the sun,' Hainy begins to introduce Lightning Ridge to Martina.

Bill and Hainy are telling Martina what I heard many times before. Maybe they are counting on me to write down their heroic tales.

'How does one become an opal miner,' asks Martina.

'You choose and survey fifty by fifty metres claim, draw a map and pay a fee to register it. Then you dig the hole.'

'How do you know where?'

'The experts agree that there is no way to tell where opal deposits are. Some try to divine opal by holding two wires in front of them. They march into the bush and the wires sometimes cross in front of them and they say that opal is underneath. Most old miners laugh at diviners because the diviners never find opal for themselves,' tells Hainy.

'Some miners look for the signs above ground; they try to guess the spot by the vegetation or the stars above them,' continues Bill. 'Wild orange tree is said to grow roots thirty metres into the ground looking for water. Where underground water was, opal could also be. Other trees are known to look for sub-moisture in the fault line where opal may form. The sandstone and rocks and sediments also tell a story to those that want to believe, but there is no sure sign.'

Bill brings a tray of barbequed chops on the table. 'Help yourselves to salads,' Martina offers.

'People like to peg next to the guys who found millions. They feel like they are standing in line for lady luck, right next to the lucky ones to be touched by providence,' says Hainy.

'Prospecting for opal is too expensive for ordinary bloke. You might drill twenty shafts and find nothing. So you wait for someone to find opal and hope to peg close. Either you are lucky or you are not,' says Bill.

'Andrew used to say that everybody has an equal chance to be lucky, 'I add. 'After ten years of playing cards we ended with the same card money we started with.' Nobody takes any notice of what Andrew used to say. I should not have mentioned Andrew. He is best forgotten.

'Miners are solitary creatures,' says Bill. 'Opal mining used to be a one-man operation. You simply couldn't trust anyone well enough to let him chip away in your mine. You can't watch a bloke all the time. You work your trench, he works his. There might be a pocket, it might be the only pocket you'll ever find and your partner might take it. There is always suspicion. There might be one solitary knobby that could change your life and you don't know if your partner would be able to resist the temptation or put it in his pocket.'

'You wouldn't do that to your friend,' says Martina.

'You don't know what you would do until you are tested,' says Bill. 'People are careful whom they pick to work with. Their life and livelihood depends on it. '

'Lead us not into temptation,' smiles Martina.

'One never really knows what one is capable of,' agrees Hainy. Is Hainy thinking about Andrew who took his opal?

'Old miners look after their mates. They know how unpredictable their livelihood is,' says Bill. You can rely on an old chum.'

'What's an old chum,' asks Martina.

'A man like Hainy. A man you can trust.' We sit in silence. John was a sort of a chum I could trust. Only John abandoned me. John and I tried to make a better world but we did not consider the world as it really is. There is a huge empty place inside me. Maybe Hainy is a chum I need. Maybe we both need to believe that we mean something to each other.

'It is easier to find opal than to find a partner,' says Bill. 'As long as you are not after the same thing you can trust your friend or your brother, but on opal everybody is greedy for the same thing. Many friendships and families are broken on account of opal.'

'People start off trusting each other, they couldn't be bothered with contracts, they work happily until they find money, but then most look again at their vague verbal agreement and try to get more for themselves out of the partnership,' says Hainy. Many years ago I was there on my own in a trench when I dug out my best stone, tells Bill. I could have put it in my pocket; it would never hurt anyone, because nobody would ever know. I could have made a fortune but I shared my luck with my partner. I would always know that I wasn't honest if I didn't. I realised that I have to live with myself. My partner and I were happily drinking and admiring the solitary nobbie all night. Everybody soon heard about it and somebody suggested to my partner that I must have filled my pockets before I showed him the one stone. There must have been more, he said. The suspicion killed our friendship. I was sorry that I have shown that stone to him. I felt that everyone suspected me of cheating my partner.'

'Working with a partner is safer because you combine the machinery and money and knowledge and work, but it is always hard to trust the man you share your life with,' says Hainy.

'The shells impregnated with specks of colour are proof that an ocean was here long time ago. There are also skeletons of dinosaurs,' I add.

'Every year miners invent new machinery and every year there are more expenses and it is harder for a small bloke to have a go on his own,' says Bill.

'Lightning Ridge was a good town in the sixties. Nobody locked their camps, there was no stealing or ratting, miners could leave their opal and equipment on the field and it would not be touched,' says Hainy.

'At the beginning miners dug shafts by pick and shovel later they used jackhammers, and in the eighties drilling rig arrived. Now they sink little mechanised diggers and loaders into the shaft to do the work,' says Bill.

'Miners are like bowerbirds; they collect everything that shines. They are telling yarns about opal in the Diggers Rest hotel to keep the hope alive.'

'You come to the pub night after night in the hope to find a girl of your dreams and your dreams turn into mateship with drinking buddies and gradually you forget why you came. Gradually you feel compelled to come to the pub to be with your mates, like husbands are compelled to come to their families night after night,' says Bill.

'Single men go out to find a wife and married men come to get away from wives who curse them for going,' says Hainy.

'You don't go to the pub much,' I turn to Hainy.

'With Bill married I will have to find new chums.'

'You need a wife to keep you home. You need someone to curse you and make your life miserable,' laughs Bill. 'Rogues, rascals and visionaries become redeemed when they find a wife.'

'Have you ever been married?' Asks Martina.

'I had a wife and a son in Austria. She heard about the opal I found so she came to surprise me. When she found me living in a camp she packed up and returned home. She didn't come to live with me, she just wanted her share,' says Hainy.

'Some little children in Austria probably talk about their rich Australian grandad,' says Martina.

I realise how little I know about people I live close to. I did not dare ask Hainy about his family. Hainy must sometimes think of a man his son became.

'This is my daughter Tina,' Martina introduces a young woman coming over.

'Jana writes stories about Lightning Ridge,' Martina tells her daughter as we shake hands.

'Tina would certainly have a story to tell,' says Bill.

'I am sure you could write it better than I,' I say to Tina.

'Maybe I will one day,' says Tina.

'You should,' says Hainy.

Hainy takes me home. We pass the camps made from old tin and hessian; lime and iron stone make stronger homes; log huts are pretty. Some miners chisel the sand stone bricks, others use clay for walls. In the eighties many brought their caravans and built shacks around them. Most have dirt floors and candle lights, many bring water in large containers and use it sparingly. The rain water tanks often run dry in hot summers and only few miners can afford to run a generator for electricity.

'Why don't you move to town,' I ask Hainy.

'I got used to the bush.'

'I don't think I could live without electricity and water.'

'You get used to anything.'

'Why did you leave Austria,' I chatter on.

'It's a long story,' he says quietly.

'Have you been back?'

'No,' Hainy shuts the door to this line of questioning.

'Any brothers and sisters?'

'I don't keep in touch.'

I am sad that Hainy does not trust me to know him. Without opal and mining we would have nothing to talk about.

'Coming in for coffee,' I invite.

'We should get a bottle of scotch to forget the places we've been to,' laughs Hainy.

'I'll find some scotch then.'

'Only if you'll join me. I don't drink on my own.'

'I don't really drink.'

'I don't really drink either but sometimes it's just the right time to drink. You are not afraid that we will become alcoholics at our age?'

'There is nothing stopping us from becoming anything we want to become,' I laugh as I pour the drinks. In this peaceful end of the day Hainy and I talk about the opal fields and mining while we remember the home and the relations that have long forgotten us. It has never been the right time yet to speak about them.

'Bill is one old chum you can trust with your life,' says Hainy.

'I have no chum here,' I say. 'I have to go home. Maybe I left my chums there.'

'Don't you remember what you left?'

'You see things differently the second time around.'

'At home people look at your family and don't see you as an individual. In Australia you can be whoever you choose to be. Especially in Lightning Ridge,' smiles Hainy.

'Tell me about your home.'

'Very ordinary town, mostly working class people.'

'What was your father like?' We are pleasantly relaxed as we sit in the dusk with the last rays of sun colouring the sunset. After a large scotch we seem less afraid of memories.

'My father volunteered himself to work for Hitler. He loved Hitler. He was on the Eastern Front. After the war Russians caught him and deported him to Siberia. '

'How long was he in prison?'

'When he came out I was a teenager living with my grandmother. When my grandmother died I emigrated to Australia.'

'Why?'

'During the war most Austrians supported Hitler but after the war most denied it. When I grew up I resented the fact that my father supported Hitler. There was a high suicide rate among the children of Hitler supporters.

'Where was your mother?'

'She died in a concentration camp. She was Jewish.'

We drink in silence. I hope Hainy will not regret opening the door on his past.

'I never told anyone about my family,' says Hainy again. He seems amazed that he told me.

'Nobody ever asked me about my family either,' I say.

'How would you feel if your father was a Nazi or a criminal or insane or a murderer?'

'I lied to my parents that I will come home next year, every year until they died waiting.'

'We have known each other for almost thirty years,' says Hainy.

'It feels like we just met,' I say. He pats my hand and the hands meet. We smile.

'Have a drink,' I offer to bridge the awkward moment.

'During the war I was made ashamed of my mother and for the rest of my life I was ashamed of my father.'

'What were your grandparents like?'

'They loved me very much. They were kind and hardworking and well respected. They were devout Catholics and the pillars of the church. The elaborate church rituals enchanted me. I grew up within the church so to speak. They made me hate Jews. They were dad's parents. They never even mentioned my mother. I was already a teenager when I found out how she died. And why.'

'So you are half Jewish?'

'I grew up as a Catholic Austrian. Nobody ever mentioned anything about me being Jewish.'

'Did you ever meet your mother's relations?'

'I believe that most were killed. Knowing what happened to mum and who my father was I do not feel right searching for them.'

'Was your father good to you?'

'I only really remember him coming home during the war wearing a shiny uniform and bringing gifts to my grandparents and me. My grandparents were very proud of him.'

'I have to return home.'

'You lived with Aboriginal tribe too long,' laughs Hainy.

'I wrote Aboriginal stories in the hope that I will merge with them and feel at home. I envied them their sense of belonging. Aborigines and I looked at the same river; we both know the river but we don't know how the other knows it. I needed them to forget that mum and dad were all this time hanging there waiting for me to return with my family. Finally I am going home,' I tell Hainy.

'I wish I could go with you.'

'Why don't you,' I whisper.

'Maybe next time.'

'There is nothing holding us back. We could go every year.'

'We might.'

Hainy comes with me to the airport.

'I will be waiting for you,' he says.

'It will be a new start for me,' I say.

'We will write our story next,' says Hainy. 'I will miss you.'

We kiss like people do as they part. We suddenly become new people. Hainy and I become WE as we hold onto each other. The road ahead is open and the sun shines on it. WE is like a ribbon around a bunch of flowers.

'I will miss you,' I repeat his words. We kiss again and no words are needed to tell how much we mean to each other.

'Take care,' says Hainy and his eyes are glistening with tears.

'Promise to come with me next time.'

'Promise.'

I feel the flood of tears trying to wash away the debris and the pain.

'Come home soon,' says Hainy.

'I am going home. Where is home?' I say through tears. I begin to smile. I have been waiting for this all my life; this is the finishing line in my obstacle race. I am going home.

'I will come home to Lightning Ridge soon, really soon,' I promise Hainy.

We follow our partners and then our children and then our grandchildren. In the end we hope that they will follow us.

My father

My neighbour Barbara and I sit with a cup of coffee for about fifteen minutes most mornings.

'Sorry Mira, but I only have milk with omega added, it smells a bit fishy,' says Barbara.

'You have to read the label on everything these days. You go to buy milk and you have to choose: soy or coconut, cow or goat, full cream or skim, long life or short, pasteurised or not, cholesterol reduced, flavoured, enriched, skimmed, etc. By the time you choose the one you want, you become worried that you made the wrong choice.'

'We came a long way since we had one kind of milk, one kind of man, and one kind of God,' says Barbara pouring fat reduced omega enriched milk into our coffees.

'It was easier when we believed that some things were forever right and others forever wrong. Like green and blue not going together.'

'Or wolf whistles being a compliment.'

'Or women saying no to sex.'

'Sex is like instant coffee these days. It offers an instant relief but you don't remember or relive it.'

'Once you satisfy your hunger it does not matter what you ate,' says Barbara.

'People with different names are much the same once you get to know them.'

'Sex is a carrot God dangles in front of us so we keep reproducing.'

'The thrill is in the hunt.'

'Men catch fish, kiss it and let it go.'

'Unless they have to feed the family.'

'Anyone who wants to eat fish goes to the fish market. Fishing is a thrill. The lures lure men to lure fish.'

'Do you believe in God,' asks Barbara.

'God almighty! Doesn't everybody?'

'But how do you know which God is the right one?'

'The one you believe in surely.'

I've known Barbara and her husband Henry for years. Henry and my husband Jack have a successful Information Technology business. Jack wanted me to work in their office but I am not an office girl; I like to negotiate and sell rather than push paper. To be truthful, I don't like to take orders from anybody, least of all from my husband.

I have a real estate agency so I can choose my hours. It gives me time for Jack, my adorable husband, and our three lovely daughters. Jane is finishing high school. Eliza has another year to go and then there is baby Natasha in kindy.

'My back, my back,' I hear Jack moaning in agony lying on the floor of our bedroom. I call to the girls to help me get him to bed.

'What happened?'

'I was putting a sock on when my back snapped.'

Jane calls the doctor. I ring my work and Jack's work to tell them that we won't be in.

Jane takes Natasha to school. She became a deputy mother to her baby sister.

It's been a week now and Jack is still bedridden. A chiropractor manipulates his back and tells him about the sciatic nerve pressing on the muscles sending pain down his leg. It is hard to believe that my six foot tall forty five years old husband can't get out of bed but it is rather cosy being in bed with him in the middle of the day.

'Sonia brought some papers for you to sign,' I call to Jack a few days later.

'Bring them up.' Sonia stays in the lounge room.

'Would you like some coffee or a cold drink while you are waiting,' I say as I return.

'Coffee would be nice.'

'Sonia is like a wildflower. Her green eyes are dancing under the long curled eyelashes. I see no trace of make up on her face. She seems as natural as a dewdrop. I know how hard it is to look natural. Women notice other beautiful women. Men become attracted to something in a woman but I don't think they ever appreciate the whole symmetry of her features.

Sonia has been my husband's secretary for over a year but we only met on a few formal occasions. Sonia always had some dashing young man in tow.

'Here we go,' I place a cup in front of Sonia. A stabbing pain in my chest stops me in mid-sentence as I lean over the coffee table. I almost drop the cup.

'Are you all right,' says Sonia?

'Fine, fine... A bit of pain in my back as well. Must have pulled a muscle as I hauled Jack to bed.' I am trying to keep my eyes from Sonia's heart shaped pendant with a small opal in the middle. Sonia's long fingers twirl her pendant absent-mindedly and finally drop it to rest under the loosely opened navy silk blouse.

'Are you sure?'

'I will be fine.'

'Nice coffee.'

'Thanks. I like the design of your pendant.'

Sonia caught my eyes following its disappearance between her slightly exposed breasts.

'Oh, thanks. It's a gift. Sentimental value.'

'From your boyfriend?'

'Sort of.'

'It matches your eyes.'

'He said that opal represents hope.'

'What is he hoping for?'

'To live happily ever after I suppose. Isn't that what we all hope for?'To get you to sleep with him, more likely, says a voice in me but I try to smile sweetly for now.

'Ever been married?'

'Marriage is not my priority. It used to be in your time,' I suppose, smiles Sonia.

'Well, marriage and family, yes, it was. It still is for some.'The bitch is telling me that I am an old woman.

'Men try to talk you into things you don't want,' smiles Sonia. 'If they think that you want to get married they run but as soon as you announce that you are not a marrying type they pester you about the body clock ticking and the time to make babies.'

'Do you want to make babies?'

'If the right man comes along.'

'There must be someone very special.'

'There always is, special for different reasons.' Sonia's eyes are cold and sad. I want her to be scared because I am going to kill her.

'Men don't like independent women,' I smile. How dare she parade my opal in front of me?

'I don't worry about what men like,' Sonia sweeps her wildly bushy blond hair back.

'Jack loved my hair when it was bushy and long like yours,' I compliment Sonia. 'When he pulled a hair out of the cake I baked, he said: Your hair is not my piece of cake. He now prefers short hair.'

'I am not trying to impress anyone,' says Sonia. The bitch is lying, of course.

'I think I saw a pendant like that at the jewellers, 'I lie.

Keep talking, keep saying things. I have to convince myself that there is a heart shaped pendant with an opal waiting for me on my fortieth birthday. I saw it in Jack's pocket before he injured his back.

'I am turning forty in a couple of weeks,' I smile.

'You don't look it,' says Sonia but I know what she thinks.

'Would you like to join us for a little celebration?'

'Are you sure?'

'It is a surprise party really.'

'I'd love to.'

'Bring a friend if you like.' I hope to poison the bitch with my birthday cake. It will also give me a chance to gather evidence. Henry phones to reassure Jack that the business is doing fine. With seven employees it almost runs itself.

'I am sick of staying home,' says Jack as Sonia brings more paperwork.

'Give it until my birthday at least. It is only a couple of days.'

'I lost all sense of time,' says Jack. 'I have to get you a gift.'

'Leave it all to me and pretend that you arranged it.'

'I love you,' says Jack. We cuddle up and make love but I hear a worm of suspicion noisily chewing my brain. Did this man, Jack, whom I know so intimately give his secretary the pendant which I believed was to be a surprise present for my fortieth birthday?I want to strangle Sonia. I want any unfaithful thought cut out of Jack's heart with the razor. I have no idea what I am going to do when the time comes. Jack and I love each other. My three girls adore daddy. They know how to make him laugh and sing and dance. They take notice of daddy. When he is not pleased they want to please him. They don't know that Jack betrayed us. I try to convince myself that there is an explanation but I am afraid to ask for it. I am afraid that Jack will tell me that he does not love me anymore. I am also afraid that he would deny it and I would always know that he lied. Maybe Jack is waiting for an opportunity to tell me that he is leaving. Jack and I took each other for granted.

I remember when Jack and I were swimming; we dared each other to go further into the surf. The ocean used to be our playground until the day the undertow caught us. The waves tossed us into the sandy bottom and lifted us onto another wave. We were toys the ocean played with. It could do anything with us or to us. Jack and I were drowning. I called God. I am not a praying person. I just called God. When I finally collapsed on the beach I thanked God. Jack also collapsed on the beach. He could not save me. We could not help each other.

'We shouldn't take the ocean for granted,' said Jack.

'Or life,' I smiled through tears of relief. Now I am drowning again.

I should never take happiness for granted. Or love. Or family. Why has Jack stopped loving me? What have I done? I try to rub out the memory of Sonia's pendant but the knowledge surfaces regularly like a knife stab.

Henry brings a box of chocolate and Jane gives me a beautiful cup with European spring flowers on it for my surprise birthday party. She knows I love cups. When one has everything one wants, one begins to collect certain items just for fun. Sonia brings me an abstract painting. I smile and kiss everybody like the opal pendant never happened. Smiles camouflage all sorts of catastrophes. Damian brings a bottle of champagne.

'I haven't seen Damian since I was thirteen. We went to school together, I introduce my childhood friend. 'He came into my office a few days ago.'

'It has been a long time,' said Damian.

'A lifetime,' I said as we hugged. I invited him to my party on the spur of the moment.

My daughters baked an exquisite cake. They decorated the house with love heart balloons and flowers. I am so lucky. The intensity of happiness brings tears to my eyes. I light the candles and then blow them all in one huge blow while my friends sing happy birthday. Jack and I hug and kiss. Our girls join the circle and we kiss each other. Henry takes a photo. A picture of total bliss. I look at Sonia for a reaction. She is talking to Damian. The bitch is pretending. The bell rings. There is a young man at the door. 'A special delivery for the birthday lady,' he says. A bouquet and a small parcel with the card. I breathe deeply into the scented roses.

'Don't keep us in suspense. Open your present,' calls Henry.

'How beautifully romantic,' says Barbara.

'Who is it from?' asks Damian.

I read the card: 'Happy birthday my darling. I love you.'

'Who do you think?'

I open the tiny parcel. In the black velvet box is a platinum heart shaped pendant with a ruby.

'Oh, darling, just what I always wanted,' I kiss Jack.

'Life begins at forty,' says Barbara.

'I am determined to make that true,' I laugh.

I am glad nobody knows about Sonia's opal. I simply can't put into words what I know. I shudder.

'Can I have a look at your opal,' says Damian to Sonia after my ruby passed inspection. Damian takes Sonia's pendant into the palm of his hand and turns it this way and that so its colour moves and changes.

'I love opals. They fascinate me; opals are like people; no two opals are the same,' says Damian.

'They say that opal brings bad luck,' says Barbara.

'Only to those that don't have it,' laughs Damian.

'What do you mean,' says Barbara.

'Miners rely on luck in Lightning Ridge. The unlucky don't find opal and remain poor.'

'I heard that it cracks,' says Barbara.

'The pure Lightning Ridge black opal does not crack. If it isn't pure or if it does not sit on black backing, it might crack eventually.'

'Or if you hit it with a hammer,' laughs Barbara.

'It's fragile like most precious things,' says Damian. 'With care it lasts forever.'

Damian tells us that he studied gemmology and has spent time in Lightning Ridge, the home of black opal. He would eventually like to become an opal miner/collector/buyer.

'Tall, blond, and adventurous. Where did you hide him?' whispers Barbara as we look at Damian and Sonia connected with her gold chain.

'We went to school together.'

Maybe opal pendant will bring Sonia and Damian together. Damian is an eligible bachelor. His boyish figure and mischievous smile make him desirable. Maybe I hoped to make Jack jealous. Maybe he is jealous of Damian and Sonia. I must play this right.

My ruby pendant is forgotten. I am forgotten. Sonia has stolen my attention. I need attention. This is my birthday. I arranged my own party and my own gift but I cannot give myself the attention I deserve. I need a double dose of attention. I don't feel loved enough. Damian, Henry and Jack become instant friends. They are about the same age, they share the interest in electronics; they are businessmen. They begin discussing sport and games.

Damian comes to see me a week after my party. He wants to buy a house.

'What made you choose Rovena?'

'I have to settle down somewhere. It's not too far from Linden and about the same size.'

'Another little satellite to Dubbo.'

I show him what is on the market. We drive around and stop for coffee in my favourite cafeteria. The flood of memories brings us into the enchanted kingdom of our childhood. Our homes, games, friends, dreams, first flirtations and all the pre-kissed fantasies return. Damian reminds me of who I was and where I came from before I met Jack who changed my life. For the better. Damian is a couple of years older; he used to be my prince charming. I dreamed little girl's dreams about him.

'How big is your family,' I ask as we inspect the houses.

'At least three children. I would also like to have a wife.'

'Forty-two and not married. That's amazing.'

'I lived with a girlfriend for a few years but she wanted to get married and I just could not make up my mind. She left and married and had three children in three years.

'You missed out.'

'I am glad she left because seeing her so happy helped me to decide to get married.'

'Who is the lucky lady?'

'I am in between as they say.'

'Not for long I am sure.'

'We must catch up on the old times and Linden.'

'I haven't been back since I left. I am rather homesick all of a sudden,' I admit. Linden will always be home although I have no one there now.'

'Those unforgettable days,' says Damian.

I forgot about Linden. No, I packed Linden in the soft tissue paper and put it away like brides store their wedding dresses. Sealed in the plastic bag taped over in the box forever. Never to be used again. A treasure in the memory bank.

I wonder how many wedding dresses lay like that forgotten in the attic. I found a wedding album on the rubbish tip the other day. How many wedding albums end there? Much of life ends on the rubbish tip. There is no room for sentimentality.

'You left suddenly,' says Damian.

'Mum enrolled me at the boarding school in Sydney.'

'Everybody comes home from time to time to reconnect. We might organise a reunion,' says Damian.

For the first time I hear temptation knocking. To be a child again at the beginning of this journey; to do it again. While there is still time. Before aging.

Damian does not know why I left Linden. Even I don't know. Dad left. I saw tears in dad's eyes as he kissed me goodbye. How could he abandon me so suddenly without explanation? I cried for my father. He has been there for me every step of the way. He read me stories, he bought me toys, and he played with me. He was my hero. My dad was the best dad any girl could wish for.

After dad left, Frank and his dog moved in with mum. Frank was my father's German friend. Mum eventually married Frank and they moved to Sydney. I have little contact with them. Years later I told mum that I want to find dad.

'You are big enough now to know that he is not your real father, explained mum. Your dad is a man I met while I worked in the Bank's Canberra branch.'

I felt betrayed and abandoned. I packed my childhood in a soft tissue paper then and never discussed it with anybody again.

I finished high school and an interior design course when Jack came into my life like a welcome drop of rain from a clear sky. We met at the dance and I married him in a state of euphoria six months later and three months pregnant. Jack became the best husband any girl could wish for. And the best father to our three girls. I love Jack. Our girls adore him. Everything was right with the world until Sonia took it away.

'I might open a business here,' Damian brings me back to the present.

'What sort?'

'Selling, I suppose. I always liked buying and selling. I have some knowledge about art and antiques and hardware and even jewellery.'

'How is your back? I ask Jack when I get home.

'Much better. Give me a hand to get up.'

'You smell delicious,' says Jack. He pulls me down and we laugh. He pulls the doona over our heads and breathes into my ear. He knows my body; he discovered every spot that excites me. I try to move out and we struggle playfully until I could no longer resist.

'Phone,' says Jack.

'Let it ring,' I say. I touch every spot that excites Jack. 'We work like a Swiss clock,' said Jack once. I hold onto Jack after we both made it on a well known road to heaven. The wellbeing of our union still brings tears to my eyes.

'It's been too long,' says Jack.

'Only a week.' I taste his hard salty body as he holds my head tight on his chest. I feel him coming alive again. This time we go slowly using every trick of our favourite game, as Jack used to say long ago. I pretend to fall asleep and he goes over my body in search of the wake up button. We enjoy our fresh new romance, a fragrance of spring almost. That's how life should be. Cover up the past with the doona and start again and again and again. Like the spring that comes again and again. And the cherry blossoms. And the future all bright in front of us. I love this boyish man who makes me feel beautiful and a little naughty.

'You better get this,' says Jack as the phone rings for the third time.

'I will be right over,' I say into the phone.

'Damian wants me to help him choose the curtains for the house tomorrow,' I say. I believed that Jack and I had what is called a solid marriage. We give each other freedom to do what we like during the workday and in the evening we are happy to come together and tell each other everything. I never had secrets. Now I have a secret. Jack's secret.

'You look radiant; must be your childhood sweetheart,' says Barbara as we meet for our morning coffee.

'Damian and I were children when we last saw each other.'

'That's what I said. Childhood sweethearts.'

'Jack has an affair,' I blurt out.

'Never. You could bet your life on Jack.'

'I would die if he told me that it is true. It would destroy us.'

'Who is she?'

'I don't want to name her until I am sure but she is ten years younger. How can I compete?'

'How can he compete with young boys that will want to sleep with her? A time will come when he will question his potency and his looks.'

I don't want to confront Jack because I don't want it to be true. I saw him looking for grey hair. He was flexing his muscles in front of the mirror. Maybe divorce is in the genes. Like mother like daughter. Nothing happened as long as Jack and I pretend that it did not happen. Sonia's pendant is dangling in front of me as I close my eyes.

'Were you ever unfaithful,' asks Barbara.

'Maybe in my mind a little,' I smile. Lately I force myself to think of something other than Jack and Sonia. I know that one day soon it will all come out in the open and hit me.

'It's good to let the bastards know that you can be tempted.'

'I never played games with Jack.'

'Games are a distraction on the way to old age.'

'Maybe Jack needs to be distracted from aging.'

I see aging in Barbara's face. She has no grey in her blond hair, her skin shows no wrinkles but the aging is obvious. Barbara's lips seem thinner; her blue eyes turned grey, her skin is tired. We are the same age. Aging. Like flowers before you throw them on the compost heap.

'Maybe Jack has noticed aging. There is a panic light flickering. Did we achieve everything we wanted to achieve? Did we succeed? Were we loved enough? Are we loved enough? Women paint their faces to cover despair. Nobody cares what is underneath the gloss and powder. Pamper the skin, stretch it, tighten it, cleanse, moisturise and hide the blemishes. However tight the bum, however big the boobs, however small the waist, once you are old nobody cares.'

Barbara and I laugh, very close to tears, both of us for different reasons.

'I can't believe that you never married,' I say to Damian casually as we go furniture shopping for his new house a couple of weeks later.'

'I was waiting for you,' he says with a laugh.

'Oh, right. For thirty years.'

'One true love,' he mocks seriousness.

We go from shop to shop, sit at different tables and on different couches.

'We look like an old married couple,' says Damian. He rolls on the bed and pulls me playfully to test it with him.

'Look at the time. Almost lunchtime.'

'Let's go home and get something to eat; I'd like to show you something,' says Damian.

'You must have had it all planned,' I tease as Damian brings out a lovely platter of goodies from the fridge.

'Always prepared' is my scout's motto,' smiles Damian. He puts on the video he made when he was last in Linden. My home, his home, the tree where we built a cubby house, the riverbank. It almost brings tears to my eyes. Damian remembers what I remember.

Damian opens a bottle of wine. 'Here is to Rovena, our new home-town.' Damian kisses me playfully with his lips still tasting of wine.

'What was that for?'

'I always wanted to do that.'

'Why?'

'I wanted to know what it feels like.'

'What does it feel like?'

'It feels like what I thought it would feel.' We remember the places and people. We laugh at silly things we did. We travel into our childhood. It is a glorious childhood; safe and warm. There is no Jack and no Sonia. Damian does not know that I am scared of losing Jack; that I want to kill Sonia. He does not know that I don't feel loved enough. Or maybe he does. His hand is over my shoulder, his lips are tempestuously close. I like the smell of Damian. I remember that smell. It is part of my growing up. He used to hold me when I cried because I had to leave Linden. We never kissed before. I am glad Damian does not know why I left home. He knows nothing about my father. He doesn't know that I do not know who my real father is.

Damian puts the music on and like in a dream I hear the song we used to sing when we were young. We begin to hum the words and stand up to dance. 'Seasons in the sun,' I whisper in his ear. Half intoxicated we hold onto each other; our cheeks hot and our bodies melting into each other. We see the world from up high.

'Those were the days,' whispers Damian. His lips are brushing my cheeks. I cannot move away. We are in our enchanted world.

'Skinned our hearts and skinned our knees,' I remember the words of the song.

'I was the black sheep of the family,' sings Damian.

'We had joy, we had fun we had seasons in the sun,' we both sing the chorus.

'But the stars we have reached were the starfish on the beach.'

'We had joy we had fun we had seasons in the sun but the hills that we climbed were just seasons out of time.'

'Goodbye papa please pray for me I was the black sheep of the family; you tried to teach me right from wrong; too much wine and too much song; I wonder how I got along.

We had joy we had fun, we had seasons in the sun but the wine and the song like the seasons have all gone.' Damian is kissing the tears running down my face.

'Too much wine,' I laugh.

'To Seasons in the sun,' toasts Damian.

'Too much wine and too much song I don't know how we got along.'

'To wine and song.'

'I haven't heard the song since I left Linden.'

'I often hear it in my mind.'

'We both liked it.'

'We were both very different people then.'

We travel on a memory lane to our other life. We are back home. We hold hands and giggle like children do. We revisit the people we once were. We only know each other as we were then. The many other persons we became, are forgotten. Tears of joy are running into our kissing as we give in to a desire to make love.

We are in bed as the brick hits the window.

I jump up in a terrified panic. The curtains are drawn but the glass from a smashed window is all over the carpet. I look out and see Jack's car leaving.

'You didn't even lock the door.'

'I never lock the door,' says Damian.

Did Jack come in and see us making love. Did he hear us giggling in bed intoxicated by wine and lust and nostalgia? Damian offers to come with me but I don't want Damian. I have to find Jack. Jack is my life, my soul mate, my family, and my best friend.

I ring Jack's office. Nobody answers. I ring Jack's mobile. It's switched off. I ring Henry and he says that Jack went to get me. He and Sonia are waiting for us. I drive home and pray out loud: 'I beg you God, I beg you. I promise it will never happen again. Please God help me.' I played my triumph ace and lost.' I cannot cry. I shake uncontrollably.

Girls are home from school. They giggle as they spread things on toast. 'Hi mum.' They don't look at me. They don't know that the world ended.

I need a shower. I need the solitary confinement to scrub away the last hour. I want to die. I deserve to die. What have I done? I went to bed with Damian for no reason at all. It wasn't me, it was a girl from Linden who never met Jack. Damian and I don't know each other apart from Linden. He is nothing to me. It was just a game, a drunken orgy. How can I ever explain that I had sex with almost a stranger in the middle of a sunny day; in the middle of a happy marriage?

'Dad is late,' says Jana.

'He had to go away,' I say buying time before my execution. I want to be dead. I have a splitting headache.

'I don't feel well. Can you get some dinner for the girls? I ask Jana.

I take two sleeping pills and wake up at three in the morning. Early morning hours are sobering. I walk into the garden and sit on the bench doubled into a foetal position. I need my mother. Like mother, like daughter. The sins of the mothers. I have to find my father. Which father? I need to know my father.

In the morning I ring my mother. 'Mira who,' says the sleepy voice in the phone. My mother obviously forgot my name and my voice. Maybe she forgot that I exist. Sorry for waking you. What time is it? Six. Is everything all right. What happened? Mum is becoming awake to danger. I need to see you. Tell me what happened. Not on the phone. Are girls all right. Can you come over. Frank left for work. My car is in the garage being serviced. Who is my father? Not that again. I have to find him. I have no idea where he is. Give me his name. I want to know everything you know about him. I need him. He does not know that you exist. He couldn't even speak English when we met. What language did he speak? Slovenian. He is probably dead. What was his last address? Maybe someone in the Slovenian club in Canberra knows about him. I called him Mick but they called him Mirko Gornik; Or something like that. I only knew him for a short time while I worked in the bank's Canberra branch. Did you always know that I was his daughter? Toni could not have children. Should I be grateful to mum and this man Mick or whatever his name is. I would not be here if they didn't, if it did not happen. I have to find Mick. Maybe it was meant to be. Maybe life is preordained. I hope someone is in charge. Once long ago mum said that she named me Mira after my father's mother. Now I know that she named me after my father.

Jana gets breakfast for the girls and walks with them to school. Thank God they have no idea. I want to buy time before they realise that their lives have changed forever. I feel paralysed. I need my father. Dad loved me; he kissed me goodbye although he didn't talk to mum. Only he knew that he wasn't my dad. Was mum jealous? Did she love him? She knew that he had no right to love me.

I ring mum again. What did dad say when you told him that I am not his daughter. Pause, silence. When did you tell him? Forget it. Forget Toni. He is nothing to you. You are lucky I got rid of the bastard before he could really ruin your life. What did he do? Thank God I stopped him. Actually Frank stopped him. What did you stop him from? Frank caught Toni touching you. Frank told me. I threatened to go to the police if Toni ever showed his face around you again. I don't believe you. He loved me. I want to talk to dad. I want to hear it from him. Toni didn't bother denying it. He just packed his bag and I never saw him again. So Frank moved in. We should all be grateful to Frank. I hate Frank. I want my real father.

'Mick went to Lightning Ridge years ago. Haven't heard from him for ages,' says the barman of the Slovenian club in Canberra when I ring.

'He hasn't got a phone on because he lives on the field,' says Lightning Ridge postmistress. I feel a little stronger knowing that somewhere on the Lightning Ridge opal fields is a man who is responsible for my being. Just knowing that my father exists is a comfort. I feel a little stronger. I try to convince myself that he will be delighted to meet me, his daughter.

I ring Jack's office. Henry wants to meet me after work. We have to talk. Where is Jack? I will tell you everything when we meet.

'I think Jack slept at Sonia's,' says Henry as we settle in the café. I almost feel relieved knowing that Jack and Sonia cheated before I did.

'He was heartbroken so Sonia offered him her spare room.'

'I know about Jack and Sonia,' I tell Henry. I saw the opal pendant in his pocket before he gave it to the bitch.

'He didn't,' says Henry. He kept it for me. I gave it to Sonia. I didn't dare bring it home because Barbara would raise hell if she found it. Sonia and I went away on business for a couple of days. I wanted to thank her for the extra work she did.'

'Oh, sure, did she do overtime in bed?'

'No, Sonia told me that she loves Jack. She always wanted Jack, but he loved you.'

'Where is Jack now?'

'I suppose he is recovering at Sonia's. Yesterday we decided to go for lunch so Jack went to get you. When he returned he was in shock. He got drunk so Sonia offered to drive him home,' says Henry.

'To her home. He is with her,' I confirm the fact to myself. I have to hear it again and again.

'I don't think they are sleeping together or anything like that. Jack is heartbroken. What exactly happened? I couldn't make any sense of him,' says Henry.

'Nothing. Nothing happened. It was nothing,' I keep on rubbing out the isolated minutes of my life. I ring Sonia and ask to speak to Jack. There is a pause. 'Just a minute.' I hear whispers from the other end. 'Jack does not want to talk to you.'

'I am coming over, you fucking slut.'

'Look who's talking. Bring Damian along as well.' Sarcasm, cold mocking condemnation. The bitch is victorious.

'You will never have Jack. He loves me,' I yell into the phone.

'Don't worry about me,' Sonia hangs up.

I have to pick the pieces of the family I broke in an insane moment. I have to beg for mercy from the one I believed had wrecked my family.

Damian comes to my office. We stare at each other like we have never seen each other before. Damian hugs me as I cry for Jack.

'I have never done it before,' I plead but it isn't Damian I should be pleading with.

'Did he?'

'I thought he did.'

'We'll work something out.'

'What could we possibly work out?'

'I thought you liked me.'

'Of course I like you. I always liked you.'

'Maybe it is for the best then. It's like I was waiting for you all my life. It was meant to happen.'

'What about the children?'

'They will get used to it in time. Children do these days. They grow up and go.'

I should be telling Damian to go away but I need someone to share my guilt. How many stupid reasons are there for people to stay together?

'We share so much,' says Damian. We remember the first buds of love that never had the opportunity to bloom; we reignited that first chapter of our lives with such ease. I am afraid that our story will end as abruptly as it began.

I ring Sonia again. 'I have to talk to Jack about the children. It is urgent.'

'I'll ask him,' concedes Sonia. I am waiting. 'He has nothing to say to you.'

'He will miss his daughters. We are his family.'

'I just decided that it is my time to make babies,' hisses Sonia.

'Our daughters will curse you for the rest of your life. You stole my family.'

'Jack's children will always be welcome in my home.'

I will kill Sonia. I need my father. In the afternoon I find Jack in his office. I ask for a few minutes of his time. I beg him not to tell the girls. They don't have to deal with it. 'Don't punish them. Do anything you like to me but don't punish our girls.'

'Should have thought about it before you spread your legs.'

I am not used to horrible words from my darling Jack. People these days don't take sex as seriously as they used to.

'It was only sex, for God's sake. I love you Jack. Yell at me, hit me, talk to me, I beg you, talk to me, we have a family.'

'No, we have no family. We don't exist anymore.'

'What about the girls? What will you tell them?'

'I'll leave it to you to tell them whatever you like. They'll hear about it; eventually they will figure it out. Nothing remains hidden forever so you better own up soon or you might lose them as well.'

'You want to take my children?'

'They can decide who they want to live with. Talk to my solicitor from now on.'

'I beg you to forgive me, it meant nothing, it will never happen again, please forgive me. Give us some time. It was nothing.'

'You risked our family for nothing?'

'I am sorry.'

'Give me some credit.'

'I love you.'

'You surely are not that callous.'

'I believed that you gave Sonia.'

'Oh, spare me the details. So you wanted to punish me before I had a chance to defend myself. My conscience is clear.

'I suspected.'

'If you can't trust me after twenty years... '

'You didn't tell me about the opal.'

'You didn't ask. I was tempted, surely I was tempted, but I would never do it to you. Now I can do as I like.'

The exchanged words are dancing on my grave. How could something so meaningless destroy everything we had? Sex is everywhere, it means nothing. Men can say that it meant nothing but women can't. What about equality? It had nothing to do with our family. I tell our girls that mummy and daddy have problems and that daddy found a room at Sonia's.

My girls mope around the house. I read it in their eyes that I am the criminal who wrecked the family. I want to pack the suitcase and escape. What would I put in a suitcase?

'Daddy came to see me at school, says Michelle. He wants us to stay with him for the weekend.'

'He can come home to be with you.'

'He does not want to, thanks to you.' Jane slams the door on my reasoning and the girls leave with an overnight bag.

What did Jack say, what does Jane know, who told her? I will have to explain one day but not now. There is no explanation just a guilty plea. Will Sonia tell them? Maybe Sonia is smarter than I am. Maybe she learned from my experience.

Damian keeps coming. I am grateful for his support. I have no sexual desire, no desire for personal survival, no need for wealth or fame or power or sex. I am not swayed in any particular direction. It meant nothing. It was nothing. I wanted to be loved. I did not feel loved enough. Jack was everything to me. We were everything to each other. Jack needs to be loved and Sonia loves him. I love him. The empty weekend is staring at me. I am not used to an empty house. I am not used to not being loved. At least I have Damian. I am reaching for the straw to save myself.

Meditation is a survival technique, I read somewhere. I go to bed and read the instructions. Close your eyes, relax, think of your toes and fingers relaxing. Breathe deeply, become aware of breathing; become alive within. Become an island happily nesting in the ocean, merge with eternity. Let peace descend. Become a part of a whole, wrap yourself into the blanket of the universe; of womanhood; nationhood, race hood, human hood, motherhood. Shield yourself against individuality.

I believed that Jack loved Sonia. Now he does.

I take a sleeping pill. And another. To make the time pass. Dreams are blurred thoughts. I am awake with my eyelids shut. I create visions of green valleys and birds and clear streams. Keep my eyes shut. No embarrassment, no anger, no jealousy no guilt. No Sonia. I force clear streams and birds and blue sky and the ocean behind my eyelids. I see mum and dad laughing, splashing in the ocean. Dad puts me on his shoulders to swim with him. Put her down, yells mum. She likes it, says dad. I said put her down. Mum's voice is angry. Why doesn't she let dad swim with me. Dad swims to the shore. He leaves soon after. The pictures are blurred. I open my eyes.

Come home Jack. It was nothing. I didn't mean to hurt you. I love you. I always loved you.

Damian is comforting me. He was comforting me before mum took me to Sydney boarding school; when she got rid of dad and took in Frank. Toni is not your real father, said mum. He is, I argued. I love daddy. Frank will be your father now. I hate Frank. Behave yourself.

I started smoking when mum left me at the boarding school. I smoked hiding in the toilets. Jack did not like me smoking so I stopped. Now it does not matter. I don't matter. I hold onto the packet of cigarettes like children hold onto their teddy bears. Damian smokes. Smoking is a sign of deterioration of one's life.

Like alcohol. Or drugs. Shame. Like adultery. Sin. Sex. I hide my sins. I pat a packet in my pocket. A promise of a better future. In the isolation I inhale and exhale and do it again and again until I become congested with the feeling of being OK. I have to escape. I need counselling; I need an anonymous stranger to take away my guilt. The receptionist schedules my appointment.

'I started smoking again,' I confess to Miss Smart counsellor of pouting lips and sexy voice who smiles professionally, patronisingly. Cool smile to fit her cool professional suit and stilettos. I hate her. Oh, be sensible, how can I hate a stranger? She makes notes. I have to be careful. Can the councillor recommend the removal of my children from my custody? I haven't been to a confession since I left Linden. I need to confess. Careful. I must not cry. Stability, control, balance. I pat the pack of cigarettes in my pocket and think of the rosy future when I will inhale again.

'I want to find my father,' I say. I came to confess infidelity. Everybody's infidelity. I need to repair my family. Stay cool and in control. I always wanted to find my father. Why did I change my mind?

'Have you ever met your father?'

'I had a father but he wasn't my real father. Mum was unfaithful to him.

'When did she tell you?

'When she packed him out of our lives.'

'Why?

'I don't know. She wanted Frank.'

'Do you like Frank?'

'We hate each other.' You are lucky that Frank saved you, said mum. Frank told me.'

'Did your dad harm you?'

'He loved me.'

'Why now?'

'I need him. Now.'

'Why now?'

'My husband left me. He is with his secretary,' I begin to cry. It is easier to confess Jack's sins. Mum's sins. Frank's sins.

The perfectly young attractive, intelligent, successful psychologist hands me a tissue box. I sniff hard, take a deep breath, and recover control and balance. What would this perfect stranger know? Is she only pretending to be perfect? Are we all pretending all the time so the world can only see perfection? Do we all hide our flaws?

On the way home I think about Jack. He is my husband, my friend, my lover, the father of our children, a breadwinner, a storyteller, a driver, a holiday-maker, a gardener, a comforter, a cheerleader. Jack is the proof of my perfect marriage, my loving family, my life. I want Jack to protect our warm nest for our children's children; I want him to have Sunday dinners with our grandchildren's families.

I only had sex with Damian. Jack only had sex with Sonia. If he did. It was a fling if it was, a dare, an adventure… Insanity. Shooting star, shining one minute and dead the next.

I buy a bottle of vodka on the way home.

I don't know what hurts more; Jack with Sonia or him not loving me.

'Jack was in shock. He would wrap himself around a dead cat for comfort,' said Henry. He probably fell asleep in Sonia's arms.' He should fall asleep in my arms. Vodka gently obscures the respectable public life. I am a tiny speck within the universe. My senses are dulled into oblivion. Life is more than my senses. I believe that I have a purpose greater than I can perceive with my senses. My body and my soul are greater than my understanding of it. The perfection of my hands, the vision of my eyes, the enormity of my dreaming, longing, knowing...My soul is reaching into dimensions unseen by human eye. I feel emotions not caused by my humanity. I hurt less. I sip vodka. There is nothing to be afraid of. God of my childhood visits. My father tells me fairy tales. It does not matter who is my father. I hover above the meaningless events. Sinful, calculating world disappears. Jack and Sonia don't matter.

Sober again I separate myself from the universe and become afraid. Sober I become a mother, a wife, an unfaithful wife, an undeserving mother. Irresponsible and unreasonable. Scared. I abandoned my respectability for a moment; I am paying the price.

The girls go to school I go to work, garbage has to be put out, toilet flushed, washing hung up, dinner cooked. Wipe, wipe, stir, stir; I turn on automatic to fit in the scheme of things. I escape into the garden to smoke so the girls would not have to deal with a bad role model.

'I am going to Lightning Ridge for a few days,' says Damian. 'Want to come?' Damian does not know that Lightning Ridge is a place where my father is waiting for me. I should not touch this last fantasy.

'What's there,' I balance my words.

'Actually it is quite unique place with adventurers from all over the world. You only need luck to get rich in Lightning Ridge. Miners believe that they are due for their fair share of luck,' Damian continues his advertisement speech for opal fields.

'Dream on.'

'Get rich so everybody will love you and want your money,' laughs Damian.

'People might get the wrong idea,' I say. 'I am deep enough as it is.'

'Isn't it best to be up front with the situation? Life goes on.' It is a school holiday and my girls are staying with Jack and

Sonia. I might as well go. The people I love have to readjust to the changed situation. It happened so fast. So unintended. Unplanned. Like it happened to someone else.

'Let me think about it,' I promise Damian.

People, who loved me, changed. I only knew Jack that was in love with me; Jack who was a part of me and my family. Jack who lives with Sonia is a stranger. I don't know Jack who hates me. The magic of love seeped through our fingers. We are left with clenched fists. My children try to please Jack and Sonia.

My mother sent me away because I loved Toni, my father; the man I believed was my father, the man who loved me. Who is my father? What was in the seed that joined my mother's egg on that fateful trip to Canberra? Did the seed of that sinful adventure plant a dimension of himself into me?

Did the man who loved me until I was fourteen know that I wasn't the fruit of his seed? Did he love me despite not being his seed; or because I wasn't. More than he should? More than my mother would allow him to? More than was appropriate for a father that wasn't a real father? Did he try to convince himself that he was my real father? Or my lover. Did he want to become a part of me?Did mum get rid of Toni because he loved me? Or because she loved Frank. Was I conceived in lust or love? Did mum have sex with an unknown man to give her husband a child to love? Did she want a child? Did Toni want a child? Did mum fall in love with the man in Canberra? Did that man reject her?

Is there anything called love? Being loved. Loving in return. Mutuality of feeling. Paid for. Returned. Exchanged. Did God prescribe the formula? Every living thing is competing for the right to mate and multiply; for the right to create and be God. The desirable is always at the same distance from me as I travel in my orbit unable to change the course? Maybe one day my daughters will understand and forgive. I don't blame my mother any more. She must have had her reasons.

The drive to Lightning Ridge is monotonous; mirages of great waters stretch into the vastness of the flat land, desolate trees look like a forest in front of us but as we come near we realise that the lonely trees are scattered in the dry land. The water was a mirage; untouched, almost barren countryside is all around; a ridge with white mullock heaps of clay opal dirt greet us at the end.

'So you call this a tourist resort.'

'People become feral in the bush. They like that about Lightning Ridge.' We stay at the Black opal motel right in the middle of the town. We settle into the basic room within a hearing distance of Digger's rest hotel.

'I feel so free here,' says Damian next morning as we speck for shiny bits of opal on the diggings. There are white clay mullocks in the desert-like countryside.

'The distance and the vastness make me forget,' says Damian.

'Forget what?'

'Constraints people place on each other in close proximity. Here you don't have to dress up or behave in any particular way. Nobody to impress. Maybe miners escaped from those they had to impress.'

'Could you live like that?'

'I would like to try.' An isolated cloud sprinkles the white opal dirt.

'Just what we need for opal to shine,' says Damian. 'It saves us licking the dust off the potch.'

'Do you know anyone here?'

'Nobody knows anyone here. Not really know. I met Peter when I was last here. He was born in Holland, grew up in Indonesia, married in America, and got divorced in Sydney. Everybody is different here. Even if you spend years with a guy, you still don't know what's going on behind the colour of his eyes. And that's just how I like it, said Peter.'

'Makes everybody the same kind of different.'

'A bunch of refugees. Multiculture.'

'Refuges must have a common bond. Like Aborigines.'

'You don't owe anyone anything. You don't even have to like or be liked. It does not matter.'

'Tell me about your family,' I say.

'Dad died a few years ago. You remember my mother. She was the important person in our family. She was the principal of our school and the sergeant of our home. You are the same as your father, mum was scolding me once. Dad winked at me. I was glad. I loved my father.'

'Men against women.'

'I learned from dad to please and obey.'

'Dad loved me,' I say without thinking. Damian does not need to know that Toni wasn't my father; Toni loved me while he was my father.

'Mum was never happy with dad and me,' says Damian. 'Mum was German, proper and industrious. I was afraid of her; maybe I didn't get married because I was afraid of women.'

'We grew up almost like brother and sister,' I say as I pick another shiny opal chip.

'I always liked you.'

'I worshiped you.'

'Why?'

'You were older, stronger and wiser. I felt that you liked me.'

'I think I was in love with you. You were so soft and cute.'

'I never thought that we would meet again.'

'Life is full of surprises. Hardly worth planning.'

'What is meant to happen and all that...'

We travel in our thoughts silently. If only I did not go to bed with Damian. If only I never found that opal pendant. If mum did not sleep with that man Mirko I would never know life. My soul would have no body. Is there a reason for everything? How could mum betray my father? He would never know the joy of being a father if she didn't. Maybe I should be grateful to mum. Maybe mum was afraid of dad's loving me. Maybe everything is as it should be. So much unknown. My two fathers and my mother complete strangers now.

Jack knows me; he knows what gives me pleasure, he knows how to love me; he stopped loving me.

'Lightning Ridge certainly is different.'

'People of different colours speak different languages but they smile the same friendly smile.'

'The colour of opal is the only colour that matters here.'

'Miners claim that they have equal chance to find opal,' says Damian.

Aborigines swagger aimlessly on the street, women with children in their prams, lots of semi black children. White women rush with urgency and purpose; miners are covered in opal dirt, fat women in shorts are miners' wives. The slim women work in offices and dress elegantly. It doesn't matter how you dress. Nothing seems to matter if no-one knows you. You don't expect anything from anybody. People who don't matter can't hurt you.

To me, mum was always this sensible, old, practical grown up; clever and well dressed. Respected. Dad must have loved her enough to accept another man's child as his own. I never heard mum and dad argue. I never saw mum cry. Do men cry? Mum must have been young and beautiful and loveable once. We had a loving home until Frank came and loving became inappropriate. We were a happy family until mum told dad to go. I was cut clean away from loving until I met Jack. I was grieving in that boarding school when Frank moved in with mum. Frank and his smelly, saliva dripping, mongrel dog. I hate Frank.

I am glad I caught him in time. Mum's words follow me. If it wasn't for Frank the bastard might still be around. Ruin your life. I told him that I will go to the police if he ever showed his face again. We should all be grateful to Frank.

Maybe mum and dad agreed for mum to be inseminated by another man so they could have a child. Did they do it because they loved each other?Did Frank lie that dad touched me inappropriately so he and his dog could move in with mum?

Mum once said that Frank paid more attention to his dog than to her. Frank and mum laughed at that so it must have been a joke. Loving a dog is funny but loving another man's child is evil. Was mum ever jealous of that saliva dripping mongrel? Did she feel loved enough?How can I explain to my daughters why I had sex with Damian? They don't know that Damian and I share the first dreams, the first loving, unspoken yet and unknowing yet, but forever written on the snow white pages of our childhood. I did not feel loved enough; I was afraid that Jack loved Sonia. I needed to attach myself to something for protection. It just happened that Damian was there. Maybe it would be easier to say that I was drunk.

'Let's go to the pub. I feel like an ice block melting in the heat,' says Damian. We go to Diggers Rest hotel. The motel maid tells us that respectable patrons drink at the other end of town but we don't care.

'Can you lend me a couple of dollars?' says an Aboriginal girl as we step into the dark smoke filled bar. I stop in surprise. I never spoke to an Aborigine before. Bold and defiant dark woman-girl. Fairly drunk. Obviously in need of another beer. I am intrigued. I have never been approached by anyone like that. Is she of legal age? Begging. Sunburnt hair-ends split, lips chaffed, hands fidgeting. Grey blue eyes. Skin the colour of milk coffee. Her strong long teeth shine out of the dark face. Yellow teeth really from up close. Clothes smelling from moth balls. Vinnie's shop. Not washed. Second hand. Not ironed.

Have a seat; I'll get you a drink.' I volunteer out of curiosity. What will you have? The girl seems suspicious of my unpredictable generosity.

'My name is Mira,' I offer my hand.

'Mia,' says the girl, shy all of a sudden. She is clearly not comfortable with my friendliness.

'Lovely name. Where does it come from?'

'After Pop.'

'How old are you,' I ask. You can ask the girl who is begging for money. She is way down in the abyss. Do I feel an affinity with the people in the abyss?

'Twenty-two,' says Mia lifting her eyes to see if I believe her. She looks seventeen but then Aborigines may age differently.

'All on your own?'

'Kids are at school.'

'You have children?'

'I had my twin girls when I was fifteen and I have two boys. That's it for me,' she suddenly cheers up expressing her decision to take control of her fertility.

'Your husband with you,' I try to get to know this unusual person.

'No,' she quietly dismisses the father of her children.

'Where do you live?'

'Got a house from Aboriginal housing. Four bedrooms. Twins like to sleep in the same room.'

Mira is shooting glances at a group of Aborigines; she probably wants them to rescue her.

Damian brings three more beers to prolong company. He winks at me.

'Where you from?'

'Rovena,' I say.

'This is my pop,' says Mia as the man with a walking stick comes to our table. With the beer and her pop at the table she relaxes. Damian gets another beer for Pop. Pop offers us opal for sale. Direct from the miner, the lowest price, will not get it cheaper anywhere, will take us to his mine tomorrow to show where it was dug out from, will make a BBQ, will tell us all about mining. All this within the ten minutes of our meeting. Instant like sex.

'Some say that opal brings bad luck.'

'Only when you lose it or brake it,' says Mick, Mia's grandfather.

'Mick,' calls a man from the bar. Wanted on the phone.

'Mirko Gornik come to the phone please,' comes through the speakers. I forget to close my mouth.

There are people and voices and movement around me. I feel stunned. This is my father, my origin, the invisible semen joined with my mother's egg in a night of illegitimate lust or love or oblivion. Is this what a father is supposed to be? Would I ever be able to feel something for this old man hobbling with a stick so people take pity on him and buy him a beer? Would this opal miner know what love is? I don't think so. Would it be appropriate for me to put my head on his shoulder and listen to him reading fairy tales? If he can read. Probably not.

It was just one night, mum dismissed my inquiry about my real dad. I wander how that one night came about. Could she explain how she chose a man to become my father?

'Want to come down the mine tomorrow,' my real father invites Damian.

'I'd be real grateful for a chance,' says Damian.

Damian and Mick are making arrangements for tomorrow's mining partnership.

'Have to go,' says my niece Mia. I can't take my eyes from my niece.

'Are you OK?' Damian is concerned.

'Maybe a slight sun stroke,' I say confused.

'We'll be going after breakfast. About eight. See you tomorrow then,' calls Mick as he follows Mia.

Did my real father invite us to mine with him and eat with him because he loves me? Does blood call out and tell who to love appropriately.

'New in town,' says a barmaid as we are about to leave.

'Just passing through.'

'Don't bet on it,' says the miner at the bar. 'Opal bug gets you and you get hooked on mining.'

'Did Mick sell you a claim yet,' says another man.

'Is Mick selling claims?' Asks Damian.

'He is always dealing and wheeling. He'd sell his own daughter to make a buck.'

'Really,' laughs Damian.

'Where does he get claims,' asks Damian.

'He has his ears to the ground. When there is a new rush, he pegs and registers. When someone drills and finds opal nearby he sells his claims. You can only have two claims registered to your name but Mick has a tribe of Aborigines and uses their names. Each miner is supposed to work in every mine eight hours a day but nobody checks that.'

'Mick convinces tourists that there are millions in his claims,' says another miner.

'Is he a crook?'

'Somewhere between a gambler and a crook. Capable of just about anything to make a buck.'

'Ever been in jail.'

'Not that kind of a crook. He'll sweet talk you into deals that pay for him.'

'Mick never misses on a tourist. The locals are harder to catch.'

Was mum in love with this man once? Was Mick in love? Are men in love the way women are? Maybe being in love is just an urge to make babies. Maybe they were both drunk. Like mother, like daughter

'Have a chop, you'll need the strength for digging,' says Mick as we arrive in the morning. Lamb chops are grilled outside on a grid iron. People with bread in their hands stand around covered in smoke.

'Have some brekkie,' encourages Mia.

'I never eat in the morning,' I say.

'You never go mining either. You have to eat for strength.'

'You'll need proper shoes to go down the ladder,' says Mick. He brings worn out boots for Damian and me.

'You have to have a helmet these days as well. Regulations, you know. Not like in the olden days. We used to go down on a rope; didn't even have ladders.'

'These are my boys,' Mick introduces two middle aged semi black men.

Peter nods an introduction. He is tall and good looking man but definitely shy. Sam, the smaller of the two moves his head in acknowledgement. He seems scared, hiding behind Peter. Smaller and darker. Both older than I. Both blue eyed like Mick. Like myself. Dark as their mother. I am pale like my mother.

'Want some old jeans,' a woman comes from the house next door.

'That's Olga, Mia's mum,' says Mick.

'Russian name?' says Damian. Olga, my older sister. Curly sunburnt blondish hair and olive skin.

'I'll be right,' I say.

'You can put them over so as not to get grease from the ladder on your slacks.' I don't want to offend Olga so I accept.

'How many children?' says Damian to Mick.

'About ten as far as I know,' laughs Mick. I think he is boasting. 'And then there are about fifty grandchildren and more great grandchildren.'

'Must be two hundred of us when we all get together,' says Mia.

'Who knows how many strays dad left all over Australia where he was working,' winks Olga. As if she knew that I was one of those poor left behind children-strays. '

'I am an only child,' I tell Mia. 'My parents came from England.'

I was a centre-stage and never dethroned by siblings. No rivalry. Totally loved, totally abandoned. No compromise, no middle way, no hand me downs, no giving way, no comparing. I always envied big families. Now I have one huge family. They will never know that I am one of them. We have nothing in common. I am still an only child of Scottish-English parents. Mum and dad must have loved each other very much once. They eloped and escaped to Australia to be together. I wonder why they had to escape to be together.

'Strength in numbers. Kinships are important to Aborigines. Minorities usually multiply more to balance the power. Migrants and Aborigines,' whispers Damien.

'I am neither of the above, I am an isolated event. Not even a minority.' We chip into the clay wall and become excited when the glassy sound tells us that I hit silica.

'I found it,' I squeal delighted. Mick hands me a screwdriver to dislodge a purple glassy stone from the clay without breaking it. He sits behind me on the ground almost touching my back as he guides me into gouging. I am mining in my real father's opal mine. His arms are around me guiding me towards the fortune. This is as close as we will probably ever come. Dirty and exhausted with pockets full of worthless nobbies and bits of colour we return to Mick's place.

Damian brings a carton of beer. People gather under the cedar tree. My brothers make the fire to sizzle sausages for lunch. My sisters bring salads and garlic bread and dips and finger food. Where did they learn to arrange the food so well? Boys and girls run around; they fight and swear at each other. My nephews and nieces, great nephews and nieces. Nobody ever swore in my home.

Mick tells about the opals he found and the money he spent.

'He could've bought half the town at one stage,' says Olga. I don't know if she is boasting or complaining.

'Instead he put it on horses,' laughs Peter. I notice that Peter's shyness evaporated after a couple of stubbies of beer. They put the music on loud and begin singing with the old westerners. What have migrants and Aborigines to do with the songs written and composed by American Country and Western singers? Maybe romantic, sad love songs and beer, go together in any language.

'Easy come easy go. I found it one day and blew it the next,' explains Mick.

'You are a bit of a gambler,' Damian turns to Mick.

'Dad would never let any of us go hungry. He always put the food on the table,' says Olga to me.

I am half-drunk from one stubby of beer. Relaxed and sisterly. Have another. I look around. Others are on the way to oblivion. Perhaps the slur of their voices is an Aboriginal dialect. Second beer tastes better. Olga puts her arm around me and we both sing.

'Is your mum with you,' I ask.

'She lives in Bourke. Got a rich farmer now,' explains Olga.

'How many children did she have with Mick?'

'Mum and dad married proper in church, says Olga. They were both very young. I am the oldest and then there is Peter and Sam. Justine was the youngest named after dad's sister. She is an Aboriginal art curator for the national gallery. Her picture was in the paper.'

'Did your parents get divorced?'

'Not really. Mum moved in a caravan after Steve was born. She moved in with Martin, dad's best friend. Actually mum had Steve with a German bloke and then she moved in with Martin. Mum and Martin had four boys but they all kept my dad's name. Mum's niece Rachel then moved in with dad. Mum had three more children and dad had four with Rachel. He also took Rachel's two children from before as his own. We have always been friends, all of us kids. Rachel later died in an accident.

I cannot follow the names or the events.

'So many mouths to feed,' says Damian joining us. Maybe Damian does not feel like one of the boys quite yet but he might. He is an adventurer. I don't know a grown up Damian. I only know the boy Damian who was my friend.

'It was hard when we were young and without welfare but dad always found a way. Sometimes he took us on the farm where he was cotton chipping or stick picking or fence mending and he made sure that the farmer fed us all. Later he organised Aborigines to work for him and he made contracts for fencing and grid making. He'd bring boxes of grog and they would drink until they spent every dollar they earned. Aborigines weren't allowed to drink in them days but dad brought drinks for them into the bush and they loved it. They played cards and lost whatever money they had left. Aborigines loved dad. They built water tanks hundreds of kilometres around.'

'Have you ever met any of your dad's relations?'

'He has a brother Janez, a big shot in Canberra. Janez is a builder and sometimes he would give dad a job to tie us over. Sometimes dad would be gone for months but he always sent money to us.'

And on one of those trips he slept with my mother. He created me, a stray. How did he meet mum? How could mum go to bed with this complete stranger? A man who didn't even speak English. People these days pretend that colour does not matter; that all races and cultures are the same. But mum knows that she is better than others. To her being English is like a seal of approval. She corrected my words every day so I learned to speak properly but she slept with a man who still does not speak proper English.

'Dad always looked after us real well. There was always food on the table,' Olga repeats herself; perhaps all drunks do.

'Have you ever met your uncle in Canberra?'

'Dad had an accident in the mine a few years ago. I went with him to hospital in Canberra. I saw his brother's family.'

'What are they like?'

'Real stuck up. They never spoke to me but they gave dad some money. They think that their shit does not smell. Janez has a wife and four children. They looked at me like I was a monkey in a zoo.'

'Have you been to their home?'

'They never invited me but dad was. Very rich and posh they are. They don't want to know us; they are ashamed of us,' says Olga. 'Big-noting themselves. Wogs. Up themselves.'

So I have cousins in Canberra. Will I ever meet my uncle? Dad always finds a way to put food on the table, Olga's words follow me. I never associated food with luck or love or goodness. I never knew what it was like not to be able to pick and choose my food. I was considered a good girl if I ate my food.

'We all look out for each other,' says Olga, my black drunk sister. What is a sister? How lucky I am that nobody knows that Mick is my father. I don't have to know this weird family. I don't have to remember all the ins and outs of their relationships. My black family. I wonder if mum ever knew what family she connected me with. I am happy I am not like them. People laugh at drunken Aborigines. Nobody laughs at me.

'Did Mick ever go back to Europe?'

'Once. Brought back a video. Real nice place. Like a postcard. Lots of mountains and rivers squeezed in between. So green. 'Not many people know where Slovenia is. I looked it up on the map.' Alps.'

'Why do I feel jealous? My father never showed me the video and explained where my Slovenian relations live. I will never know how they live and think. My father will never know that I am his daughter. I don't want to be his daughter. I am ashamed of him and his family. I can go to Slovenia if and when I like. I'd rather go to England and visit mum's family. Only she tells me that she lost touch with her relations.

'Since the accident dad has a bad leg,' continues Olga. 'When he is on opal he forgets about it but when he is broke he takes a stick and hobbles to the pub. People buy him a beer,' laughs Olga. No shame in begging or hobbling. No pride. Mum would die of shame if she saw a man she once slept with.

'He would do anything for his family,' says Olga. 'When mum left, dad brought the food home and cooked it for us.' It is obvious that all these people love Mick. They are actually proud of their dad.

'I think Damian is already hooked on opal,' I say to Olga.

'We all grew up with opal. We started specking as soon as we started walking,' says Olga.

'Where did your parents meet?'

'Mum was born here. Dad came as a nineteen year old from Slovenia.'

'Why did he come here?'

'He did not speak a word of English so it was easier for him to work on his own. Or with his own people. He escaped from Hitler or Tito or something. We've all been baptised because they Catholics where dad comes from.'

Olga's voice is Aboriginal, I decide. She leaves out the unnecessary words. Is this from her migrant father or from her Aboriginal mother.

'Do you go to church?'

'Dad never either.' So Mick is Catholic. I am Anglican brought up by Catholic nuns. They all teach Jesus love. They all pray Lord's Prayer in parliament before question time. What is the difference? So many branches of the same Jesus. So much politics. Do they all believe in God? What do I believe? I call on God in my despair, I thank him for exquisite joys. Mick had his children baptised; he will need a priest for a funeral.

'You are lucky to have such a big family,' I try to be positive.

'Dad is very proud of all of us.' I wonder what there is to be proud of.

'Your family still in Slovenia,' I turn to Mick, my father.

'Can't keep track of where they are.'

'His parents died in the war,' tells Olga.

'How?'

'In 1943, I was about fourteen, my school friends and I became partisans,' Mick begins his story. 'One night we sneaked out and went into hiding. Dad reported to German police that partisans took me. Dad was in a wheelchair and terrified of

Germans. They captured us but let me go as a favour to dad who reported us.'

'Was dad working for Germans?'

'He could not work for anybody; he could not even walk but he was more scared of Germans than of partisans.'

'Which side was he on?'

'It wasn't like that. Men were taken. They had no choice. Some were taken by Germans others were taken by partisans. I had no idea who was who. Or what they were fighting for. Mum was a pious woman and the priest told her that partisans were communists who hated God. She was terrified of Germans because they burned homes and shot the families that supported partisans.'

'She was between the brick wall and the hard place,' I smile listening to my father.

'Anyway,' continues Mick. 'My friend, Tone, our neighbour, escaped from Germans. The next morning he came to our home. Mum showed him a chair at the table and invited him to eat with us. She didn't even know that he was with me when Germans caught us. Tone stood there for a moment without saying a word. I remember him looking at me as I lifted my head and carried the beans and sauerkraut to my mouth. We locked eyes somehow before he pulled out a gun from under his coat and aimed. We froze; it was unreal; nobody moved or said anything. I still keep seeing it all in a slow motion. He shot mum in the chest. Her blood sprinkled the food and our faces. I sat next to mum and I wiped mum's blood from my face in an automatic movement. Tone made a step forward and shot her again in the head. Mum's head fell on the table. He then turned around and saw dad in his wheelchair in the corner and said: traitor, as he shot him. Tone was gone before we began screaming. I ran for the doctor but both my parents were dead, of course. Relations and farmers took my younger brothers and sisters as servants to earn their keep until they were old enough to look after themselves. One of them, my brother in Canberra, even became a carpenter. He is a top man in Canberra. A builder. Built half of Canberra I believe. Whenever we were short I'd go to Canberra and he'd find work for me.'

'Do you write home?'

'I used to send money to them when they were little but later we lost touch.'

'What else do you remember about home?'

'I remember being hungry before the war and during the war. We ate fast because we were scared that there will not be enough. Mostly we ate beans and sauerkraut.'

'Now we eat fast food fast and feel guilty because we eat more than is good for us. We work less and eat more and we can afford to eat what we like. We are growing fat and unhappy,' I blabber. I look at this strange, old, blue eyed, blond, greying, tall and slightly bent man, my father. He must have been handsome forty years ago. I recognize the shape of the face. I inherited his eyes and his eyebrows. I watch for little familiar gestures. I spy with my little eye; I am looking at my self -image. I am afraid that somebody will spot the resemblance.

'I am surprised that you did not marry a Slovenian girl.'

'What Slovenian girl? When I came to Australia migrants were men. Twenty men to one woman. Fifty Slovenian men to one single Slovenian girl.'

'Lucky women,' I smile.

'Men were so jealous they would not let their women out of sight.'

'Poor men.'

'We were so young and no girls. English girls were so up themselves. They laughed at us because we didn't speak English,' says Mick. I wonder if Mick ever spoke of these things with anyone before.

'Many men have Pilipino wives,' I add.

'They do now but in them days Pilipino girls weren't allowed to Australia. White Australia policy. Pilipino did not count as white. They are lovely women, Filipinos; polite, hardworking; religious and obedient. A lot of lonely old men go there now to find a young girl for a wife.'

'What about your brother.'

'He brought a beautiful Slovenian girl with him. She cried every time I came down to Canberra.'

'Why?'

'My brother treats her like dirt. I think he is scared to lose her so he acts like a sergeant to keep her down.'

'Why doesn't she leave? Plenty of fish in the sea.'

'They have a family. Kids have no other relations so they stuck together.'

'They have you.'

'They don't really want to know my family. Not good enough for them.' I feel sorry for my father. Mick convinces Damian to stay a few more days. He might find red on black. I am glad that Damian and Mick get along.

'You never know what's behind the next slab of clay dirt,' says Mick. Stories go on and on about someone who left the mine only to leave the gem just centimetres from the surface. Damian convinces me to stay a few more days. It is going to be Mick's birthday and everybody will be there. I bet Mick hopes to sell a claim to Damien. Damian hopes that eventually we will become opal miners. Opal with bad luck attached. I want to know more about my father.

'What can I bring,' I ask Olga the day before Mick's birthday party.

'Men bring drinks.'

'What would he like as a present?'

'You mean a cake or something?' Olga considers my question.

'Anything.'

'You don't have to though. Women bring food. We all pitch in.'

'What sort of cake?'

'It does not matter. He'll probably let little ones have it. That's how he is.' They all come; men carry cartons of beer or bottles of wine; women bring food. Nobody takes notice of Damian and me or our donations. We blend in. How will I ever be a daughter to this strange man who has a family of two hundred? There is no time to get to know all that life connects us with. Part of me wants to escape while the other part wants to anonymously attach itself to Mick's family.

'We could start our new life here,' smiles Damien.

'I have a business and my family in Rovena.'

'We'll see how we go,' says Damian.

'Lightning Ridge is truly multicultural,' I venture. There is hardly a reason for discrimination where one is as different as another.' What do I know about prejudice or discrimination; I never had a reason to feel prejudiced or discriminated against.

Damian finds an opal. He wants me to have it for an engagement ring. We are not engaged but I accept his expression of love. We decide to stay in Lightning Ridge for another week. I rang Jack and arranged for our daughters to stay with him and Sonia. Will I ever stop aching for my family? Will they get used to live in a broken family?The events follow an invisible script. Damian is mining with my father. I spend a morning in a motel room watching erotic videos. I cannot sleep so I take a tranquiliser. I feel balanced until the effect of the tablet wears off. I have to find a substance that will keep me permanently cheerful. I want to dance and sing with total abandon like Mick's family does. I don't really want to be like my Aboriginal sisters who begin a day with a stubby of beer. Maybe their happiness only lasts as long as the beer. Mia begged for money from a stranger. How low is that? She did not know that I am her aunt. She will never know. I have never been asked for money from a complete stranger. I am ashamed of my family. Damian tells me that he loves me and I tell him that I love him. We make love. I took a bite of the apple I might as well eat it. I ache for my family.

I join Mick's children under the cedar tree. We smoke and laugh and tell yarns. I don't have to impress anyone. Nobody cares what I do. Mick and Damian return from work and grab a beer each before they settle in a family circle.

Next morning I watch the evangelists on television. It is Sunday, a day of prayer.

'Jesus will prepare the table for you among your enemies,' promises the elegant, eloquent preacher. People buy Jesus manuals. Millions of books are written about Jesus. Video, audio and donations to Jesus merchants who love themselves in their spotless preacher outfits driving their faultless preacher's limousines.

'Your sin will find you out,' said the Lord. My sin follows me into my dreams. Love your enemies, says the preacher. Sonia is my enemy. I dream of an ideal world in which Sonia is dead and Jack loves me. Does Satan work in mysterious ways like God?The more I panic the more I subscribe to Jesus and then I blush and then I try to love my neighbour. And make a fool of myself in the presence of Jesus all over again. I hate Sonia. I wish her dead. Jack and I were in heaven until she tore us apart. I never stopped loving Jack; I just gave in to nostalgia. Sex has nothing to do with love. I move but do not feel alive. I don't know where I am going. When a queen ant dies the colony of ants moves without direction until they choose a new queen. Is keeping life alive the only purpose of life?

'You will find Jesus when he brings you down to your knees,' says the preacher on TV. We met. Jesus and I. I am suitably scared. I smile into the mirror. People smile to cover the murder in their hearts. I was born as a mistake.

'Opal bug got Damian,' says Mick. 'Why don't you stay? I have a spare room until you find something.'

Damien stays but I return home. I need to decide what kind of future I want. I love Jack and Damian. Can one woman love two men? Can Jack love me and Sonia? Sex became a national sport yet one moment of sex destroyed the lives of everyone I love. A mad moment of sex? Is there a way to erase this event? People commit crimes while intoxicated and the judge takes their intoxication in consideration. No intent. Damien and I were intoxicated by the wine and memories. I plead diminished responsibility.

My daughter Jana began university studies in Sydney. Eliza wants to live with her and do year twelve in Sydney as well. Natasha seems as happy with me as with Jack and Sonia. Jack, Sonia and I compete with affection and she laps it up. She cried at the beginning but she adjusted. She is loved enough.

Jack and I decide to put our house on the market. I remember the heady romantic days when we bought it. I was twenty and pregnant with Jana. We spent twenty happy years in this house. Neither of us needs a reminder of the past.

Twenty years ago a letter came from a solicitor informing me that my English grandfather left me a small fortune. Jana was a year old and I was pregnant with Eliza. Why did Granddad leave everything to a grandchild he never met? Jack and I did not need the money so I put it in the trust account for my girls. Maybe that's how generations get linked. I told mum about the money. 'I know,' she said flatly. 'Why didn't he leave the money to you?' 'He punished me because Toni and I escaped to Australia.' Escaped from what?' 'The bastard.' 'What did he do?' 'Forget him.' 'Tell me about him.' 'Nothing to tell.'

So much unknown in one family.

Mum and Frank must have been furious. People insist that they don't expect to inherit anything but one can't help to feel jealous and angry and sad when left out. Is the size of inheritance a measure of love? Maybe mum did not feel loved enough or loved appropriately. Are we ever loved enough?

Barbara and I go Christmas shopping as I return from Lightning Ridge.

'People spend money they don't have to buy things they don't need to impress people they don't like,' Jana quotes someone.

'I have no-one to impress.'

'Always a missing ingredient. Life is like that,' sighs Barbara.

'Life is an enemy.'

'Sexually transmitted and terminal,' laughs Barbara.

'Keeps the food chain unchanged.'

'Every link is bent on destroying the chain.'

'Nobody is safe.'

It is imprinted on every living thing to multiply and fill the earth.

'People call this love.'

'We don't know what animals call it.'

'An eye meets its image and the romance is born.'

'Romance is a high. Nobody is high all the time. The higher you are the harder you fall.'

'Everybody wants to be loved more than they are and more than they deserve.'

'Maybe one should not wish to be the shiniest star.'

'But one does.'

Damian rings that he and Mick are on colour. Opal fever really got my easy going adventurer. He never opened a business in Rovena. He let his house to tenants and went opal mining. Maybe opal really brings bad luck. It all started to go wrong when I found that opal pendant in Jack's pocket.

Damian once said that he wants at least three children. How can I have three babies at forty? It is so unfair. Men can have babies into the old age but women have to be young. Was Damian joking? Was he joking about waiting for me as well? Did he think I wanted to hear him say that he was waiting for me? Am I so naïve? How many times did Damian say those words to how many women? How many times did he make love to different women in the middle of a sunny afternoon? He is used to being single. He was single all his life. He survived on take away food and take away sex?Is he sleeping with my black sisters or their daughters now? Does he buy them a beer before they consent to have sex with him?I don't know how to be single. I have never been single. I stopped being a child when I became a wife and mother.

'Mick and I finally found a nice patch of opal. We are going overseas to look at the opal market,' says Damian on the phone. He rings every day.

'Lucky you.'

'Mick wants to visit his sister in Slovenia as well. She is dying apparently. I might stop in Germany to see where mum was born. Would you come with us?'

'Have you forgotten that I have children?'

'Would they like to come as well?'

'They go to school.'

Eliza and Jana are boarding but Natasha should come.

'She would miss school.'

'She will learn more on the trip than at school. I would also like to go to Disneyland. I missed out when I was little. She would keep me company.'

'Don't tempt me.'

'Hawaii is nice this time of the year.'

'I am not prepared.'

'What is there to prepare. Think of it as a business venture. You can keep us organised. Say you will come. Consider it my Christmas present.'

'When?'

'We have this trace. Gem colour. As soon as we dig it out we will start cutting. Come up and we will celebrate together.'

'Maybe after Christmas.'

'We can plan the itinerary while you are here,' says Damian. Going home with my father! The idea excites and frightens me. It is not my idea. Was it written? Was my infidelity part of a bigger plan? Whose plan?People who loved me don't love me anymore. I need to be loved. I need Damian.

Girls spend Christmas Eve with me. We go to the evening mass like we used to when we were a family. We were not regular church goers but Christmas Eve mass became a tradition. The magic of growing up and Jesus born every year. The girls hum Christmas carols. We drive through town to look at the lights and the decorations before we go home to open presents and pretend to be delighted. We remember the excitements of other years, the Barbie dolls, the first bikes, the Nintendo, the first make up.

'We are going to Sydney tomorrow,' says Jana. They are going with their daddy and Sonia. I don't want to know about Jack and Sonia's plans.

'I will go to Lightning Ridge,' I announce. Nobody is interested in my plans. I spent my whole life building fences around my home and then in a moment of madness all the boundaries collapsed. There are new adventures in front of my daughters; they don't want to look back yet. Do children and their parents ever really get to know each other?

'We might as well spend what we found,' says Damian. 'What you can enjoy today never put off until tomorrow. That's my motto.'

Going home with my father and my lover. I tuck my little secret safely away from prying eyes. My father and I will return home to meet our family. Yesterday is gone and tomorrow may never happen. It is my turn to draw that magic line in the sand. This might be my second chance.

'How was your Christmas.' asks Barbara

'We muddle along, I say. 'My parents muddled along and produced me. I am a product of a blunder.'

'Life would be dull without the blunders,' says Barbara.

Do people ever really forgive; do generations ever meet? Will my mother and father ever know each other? Should they? I believe that generations are connected by the mistakes they make.

It takes a lot of courage to show your dreams to someone else.

~Erma Bombeck~

Odd Socks

'My name is Michael. I am new in town so I would like to open a post office box,' says a man smiling at me across the post office counter. His hand is reaching towards me and I feel compelled to shake it.

'I am Emma,' I point at my badge as I hand him the key for his post office box.

A few days later I find Michael leaning on my car as I am about to go home. He opens the door for me and touches my arm. Was he waiting for me?

'Do you mind if I call you Emma?'

'Everybody calls me Emma.'

Michael tells me that he built himself a camp. He is going to stay for a while. Michael came to Lightning Ridge like fortune hunters do when a new opal mining rush is on. He looks forty something; I try not to look fifty.

'I missed you over the weekend,' says Michael on Monday. 'Will you be in town tomorrow,' he says on Friday with the same normality old friends discuss weather.

'Have to go to the library in the morning.'

'Might see you there,' he says walking away. I wonder if we just made a date. I often go to the library on Saturday mornings but I do not go this time. I am so ordinary and my family so well respected that nobody would ever accuse me of having impure thoughts. I admit that I am a dreamer but I never allow dreams to complicate my reality. I like to play with the idea of an ideal man but men around me seem branded by experience, they are marked by sadness and disappointment. I often hear migrant miners say that they will bring a young virgin from their hometown when they find opal. Most miners seem to be migrants coming from God knows where and going God knows where. Most came during the sixties and seventies to get rich quick but decades later most still live in their camps in the bush. People say that many of them are millionaires but they don't look rich to me.

'Odd socks. Freaks of nature most of them. Damaged people, weirdoes, geniuses, adventurers, vagabonds, artists; the town is full of men,' laughs my friend Melanie.

'A great big pile of odd socks,' I agree.

'One always hopes that another sock would be a perfect match to the lost one,' says Melanie.

'I wonder where all the matching socks disappear.'

'I bet they gather in some other mismatched, weird place, like Lightning Ridge?' Maybe we all long for someone undamaged by life. I am damaged myself, of course. I feel like a worn out shoe that was forced to lean to the side because the person who wore it was a little bent. I wonder what irreparable damage Michael hides underneath the brave exterior.

'What are you reading,' I ask as Michael and I meet at the library on Tuesday afternoon.

'I study etymology, are you familiar with etymology?'

Should I know the word, I wander if it is about butterflies or insects.

'Vaguely.' Michael and I allow our eyes to meet for a split second.

On Friday Michael and I stand in front of the post office; he suggests that we move into the shade; he touches my elbow as he guides me towards the tree on the side of the road. A shiver goes through me. Startled I look at him and the knowledge passes between us. I know that I am burnt, deliciously burnt. I begin to look for Michael as I drive through town. I pass his camp on the opal field. I see him washing under the tree, splashing water from the basin over his naked top and then rubbing it with the towel. He only has army disposal trousers on. Hidden by the trees I imagine rubbing his body dry for him. I return home breathless, lie on the bed, close my eyes and relive the moment our eyes met. I lay there with a smile on my face like an idiot. I weave a fantasy that couldn't be tempered with reality or knowing.

Michael writes me a letter. He says that he is enchanted by my beauty and my wisdom and that he wants to spend time with me and get to know me.

Of course I wouldn't write letters to a stranger. I am a married woman. I didn't get a love letter for decades. It feels deliciously funny. Is it a love letter? I become cheerfully juvenile. I meet Michael in front of the post office almost every day. He pretends to be checking for mail but I know that he has none.

'I found a good trace on Green Acres. Want to see the colour?'

I can't refuse because Michael already has his hand with the opal in front of my eyes.

'Nice colour,' I say.

'It's not much but it's a solid claim.'

'I wish you luck.'

Michael probably fantasises about finding opal which will bring him admiration and adoration. Maybe he will not want my admiration if he finds opal. Everybody here adores men who are on opal.

'Come and see me sometimes?'

'Why?'

'To talk.'

'I don't know you.'

'We will get to know each other.'

We smile and know unmistakably everything we need to know. I will be careful, I promise myself. Just a chance meeting on the street that is all it will ever be. In the privacy of my bed I wonder if he ever said I love you to me in his heart.

'Why do you study etymology?' I looked the word up in a dictionary.

'The powers to be change the meaning of the words for their own ends. I'd like to challenge them,' says Michael.

'How?'

'For example, in the old English a word MAN stood for men and women. St Paul said: no woe man will teach the man. A woe man was a man who was disobedient to God. St. Paul wanted to say that a teacher must be a good person to be an example to his students. The Greek philosophers insisted that one must become a better person after time spent with his teacher. Men stuck a prefix wo onto females and you read it in the Bible now that apostle Paul said: no woman should teach a man,' explains Michael. Michael and I meet on predictable corners at predictable times to have most unpredictable little conversations because we don't know each other well enough to talk about ordinary things.

'You said that you studied theology.'

'I am fascinated with God.'

'Do you believe in God,' I ask.

'We believe what we learn to believe. Only God knows the truth.'

'How do you explain life?'

'God wrote a role for each of us. We change his script sometimes but it's never right at the end,' says Michael.

'How do I know the script?'

'Your story is written on your heart,' smiles Michael and touches my hand by accident. 'Everything you do is everything you are. Every step you take brings you a little closer to where you are heading. Everybody you meet tells you a little about who you are.'

One hot afternoon I find a card stuck on my windshield. A picture of a man and a woman dancing; four lines are handwritten inside.

A daydream often steals away
Many moments through the day
And in that dream you hold the sway
My heart as harp you sweetly play.

The card is sighed M

'Did you get my Valentine card,' asks Michael as he pokes his head into my car.

'I didn't even remember Valentine.'

'I wish you wrote me a letter.'

'I wish I could.' The eyes do the trick. I feel the proverbial arrow lodged firmly in my heart. The lightning from the blue of his eyes. We lock eyes for ten seconds too long. We melt into one and feel complete; joyously together; I wake up from my sleepwalking existence. Is that what they call love. Is that what people who were in a coma experience as they wake up and suddenly all their senses burst into awareness?I drive home like a wounded bird. The exquisite pain makes me forget all that is wrong in my life.

In love there are no flaws, no time, no age, there is only sun wanting to shine. There is excellence and light and angels singing. I see pictures of waterfall cascading over us as we want to merge like two magnets that cannot be pulled apart. My heart strings love words together but my mind tells me that there is no love; there is nothing flawless or splendid. I am not a Snow white, he is nothing but some sort of a mysterious tramp. A love mirage in the loveless desert. I remind myself that Michael could be a murderer, a conman or a thief.

I look for Michael and find him everywhere. We exchange greetings but I am scared to stop and look at his blue eyes again. I try to laugh at myself but my laugh sounds sick. People smile at sixteen years olds in love, knowing that they will soon grow out of it. They would laugh at fifty years old in love. A married fifty years old. My friends would love to spread the joke around. Sensible Emma fell in love. Don't be ridiculous. Get real. Just as well I am sensible about it. I try to reconcile myself with my mirror image. Could Michael really love my face? Or my body. I feel neither wise nor beautiful. What would we see after we exhausted ourselves with lovemaking? I don't want to know. I write a pretend letter to Michael at the end of the recipe file on my computer. Nobody would look there.

I cannot write you a letter; I am afraid of the ridiculous words that would tell you what I would never want anyone to know. I don't love you. How could I, I don't even know you. But then I don't even know myself. It seems that you like me better than I like myself. I like that about you.

I am suffering from a strange sickness. The symptoms include chest pain, delusions and illusions, disorientation, diminished mental ability, lack of concentration, dizziness, light headedness, forgetfulness, sleeplessness,

The tendency to stare into space,

And the compulsion to whisper: Michael.

I ignore friends and loved ones. I dwell on the memory of that fire in our eyes as we first began this dangerous game. I know it's an illusion but life itself is only a pretence.

Your name forbidden on my lips
Like chocolate chips

And autumn fruit
So ripe and sweet
I will just look
But never eat
It's only when I close my eyes
Like spies my thoughts
Go through your smiles
My hands feel
Tingling touches of your skin
I hold you still within
But when in clear light of day
We walk on busy street
Our talk is brave
Our love is hidden far away

Are my thoughts of you
Keeping you awake
Are you searching for me,
Am I in your heart saying things
You want to hear

I close my eyes to see
The blue of your eyes
As we meet on the street
The heat of the summer
Dusty sweat of rushing
Mixed with the splendour
Of our giving
To each other
The essence of our being
Oh how blue are your eyes
As we meet

On the one way road
I am scratching footprints
On the footpath
To engrave the traces of our passing
I want to be a mirror for you
So you will see in me
How good you are

I wanted that dress
Displayed at
The price
Below cost
In the shop
Where we met
I first saw your face
Through its gossamer lace
Alone now I stand
To admire the lace
The sun in the window
Did its best
The colours failed
The test of time
On top
And beneath the lace
Stay on display you beautiful little dress
I don't want you to impress my lover
I confess I am out of contest
You look better where you rest
I look better than my dress

You will never know the words I whispered
To that silly moon,

The promises I made to stars,
Have nothing to do with you
I will not miss what I never had
It will be easy to forget
If there is nothing to remember

I should know better
I know better
There is a boogie man in the scrub
Run Little Red Riding Hood
The wolf is coming
I have to go home
I have a job to do
A life to live
A fish has to swim
So if you please
Unhook me
I am not your fish

We never once said that we love each other.
We talked about God but our eyes were saying love.

My husband Robert returns from work an hour after me. I kiss him at the door. I became more affectionate. I prepare dinner carefully to keep Robert contented.

'The rice is soggy,' says Robert. 'Can't you do anything right.'

'Don't worry, have bread with the stew instead,' I try to diffuse the situation.

'How many times do I have to tell you that I don't like overcooked rice?

'Don't eat it.'

'You are too lazy to wash and dry rice before cooking. How many times do I have to tell you that I like grains separated?'

'Why don't you cook sometimes?

'At least you could learn to cook; since you can't do anything else.'

'I do more than you do.' After our children left home I continue to serve Robert so he allows me the luxury of going to work.

'Post office pays you peanuts,' says Robert. 'Monkeys deserve peanuts.'

'Go fuck yourself,' I say for the first time in my life. My words frighten me. What possessed me? Instinctively I move to the door. Robert grabs my arm and pushes me to the floor.

'That's the last time you hit me, you bastard,' I hiss. I never dreamed of being so rude and reckless.

'You are asking for it, says Robert pulling his belt out. Afraid that he will belt me again I get up but Robert pushes me down and falls on me. Pulling on my hair with one hand he tears down my panties with the other and rapes me.

'That's the last time you fucked me,' I say.

'I will fuck you whenever I damn want. You will beg me to fuck you like you begged me after every stupid argument,' Robert snarls through bloody teeth. He bit my breast. The blood on his teeth terrifies me. Things went out of hand; nothing like that ever happened. Robert never used a belt on me and he never raped me before. I never before back-chatted Robert. I never provoked him intentionally. Does he know? Did he read behind my recipes on the computer?Robert waits for me to apologise. I always apologised; he loved me when I begged.

'Lovemaking after a fight is best,' Robert told his friend.

'Women are much like tiles. Lay them down well in the first place and you will be able to walk on them for the rest of your life,' said his friend.

'You have to hit the horse that pulls well or it will go bad.' Robert shuts himself in a spare bedroom. He knows that I will come to apologise. I drive to town not knowing whether to go to the police or to the doctor. I sit in the car, my head leaning on the steering wheel. Michael taps on the window.

'Go away.'

'What have I done?'

'Nothing and you never will.'

'I thought that we...'

'There is no we.'

'I thought we had an understanding.'

'We had nothing, we will never have anything.' It is all Michael's fault. I would never say those words if Michael did not make me feel that I could.

Michael left town. I search the streets for him. Robert and I barely spoke to each other since the incident.

A month later I find Robert leaning over the toilet. There is an empty wine bottle on the kitchen table. There are painkilling tablets. He must have been sick. Or drunk. Robert sways and falls. Did he take too many tablets? Did he want to commit suicide?My God, did he find out about Michael. Thank God that there is nothing to find out. Michael only lived in my mind and heart. Is there such a place? Does it matter who lives there.

'Are you OK?'

'Can't you see I am sick,' says Robert and his speech is slurred?

'What's wrong?' I kneel next to Robert cradling his head.

'Get a doctor.' I ring for ambulance. Robert suffers a stroke. It is my fault. Lately he lost his temper more frequently. Poor man. Thank God Michael left.

Robert never hit me again and we never made love again. In time we became friends. People are amazed how well I serve Robert and what a lovely family we are. Robert wants me to stop working and stay with him but as long as I stay at the post office there is a chance that Michael will return.

When I was seventeen I ran away from home because my father belted mum and us kids when he was drunk. He was drunk most of the time. Robert found the room for me as well as offered me a job as a receptionist in his business. He told me what to do, how to do it and when. He was pleased because he could rely on me to follow his orders. I was flattered when he praised me. I loved his little gifts of appreciation. I felt important since this older businessman relied on me. I felt that I had to keep pleasing him so I married him.

Robert was a loving, generous man. Sometimes he lifted me up and carried me around, singing and dancing. He told me how much he loved me and how he could not live without me. He would rather shoot himself than live without me. He would rather shoot us both. That sounded so tragically romantic. Just as suddenly he sometimes pushed me away, telling me that I am stupid, good for nothing. Robert was the same with our children. We never knew when or why he will become angry. An angel one moment and a devil the next. Slapping started after the twins were born. He became annoyed by their crying, I suppose. Robert very rarely slapped me and he was always sorry afterwards as we made love. He often threatened to shoot himself because he felt so bad. How could we live knowing that he killed himself? I always managed to convince him that I could not live without him. It would clearly be my fault if our children lost their father.

People told me that Robert's father hung himself eventually. Robert does not want to talk about his father. Maybe Robert was born like that; maybe he learned from his father; maybe he was sick. He often complained that he had headaches. He simply could not control his temper. Anything could trigger his anger. We learned to be careful. Maybe men are like that. I know nothing about other men. Dad was like that but only when he was drunk.

After the stroke Robert became a sad old man.

Amy, our oldest daughter returns when I tell her about dad. She looks at him cautiously at first but then he smiles, half his mouth hanging down, his hands limp on his lap. His eyes mist and she comes closer touching his hands. Silently the tears run down his cheeks unchecked. Slowly she kneels beside him and puts her head on his lap. He caresses her with one hand. Amy's three little girls watch a bit shy but soon they join mummy. There they are on their knees with their heads in Robert's lap like a holy family. Robert never saw his grandchildren before. Amy ran away at the age of eighteen. After he belted her for the last time.

Peter and Paul, our twenty five years old twins return with their girlfriends. We love Robert now for not being who he was. We are no longer afraid to show love. You cannot hate a cripple

I often threatened to leave Robert. He lived under threat all his life, poor darling. Maybe I needed Robert more than I knew. I needed the fences he built around me. There was nobody else ever. I can see it all now; it wasn't Robert's fault. Everybody hated Robert; his father drank; his mother worked to feed her seven children. She often said that the kids were her cross. I am glad everybody loves Robert now. Amy and her daughters come and sit with him almost every weekend. He loves his granddaughters. They run to him when they discover something new or when they need someone to kiss the pain away. Robert and I are the only people that will ever rejoice looking at the smiling faces of our grandchildren. My precious family is my blessing.

Michael could never love my grandchildren like Robert does. But then Michael is only a fantasy.

I still write letters for Michael behind my recipe file sometimes:

'I know that no man can possess the strength and wisdom, gentleness and sincerity, love and compassion that I imagined you to possess. I only tried these virtues on you, you never had them, you were never really expected to have them; I would never let you close enough to show me who you really are. I don't even love myself as I would have you love me.

I remember your raised hand as you plodded along. That wave told me that I am as alive for you as you are for me. I pray for you. Even my God tells me that I am a better person for knowing you.

Are your eyes blue or do I remember the sky from the day we once looked at each other for a few seconds too long.

Are you a victim or a criminal, a hunter or the hunted? Where did you come from and where are you going.'

'I might retire for Christmas, I say to my friend Melanie.

'You will have time for your darling Robert. And for your children and grandchildren.'

'I will miss my job though.'

'You will find yourself a nice hobby.'

'Like painting,' I smile at my painter friend Melanie.

'While I mix the colours I can't possibly have any impure thoughts,' laughs Melanie.

'What sort of impure thoughts,' I ask surprised.

'Oh, you know, of what might have been. It's best to accept that what is, was meant to be. I believe that even what's yet to come has been arranged by some higher power. Like the colours of the flowers I am painting. I paint what is in front of me.'

'One cannot shut one's eyes to things not seen by eyes,' I read on the poster above the book shop.

I see a man looking at me. His lopsided smile did not change. Nothing changed. The way my heart jumps, the way I want to sing. Michael.

'You came back;' I cannot hide the happiness.

The outstretched arms return to their sides. We do not embrace like old friends do. We were never friends. We never touched each other.

'Nothing changed,' says Michael.

'Where did you go?'

'I was at sea.'

'Are you a sailor?'

'A seaman.'

'Is there a difference?'

'I worked as an engineer.'

'You were at sea while I lived in the cage.'

'How is that?'

'It's a long story.'

'I'd like to hear it. Maybe we could have dinner sometimes.'

'I'd love to but it is a bit complicated.'

'You have somebody else?'

'An obligation, yes.'

'Was it like that last time?'

'A bit different.'

Michael helped me survive the last eight years. I built a fairy-tale around him. Now he is a reality again. Could I deal with reality?Michael and I bump into each other almost daily.

'What are you doing these days,' I ask.

'I read.'

'What do you read?'

'Old philosophers. And the Bible.' Is Michael trying to impress me?

'I read Conversations with God. Everybody seems to be reading them.'

'What is that about?'

'It talks about everything being a part of everything else, sort of.'

'Why don't you read the Bible?'

'Old men excluded women from the Bible.'

'A new age feminist.'

'Bible is not much fun.'

'Only for those that don't care to understand it.'

Michael apparently considers himself one of those rare wise guys who do. He reads old philosophers while I read new age conversations with God. Old wine and young wine. Old money and newly rich. Since Robert became an invalid he sleeps in his bed in his room. I have the freedom of my own room and bed. I can watch the love stories on television and dream about Michael. I feel the tingling sensation as my hands caress my skin the way I would like Michael to caress me.

I don't want my dreams to come true. King Midas was so unhappy when his dreams came true and everything he touched turned into gold. If all my dreams came true, I would have nothing to dream about. The fantasies shine inside me like the stars in the silence of the night. What would I do with a star in my lap? I need the wonderland of wishing for the star. Like a drowning person I hold on the straw but the straw and I obey the current and float down the stream, a part of the current, a drop in the ocean. I sneak behind my recipe file and write pretend words for Michael.

Let's not temper with fantasy
Let's not change the scenery
Let's never promise anything to each other

Let's enjoy our moments in time
Let's remain
Two strangers on the road
Never afraid of
Not being loved
Or not loving
Never afraid of leaving
Or dying

I do not love you
Like you want me
To love you
You have nothing
I like
Or want
Seeing you
Just makes me want to dance

We are both at sea
We do not know what to do
With each other
I am homeward bound
I am not a seaman
I see no future
With you
I love the moments we share

You are just a fantasy. I need to serve my master. I wanted to change you into my master but you could never scare me like Robert does. I wanted to leave my kingdom to find a more worthy and noble king but I realise that kings are not noble but only powerful.

God
Do you remember the time
Before you became a creator
When things were not yet
As they are
The time when you were
Just happy to be

God
Do you remember us two
As we met
On top of that hill
I saw you looking at me
Your face clear in the sky
Through the umbrella
Of spring branches
Talking to me
As I sat on the moss
Looking down at my home
The bees in the flowers
The birds in the nests
You and I met
For the first time

Do you also long
For the paradise lost
For that place where we met
For what we once had

It has been months since I last saw Michael. I let my life run within its banks. I stand aside so it does not hit me. Sometimes when it rushes over the cliff I stop and want to rush with it but then I remember that it will come back. I let it run like a river towards the ocean, I want it to be surprised; to see how it feels and what it looks like where it is going while dreaming about the places it has seen. I stay on the riverbank. One day maybe the river will rise and flood the days covered in dust; it might cover its banks with debris and mud. Maybe the river bank, nourished with rain will wake up the life that forgot to live. I know Robert loves me now. He always loved me. Maybe he did not love me well; maybe I did not love him well.

Our twins Peter and Paul are getting married on their thirtieth birthday. It's going to be a huge celebration; two brides' families and us with all our friends.

Amy's daughters will be bridesmaids. A bit young yet but ever so beautiful. Their uncles Peter and Paul adore them. Robert is so proud. He showers them with gifts and affection. They love poppy and nanny. We have never been so contented. Maybe the precious moments Michael and I shared saved my precious family. Having a family around means a lot to all of us.

In a remote little part of me I still wait for Michael.

I know he will come when I will least expect him. When alone I write little notes at the end of my recipe file for him.

My thoughts like foxes hunting in the night
Are searching through the secret places in my heart
I am the only one to see
My hidden webs of inconsistency
Let's pretend to be
Lovers forever
And never, never afraid
Of going, going away
Play on piped piper
Happy land is around the corner

The same piped piper
Piping the same pipe dream
Forever
The road is all
One way traffic
A glimpse of truth
A hint of perfection
And the ashes
Every word that you said
Our eyes as they met
Our souls
As we parted
All that we had
Ashes
Ashes Cinderella
Ashes to wade through
On the way to heaven
The prince is dancing without me
On his way through hell
On his way to heaven
Play on piped piper
Happy land is around the corner
Prince charming and Cinderella dance
Happily ever after
Snow White is waiting
In the forest
Of my mind
A Little Red Riding Hood
Never afraid never growing old
Like God

Daydreams

Whoever at anytime has undertaken to build a new heaven has found the strength for it in his own hell.

—Friederich Nietzsche

Daydreams

The end of the school-year play was called Daydreams. Our teacher asked us to act out what we would like to be when we grow up. I do not dream about the future right now but I often daydream about last Christmas because everything was just right in our home then. Mum and dad paid off the mortgage on the house and we went out to celebrate.

'What I really want now is a new washing machine,' said mum.

'Why not a new bed as well,' said dad squeezing mum's shoulders.

'What about a fridge,' mum looks at dad all excited.

'If we take another loan we might as well get everything we need,' said dad.

We went shopping for the king sized bed. Mum and dad rolled like two huge beached whales on every king-sized bed at Harvey Norman's. How embarrassing.

We bought a load of Christmas goodies to fill up the new fridge.

'Stop admiring the inside of the fridge,' said dad but he did it too and so did mum.

When they delivered a spanking brand new washing machine mum looked quite pretty. There was a permanent grin on her face. She was hanging out her first load of washing when dad came behind her, took her in a bear hug and turned her around. They stood there like two fat idiots holding onto each other.

I looked around to see that the neighbours were not watching. It would be soooo embarrassing to see two oldies standing there with the wind wrapping the washing over them. Mum's nightie was pulled high when she lifted her arms to hug dad. I could see the blue veins on the inside of her thighs. She is soooo embarrassed about those veins that she does not want to be seen in swimmers.

Dad's boxer shorts came down to unveil half of his fat bottom and mum's hand held it like it was her gold medal.

My sister Mia came behind me and pushed me into the window. 'Perving perving,' she sang and I told her to piss off. I pushed Mia towards the new washing machine and she cried out.

'Watch your language,' mum yelled out.

'Let's go and get that dog then,' said dad to me; he was laughing as he came in. I was grateful that for once Mia did not come with us. The dog was my Christmas gift; it was my shopping with my dad; a men's business.

There are about twenty puppies to choose from. Dad repeats to me everything the kennel owner says. Dad is a bit excited and forgets that I understand English. Of course I can follow what the kennel keeper says but no, dad has to repeat and explain it to me again. I am not a baby.

Don't treat me like a five year old, I want to say but I just say yes because I feel a bit grateful and generous.

One of the pups sniffs my hand and takes no notice of anybody else so I choose him. I am glad women are left at home. Dad tells me to think hard before I decide because you don't get a dog every day of your life. I know all that, I want to tell him. Wasn't I waiting for this since I could utter the word doggy?

'I would like mum to help us decide. She will have to help you look after the dog after all,' says dad as I cuddle my chosen puppy.

'We have to keep women happy,' dad puts his hand on my shoulder like I was one of the men.

I want to be like dad and keep the women happy.

'I think it's best if everybody is happy with your decision, don't you,' says dad.

Maybe dad wants to please mum. I don't like mum and Mia having a say but at this stage I would do anything to get that pup. It is a bit annoying when a grown up person like dad can't decide without a woman. It is my present, my Christmas after all and he told me to decide. But no, I believe that dad is a big sissy as far as decisions go.

It is nothing new really. Dad goes shopping but he never buys anything on his own. He has to talk to mum about it. Come to think, mum is a bit like that too. Why can't they make up their minds on their own? It's like they are half of a person walking through the shops and they need the other half to actually do something useful.

'You don't mind if we get mum and Mia to help us decide. We will reserve this one for an hour,' said dad sheepishly.

Of course I mind bitterly but I don't want to spoil the Christmas and my chances of getting the pup. If I do something unpredictable dad might change his mind. I really hate Mia having any say about which pup dad will buy for me. It's all too much but I say that's ok dad and I even allow dad to hold my hand. It feels kind of awkward holding dad's hand since I am almost as tall as he is.

I know mum will ask me which pup I want and when I will tell her which one I want all over again Mia will say that the other one is cuter just to annoy me. We will end up arguing, I bet. Mia can't really overturn my decision since the pup is my present. She will choose her present and I don't even want to know what it is going to be.

'You and I do things outside and the girls have what's inside,' said dad once. My dog is going to be with us outside. He will sit next to us as we fix things.

'I want that garage fixed before Christmas,' mum ordered and her voice had that unpleasant annoyed shrill to it.

'You going to help clean the garage,' dad pats my shoulder.

I love fixing the garage. Dad and I go to garage sales on Saturdays and we buy good stuff really cheap. There is no room left in the garage for the car so mum gets a bit stroppy.

'It saves time and money when you need to fix things,' says dad. 'I don't have to run to the shop for every screw and then every screw is a dollar,' dad argues with mum. We heard it all before. Dad has millions of jars of screws he bought really cheap. He has every tool a man needs.

'Sort it out,' says mum as she closes the door with a little slam.

Mum sometimes complains that dad is forever looking for the right screw and that it would be cheaper to just go to the shop and get it when he needs one. I think dad likes looking for things in the garage.

'Garage is where a car is supposed to be. I can't even get in without breaking my leg,' said mum.

I am not sure if she is seriously annoyed with dad or not.

'All that junk. Get rid of the mess. One day I will take it all to the tip,' said mum a few months ago.

'Try it and I will take your junk from the bathroom to the tip,' said dad in a sharp voice. 'You don't touch my staff and I won't touch yours, dad added in a little friendlier tone. Mum put her head down and went inside.

It wasn't the first time either. Mum once actually dropped some of dad's things in a rubbish bin and when dad wheeled the bin onto the road he discovered his favourite pants and some pliers or something. A really bad row followed. Dad told mum that she does not appreciate his work and mum said that she works just the same. They were getting noisier and noisier until dad told me to get in and read. Every time they have a row they send Mia and me to read in our bedrooms. I hold the book in my hands but I listen to what they are arguing about.

Dad did not come in to cook lunch. Mum made sandwiches and dad did not even have one. Everything was really quiet for a few hours. Just as well Nan and Pop came in the afternoon and we all hugged real hard and smiled and dad offered to cook dinner for everybody. Mum set the table and served drinks and said that dad is the best cook. Nobody would guess that they looked daggers at each other only hours before.

Mum even cracked a joke on behalf of dad's old pants she threw in the bin.

'I bought him new ones because you could see half of his bottom through the cracks in the ones I threw away,' she laughed and then dad also smiled and said that he is going to throw away the grease jars mum keeps in the bathroom.

I was sort of happy that they were only teasing and I told Mia that I will clean her beauty case. 'Beauty what,' I teased. She hit me, I yelled then to warn the oldies before I pinched her. She jumped at me then and stuck her claws into my arm. She made me bleed.

'Both of you to your room and read,' ordered dad.

Dad pretends that he is the boss when Nan and Pop are here. Reading is the worst punishment he can think of.

'She started it,' I protest.

'It's all his fault,' whined Mia. We stuck our tongues out at each other and left.

I hate reading. They talk a lot about my dyslexia and colour blindness and double vision and how they will have to do something about it but they never do and I don't know what is really going on.

As I predicted Mia did not like my choice of a dog but mum told her that it was my present and I had my choice. Mia called the pup a mangy mongrel and mum told her to behave herself.

'Which one would you choose,' asked dad and I was scared that mum would make me choose again.

'I don't care,' she decided and I was almost grateful although it took some of the joy away from having a pup.

Maybe I remember last Christmas because last Christmas I still had my family. My family is broken now.

It doesn't really matter what they get me this Christmas. Mum and dad will get me what I tell them to get me because both of them want Mia and me to live with them. The court will decide where we will live because mum and dad are too stubborn to decide for themselves. I want to stay with dad but I know that Mia will want what I get so there is no chance of her staying with mum. Women should stay together I reckon but no, what I have Mia must have.

'I don't want to split you,' said dad because he is a bit soft in the head about Mia. I know it and Mia knows it. So where one of us will live the other will too.

'In your dreams,' said my sister when I proposed that she stay with mum while I go with dad.

'You would miss each other,' said dad.

Of course we would miss each other, we miss mum and dad living together but they wouldn't even talk to each other. They expect us kids to be sensible about things. Why can't they be sensible? We could at least go together to buy Christmas stuff.

Mum is dragging us through courts instead.

'We spent over twenty thousand each for court orders and solicitors and counsellors,' said dad.

They are paying for counselling for Mia and me so we don't end up messed up through the divorce. What's the use us going to counselling if mum and dad can't even say hello to each other? The counsellor keeps saying that the divorce has nothing to do with us and that mum and dad love us. She knows nothing. My parents have a funny way of showing love. I wish they could be normal, say sorry and shake hands. Counsellors should talk to parents and make them see what they are doing but they expect us to be more responsible than our parents. It's all too weird.

Looking back now I can see that mum and dad acted kind of funny even right through last Christmas holidays. They did not argue like usual. Dad tried to cuddle mum at every opportunity and she sniffed a bit every time he took her in his arms. Maybe cuddling and crying is the way to go when you are happy. They cuddled Mia and me as we opened Christmas presents and mum sniffed.

One day I asked her if she was crying but she said that she caught a bit of a cold. I knew she was lying. These days Dad buys me all sorts of computer stuff and he lets me sit at the computer for hours. I don't care really what I get for Christmas. I think dad is going to get me some more computer games.

I love computer games; especially neo-pets. You get four pets, which are really different forms of creatures like monsters, and you get your team to compete against the other teams. I always play war games because I love to listen to the weird sounds people make when they die. You learn strategies to avoid getting killed and win the game. I also like the game called worms. You get a can of worms to fight other worms. It is sad to see your worms getting killed but when your worms kill other worms it is just so exciting. You learn a lot and you get better at killing other worms.

I am glad the school is over and I never have to go back. I am going to high school next year.

I hated Brendan, he is a stuck up poof and I am going to kill him one day. He pisses me off severely. I wanted to get him on the last school day but dad did not let me go to school. You see we have these groups and Brendan sticks up with girls like a poof. He and Craig, they are the biggest weirdos; they think they know everything and when they see me they make faces and I just have to hit them. Reece and Lee are on my side but they are Korean and adopted and Brendan is a racist.

Craig's mother comes to school and complains to the principle that this big fat boy bullies her baby boy. One day I am going to kill Craig's mother. Craig keeps running to the teachers. When he gets me in trouble he walks past me and makes these weird noises screwing his face.

It got worse a couple of months ago. I brought half a pizza to school. We ate the other half for tea the night before. I woke up late and did not have time for breakfast. I took the pizza out before school and walked with it on the playground. Craig came from around the corner and he tripped me. I fell and my face landed on the pizza. I tried to cover my face with my hand as I fell into the gravel. Brendan came behind Craig and laughed. Some girls came with him and they laughed as well. Someone yelled: pizza king. I punched Craig then and shoved the pizza into his face.

I am the tallest boy in the school so I could not possibly cry. One of the girls ran for the teacher and Brendan said: fatso fatso pizza king.

I did not have time to get him before the teacher grabbed my arm. I swung to get free but the teacher twisted my arm behind my back and I told him to f off. He marched me to the office and everybody watched.

Mum was called and she said that I am not a violent boy and that I would not hurt a fly if they didn't provoke me.

I got suspended for two days and on the way home mum asked me what it was all about. I told her that Craig started it.

Mum got enough problems right now. She keeps on dusting and ironing all the time when she is not working. She buys something on the way from work for tea and we spread the paper on the table and eat it with our hands as we watch television. Mum never cooks. Cooking reminds her of dad, I suppose, because dad always cooked. She does not touch the kitchen. I think she is on a diet herself. She goes out the back and smokes because she is giving up smoking but can't. Dad moved out and mum got an AVO against him.

My sister Mia and I stay in after school care until six and then mum picks us up on the way from work and we are all tired and hungry. I loved pizza and mum got it for us almost every day. Since this thing at school I hate pizza. I told mum that my stomach hurts after pizza so she switched to chicken and sometimes she buys Kentucky or Mc Donald's. I watch television and videos at mums all the time. She does not feel like talking most of the time.

When mum drove home from dad's place one-day, she didn't want to talk to me. I kept asking her what was wrong and I told her that I loved her but she just drove in silence looking straight ahead. I kept on asking what happened and she ignored me so I pulled the hand brake. The car swerved and hit the tree. It almost tipped over and the blood kept running from my lip. Someone stopped and rang the ambulance and the police. They took me to hospital and mum sat with me all night. They stitched my lips and put my arm in a sling. I was the only one injured. I took off my seat belt to reach for the handbrake so my head hit the dashboard.

Mum was very sorry and I felt really angry and I did not want to cry.

Mum said sorry and I said sorry. I wanted to ask her why she was upset but I could not. I saw her cry next to me in bed and I kept my eyes shut so I would not cry. I hated mum because she would not answer when I told her that I loved her. She took my hand then and we both said sorry again almost at the same time.

I wish mum and dad would say sorry to each other. That would be the bestest Christmas present really but they will not. 'Over my dead body,' says mum.

It is exciting opening Christmas gifts but I would much rather go fishing with dad. And mum.

It is good fun to be with dad. Sometimes he embarrasses me though. Like that time he started singing jingle bells real loud in the shopping mall. One of the girls from school walked past with her mum and I walked to the other side and pretended I did not know dad.

'Oh my little baby is embarrassed,' dad caught up with me and tried to hold my hand. How embarrassing. Once I embarrassed myself bad. I spoke out real loud in class right in the middle of the lesson. I was thinking of something that happened at home and I just yelled out. I almost died of embarrassment but I told the teacher that Craig and Brendan made faces at me. They did really but just at the end of the playtime and I could not get them and punch them.

Mia is a big fat brat. She is the youngest in our family but she always wins. She sulks until everybody gives in. Nobody takes time to wait for her to get over it. Whenever I get a present she has to have the same one or two or better one or bigger one. She sulks if she does not get her way. Mum once called Mia a bitch. She hissed the word in a half whisper actually. Dad thinks that the sun shines out of Mia's you know what. He let her get away with murder. They are too busy to make her behave.

As I came into the kitchen one morning dad told mum that he had a dream how he baked the cake and the crust rose up and separated from the cake. There was a huge empty space between the crust and the cake.

I stood in the doorway listening. Dad tried to hug mum. 'We haven't slept together for weeks,' he said.

Of course they did, sort of, king-sized bed is big enough to sleep together or separate.

'It's like we are no longer together,' said dad.

'It's all your fault. Go to your computer sluts,' said mum.

I announced my good morning and they put their best faces on and they smiled and chatted like the dream wasn't there.

Joy to the world goes on in every shop as mum drags Mia and me shopping this Christmas.

As I said before, things began to change after last Christmas. I should have realised it before but I thought mum and dad were just going through a phase until one evening mum and dad had this terrific row. They behaved really peculiar.

'Get out of my face,' mum told dad. 'Keep away from me you porno maniac. I know everything about you and I am going to tell everybody.'

Dad tried to kiss her.

'What did I do, tell me what do you know, what did I do,' dad kept saying. He looked like a little boy who was scared to have his butt smacked and I wanted to help him get out of trouble but mum put her face right up dad's face and said: 'liar liar liar.'

'Tell me what I did,' dad begged.

'Get fucked,' said mum and even she flinched as she said it. I never heard this terrible word in our house before. It was fine to say the word when I played footy but it was shocking coming from mum in our kitchen.

'Go to your room,' said dad to Mia and me. We left the door ajar and heard every word. For the first time dad did not say go to your room and read. Something serious was going on.

'I wish you were dead. I will not be happy until you are dead, you bastard,' hissed mum.

Mia grabbed my hand then and I felt it tremble. I think it was the first time Mia and I hugged each other without a reason.

'Just tell me why you are upset and I will explain,' dad begged mum. We hoped she would let him explain. She always insisted that people have to talk about their problems and tell each other how they feel. She said that everybody has to give in a little so everybody is happy.

'Please darling you know I love you,' begged dad.

He must have done something really bad to go begging like that.

'How long has this been going on, you bastard?'

'Going on what,' dad tried to sound innocent and big eyed.

'I read all your secrets. You have no time to clean the garage because you are chatting to those sluts.'

'But that is just a joke. We used to do it together to relax, for fun. Remember?'

'Do what? Talk about your sexual habits, you maniac. I never talk like that to my best friends.'

'I wouldn't tell my friends but this is just a chat-room,' tried dad.

Mia and I still held hands and I wondered what secrets mum found on the computer. Would dad use swear words? He told me never to swear because any dumb person could swear better.

'It is better to baffle others with intelligence,' said dad. He taught us how to be sarcastic instead and ridicule those that used swear words.

During the last year I heard dad swear a lot at a lot of people who annoyed him. Especially mum.

'Dad has a girlfriend,' whispered Mia.

'Don't be stupid,' I pressed my hand on her mouth. 'It's about computer.'

'I heard mum say that dad has cyber sex,' Mia squeezes the words through my fingers.

'Close the door and go to bed,' ordered dad.

We are both far from sleepy.

We glue our ears to the wall but soon both mum and dad go to bed.

In the morning both of them kiss us and ask how we slept. They don't usually do that. They are quietly polite to each other.

I keep wondering what will happen in the evening.

What I really want for Christmas is to see mum and dad standing under that hoist with the fresh washing flapping all over them with arms around each other like an enormous fat tree ignoring the rest of the world. I know this will never happen but I still hope it does.

Mum told the court that she wanted dad to move out so the children will not witness their arguing. I hate mum for it. She treats me like I have no idea what's going on. Why can't they tell me what is going on. On the last day of school we came home and mum stood in the doorway speechless.

'What's wrong,' I asked.

'We were robbed,' she broke the spell.

We follow each other from room to room in silence. The food we had in the fridge is stacked in the laundry tub covered in ice. There is no fridge in the kitchen; there is no washing machine in the laundry. Mia is reaching for my hand. We follow mum into her bedroom. The king-sized bed is not there.

'Phone,' I break the silence and we follow the trail towards the lounge. Mum's hand moves towards the phone. The message comes on and it is dad and I feel happy that he is there with us.

'I have split our personal property. I have been asking you to do that together but you refused. I am only taking the items I am still paying for. You can have the rest. The settlement for the house is due in the next few days so this will make it easier for you to move out of the house.'

Dad's message lingered on our minds. We stand there like some dumb pillars waiting for everything to go away. Only the silence follows. Mum moves to the window and bangs her hand on the ledge.

'Bastard, bastard, bastard, fucking bastard,' she chants in the smallest voice ever but it sort of hisses into the silence like bullets through the still air. Mia and I move closer to mum and for a moment mum moves her hands towards us but then she lifts the phone and rings her mum and dad. I suppose even grownups need mum and dad in times like this.

'The bastard took everything,' says mum into the phone.

'What can the police do,' she says after a minute.

Mia and I hold hands; we do that a lot lately.

'Why did dad do that,' Mia wants to know.

'Because he is a mean bastard, I told you he is a bastard and you wouldn't believe me. He brainwashed you. Now you know. You never believed me,' says mum spreading her arms around us and I am sorry for not believing her before and for wanting to live with dad.

'Dean wants to live with dad,' tells Mia at just this wrong moment.

'Over my dead body,' says mum pressing my head onto her chest. 'Over his dead body,' she says suddenly. People say things they don't mean. I said these things to Mia and she is all I have now. My hope that mum and dad will come to their senses is evaporating rapidly. Say sorry and shake hands, people keep saying to kids. Why can't grownups do the same?

People keep asking me what I want for Christmas and I wish I could tell them that I want someone to take away everything I have and make us go back to the last Christmas. I want mum and dad to say sorry to each other and shake hands and hug and kiss and start again.

They sold our home and they are going to spend the money to pay for courts that will decide who we are going to live with.

'I am going all the way with this,' mum keeps saying. 'I will make sure that he never spends another minute with you,' she promises as she plats Mia's hair.

One morning I took the leftovers to my dog and he wasn't there. He often jumps the fence. Sometimes we go to find him and sometimes he comes back on his own. I tell mum and she says that she couldn't care less where the dog is. 'Get dressed we have to go,' she says.

At school I was thinking about my dog all day. I rang dad after school and he said that it was mum's responsibility since she took the house and everything off him and got an AVO against him and he wasn't allowed to get anywhere near the house.

'Maybe she let the dog go herself,' I say to dad.

'I wouldn't put it past her,' says dad.

What is AVO, I want to know but they tell me that mum is just trying to keep dad away from Mia and me.

Mum keeps saying over my dead body a lot. She bought Mia a scooter so they cuddled and it made me sick. Mia is only thinking of presents.

'Don't worry about mum,' says dad. 'She is scared to lose you so she says bad things about me. She wants to stop me from seeing you. She wants you all to herself.'

'I am going to run away if she does,' says Mia.

I think I will too.

'What is going on,' I ask mum but she says that there is nothing for me to worry because she loves me. She has a funny way of showing it. She has no idea. Nobody has. I am not going to listen to stupid counsellors.

Court first ordered that my sister and I spend half the time with dad and half with mum. Mum wasn't happy with that so in the final hearing the judge said that I am old enough to decide where I wanted to live. I decided to live with dad. Mum got Mia. Our lives became a court order.

Though nothing can bring back the hour of splendour in the grass, of glory in the flower.

Wordsworth

My Beautiful Sister

'No place like home,' says Stan as we return from a holiday on the Gold coast.

'Home, beautiful home,' I agree. Autumn leaves covered the lawn while we were away. Canberra changes colour every season.

'It's the phone,' I rush into the house.

'Are you ready for another holiday,' I say as Stan comes in. I am actually bursting with excitement.

'What do you mean?'

'It was Hana. She is begging us to come home.'

'Why?'

'Toni is running for parliament. If he wins we will have our own politician.'

'He always wins,' Stan dismisses my news. He is not over the moon about my sister Hana nor her husband Toni.

'Freddy persuaded him to run.'

'Freddy and Toni always ruled the roost,' says Stan.

'We could, really, couldn't we? Go home, I mean.'

'What about your job?'

'I could take a month off, I suppose.'

'Why not stop working all together,' Stan decides out of the blue. 'We don't need the money. You always said how lucky Hana is because she does not have to work.'

Maybe Stan does not like me thinking that Hana is lucky. Maybe he thinks that I want to be Hana and be married to Toni. Maybe he wants to be Toni and rule the roost.

'I would be bored without work.'

'Something else will come along. Something always does,' says Stan. 'Why work, we have more than we will ever need.'

'Why indeed? We were mad to work so hard.'

'Someone had to.'

I am excited at the thought of change. Stan was afraid to go home while Yugoslav regime was in power but going home was always at the back of my mind.

'They might still get me,' says Stan.

'Not likely. Everybody has been home since Slovenia became independent.'

'Your work always held us back.'

Stan is a self-employed builder; he can take time off when he wants to. He slowed down lately. I feel bold and brave as I tell my employers that I wish to retire.

'Whatever will be, will be,' I say to Stan on the first day of my retirement.

'Now you can do whatever you ever wanted to do.'

I am simply not used to not being busy. I was never alone before either. Stan and I did everything together. During our work hours we were with other people but we spent our free time together. Stan and I mean everything to each other. I hear the silence of my home now. I feel the aloneness and the distance. My life is spinning into an unknown. I have to search for the new purpose and establish a new routine. I watch the bird pecking at her image in the window. I watch the leaves falling. The garden will appreciate some rearranging. I don't know how to sit without work. Keep busy is the best I can do. Keep busy and don't think about it. Thinking gets you nowhere. Working and saving and getting rich used to make me feel essential. There is no need to save or to work anymore. I always kept the filing cabinet for Stan's business and our home accounts neatly organised but personal papers roamed around the house until they ended in boxes to be sorted one day. For ages I wanted to put our photos in a chronological order so people could come to look at my life neatly framed in the slots of the album. Now I wonder if anyone would want to look at our life. Stan and I know other Slovenians in Canberra but I doubt any one of them would really want to follow the events of our lives. People save their images on computer these days. I look at yellowish old bits of paper. Much time has passed without ever taking time to remember. Here is a picture of Hana and myself as we played with homemade dolls. I always thought of Hana as beautiful. I was definitely ordinary. Mum used to make our clothes until she became too sick. I was about thirteen when I first ventured into a dress shop. My little brand new breasts started pushing forward into my little girl school dress so I needed a new one.

'Try it on,' the man in the shop urged me. He held the curtain of the dressing cubicle open for me. When he dropped the curtain I put the dress on. The salesman squeezed into the cubicle and smoothed the dress over my chest. His hands were shaking uncontrollably. He became red in the face and began stuttering. Another customer entered the shop so the salesman left my cubicle. I quickly got out of the dress and out of the shop. I was shaking. I had no idea what I did wrong but I became ashamed. Since then I never liked dressing rooms.

Being the oldest I was privileged to wear crisp new garments but my sisters wore mostly hand me downs. When Hana became a teenager our relations let her choose her own bits of clothing because she was so obviously different, exotically fragile and hauntingly beautiful.

Mum's relations moved to Vienna soon after the war. When Hana was thirteen they invited her to stay with them for a while. She was a different person when she returned at fifteen. Hana learned to play the piano and the steps of ballet. She wrote poetry, knew about arts, was introduced to German and Italian and she sprinkled her speech with French expressions we never heard of. She looked rather vulnerable but maybe they taught her how to look vulnerable so she didn't have to pull her weight when any manual tasks had to be done at home.

The photos of mum and dad remind me of the love they had for us and for each other. It's not like me to cry over photos. It's the change, I suppose. Life is so short. Suddenly I am back where life meant so much and the future looked so rosy.

It is no use wondering if I made the right choices. It would be useless to go over all the reasons, yet in my aloneness I wonder about the meaning of it all. Was the life I had my destiny? What is the essential me if there is any such thing? Am I just a reflection of unplanned little events and people I met?

I was sixteen. We were swimming in the river when I got caught under the branches of the willows. Toni rescued me. He carried me onto the riverbank and placed me into the tall flowery grass. As I recovered he kissed me. Just a playful kiss but I almost drowned in happiness. Since then I followed Toni from the distance. In a daze. Was this first kiss a kiss of life? It marked me for life. Toni became my hero. He was my whole life. Two years older he seemed a wise grown up man. He bought me a beautiful shiny copper hairpin from the stall when we went on a pilgrimage to the little church on the mountain. I wore that pin like women in love wear their engagement rings. I was in love with Toni. One can only be so totally hopelessly in love once in a lifetime. My love for Toni was all in my head until for my seventeenth birthday Toni invited me to see a play in the town hall. It was to be our first real date. I was breathless with excitement. I waited for Toni to kiss me again and finally declare his love. I think everybody knew how much in love I was with Toni.

Then there was Hana.

Mum insisted that my little sister come with Toni and me to see the play. Hana came out in a silky pink dress. Her hair was tied on top of her head with a huge matching pink ribbon. She wore red sandals with slightly raised heels. My little sister took our breath away. Even Toni seemed stunned by Hana's beauty. There we stood, my seventeenth birthday forgotten, as we admired the blossoming of my fifteen years old sister. Hana's childhood ended and suddenly she became a beautiful young woman.

The picture of my beautiful sister standing there all newly grown up and pink, remained with me forever. Toni came to our home frequently since my seventeenth birthday. We became firm friends. When Toni came Hana found some excuse to get away. She did not like Toni. Sometimes she teased him about the girls that wanted to go with him.

One day I saw Toni kissing Hana under the flowering cherry tree. They looked like an enchanted couple from my father's fairy tale. I couldn't move. The bitter pain of jealousy was mixed with sweet pain of admiration. I knew that it was inevitable that Toni would choose Hana. I was almost happy that Toni would become part of my family and so stay close to me. Nobody was surprised that Toni chose Hana. Her long blond curls, her forget me not blue eyes, and her shy smile enchanted him.

When Hana and I walked to school, boys tried to catch up with us to be with Hana. I was just one of Hana's sisters. Nobody took notice of me. Are you Hana's sister, people used to ask me in total disbelief. I am also Emil's sister and Tereza's sister but nobody ever mentioned that. We are ordinary and we married ordinary people. We are not beautiful or talented but everybody knows that Hana is all those things. Stan must have sensed my feelings for Toni but he never said a word. There was no reason. I sometimes wonder if Hana really belongs to our family. There is certain preciousness about her.

'She will never grow up. She will be cute and charming all her life,' complained Tereza. Hana displayed her childish playful coquettishness in a flirtatious way that would make me look stupid but then I don't look the part. I was never precious. I never told anyone about my crush on Toni. Nobody ever knew about my first kiss, hidden deep in my subconscious like photos in this shoebox. My first puppy love. I pretended that it never happened. Even years later I sometimes dreamt about Toni. I woke up with a strange tingling sensation. I kept my eyes closed for a few more minutes to recreate a dream. I could never compete with Hana. I admired Toni as much as I admired my sister. Hana was glad that I liked Toni because I was the only family member that liked him. I could not understand why my parents worried about Hana's marriage to Toni. Maybe Hana was just so precious to my family. Nobody worried when I married Stan. Stan was twenty and I was eighteen when we started dating. I was grateful to good old Stan for wanting me. He loved me and I felt safe and whole with him. There was never another man in my life. I don't think there was ever another woman in Stan's life either. Stan was an ordinary carpenter at home. In Australia he became a builder which is much the same thing. Stan is a hardworking, faithful man and we have everything we need. Stan drives his utility because he is delivering material for his buildings. I do Stan's accounts in my spare time so he never has to worry about bills or money. We know exactly where every dollar goes. We are contented with our arrangement. We are comfortable. We don't have to agonise about other people.

I was the oldest of four children so I learnt from the very beginning to be sensible and act responsibly. Even my name, Maria, seems common and sensible. At the age of six I became a chief baby sitter for my two younger sisters and a brother. Emil was the youngest. I suppose my parents had to have a boy before they stopped reproducing.

Mum and dad married just before the war. Dad's parents were rich respected farmers then but for an unknown reason after the war landowners became despised in communist Yugoslavia. People working on the land were considered stupid peasants. Communists took most of my grandparent's land and distributed it among the poor. Dad's parents were the pillars of the church but the new regime considered church going people backward and superstitious. Dad's parents blamed mum and dad in some way for the new government.

Dad became a war hero during the communist revolution. He was badly injured and has since then spent much of his time in bed or in hospital. Mum and dad never talked about the war or about the revolution. Not in front of us children. I never knew how mum and dad felt about the church or the government. I sensed that they did not dare talk about politics or religion. I wish I asked them. I wish I knew them better.

Mum's family did not want to have anything to do with us. I heard mum's mother say that her daughter deserved better but not once did mum complain about hard work on the land. She took us kids to the field with her; she spread a rug under the tree and left us in my care while she worked. Once I heard a woman say to her friend as they looked in mum's direction:

> "About time the high and mighty dipped her dainty fingers in the soil.' I really know nothing about mum being high or mighty. I suppose mum was a bit dainty

> though. She was a shire secretary when she married her handsome rich farmer but neither the handsome nor the rich lasted long. Dad could barely walk with a stick since he became a war hero.

'You better do as mum tells you. She is the clever one,' dad often said. I believe that mum was much like Hana once. She became sensible, of course, but she actually encouraged Hana to be a bit precious. Dad adored Hana. I think she reminded him of mum. I felt protective towards mum from the beginning. I took care of mum's children and of our dad to give mum a chance to provide food for us. She gave some of the remaining land to poor people to work on and they gave her half of the produce.

I believe that dad was the love of mum's life. It was plainly written in the way they looked at each other and touched each other. When all her work was done mum would sit next to dad's bed and hold his hand.

During the winter before I started school dad taught me to read. He had nothing else to do in the long winter months, I suppose. I sat on his bed and read every evening. Other children listened to my reading and we all cuddled around dad while mum fed the pigs and the cows and the chooks. I still remember the smell of this closeness. Dad said that we were his bunch of wild flowers. I can still hear dad's voice as he lulled us away into the magic land of his stories.

Dad loved to make up stories and we listened, mesmerised by his words. He taught me to write and encouraged me to write down the stories he made up. I think dad trained me to take over from him and become a man of the house. I fed the kids and brought food for dad but mum and I ate whatever was left over. It was understood by everyone that mum and I had a duty to take care of the family. Hana was a delicate baby and we all admired her first smiles and words. Everybody was chirping over Hana. Tereza was a real disappointment because mum and dad must have sorely wanted a boy by then, so they could give up having children. Emil was a cry-baby. As the only boy he became a spoilt brat but he quickly had to grow out of his preciousness after dad died.

Mum cried a lot after dad died. The light has gone out of her eyes and she eventually got sick. I was eleven then and there was much to do. Mum began going to church regularly after dad died. She spent more and more time praying. Dad's family became very kind to us and I believe that they finally accepted mum.

For Sunday dinner a chook had to be killed and plucked. Mum did it without fuss and we enjoyed the smells of a roasting fowl. As Mum got sicker she asked me to kill a chook. It had to be done. I had a certain air of importance taking mum's place at the age of twelve. I almost felt heroic; at least I tried to look heroic. If you want to eat the Sunday roast you better kill the chook. If mum could do it so could I. Hana could not even watch the killing so it was useless to pretend that I was brave. Tereza and Emil expected me to be a deputy parent for them since I looked after them from the beginning. I held the chook between my legs, its head in one hand and the knife in the other. Mum said that the chook dies quickest if you turn the knife into its eye. I poked the little sharp knife into the chook's eye, closed my eyes and turned the knife to squash the chook's brain. I opened my eyes to catch the splattering blood into a pot so we could bake it for breakfast. Even Hana enjoyed this delicacy. There was an awful pain in my stomach as I stuck the knife into the eye of the chook for the first time. I had to pull myself together. When the blood stopped dripping in the pot and the chook stopped struggling I dropped it on the ground but the chook began to run away with its head hanging to the ground. I panicked and grabbed it to have another go at killing. As I held it between my legs again, it slowly went limp and I knew that it wasn't only pretending to be dead.

Sometimes mum dropped the chook into the boiling water for a minute to make the plucking easier but this time she wanted me to pluck it dry and save the feathers. During long winter months we picked the feathers for doonas and pillows.

When the chook was ready for roasting I filled it with spicy stuffing and placed it in the oven. After a few minutes the sweet aroma brought admirers to the kitchen. Hana couldn't wait to peel off the chook's golden crunchy skin.

The smells of my childhood follow me.

Nobody took any notice of my fear of cockroaches. They were a part of life. One has to live with pests one could not destroy. Mum insisted that cockroaches came from the neighbours since we regularly killed the ones in our house. Sometimes they could be heard chirping behind the bench around the stove during the day but in the evening they ventured onto the ceiling. As the light was turned on, they scuttled to the corners and sat in clusters quietly. Mum crept close to them and in one quick strike killed them with the broom. But others came the following night.

When the floorboards of our kitchen were replaced we discovered that cockroaches had a cosy home right under the old floorboards. Mum still insisted that they all came from our neighbours but the horrible masses of black beetles felt quite at home until we so rudely disturbed their dwelling. They began to run in all directions in their hundreds looking for safety and the new hiding places. We armed ourselves with spades and brooms and killed them like fire-fighters kill the fire that is threatening to destroy the house. For many months since this assault I had nightmares about cockroaches crawling over my body. Nobody took any notice of my crying at night. I silently watched and listened for the left over cockies. Phobias were not heard of and being scared of the small creatures was considered plain silly.

At school we put our lunches in the drawer under our desks. When I opened the drawer I found cockroaches eating my lump of bread contentedly. Other sensible kids just brushed the unwelcome guests away like one brushes the fly from one's face. I could not eat the cockies' leftovers.

I listened to the teacher explaining that we had to be grateful to the communist revolutionaries who liberated us and brought us freedom and prosperity. I watched the floorboards. I was convinced that under the floorboards rested other millions of my enemies contentedly waiting to eat my lunch. I stopped bringing lunch to school and hoped that cockroaches would die from deprivation.

Soon after the war the beetle brought from Colorado attacked our potato crops. We tried to kill this Colorado potato beetle manually at first. School children were sent on the fields to check for and squash the unwelcome tourist. The village co-op provided a prize for every creature we brought to them, dead or alive. Any prize was welcome in those poor, after war, times, so we, children, swarmed over the potato fields like locust.

Eventually America provided DDT powder that would kill any beetle. We dusted the fields and Mum sprinkled DDT powder in every hidden corner of our house as well. Mum was just so sensible. We were finally liberated from cockroaches. I was so proud of my home and my mum. I felt superior. We were clean. We looked down on neighbours who did not liberate their homes.

'People will never get rid of cockroaches. They were here before us,' said our neighbours.

One day a kind neighbour brought us a jar of cream because our cow was having a calf and did not produce milk. I gratefully dipped a piece of bread into the thick cream. When I pulled it out there were the huge tentacles of the cockroach attached to my bread. I screamed and threw the bread away, the jar tipped over and mum told me not to be silly. Nobody considered my aversion to cockies an issue. It would surely develop into phobia if anyone allowed for it. Or knew about it.

Mum told the neighbour then about the magic of DDT powder in the hope that our neighbourhood would become liberated from the pests. Having pests in the house was shameful to mum rather than terrifying. The rest of the family ignored them.

Mum considered our family better than people around us. Especially since she cleaned our house of cockroaches.

In the box of old papers I find a diary I began thirty five years ago when Stan and I came to Australia with our two little boys. We didn't understand English and nobody understood us so I began talking to myself by writing the diary.

Stan and I came to Australia with our two babies and a cardboard suitcase. We were broke. Stan heard that one could earn good money cutting sugar cane in Queensland. Queensland meant sandy beaches and everlasting sunshine. The smell of frangipani blossoms and the sight of the clear blue surf impressed us. The freshness of the vast fields inspired me to daydream alone in the middle of the universe.

I open the tattered old diary and start to read what I wrote when I was still a young girl in the Australian summer of 1964.

The gang of Spanish cutters was willing to take Stan as a partner if I would cook Spanish food for them. Can you cook Spanish food, a man asked me. Of course, I said. Food is food and it has to be cooked. It is natural that a woman would know how to cook. It comes with the gender like cutting sugar cane comes natural to men. In return for my cooking we lived for free. The babies and the cooking will keep you busy, said Stan.

The Spanish sugar cane farmer provided living quarters for his cane cutters. I knew a few English words and so did the Spanish farmer and his cutters. They told me that everything I would need is in the cupboard. As the men left for work in the morning I inspected the cupboard for provisions. Everything was covered in black. I shuddered and shut the door quickly. As I recovered I stilled myself for longer inspection. The cockroaches scuttled into the corners as the sunrays hit them. The butter underneath was all nibbled by them and the jar of sugar still held a few big brave ones that did not feel intimidated by my presence. In the crevices of the bread moved the long tentacles and munched away. I closed the door and took a broom and banged it on the door. I wanted to scare the living daylights out of them. I was angry because the cockies refused to be scared of me. When I opened the door again the clusters of moving black wings and tentacles hung onto the corners but the food was free. I took everything out of the cupboard and let the sun shine on the monstrosity of black clusters of cockies hanging in the corner of the cupboard from the ceiling to the floor. Like me they were probably considering a new strategy of attack. We knew that we were enemies, deadly enemies. I took the hose and sprayed hard into every crevice in the cupboard. They ran in their hundreds and I swept them out and brushed them into the bin where they were supposed to suffocate and never return. Luckily I had a hose and enough water to drown the buggers. There seemed no end of them. They kept coming huge and ugly from tiny cracks in the walls. I kept drowning them all day and by the time men returned my kitchen was clean.

It was no use telling men about my predicament. Living with cockroaches was obviously no problem for them. I had to be sensible and find a way to fit into cohabitation with the rest. It was my problem if I couldn't stand the long, fast moving black monsters. Men just brushed them aside casually. They are all a fact of life. You can never get rid of cockroaches, they have been there before humans and will probably remain after we become extinct, I remembered from the past.

'The climate suits them and there is plenty of food,' was all Stan said. No use crying or waiting for help. I couldn't sleep at night. As I closed my eyes millions of black enemy came dancing in front of my eyes. I sat in the car all night. The car was the only sanctuary not yet infested by my mortal enemy. In the morning I returned to my clean kitchen to prepare breakfast for my men who had a hard day's work in front of them. I opened the cupboard and my heart sank. I could feel tears running down my cheeks. I lost my battle. Either the cockroaches I drowned rose from the dead or their relations replaced them and settled on the clean shelves over the sugar and butter and bread. I closed the cupboard door and banged on it with the wooden spoon to frighten them away. Cockies understood and moved into the corners so I could reach the food. When alone, I began to consider my future. I could either leave the place and let cockroaches defeat me or find new strategies to destroy them.

I went to the local grocery shop and asked for poison.

'Not that it helps much,' said the shopkeeper. 'I spray every evening and I sweep them out in the morning but new ones will come. They multiply.' Australians are sensible about pests. They continually try to get rid of them but they don't lose sleep over them. I believe cockroaches figured out how to win against Queenslanders; they became immune and grew stronger than poison.

'What fails to kill you makes you stronger,' said the newsreader on the radio. Some bacteria apparently grew stronger than antibiotics. My home is an invisible killing field. The surviving cockies grow big and angry. They want to punish me for trying to eradicate them. Flies and rats and viruses, termites and ants and bacteria multiply incessantly because they know there is strength in numbers. I have to find a stronger poison.

'What about DDT,' I asked the grocer.

'Not allowed to use it near food. Too dangerous.'

'I want to poison ants outside,' I lied. So I got the magic powder and sprinkled it outside and inside the house. I filled in every crevice on the wall and on the floor. They must not grow stronger. Every morning since then I swept dead creatures away. After a couple of weeks only an occasional cocky came to die in my kitchen. I did not tell anyone about DDT. I watched the men for signs of poisoning but the cane cutters survived. I remain on the lookout for cockies wherever I go. Especially in the sunny Queensland where the food is plentiful and the days are warm. Everything grows and multiplies in the warm, humid coastal resorts. I suppose one has to be sensible about these things.

The grocer told me to call him George. He was an older Greek man well over thirty. He seemed used to dealing with people who knew even less English than he did. We both smiled in places where we could not find the word and we used our hands a lot. I was as foreign to George as he was to me but we were probably closer to each other than we were to most. George and I lived out on the fringe, equally out of place and that made it easier for us to be comfortable with each other. I did not understand a word of Greek and George did not understand any Slovenian. He belonged to Greek Church and I am a Catholic but actually neither of us went to any church at the time. I bought food every day from George and put it on the account for cane cutters to pay.

A man came in the shop one day with a crate of lemons to sell to George. He gave me a few lemons and said: 'When life offers you lemons make lemonade.' I made lemonade. He was a kindly Italian man over forty years old and must have sensed that life had many lemons in store for me. I wonder who the man was and where he is now. He left part of himself with me in his little offering of wisdom.

I turn the brittle pages of my old diary.

3.11.64

'How is your husband coping,' asks George. Cane cutting is considered the hardest job. George is the only person I come in contact with, so I consider him a friend. I keep chatting with him to practice my English. I don't know why he keeps on chatting. He is not busy and I buy lots of groceries for the cutters. I realise that I never even asked Stan how he is coping. I am too busy coping. Stan does not complain. His hands are blistered but he says that he has to get used to the machete. When the blisters harden they don't bleed any more. I was so preoccupied with killing cockroaches that I even forgot my boys. The farmer's wife, a dark haired Spanish little lady, takes them almost every day to play with her little boys. My boys began to speak but the words they say I have never heard before. Mark points to the water but he says aqua. He points to the farmer's house and says cassia. I realise that my boys' first language is Spanish.

29.11 64

We are coping better every day. In the morning I fry eggs and bacon and make toast. I put a coffeepot and a jug of juice on the table. The men like their standard breakfast. Maybe it is Spanish, maybe it isn't. As I clean after breakfast, I smell the fires. The cutters burn the cane fields so the fire strips the leaves. The blackened stocks are then cut with machetes and chopped into pieces and loaded on train carriages to be taken to the mill. At lunchtime six blackened men descend into the kitchen and I serve lunch which they wash down with beer. Almost every day they eat soup and steak and vegetables. Every day they have custard with fruit. It is dry fruit, which I soak for a few hours and place on top of the custard. This must be Spanish menu because Spanish lady showed me what to cook the first day and I cook it every day and nobody complains.

Each of the men takes a water bag and off they go again. In the evening they return, wash themselves under the tap of the water tank. They eat more slowly. For dinner I roast the meat and bake potatoes. The farmer's wife provides greens for the salad. Sometimes the men go to the pub and have a few beers afterwards but most of the time they just drop onto their beds.

After six months the cane season finished so we move south to look for a suitable place to settle down. North in Australia is hot and South should be more suitable.

18.12.64

We are on the way down South and it is going to be Christmas and we have no home. We sleep in a car. Stan heard from other migrants that one could earn good money in Snowy Mountains. Anything with the name snowy is welcome after the heat of Queensland summer.

Just before Christmas 1964 Stan began to work in the tunnel. I remember those heady days in the Snowy Mountains. This great engineering project fascinated Stan.

In 1949 the Australian Prime Minister fired the first plug of dynamite to commemorate the start of The Snowy Mountains Scheme. The water from mountain streams was first directed through a series of tunnels to power stations where it generated enormous amounts of electricity. The water was later made available for irrigation.

The first wave of non-English speaking migrants from Europe came to work on the gigantic hydro-electric project. Cooma, the sleepy Anglo-Saxon rural town at the bottom of the Snowy Mountains, soon became the multicultural metropolis of Australia. The smell of the cappuccino and salami wafting in the air on the main street was a welcome reminder of Europe for lonely men who had left behind their country, family and sweethearts. In Cooma one could hope to meet someone from home or at least from the same continent.

Snowy Mountains project became a memorial to migrants of the sixties and most of those involved in it remember it with pride. Men reminisce about the wild freedom of the bush, the drinking in the pub, the hunting and the fishing. Many travelled to Cooma or Sydney on their paydays to find girls, grog and gambling.

Early migrants had their travel to Australia paid by Australian government. In return they had to work in Australia for two years. Most non-English speaking migrants were sent to the factories and shipyards or to work on the farms. Many stayed in their first job until they retired. Very few ever left Australia. More adventurous quickly discovered that they did not have to go where they were given a job. As long as they could provide for themselves or find their own employment they were free to roam the vast continent.

When the project finished in 1974 the Snowy Mountains national parks made attractive tourist destinations. The man made mountain lakes, scattered through the Snowy Mountains are overgrown by native fauna and look like they were there from the beginning.

I wrote a diary and I read the yellow pages of many years ago. I remember writing the diary as I sat under the poplars in

Tumut. Stan and the boys went fishing along the mighty Tumut River, which was rich with trout. Sometimes we camped on the riverbank. The chirping birds in the poplars and the sound of the river rushing by made me feel quite homesick for the river and the village I left behind. In the evenings we sat on the riverbank and watched the moon's reflection in the water and the stars in the brilliantly clear sky.

We fell in love with the wholesomeness of the untouched bush. We tuned in with the sounds and the silence while watching the birds build nests on the riverbank protected by raspberry and rose-hip bushes. The ducks scattered as we approached, but the platypus could be seen wading unperturbed in the deep of the cool clear water. The bush around Tumut created a sanctuary for platypus. The huge white gum trunks hollowed by termites were teeming with life. Termites rarely killed the trees; the birds nesting in the hollows fertilised the shell of the tree with their droppings and the tree survived. The young trees surrounded the healthy mature ones and saplings grew out of the dying trunks. In an everlasting undisturbed cycle of reincarnation they swayed in the breeze. The wallabies and wombats looked for food and white cockatoos and galahs screeched into the silence without disturbing anyone.

Gradually ambitious hard working Europeans created their little Europe around Tumut. The hills became orchards of apples, pears, chestnuts and walnuts. The sheep paddocks along the Tumut River were ploughed into the fields of corn and other vegetables. The weeping willows along the river and the poplars along the road were planted by Europeans who built houses in the valley nestling among the hills. In the last century they made a stamp on the land where Aborigines lived for thousands of years without disturbing or changing anything. Only the few scattered trees were left and their branches were eaten by stock to a metre off the ground. These trees looked like lonely ballerinas dancing over the dead logs that farmers ring barked to clear the land for more cattle and sheep. The farmers cut deeper and deeper into the bush. The clearings, scattered with fallen trunks, looked like a battlefield with massacred tree bodies.

During dry summers sheep and cattle ate into the roots of the new growth and the hills became brown and desert like as the wind lifted the soil that accumulated there through millenniums. During the last two hundred years many back-packers walked along Tumut River in search of riches. In the middle of the nineteenth century the nearby Kiandra and Adelong yielded tons of gold. The abandoned mines covered in new growth blended into the eternity of the bush to add to the picturesque beauty. The waterfalls and over two hundred caves provide the mysterious, sacred spirituality for the countryside.

The hills covered with snow in winter protected the valley from cold and wind. Skiing in Australia began in the middle of nineteenth century in Kiandra near Tumut. The European gold miners first used skiing as a mode of transport but later it began to be the main entertainment for gold diggers during the long harsh winters.

We liked the smell of the wild rosemary; we watched the daisies of all colours and sizes with their open unspoiled smiling faces looking for the sun. Exotic scents of shrubs were mingling in the untouched mountain air. The moss-covered ground was sprinkled with tiny flowers; the bigger ones grew up over them. The longer we looked the more varieties of flowers we found.

The trips to Tumut became our yearly pilgrimage. We are rather sad to see developers cash on the natural beauty of the virgin bush. The mighty Tumut River is still cool, clear and deep but the riverbank is now covered by tents, caravans, cars and people. The surrounding lakes also entice the tourists who enjoy water skiing, wind surfing, boating, yachting and fishing. Everything changed. The bush walkers trample the bush flowers, the birds and wallabies are scared away, the platypus is hiding in the water holes.

'Tumut offers fun for the whole family all year round,' says the advertisement.

I was never able to quite separate the memory of the beautiful countryside from the rats and mice I had to live with. And the terrible aloneness.

I read the diary from 5.1.65.

We moved into the five-bedroom old farmhouse in the old Jindabyne. The owners of the old houses from Jindabyne down in the valley moved up on the hill where they build a new Jindabyne. The old homes are made available to workers on the Snowy Mountains Scheme. They will flood the old town and cover up all the dirt with beautiful blue water when the project will be finished.

The fibro walls have holes in them but we feel lucky that we have a roof over our heads. We found some old pots and crockery and cutlery abandoned in the shed. We also found an old mattress and some clothes people left behind.

There is no water supply. Australia has no water springs like Europe. You can't even dig a well. Stan patched and cleaned the old empty rainwater tank; he took out dead birds and cats and smaller unidentifiable animals. He didn't even let me see all the rubbish he took out. I brought buckets of water from the Snowy River to wash the tank and now we are waiting for the rain to fill it with fresh, clean rainwater.

'Any rats,' asked a man who passed by as Stan cleaned the water tank.

'No,' said Stan. I never saw a rat in my life so I took no notice.

'They come inside during winter for warmth,' said the man.

Jindabyne 16.3.65

I am in hospital with my third baby. Stan has to work a double shift. They wanted him to do the third shift because the man did not turn for work but Stan said that he had to go to the hospital so the supervisor took his place. Stan was dirty and wet as he slumped onto the hospital bed. He didn't ask about our new baby. He was shaking.

'There was an accident just after I left,' Stan told me after a while. Explosion. A man lost his legs. Another man had his chest crushed by a rock. 'If I stayed a few more minutes I could be dead.'

'How did it happen,' I asked

'The detonator didn't explode,' said Stan.

'What do you mean?

'You know nothing about the things I have to do,' said Stan. I know only that Stan works on the face of the tunnel preparing the platform for miners before they blast another metre of the mountain to make the tunnel.

'I want to know.' I hold his hand. He came to see our baby, he was supposed to comfort me but I know that he needs comforting. He saw it all happen. The nurse brought our baby and while he suckled at my breast, Stan told me about his work.

'There is a two-story platform at the face of the tunnel. The big jumbo drilling rig with about a dozen air drills comes and the miners set the drills to drill about four metres into the rock. There is a big hole in the middle and about sixty or more smaller holes on the face of the tunnel around the big hole. The miners place gelignite and a detonator into each hole. The air pressure pushes it to the end of the hole. Then they fill the hole with the nitrogen powder mixed with diesel. Next they place another gelignite and detonator at the end of the hole.

All detonators are connected to the wires and to the firing switch. The switch is under the lock so nobody could turn it on accidentally. When all the holes are ready, the jumbo drill and the wagon with the gelignite and the miners are taken back about half a kilometre where the firing switch is. The supervisor checks that everything is in order before he turns the switch. Each hole has a number. The holes around the big hole in the middle explode first, then those next to it and so on. The whole lot crushes and caves towards the middle where a big hole was drilled. After the explosion the face electrician is the first to go towards the face of the tunnel to install the lights. He can't see in front. Rocks are hanging loosely from the ceiling and can kill you. After the electrician installs the lights, the man called chip monkey, dislocates and removes the loose rocks from the ceiling. The loader comes to load the rocks on the carriages and clear the ground for the next drilling.

'What went wrong,' I ask. It is hard for me to comprehend and visualise every detail of the operation.

'There is a strict rule that miners should never drill into the existing holes because the first detonator and the gelignite in the hole may still be alive. It rarely happens but it did. One of the miners drilled into the old hole and it exploded into his face. The rocks were flying all over the face of the tunnel.'

'How could he?'

'We were all tired. After the miner prepares his set of holes he can take a nap. One miner took a short cut. He was sleepy, I suppose. Drilling into the old hole saved time.'

'Do you know which miner?'

'It isn't important; we all learned a lesson. I was on the way out when they called me back to help.'

'How long ago was it?'

'Less than an hour.'

'Go home and have a rest,' I said. Stan never asked how long the labour took and how heavy the baby was. Those are the luxuries we will talk about later. I hate it when Stan is on a night shift. I am scared to sleep in the isolated house. During the day Stan sleeps and I keep the children quiet so he gets his rest. If I am lucky they all go to sleep for a few minutes and I sleep with them.

30.5.65

We are waiting for the rain. Stan junior is at school and three years old Mark follows me half a kilometre to the Snowy River to get a bucket of water every morning and every afternoon when our baby sleeps. I couldn't carry the baby and the bucket. As I get water, I also wash the rags we wear and the rags that I use as nappies. I found old sheets in the shed and tore them for nappies.

I rinse them in the river in the morning, soap them and spread them on the branches of the trees to sun bleach them during the day. In the afternoon I rinse them out and hang them on the branches to dry.

On Sunday we went to church and prayed for rain.

'We should take a bucket with us to church so God could give us water,' suggested Stan junior. He learned about God providing water during scripture lessons at school. I found a box of comics and short stories abandoned in the shed. The little Mills and Boon romances are easy to read and bit by bit I learn the words and their meaning. The books are half eaten by rats and mice, they were covered in dust and cobwebs but I cleaned them. These romances saved my sanity. Luckily we brought the dictionary with us. I read to my boys and Stan junior tells me when I don't say the word properly. We all learn English. Seven years old Stan is our teacher. I read to him every scrap of writing he brings from school.

We bought a new mattress and found an old frame for the bed. This is a great improvement. My babies are growing up beautifully. We named little Joe after my father. I remember my parents whenever I am alone. Dad told me that the magic land is always within me. This helps me survive.

28.6.65

We had the first snow. Stan cut a pile of wood to keep us warm through the winter. While Stan was on a night shift I put the baby in the basket near the fireplace while the older boys were asleep. I took a book and sat near the fire. I heard a sound and looked up. There were two pairs of beady eyes looking back at me. They didn't blink and neither did I. I sat frozen to the chair. A tail hanging out of the hole in the fibro wall suddenly moved, the heads of the creatures nodded to each other and moved towards the basket with my baby. I grabbed the baby and ran out into the freezing night. I stopped up on the hill, leaned on the tree and cried. I could hear the ice forming on the branches. The crisp snow crunched under my feet. I shivered. The wind touched my bones. Suddenly I remembered the boys asleep alone amongst rats. I took the baby and a stick and returned to the house. I rattled all the walls to frighten the rats away before I sat in the middle of my bed with my children around me. I read out loud to frighten the ghosts and the rats away. I read and re-read the books until I knew them almost by heart. I told Stan but he is not worried about the rats. He bought the poison and spread it into every hole.

26.8.65

In the middle of last night I heard the footsteps under the window. I looked out and saw a man. I grabbed the gun, turned the light off and waited. The man went to the back of the house. There is a little slope and the ice formed on it. The man slipped and came crashing on the back door. I had no strength to hold the gun straight, let alone shoot. When I heard the man's footsteps running away I crumpled to the floor. I never again closed my eyes until Stan returned from the night shift.

I told Stan about the man. That scared him.

'I am going to resign,' said Stan. 'We saved enough to put a deposit on a place in Sydney.'

I sit in my kitchen sometimes and watch mice play on the old black wood stove. There are about half a dozen of them jumping from one pot onto another looking for morsels of leftover food. They take tiny crumbs into their dainty hands and nibble like little children. They became my pets.

'We are going away,' I tell the mice. I am overjoyed. Spring is here, wild flowers are everywhere; the rats moved out. Maybe Stan poisoned them and they lie somewhere behind the fibro walls rotting away. I want to believe that they moved out. They would enjoy the sunshine.

7.10.65. Today we got a letter from Toni. He sold our home in Slovenia. All we have to do is sign a contract of sale and verify our signature at the Yugoslav Embassy in Canberra.

Toni will then deposit the money on our bank account. It seems that Toni guides our lives with an invisible remote hand. I am happy that he sold our house so we could finally rebuild our lives in Australia.

20.11.65

The trip to Canberra was a catalyst. Stan and I fell in love with Australian Capital Territory. To us it is definitely a promised land. The cool orderly modern design and the clean, symmetric beauty of Australian capital city overwhelmed me. We both firmly believe that Canberra is the most beautiful city in the world.

'Forget Sydney, I want to live here,' I said to Stan right then and there.

'You could do worse than buy a piece of land right next to the Australian Parliament House,' he agreed.

We had about eight thousand pounds from the sale of our house in Slovenia and we saved almost two thousand. Land was cheap. Ordinary blocks of land in the suburbs could be bought for a pound each but Stan wanted to buy close to the Australian Prime Minister. This was the most daring thing Stan ever did.

'I don't know anyone in Canberra and I have no idea which suburb is best but what is good enough for the prime minister is good enough for us,' Stan said. So for Christmas 1965 we paid four thousand pounds for the magnificent block of land from which one could see all over Canberra. It was the most expensive block of land in Canberra ever sold until then. Our name and picture was in Canberra Times so all Canberra Slovenians read about us. Every Slovenian in Canberra also found out that we were at the Yugo Embassy and that we bought a block of land in the same street. We were totally unaware of what role Yugo embassy played in Slovenian community in Canberra. Stan never had time for politics and I had no reason to become involved in it. We visited the embassy so they would witness our signatures on the transfer papers of the house Toni sold for us in Slovenia. At the Embassy we met the first Slovenians in Australia. We felt close to Ivan immediately after he said 'dober dan.' To hear an ordinary greeting in your own language sounded miraculous. Ivan was at the Embassy to get a visa for Slovenia, because his family wanted to return to Slovenia. Stan was surprised that

Slovenians had to ask permission to return to the country of their birth but that's how it was then.

Stan believed that the land close to the Australian parliament would be a good investment. He built a beautiful mansion because the land was expensive and surrounded by beautiful houses. We took a loan half way through to complete the six bedroom three bathroom place but we could never really afford to move into it. We rented it to an African Embassy so the rent paid off the loan.

We didn't even realise that most of the streets around Parliament house were known as the Embassy district. Unbeknown to us we ended up closer to Yugoslav Embassy than to the parliament house. Stan did carpentry works for other tradesmen who as a payment built our house. We never saw any money from his work for years. After Stan finished our magnificent home it was easy for him to get the building licence and the loans from the bank.

We lived in a rented backyard flat of the house owned by a sick old Polish migrant. I had to clean and cook and garden for him so we did not have to pay rent. Times were tough. I had three young children at the time and people weren't keen to rent places to families with little children. I heard that most Australians did not want anything to do with foreigners. I believe that they were a bit scared of migrants although we were as much foreigners to them as they were to us. One never knows what to expect from a foreigner. It was probably easier for them since they were in majority.

Australia was full of foreigners in the sixties. Even Slovenians in Canberra seemed foreign to us. They came from different regions, backgrounds, religions and political persuasion. Slovenian Franciscan priest came from Sydney every third Sunday and most Slovenians came to Slovenian mass. We wanted to see each other; even those that disliked each other and those that did not really believe in God came to mass to see each other. I suppose just seeing a group of Slovenian faces was comforting. During the mass the priest told us to offer a sign of peace to each other. We sat next to Joe, a very pious man. When the sign of peace was to be offered Stan extended his hand towards Joe but Joe ignored Stan and turned the other way. We later learned that Joe was spreading rumours about us being Embassy's spies. 'Where else would a young couple with three children get the money to buy the dearest block of land in Canberra,' reasoned Joe.

Ivan invited us home to meet his wife Meta and their family. We became instant friends. Ivan was also a builder. I learned much later that Ivan was a spy for Yugoslav Embassy. Apparently his time expired. We heard a rumour that my Stan took Ivan's place as a spy and that Yugoslav Embassy paid for our house so we would spy on the activities of other Slovenians in Canberra. We did not dare tell anyone that we were ourselves scared of Yugoslav Embassy. We were also afraid to tell anyone how we came to have the money. Slovenians were suspicious from the beginning because we became friends with Ivan's family. Apparently anyone on friendly terms with the ambassador or Ivan was a communist. We were forever known as the owners of that magnificent, expensive block of land with that pretentious mansion on it. Slovenians in Canberra never fully trusted us. Few of them trusted each other. I learned that the two opposing political groups of Slovenians even sat far apart in the strategic positions in the church so that they did not have to shake hands with their political enemies at Easter or Christmas.

Someone apparently even found out that my father was a war hero and that Toni, my sister's husband, was a chief of police. Our fate was sealed. We were forever referred to as Embassy's agents. The pillars of the church never trusted us and we did not trust the friends of the Embassy.

I took an evening job in a local club. As a barmaid I met with Australians for the first time. The men leaning on the bar were eager to talk. They introduced themselves as Jack and Sam and Tom and Dave. They asked my name and I said: 'My name is Mrs. Bregar.' They burst out laughing.

'I know you are Mrs. Bregar but what is your name,' asked Dave. Incredulous.

'Maria,' I said and felt like a woman who has committed adultery for the first time because I revealed my first name to an almost complete stranger. I later learned that Jack was an important man in the government. Men were friendly, I suppose anybody is friendly with a young barmaid while they have a glass of beer in their hand. I liked to talk because I wanted to learn English fast. Broken English was not a deterrent for a pretty young barmaid as much as it was for tradesmen. Stan complained about the English speaking co-workers who mumbled their sentences so fast that he could not catch their meaning. The men came to the club at exactly the same time and left at the same time to go home for dinner and to kiss their kids good night. Stan kissed our boys goodnight while I worked. Most men spent a couple of hours after work in the club and would have two to three beers. Anything over that may lead into the change of home-going routine and trouble at home. They were older men all of them. Any man over thirty was an older man at the time because I was so young. Some of these older men held high positions in the government but to me they were known only by their first names and by the size of beer they drank. They appreciated my eagerness and good memory. I would see a man at the door and by the time he came to the bar his drink would be waiting for him.

Kathy, another young mother, who worked with me, invited me to her home. Her home was the first Australian home I ever visited.

'Coffee?' asked Kathy as we sat down.

'Oh, you don't have to,' I dismissed the invitation, convinced that she will ask again and at least once more urge me to partake of the coffee with her.

'You don't mind if I have one,' said Kathy unaware of my expectations. She made herself a cup of coffee and accepted my refusal of her hospitality without a sign of discomfort.

I never needed a cup of coffee more than at that moment but I couldn't ask for it. I never again refused a drink of any kind from Australian hosts when I wanted one. You don't get a second chance. Whatever they offer they want to share with you but they never offer twice in the same sitting. There was so much for me to learn fast.

'What you see is what you get in Australia,' explained Meta. 'They don't beat about the bush like we do.'

On a big dance night in the club a man asked for many fancy drinks and I felt good that I knew how to make all of them. Before he left the bar he asked for the screwdriver. I was glad that I knew exactly what he wanted. Having a carpenter for a husband makes you aware of the tools. I brought a half metre long screwdriver that I previously saw sitting at the back on the beer keg. I placed it in front of my customer but he opened his mouth wide and looked at his friends. They burst out laughing. The music stopped and everybody looked at me. I was the only dummy who didn't know that vodka with orange juice is also called a screwdriver.

I felt embarrassed but looking back I think they liked the opportunity to laugh. They remembered and retold the story. People are usually grateful to those who make fools of themselves. Gradually I began to laugh with them and laughed at myself making mistakes. There are millions of opportunities to make a fool of yourself when you are transplanted into another continent and society.

After the children started school there was no need for me to be home during the day so I began looking for a day job. Luckily all my children were born in the first half of the year so they were allowed to enter school at the beginning of the school year in February before they turned five. Children born after July had to wait until they were over five. It saved us money on child minding.

Before Ivan and his wife Meta left for Slovenia they invited us to a farewell dinner.

'Paula lives next to your new house,' Meta introduced me to her friend.

'What a coincidence,' said Paula. 'We will be neighbours.'

We never became neighbours because my family never lived in our magnificent mansion but Paula and I became lifelong friends. Paula is an elegant, confident lady, about ten years older and much more educated than I am. Paula was born in Australia a year after her parents arrived from Austria. She remembers how difficult life in Australia was for her parents before they learned English.

'European migrants brought skills, culture and ingenuity to Australia after the war,' said Paula confidently.

Paula never worked. Her husband Ron is a parliamentarian and he probably earns enough. Paula buys the best quality clothes. Her son Damian is older than my boys so my boys wear Damian's expensive hand me downs. Paula told me about the shop in Manuka, where Embassy ladies buy clothes of international designs.

'They need a sales assistant,' said Paula. Working in this shop will be a good experience for you. Most of the customers are from foreign embassies so your European accent will be welcome.' Paula introduced me to her friend Eva, the owner of the shop.

'Eva will tell you what to wear and how to walk and talk,' Paula smiled. 'You listen to Eva, she knows what she is talking about.'

'You don't have to be beautiful but you must always be perfectly groomed and elegant,' Eva said in a firm German accented voice. I carefully followed Eva's instructions. Gradually she introduced me to her important clients in a whispering but clear voice. Later Eva told me madam's name, the country madam represents, and what colours and designs suit madam.

I wrote down all the information and later at home tried to find further information about madam's country of origin and the place of her embassy in the Red Hill Embassy district. I asked Eva how to spell madam's name and I practiced its pronunciation.

'People are particular about their names and their home countries. One should not mix Slovenia and Bosnia just because they were both part of Yugoslavia,' said Eva. 'In the same way you must never mix Thailand and Taiwan because people of any country think themselves a bit better.'

'I asked madams questions about their countries and their fashions. I am getting to know the customers,' I said to Eva.

'They are not customers, they are clients. In a supermarket you have customers but in a place like this we have clients,' Eva corrected me.

I still do not properly understand the difference but I understand that it is important.

In my old diary I read an entry I wrote in 1970:

Every day I drive my little Ford to the boutique where I sell clothes to the rich old ladies. I smile at them because they are the only women that can afford the dresses I sell. I tell them how appropriately elegant they look. I know that nobody cares how old ladies look but they have to maintain the status of rich elegance even when nobody takes any notice. These ladies would not touch anything made of synthetics. Natural fibre is like a mark of respect to them. Their clothes carry designer labels and different designer labels suit them for different times of the day. I have to remember what they believe suits them so that I can tell them what suits them and then they appreciate my good taste and knowledge. They change for dinner and for coffee and for casual visiting or shopping.

Eva chose a designer dress for me to work in, to show these ladies that I know what is appropriate. I feel more like them in a designer dress. Eva lets me have these dresses at a fraction of the real price.

'You are the right size,' said Eva as I tried the dress on.

I am an unnoticeable size with a civilised body that is not too big or too small in any particular place. The same goes for the rest of me. People have a better chance to remember the dress I wear than my face. I never put a foot wrong in a really big way.

I earn a reasonable salary so we moved into a two bedroom flat where we stayed until in 1971 Stan built another, much more modest four bedroom home for us on a cheaper piece of land in the suburb of Deakin. Gradually Deakin also became a prestige suburb. I just love the views and the spacious simplicity of our home. We can see most of Canberra. I believe that they chose Canberra as a capital because it is surrounded by hills. The rich people like to look over the valleys where poorer people live.

Apparently Australians could not agree if Sydney or Melbourne should become the capital after Australian states united in 1901 so they decided to find a suitable place between the two cities and built a capital.

Canberra is spotlessly clean. Some say that it is a cold, unfriendly, boring place but to me it is refreshingly cool. People also complain that it is an impersonal, sterile environment but I love sterile and impersonal. It liberates you like DDT. I have never seen a cockroach or a rat in Canberra. I suppose rats and cockroaches do not like sterile. Canberra people never even mention rats and cockroaches. They may have phobias about spiders or frogs but rats and cockroaches hide respectfully in the dark corners of their consciousness. I am glad that I made a clean break from the sneaky black monsters.

Flies bother people even in Canberra. I suppose they are left over from the time when the land was a sheep and cattle paddock only a few years ago. Ants annoy some. I suppose ants and flies are really miniature cockroaches but a lot friendlier and socially acceptable. They are also a lot less scared of people.

Stan is sub-contracting many building jobs to other Slovenians. They finally cautiously accepted us but I know that they don't really trust us. They can't figure out where we got the money and we can't tell them.

In 1969 the government gave Slovenians in Canberra a beautiful block of land to build their club. Stan spent many weekends building the club with other Slovenians. They rewarded him for his work with life membership to the club but they never elected him as a president.

Since the club opened we had many wonderful nights dancing and singing there. Slovenian music created a magic feeling of being at home. Women dressed in their finery, teased their hair into a balloon like hairdos, painted their eyelids blue and their lips red. On the dance floor we were the actresses as well as each other's audience. Women were careful never to wear the same dress as any other woman. It is all right for men to wear the same clothes, I suppose, since they all look like identical penguins in their dark suits and white shirts. Men expressed their individuality with their political views, their work, hobbies and neckties.

Slovenian club became a place of our rituals and celebrations. It was our little Slovenia. We blossomed there; we provided the recognition that we were alive at the time when we barely existed in the minds of other Australians. There was no other place where we could dance and sing, flirt and remember, and specially be recognised for who we were.

Canberra is a family city with monumental public buildings and beautiful homes. There is no nightlife in Canberra because Canberra families sleep with their children at home and go to work in the morning. Everybody in Canberra seems ordinary except perhaps the foreign embassy people who frequent Manuka prestige shopping centre where they can drink real Vienna coffee and eat food that reminds them of home.

Migrants from all over the world built Canberra and they provide services for the politicians and public servants whose parents or grandparents came mostly from Great Britain.

During the Independence War in Slovenia in 1991 Slovenians at home and abroad united. I suppose common enemy is the best reason for unity. Canberra Slovenians celebrated the independence united in our club. We almost became friends and relaxed in our love for Slovenia.

I was so young in so many ways. Young people follow fashions. We worked hard and saved and never wasted time or money. We cleaned and sterilised ourselves, our homes and our gardens to impress each other. We believed that cleanliness and purity was an essential part of civilisation and culture; like a baby formula that became the fashion when my boys were born. Most young mothers began to shun breast-feeding as old fashioned.

'You ironed and washed and wiped all the time,' my son tells me. 'I never remember those ironed shirts but I like to remember going fishing with dad and getting dirty.'

Perhaps I valued cleanliness more than I should and more than games our children wanted me to play. God forbid that another Slovenian would run a finger over my furniture and find it dusty. Cleanliness was very important to mum. It was a sign that she was better than those around her.

Most of us are slightly sorry now that we didn't waste a bit of time on our children and their activities. Perhaps we should have gone to watch their games and admire their trophies and be there on school presentation nights. But most of us didn't. Most of us never talked to the teachers our children spent years with. We didn't cheer them on the football oval or swimming carnivals. We couldn't waste time.

Now we have all the time we want but our children left and they lead their own lives. I want to spend time with my grandchildren but they live far away and when they come they would rather play computer games and chat on the Internet. I am a virtual stranger to my own grandchildren. I send gifts for birthdays and Christmas. I want to grow closer to them; they are polite but not really interested. Young people talk mostly to strangers these days. I find it amazing that children can sit at the computer for hours chatting to American friends one minute and then turn to Europe the next. This is a new kind of friendship for us who were taught never to talk to strangers.

'My sister Hana would like us to come home,' I tell Paula.

'I wish I met Hana.'

'Everybody likes Hana. She had the nicest boyfriend and married him. I suppose one perfect life in a family is enough.'

'She sounds special,' says Paula.

'She is.'

'I hope she knows it.'

'I am sure she does.'

'Were you jealous?'

'More proud than jealous. She made our family special. I always admired her life.'

I never had to impress Paula. To her I could say things I would not say to Slovenians.

During 1999 Paula's husband Ron developed Alzheimer's disease. I was not at all familiar with this disease. To me it was just old age forgetfulness.

'He can't swallow food or medicine. He won't last long,' said Paula.

'Why doesn't he go to hospital?'

'He doesn't like hospitals.'

'Can I help?'

'I have a nurse visiting every day. He is incontinent and she helps to bath and change him,' says Paula.

At Ron's funeral many dignitaries speak glowingly about Ron's life. Elegant mourners express sympathy to Paula. They praise her for her excellent care.

'I feel guilty because I never did anything to help you with Ron,' I say when we meet weeks after the funeral.

'You have always been my refuge,' Paula hugs me.

'I envied you because you did not have to work but I am really grateful for the job you found for me.'

'I wish I had your job but Ron would never hear of it,' says Paula. 'I suppose I wanted to work so I could be with other old ladies who observed propriety. The right dress, the right manners, the right place, the right words. Only old ladies still observe propriety.'

'I like things in the proper order too.'

I searched for order and perfection all my life. I suppose we want things to continue the way they were as we grew up. Marriages used to last forever. Family traditions and heirlooms were passed down; there was a sense of continuity. I am frightened of the changed world. The chaotic confusion eats people.

Paula and I bake a cake for Stan's birthday. We listen to the radio talkback where they are discussing the pros and cons of private and government nursing care.

'It is not right that rich old people have luxury nursing care while the poor have to be grateful for whatever the government provides,' says a caller.

'They want to punish me because I saved for my old age while others spent on pleasures of their youth,' says Paula. 'They ate their cake and now they make me feel guilty for saving mine.'

'The talk back host is going to be on the side of the poor, because the poor are a majority of his listeners,' I smile.

'He gets a million dollars a year to be on the side of the poor and talk about equality.'

'He will hire a nursing staff and be nursed at his mansion.'

'I nursed a man who forgot my name and his name. I didn't ask the government for help. I saved the government a lot of money,' says Paula. I changed my kids' nappies and then my grandchildren's and for the last six months I changed my husband's. Now they insist that I wear the same nappies and be fed the same mash as everybody else to prolong my misery.'

'The same nurses will be telling us how young we look and how much better we are every day,' I laugh.

'I cried all night when they finally had to take Ron away because he couldn't swallow or pee or poo any longer. He couldn't help it, poor darling.'

'You were a real angel to him.'

'I cursed his senility and his demented Alzheimer's and Ron himself. Then I felt guilty so I nursed and nursed to make up for my cursing. He used to hit me in the end when I wiped his bottom. He spat at me the food I tried to push into his mouth. Damian urged me to have him put into a nursing home earlier but I would never forgive myself for not caring for him.'

Paula changed since Ron died. We never talked about Ron before. Maybe I never really knew Paula.

'Sometimes I just want to die,' smiles Paula. 'I am not depressed or even sad about it; I just think it is time for me to go. I have done what I came here to do.'

'I need you,' I say a little scared of losing my only real friend.

'I wish the world would stop long enough to give young people time to attach themselves to something. I believe that God shaped a special corner for himself in every person's soul. When that place is empty people become desperate,' says Paula.

'I think we all feel desolate and sad sometimes,' I try to comfort Paula.

'I seem totally stuck in the mud,' says Paula; 'I have no power to move my feet or my thoughts; I feel nothing; I want nothing; I love no-one. Perhaps all old widowed people feel the same; never satisfied with what they achieved; never loved enough. And less every day. It feels like I laid myself into the coffin just to see if it feels like something there. I am waiting for something but do not know what I am waiting for.'

Paula has never been religious but since Ron's death she often talks about God.

'Have you heard from Sonia,' I ask. Paula's daughter Sonia ran away from home at sixteen and she never returned.

'She did not make it to the funeral. I told people that she was not well. I lied all my life. I suppose you have to when you are the one that has to cover all the shit that goes on in a family. My daughter never forgave her father. Serves him right, the pig, she said when I told her that he got sick.'

'Damian's family came.'

'Damian always did the right thing, he has to, I suppose, being a lawyer. People would talk. It was the worst for Damian really. I have nightmares about Damian pleading with me to protect him from his father. He was a tiny boy and Ron belted all the rebellion out of him. I think we all prayed then that the bastard would drop dead. I didn't dare admit it even to myself but I wanted him dead. I felt guilty and sorry for wishing him dead so I nursed the bastard until he could not poo and pee any more in his nappy.'

'There is a lot of poo in every family,' I smile to soften Paula's memories.

'It was almost a relief when Ron no longer recognised me.'

'Christmas is coming and everybody will be here to cheer us,' I change the subject.

'Damian and Julie are going through a difficult time.'

'I am sure they will make up for Christmas. People act civilised all year round so they can turn feral at Christmas,' I try to reason.

'I hate Christmas,' says Paula as we meet after the festive season. 'Everybody eats too much and farts too much. Kid's ears are plugged to their smart phones. At least I don't have to listen to their crappy music.'

'This is a new normal; they don't know any different,' I reason.

'On Christmas eve I watched a television show: The meaning of life. A man said that happiness to him means being able to tell everyone to fuck off. For Christmas. That really depressed me,' says Paula. 'Later on I realised that finally I can myself tell everybody to fuck off. That cheered me.'

I can't get over the change in Paula. Swearing became a part of most television shows but to hear Paula say the f word seems like blasphemy. Paula is no longer a proper lady.

Since I retired from my work Paula comes every day and we sit with our cups of coffee and I listen to Paula's reports on the Damian-Julie saga which became more intense than Bold and Beautiful soap opera on TV. Paula's son Damian and Julie have been married for eighteen years.

'Julie told me that she wants Damian dead. How could she tell ME, Damian's mother, that she will never be happy until Damian is dead. Damian is all I have,' says Paula.

'I think people who are wanted dead, live the longest.'

'Julie told me that Damian found his soul mate on the Internet.'

'Funny thing, the soul,' I say. 'As illusive and mysterious as God. When I was a little girl alone in the fields I felt an overwhelming awesomeness of God and soul.

'My granddaughter told me that mum does not like daddy because he has cyber sex,' Paula continues. 'I didn't even dare ask her what cyber sex is. I am appalled that a nine years old girl knows the word sex, let alone cyber sex,' says Paula. 'I am too shy to ask her what she means.'

'What is cyber sex?'

'I don't really know myself what she means by it. As far as I know Damian wrote to a girl and Julie found messages on the computer.'

'The world has gone mad.'

'I asked Damian about it.'

'I correspond with an online friend. On the Net I feel free to say exactly how I feel and nobody bites my head off,' said Damian.

'But cyber friends are not real people.'

'Maybe when you are not face to face it is easier to be who you want to be. You relate only to the part of the person you want to know, reasons Paula. Maybe neither Damian nor the girl are who they say they are.'

'Maybe Julie should find herself a cyber friend.'

'I wish I had a cyber friend,' smiles Paula. 'I buried my essential self so it wouldn't interfere with propriety and with what Ron was and wanted me to be. My body was doing the appropriate stuff with Ron but my soul wasn't.'

'You looked happy.'

'There was a decorum to be observed and the duties to be fulfilled,' says Paula. 'In my time one was only allowed to fantasise about being who you are.'

'Computer chats are essentially a fantasy.'

'Romance is essentially a fantasy. Marriage on the other hand is a contract with duties and rights.'

'You have to give and take,' I say.

'People these days feel entitled to more love than they give or deserve,' says Paula.

'I believed that your family was perfect,' I confess.

'My job was to keep us looking respectable. We had to look contented. Since Ron became impotent and then lost his mind he became an impossible grumpy old man. I wished him dead and that bothers me more than what I went through. The guilt and the fear of punishment. I served to atone for my evil thoughts. Maybe it was wrong or maybe it wasn't.'

'I suppose we are all killed off in someone's thoughts sometimes.'

'I will never be able to forget that Julie wants Damian dead. Her words are my punishment. I hate Julie for hating my son.'

'Nothing I do is good enough,' says Damian. 'She keeps telling me how unhappy I make her. What does she want from me?'

'Divorce is never pretty.'

'Julie told me that Damian always has one foot outside. I am on my own all day,' she complains. 'This is not good enough and I won't have it. The girl on the computer does not have to deal with naughty kids, blocked toilet, runaway dog, dead lawn mower or a plague of spiders. I cry myself to sleep most nights. He gets his titillation on the computer, and then he wants me to enjoy sex.'

'Nothing I do is good enough,' says Damian. I am under attack all the time so I stay at work. She makes me feel guilty for whatever is making her unhappy. I am not happy.'

'I suggested to Julie that part time work might give her a chance to meet people,' says Paula. 'She is a trained, registered nurse.'

'Damian would want me to go to work so he would not have to pay maintenance,' says Julie. 'I am going to make it really uncomfortable for him to strut around with any other woman. I was there for him when he needed me. Why should some girl, who has never lifted a finger for him, spend his money? I hate him.'

'Damian tells me, that Julie tells the kids that they are no better than their father,' says Paula.

'I can't go on like this, Julie says. 'It is better that he moves out of the house and out of my life.'

'I am never home anyway,' says Damian. 'All she wants is to deprive me of my children and my home.'

'The lawyers and judges make sure that the wife of a lawyer loses everything,' says Julie. They don't let one of theirs lose. They would collectively stone a woman who would dare to sue a lawyer. I know I will never be happy while he is alive.'

'Who is this other woman,' I ask Paula.

'Damian said that there is no other woman. There are several people I chat with on the computer, he said. Actually a girl asked me to make a clean break and come to her. Julie found her message. There is nothing clean about breaking the family, leaving the children and the home. How can I break away from the business that I built for twenty years? What will I do in Perth? I can't keep two homes. I will have nothing left by the time I pay the maintenance and child support. So there is no other woman.'

'Perth is thousands of kilometres away,' I say.

'I don't know what Julie does all day. I really don't, says Damian. She can't cook a simple meal without moaning about the sacrifice she made for her family. I am sick of doing the same thing over and over,' says Julie. Damian never notices if the place is clean or filthy. He just moves into his office and writes to his sweetheart. He doesn't even bother to argue.'

'I argue in court all day so I want to give it a rest at home,' Damian told me. 'I have to do my work properly to get paid, why can't she do hers. Our house is a mess, our garden is overgrown with weeds, we don't call friends over because we are ashamed for them to see how we live. She should get off her fat behind,' says Damian.

'He calls me fat,' complains Julie. 'For the first ten years I was either pregnant or breast feeding so I ate for two. I still eat for two. I hate myself. I am fat. I couldn't be bothered with housework. Kids enjoy the mess we live in and Damian is never home anyway.'

'What am I to do,' sighs Paula.

'Sonia and Damian are lucky to have you as their sounding board,' I say.

'This sounding board is worn out. I wish they were like Stan and you, so perfectly sane and calm,' smiles Paula.

'We don't expect too much from each other.'

'Is that your secret?'

'It's no secret. We are realistic.'

'You go to church,' says Paula. 'What do you believe?'

'I believe that there is a reason and a purpose for everything. I also believe that it isn't given to me to understand God's plan and purpose for me.'

'I am getting clumsy. My leg is in plaster,' Paula rings me from the hospital.

I bring Paula home a week later. They had to operate on her ankle and insert a bolt to hold it in place. She tries to smile but

I can see that she is still in pain. I realise that my friend became a frail old lady. I visit her every day, cook for her and tidy her house. I am happy that finally I can do something for her.

'The pain is not even where they operated, it feels like the vain under my knee is hurting,' says Paula. I take her for a check-up at our new Woden Valley hospital. They find a blood clot and prescribe medication. It is going to be fine. Blood cloths happen after operations, the doctor assures us.

'I haven't been to hospital so much in my entire life,' I tease as I visit Paula.

'I hope that I won't have to return the favour,' says Paula.

'You have never been sick or in hospital before either.'

'Actually I had a mastectomy fifteen years ago. I did not tell anyone. Maybe I hoped that it didn't happen if nobody knew about it.'

'I don't even remember you being in hospital.'

'I told you that I was visiting my sister in Melbourne. I couldn't stand anyone knowing. Or being sorry for me. Or feeling smug because it didn't happen to them.'

'Did they take it off?'

'They took both of them. I had a complete breast restructuring and you can hardly notice it. After the therapy I never had any problems.'

'You never told me.'

'Maybe I was protecting Ron. I didn't want him to have to deal with it.'

'How?'

'A wife with no breasts. Pity, I suppose; Ron couldn't cope with pity. Actually he suggested that we keep it to ourselves.'

Paula comes home and is ordered to rest. Julie offers to stay with her. Two days later Julie rings to say that the ambulance took Paula for a check-up again. The pain didn't go away as promised.

I pass the hospital cafeteria on my way to Paula. I see Damian and Julie. Damian's face is cupped in his hands and Julie is running her fingers through his hair. I don't want to intrude. No doubt Paula will tell me what happened. Underneath the pride and anger and jealousy there is also love and caring and forgiveness.

'I saw Damian and Julie in the cafeteria,' I tell Paula.

'I had to break my leg to get them sorted,' smiles Paula.

'I hope they will remember not to do it again. You are not used to all this pampering,' I tease.

'So much vanity and nonsense.'

'We are going for a drive to Tumut on Sunday and you are coming with us. Fresh air will put a spark into your eyes.'

'I don't know if they will let me out.'

'As soon as you are better then.'

'I don't know when I will be better. They made tests.'

'What tests?'

'The blood clothing medication did not work so they tested for cancer. It has spread. I only have months. If that.'

'Why did they check for cancer?' I try to blame the doctor for finding Paula's mortality.

'Apparently the blood clothing should have stopped and when it didn't, they knew that it was cancer. Deep inside I was expecting it anyway. You see once you have it you carry it in your mind.'

'But they cut it out,' I try.

'They cut it out of my body but not out of my mind.'

What can I say? Do I complain that it is unfair that my best friend will be snatched away from me because she broke her leg? Paula never asked for anything, she just was there. Only now I realise that she was the central part of my life in Canberra. She took me under her wing and became my surrogate mother, my sister and my friend. My only real friend.

'Time to go,' smiles Paula patting my hand.

'No, you can't just go, It's not fair. You only broke your leg.'

Paula is the same strong sensible lady I first met. I expect her to tell me what to do and say. Her eyes are sunken and her skin is transparent. How come I did not see that straight away? I hear words but I do not look at things with my eyes. Maybe I am my dad's daughter after all. He didn't look at things with his eyes. 'Close your eyes so you can see the magic land,' he said.

'I was in remission for fifteen years.'

'You recovered,' I argue.

'One carries the torch until someone else takes over. There is always someone else.'

'You will get better. You must get better.'

'Everything makes sense when you finally surrender. You orbit for a while with the rest of the universe and then you change into dust and orbit again. Someone created these orbits. The smallest and the biggest mirror each other. The biggest is as essential as the smallest but we don't know either. Someone must know why things are as they are. God calls us one by one and the chain of life continues. There is a reason for everything. Damian and Julie made up. Maybe they realised how lucky they are to be alive. Perhaps the reason for my life was to persevere in my imperfect family.'

'No family is perfect.'

'I am glad you are going home to see your family now.'

Damian is holding Julie's hand as they come in. Their eyes are red.

I walk into the cafeteria. There is an enormous aloneness inside of me. I need to cry but cannot cry alone.

'The priest just left,' says Paula the next day. 'I made my peace with God. I never bothered with religion much but the words attributed to Jesus make sense now. I am the way the truth and the life. If Jesus did live and if he was a son of God and if he said these words, then I am on the right path.'

'I don't think Jesus would have lied.'

'I was never good at praying. It seemed senseless bothering God but when you have to prepare to meet your maker it is easy to prey,' says Paula. 'I shouldn't blame him for not making me more perfect.'

'You were always perfect,' I say to Paula.

'I failed to appreciate perfection. I chose to concentrate on my miseries.'

Maybe it is easier to concentrate on miseries. Why do we choose to ignore the perfection we are given? I remember my photo albums. Hana and I look so alike yet I never thought of myself as beautiful or special. Maybe even Hana does not know how beautiful she is.

'The priest told me to put my life in the hands of Jesus if I want it to count for something,' smiles Paula.

'Stan and I once watched football and the spectator called out: 'The ball in his hand is worth a million.' The same ball in my hands would be worthless.'

'Perhaps we should all put our lives into the hands of the almighty.'

Paula died, I ring my boys but they barely knew her. She was just that Red Hill lady when they grew up. Mum's friend. Children only notice other children because they are at their eye level. We only see our own size. People like us. I have no one like me. Maybe even at home there is nobody like me anymore. It has been so long yet it seems like yesterday. In retrospect one's lifetime becomes a fleeting adventure. Memories, like fireflies, illuminate the darkness but they don't show the way. I am alone. Stan was never close to Paula. Maybe he is close to someone I don't even know. Maybe men don't need this kind of closeness.

In Australia people become friends while they live close to each other but then they move or die. Never to be remembered. I panic when I think that nobody will remember me after I am gone. I have lost myself somewhere. I am not connected to anyone.

We finally made arrangements to go home but then Toni rings.

'Toni and Hana are coming to Australia,' I tell Stan.

'When? Why?'

'Soon,' I think. We might stay for good if we like it, said Toni.

'What about the election?' Asks Stan.

'He said that he dropped out.'

'Was probably kicked out,' says Stan. 'Maybe former communists aren't so popular these days.'

'Toni dropped out of the party ages ago,' I defend my brother in law.

'Communists infiltrated other parties to cause trouble,' says Stan.

'Toni was never a real communist.'

'None of them were ever real communists but they will always be opportunists,' says Stan. 'Old friends still share old habits regardless of what party they are in at the moment.'

Stan was never thrilled about Toni or Hana. He just can't see what is so special about them. Men are jealous and petty. I need Hana. I need to be close to someone. Stan is a reasonable man but there is something that irks him about Toni. I hate it when he is so negative but now is not the time to argue. I want Hana and Toni to admire our life. I wonder what Toni is like now. I have to contain my excitement. Maybe God arranged Hana's visit to ease the pain of losing Paula. Hana is family; she will never stop being my sister. It would be just great if they would stay in Australia.

'They might not like Australian food,' I say to Stan.

'They can buy whatever they like and cook it the way they like it.'

Stan can't understand why I am worried. Stan and I hated Australian food at the beginning but it has improved with the influx of international cuisine. We can order anything at the restaurants but Stan still likes my old-fashioned cooking. I think he really likes the food his mother cooked in our village when he was a little boy. I am only an extension of his mum. I cook what she got him used to.

We are waiting at the airport. Stan must be excited because he doesn't even notice that I am crying as we see them coming through the customs. Hana is as beautifully elegant as ever. There is something glamorous about both of them. They say that the beauty is in the eye of the beholder but I believe that everybody would notice how radiant Hana and Toni are. Hana's hair sways as she walks. Half of her face seems covered by her blond curls.

Toni hugs Stan and congratulates him on his good looks before he sweeps me off my feet and tells me that I haven't changed at all. No wonder Toni is so popular.

'If Mohamed doesn't come to the mountain the mountain comes to Mohamed,' laughs Toni. 'Everybody is coming home for holidays except you.'

'We were planning to come. Actually I retired so we could come.'

'Took you a long time. Stan always needed a little push,' laughs Toni slapping Stan's shoulder.

'At the beginning we had no money, later the babies came, then schools and weddings and grandchildren and everything.

'There is always something going on,' I keep explaining because I know Stan heard the words: needed a push. He would not like that. One becomes sensitive to the person one lives with for forty years. Toni pushed us out of Slovenia. Maybe Stan does not like being pushed.

'We wanted to go together but we could never all agree on the right time,' says Stan.

'I am so happy to see you again,' whispers Hana. I feel her tears but her face is not changed. My face is a mess as I sob openly. We drive over the hills of Canberra and they seem suitably impressed with my favourite city. I think both are speechless looking down on Canberra from our place.

'I don't know if you will like our food,' I apologise, as I serve dinner.

'Stop fussing, you are the best cook,' says Stan.

I will have to be careful not to cause friction. We keep talking about the trip and about the reasons for their visit and we tell each other over and over how delighted we are to be together and how wonderful we look.

'We will let you settle down and freshen up. Come down when you feel like it.' I show them to their room and the bathroom. Stan and I bring up their luggage. Later Toni comes down but Hana wants to rest.

'How come you dropped out of the election,' I ask Toni as we sit down with a drink.

'I never had time for my family. It's time to get my priorities right,' says Toni.

'Before it is too late,' I say. 'Stan and I have been thinking the same. We have always been too busy; we never took time to be with our boys. Maybe we can make up for it with our grandchildren. We were going to visit them but then you invited us home.'

'Are you a grandfather yet?' Asks Stan.

'It's not so easy these days to become a grandfather,' laughs Toni. 'Young ones have too much fun without children.'

I always get up early to prepare breakfast for Stan. After Stan leaves for work next morning, Toni comes in the kitchen with a finger on his lips. 'Hana likes to sleep in,' he explains.

'Have some coffee?'

'Could we go shopping after? I would like to buy a few things for Hana.'

'What are you looking for?'

'We'll see what they have.'

In the grocery shop Toni selects a box of Swiss chocolate and a few bottles of wine. He picks a bottle of vodka and reads the label. 'Hana likes a bit of vodka in her orange juice,' he says. 'She stopped smoking so she needs something to relax with.' He puts two bottles of vodka in the shopping trolley. As we move through the shops, Toni picks a sexy looking nightie and runs his fingers through the silky material. 'Do you think she will like that,' he says as he takes it to the cashier. 'What is your favourite scent,' Toni asks as we pass the cosmetic counter. He buys one for me and one for Hana. 'That will cost you a fortune,' I protest. 'This is for being my guide,' he squizzes my elbow. On the way home Toni stops at the florists and picks a bunch of white roses. 'White is Hana's colour,' he smiles.

When Stan comes home he opens a stubby of beer to relax with. He has one stubby every day, on rare occasion he has a couple. We have a glass of wine on festive occasions but I usually drink coffee.

'Toni bought these for Hana,' I point to the roses.

'You have the garden full of flowers,' laughs Stan. I wonder if he feels chastised. Stan never buys me flowers. We grow our own, I suppose, but it would be nice to be surprised with a bunch of roses. Stan is becoming irritable. Maybe he wants me to be like

Hana. Maybe he wants me to be Hana. I decide not to tell Stan that Toni bought me the perfume. I feel a little guilty. Irresistible, says on the heart shaped bottle.

Hana sits in the big armchair like a kitten. Her eyes are half closed like she lives in another world. Dad was like that. He never raised his voice or lost his temper or become moody. He said that there is another wonderful world if you only closed your eyes.

Toni pours Hana a drink and she sips it lazily. She smiles as Toni pats her hand. She is like a mirror; smiling when others smile. She is like a sponge that soaks up everything around her. I wonder where her thoughts are and how she feels. Perhaps she is not bothered with feelings and thoughts. I feel obliged to keep the conversation going but Hana just nods this way and that. Toni speaks for her.

Stan invites Toni and Hana to our Slovenian club but Hana does not feel like going. I stay with Hana. It isn't easy to become intimate with someone you didn't see for close to forty years. I ask Hana about the tablets she takes with her drink. She explains about hormonal imbalance and arthritis and calcium and iron. She is surprised that I never take anything. I just put up with things.

'I am less anxious since I began taking the happy pill,' smiles Hana as she passes a bottle of Prozac to me.

'I was always so proud of you; you were our shining star,' I say.

'I always wanted to be like you,' says Hana.

'No, you didn't. Nobody ever does. Everybody wants to be like you,' I insist.

'You had a common sense.'

'Everybody has common sense that's why it is called common. When you have nothing else you remember your common sense and use it.'

'You manage to be in control while I agonise about my problems.'

'I suppose it is easier to be ordinary like me than to shine like you. I put up with things and pay my dues.'

'I think I will take a nap. I am still a bit jetlagged,' says Hana.

'I roast and bake and shop to give the best I have to my sister. Stan is tired of my admiration and subservience.

'You are not yourself, says Stan. I don't know what you want to prove to them.'

'You don't try so I have to,' I defend my behaviour.

'What would you like me to do? I drive them around, buy drinks, and introduce them to Slovenians. What more do you want from me.'

'Toni and Hana are as much in love as they were at the beginning.'

'It's all a show,' says Stan. 'I think Toni is a clown.'

Toni and Hana have cast a shadow over our ordinary lives. The more I try to be neutral and natural the more self-conscious I become. I feel like a proverbial centipede wondering which foot comes after which.

'Stop acting like a mother to everybody,' says Stan when I ask Toni if the bed suits him and if they slept well.

'She is just being kind,' Toni defends me.

'She is not your mother.' Does Stan feel isolated or jealous? There is nothing to be jealous about.

'I am amazed how well your boys speak Slovenian, says Hana when Stan junior and Mark and Joe arrive to see their famous relations.

'Stan insisted,' I explain. 'He also arranged that they all have Slovenian citizenship just in case they ever want to go home.'

'It can never hurt to know another language. The more you know the better,' explains Stan.

'Dad wouldn't speak English so we had to learn,' says Mark.

'They speak only Slovenian with Stan. I suppose it became a habit, I give a pat on the back to the man that made it possible for boys to know their mother's tongue. 'They actually learned everything from Stan,' I add. 'They finished uni, of course, but you don't learn there how to fix a shelf on the wall or repair a leaking tap.

'When they grew up I bought them an old car each so they learned how cars work. Now they can put a car to pieces to check which piece is faulty and repair or replace it,' says Stan.

I am glad Stan can boast about his success with his boys. He deserves to be proud.

'These days everything is electronic and replaceable. Nobody repairs things anymore,' says Toni.

'There are still heaps of things one can do in a home,' I stand on Stan's side.

'Most things are best left to experts. It's cheaper in the end,' laughs Toni. Maybe he is right. No doubt Toni knows best, he always had the best from cars to homes to women. Toni makes Stan look insignificant. My family seems less successful. I feel put down. Toni and Stan are like two bulls in the same paddock. Small paddock. I don't know how to fix their relationship.

'Maybe nothing is worth fixing anymore,' I say for no reason at all.

I remember meeting an old man who knew our boys when they were little. 'And how are the boys? Are they in or out of jail?' the man asked. I was shocked and even offended at first but later I felt relieved because our sons have never been in jail. They get along doing what boys are supposed to do.

There is nothing wrong with my family. Why should I feel inferior?

Stan and Toni often go to Slovenian club. Slovenians have taken to Toni immediately and wholeheartedly. He has a knack of being everything to everybody. He buys drinks and pays compliments to men and women. They tell yarns and sing and remember. Toni tells me that Slovenians teased Stan about finally getting permission to come for a drink. Toni looks at Stan for reaction. I know that Stan resents everything Toni says and does.

'Like I would not allow him,' I laugh.

On Saturday night we go to the club for dinner. I want Hana to meet our friends

'You two look like twins,' says Zinka.

'Like cheese and chalk,' I protest.

The thought that I look anything like Hana seems absurd. My hair is straight and short and brown while Hana's wild long honey blond curls are bouncing off her shoulders.

'Wrap your hair in a towel and look at yourself in the mirror,' says Zinka. I wouldn't dream of comparing myself to my sister. While home alone Hana and I gradually return to our childhood. We have to pick up where we left a lifetime ago.

'We all looked up to you when we grew up,' says Hana affectionately.

'I suppose Mum trained me early to put up with you.'

'You have your life beautifully organised.'

'Organised is the best I can do. We get along.'

'Toni said that people who just get along never make a mark. You have to take risks and break the rules. He says that the fighters rule the world,' tells Hana.

'We live by different rules. Comfort and peace mean a lot to us,' I say feeling slightly offended.

'I really like your life and I love Australia,' says Hana.

'People are literally dying to come to Australia. There are boatloads of Asians and Africans; people from the Middle East are risking their lives to get in. Australia is the second America.'

'You are lucky to have two countries to call home.'

'I am.'

'You should be proud of your boys,' says Hana.

'I am.' I bring out my albums and begin the story of my family. Just as well I got the photos sorted so my sister can admire my life.

Joe is the youngest but he was the first to get married. He has two gorgeous daughters. Marko married a year later and has three children. Stan junior has a girlfriend. Have you any photos,' I give Hana a chance to tell about her family.

'Sofija and Janez are very independent and career minded.' Hana picks a family photo from her wallet. Toni loves his family. Sometimes it frightens me how protective he is, says Hana. I think he would kill to protect us.'

'You are lucky,' I say.

'Kids think that he is bee's knees.'

'I am happy for you.'

'I wish I was more like you,' Hana's voice suddenly breaks. She is on the verge of tears. 'You were always so sensible and cool while I let others run my life.'

'Perhaps everybody sometimes wants something else, be somewhere else, do something else, be with somebody else.'

'But you always made sensible choices,' says Hana with her eyes half closed; sipping her drink.

'I didn't have as many choices as you did,' I smile.

'I am waiting for the big event called life. I want to remember one moment and say: this is my life. I feel like my soul has been disfigured and pushed aside. What was your big event? What made life worth living?'

'The little things were as important as big events. Family, coming to Canberra, new experiences.'

'I don't know what I am waiting for;it feels like I am serving a life sentence with no parole in sight.'

'We are all paddling in the same canoe. Serving.'

'I am wasting time,' says Hana.

'You can't save time and put it in the bank,' I joke. 'Seriously though, I never wasted time. Since I retired I can do what I like but there is so much to do and see and experience.'

'Toni and I nurture our fragile relationship which is like a millstone around our necks.'

'I had a wonderful friend Paula. I keep looking at the door hoping that she will come like she did almost every day. I believed that she will be with me forever but she died suddenly. One way or another relationships die. Even love dies.'

'I am sorry to bother you with my miseries,' says Hana.

'You are not. Paula shared her miseries with me.'

'I want to punish Toni but I don't even know what for. He had affairs but they never meant anything to him or to me. I could have left him but some other girl would be only too happy to grab him. Toni lived on the edge; he likes big houses, big cars, big parties. He is a real daredevil. At the beginning I was attracted to that.'

'Men are like that,' I say but what do I know of men. Stan is not like that.

'I will never be myself while I am with Toni.'

'Australians have this famous saying: You can't have your cake and eat it.'

'Toni solves my problems; he never needs my help or my opinion. I wish he disappeared from my life.'

'Paula wished her husband dead and her daughter in law wanted Paula's son dead,' I remember. 'Both also loved their men. They just didn't feel loved enough at times.'

'I am trapped in Toni's life. Toni is the king and I am his shadow. I never know where I am going but I follow.'

'It is easier to follow than to choose your own path. As long as you don't make the rules you have no responsibility, you cannot be blamed.'

'Leave it all to me, is Toni's favourite saying. Once we were out dining and he said to Sasha: don't worry your pretty head about it. Leave it to me. Sasha laughed into Toni's face: if I leave anything to you, I might find you hanging on the end of your own rope. You'd be hanging on the other end, laughed Toni.

'Sasha likes to tease Toni but he takes notice of what she says. When I express an opinion, Toni smiles at me, messes my hair, tweaks my nose, pats my hand, buys me vodka or roses or lingerie.'

'He is generous.'

'It amuses him to see people notice how generous he is.'

'You trained him to be who he is.'

'I always blamed myself for who he is. At the moment everything seems to be against him so I don't want to make it harder for him. He is the father of my children. I have a premonition that something dreadful will happen.'

'What is meant to happen will happen.'

'I have recurrent dreams about a woman who tries to hit me with her walking stick. I try to escape but I get stuck in the mud and cannot lift my feet. I turn off the road and hide in a tunnel. The tunnel turns into a tarpaulin bag squeezing me until I can no longer move. I am suffocating. I wake up from the agony of my struggle. Something is going to happen. The woman with a stick keeps following me.'

Hana sips her drink and smiles as if she was telling a fairy tale.

'Dreams are dreams. I have weird dreams during the full moon but I know that they will go away.'

'Everything becomes more intense in the silence of the night. I hear the sounds of my heart beating. I become afraid of the world closing down on me. Swallowing me. I think of death. Am I going mad?' Hana tries to smile but I see real fear in her face.

'The world goes to sleep but the dream-world wakes up. God lets the angels hover over the world at night, dad used to say. I wonder what he meant.'

'I can put up with Toni and Sasha but I cannot put up with what's going on in my head.'

'What is in your head?'

'Toni is suffocating me with gifts and compliments. At home he lived his life and I lived mine. Now I am all he has and he wants me with him all the time.'

'Maybe he really put his priorities in order. Paula's son Damian and his wife Julie were heading for a divorce when Paula became sick. Paula said that she had to break her leg to sort them out. Maybe we have to break something to mend something else.'

'Do you like Australia?'

'You give up something so you can have something else. Stan says that we would never see Australia if it wasn't for Toni.'

'Toni also arranged your life,' smiles Hana.

'We were so young then. Stan did what Toni told him to do. Toni made an offer and Stan couldn't resist it.'

'I feel that Stan resents Toni. Maybe he never forgave him. Are you sorry for leaving Slovenia?'

'I sometimes wonder how things would be if Toni wasn't in our lives.'

'Is Stan happy in Australia?'

'We manage.'

'You managed well without Toni all these years.'

'Toni was there in the background all this time. Everything started with Toni.'

'It was a lifetime ago,' sighs Hana.

'Stan and I have only been married a few months. I was pregnant with Stan junior when Stan decided to go to Germany for a few months to earn the money for a car. I hated being on my own. After six months Stan returned with an old car. Toni offered to buy it from him at a profit. Stan returned to Germany by train and brought another car and another. Stan brought fourteen cars for Toni in two years. We had two children while I lived on my own for those first two years of our marriage. The cars were full of other stuff like radios and cameras and clothes, which Toni sold to his friends.'

'They made plenty of money,' says Hana. 'Toni was always good at making money. He is happiest when he makes money. Dealing and wheeling gives him a buzz. He makes money for the thrill of it. Our family wasn't ambitious, our lot has not half the drive Toni has,' says Hana. 'At the beginning I enjoyed the prestige and wealth but then I just accepted whatever happened. I suppose I gave up on myself. Toni bulldozes anyone who stands in his way. He makes people feel that he is smarter than they are and if that doesn't work he reminds them of the risks they are taking in trying to outsmart him. If nothing else works he loses his temper and makes them ashamed of their stupidity. I have actually seen his eyes turn green as he lost his temper with the man who tried to outsmart him,' says Hana.

'The last car Stan brought for Toni was a new Mercedes and it came to the attention of the police. We just settled in the new home with our two boys when Toni brought our passports and plane tickets. He told us to pack up and go to Germany. UDBA began investigating our incomes. From there we applied to migrate to Australia.'

'Toni sold your house and placed the money into a German bank account before the government could confiscate it. I wonder if Stan ever forgave Toni for sending you away.'

'We came to Canberra to sign some papers in order to collect that money. When we got the money from the house we bought a block of land close to the Parliament house in Canberra. I think Stan forgave Toni then.'

'You became very successful.'

'Slovenians were suspicious because we had money and came with passports. If the government gave us passports we must have been spies. We felt very isolated at the beginning. They called us UDBA. We were too scared to tell them that we escaped from UDBA.'

'They were jealous,' says Hana.

'Slovenians were the only important people for us at the time. We wanted them to like us. Australians had nothing to remember with us, we had nothing in common with them. They did not hate us or love us or admire our efforts. They weren't jealous or envious. We weren't a part of their life and they weren't a part of ours. It was nobody's fault but that's how things were.'

'I am sorry.'

'Stan spent many days building Slovenian club in Canberra but Slovenians kept their distance. They forever connected us to Yugoslav embassy. We became regular churchgoers and we did not make friends with the ambassador but Slovenians still did not trust us. We tried to keep neutral in their political squabbles but our neutrality did not please anyone. I did not dare tell anyone that we were afraid of Yugoslav government, Yugoslav embassy and UDBA. Or about the cars Stan brought from Germany.'

'Toni fixed everything at home and you were quickly forgotten,' says Hana.

'Everybody around you is your friend at home but Paula was my only real friend here. You wouldn't understand what it means not having anyone of your own.'

'Toni left the police force soon after you left. He became a director of the petrol service station and became known as the man who could get you anything from cars to chocolates to tractors, radios and televisions. Nobody asked where Toni got those things. He had connections. As a policeman and a director he knew who was worth knowing. Toni could supply anything from the East to the Middle East to the West. 'Trafficking goes with traffic,' said Toni's friend Freddy. Toni can get you jewels and girls and cars and clothes. People who travel have to stop at the petrol station to get information and fuel. Western tourists sold Toni currency and he sold that currency to people travelling to the West. Soon after Slovenia became independent Toni retired from the petrol station and dedicated himself to politics. People liked him, they owed him favours and expected more favours.'

'Why did he drop out?'

'It's a long story,' sighs Hana. 'I only know little bits I hear and read about it. The place is full of rumours, lies, intrigues and half-truths. I don't know what to believe. We escaped to Australia in the hope that people will forget us.'

'Tell me all about it.'

'Everything changed after Sasha's husband, Freddy, was murdered.'

'Who are Freddy and Sasha?'

'Sasha and I were in the same class at school. I think Sasha had a crush on Toni even then. When Toni and I began dating, Sasha began ignoring both of us. When she started going with

Toni's friend Freddy we became friends. People used to say that Sasha was born with a silver spoon in her mouth. Her father was the director of Plastika, the only factory in town. Just before Slovenia won independence in 1991 the factory was going broke. Sasha's father bought it at a fraction of its value for his daughter. He retired and Freddy became the director.'

'What is Freddy like?'

'Toni and Freddy did a lot of business together. We dined together, we even went on holidays together in those heady good days.'

'Are you still friends?'

'There are rumours that Toni murdered Freddy so he could marry Sasha.'

'Is Toni having an affair?'

'It's complicated. Freddy's BMW car was stolen. Freddy claimed the loss on the insurance. He told them that his key is where he always had it hanging in his bedroom. The factory checked his key and told him that it wasn't the original key. Someone stole his key and had a duplicate made and hung it back on Freddy's wall. The makers of the car informed the police that the car could not be driven without the original key. A special coding in-built in the car also monitored the car's movements. I don't understand how it works but they traced the car. If Robert had anything to do with it, I will kill him, Freddy said to Sasha.'

'Who is Robert?'

'Their only child. Robert admitted that he took the key. He hoped that his father would be able to claim the car on the insurance. He did not know that police could trace the car.'

'Why did Robert take the key?'

'Robert dropped out of school and became involved in illegal activities with other dropouts. There were wild rumours about his activities. He became a truck driver. I heard that police caught him smuggling Iraqi refugees. The refugees apparently paid him to take them to Germany but he left them in Slovenia. I heard that they threatened to kill Robert if he did not provide the car.'

'Why did Robert drop the refugees in Slovenia?'

'He parked the truck in front of his house and the refugees were asleep in the garage. The police must have been informed about his activities, they searched the truck and found money and drugs. They arrested Robert for drug trafficking. They did not know about refugees at the time. Robert claimed that he was only delivering things for his boss and did not know anything about the money or the drugs. Anyway he was bailed out soon after Freddy's murder.'

'Who was Robert's boss?'

'His friend Milos hired him as a delivery driver. After Freddy was murdered Sasha hired Milos as a new director for her factory.'

'Who is Milos?'

'Milos' father was a Serb general or something. After Slovenian independence in 1991 the family moved to Serbia. Milos, Freddy and Toni were friends or business associates.

'Why did Robert drop out of school?'

'Sasha and Freddy led their separate lives for a long time but when Freddy's girlfriend, Veronika, became pregnant Freddy spent most of his time with her. Robert began drifting along with his dropout friends.'

'Is Toni involved with Sasha?'

'I believe Sasha is blackmailing him.'

'Is that why Toni dropped out of the politics?'

'There are enemies everywhere when you stand for a political office. They dig dirt. Slovenia has more political parties at the moment than ever before.

'Toni was always so popular.'

'Sasha leaks bits of information about him through her confidants but when the police question her about it she denies it. There is a rumour that Toni sold Sasha the gun Freddy was shot with.'

'Did he?'

'Toni had no reason to shoot Freddy. They really liked each other. Freddy was much like Toni, popular and powerful,' says Hana. 'Freddy promised Toni full backing if he entered politics.

I sip coffee and Hana sips her orange and vodka.

'When did you start drinking vodka? I ask.'

'When I stopped smoking.'

'I am glad you stopped smoking.'

'I began taking pills but it annoyed Toni. I switched to vodka,' smiles Hana. 'He is very generous with vodka.'

'You are not taking pills anymore.'

'Actually I do but Toni does not know that. They help me pass the time. I like to watch the time passing. I am more aware when time walks with me slowly.

'You don't sound happy.'

'I am Toni's wife. I have no friends. I am nothing. I am afraid,' says Hana. 'There comes the time when the big questions have to be faced. I have no answers.'

'What questions?'

'Why am I here, what have I done, who am I.'

'There are no answers.'

'Our marriage died long ago. I don't know why we are going through this charade of married bliss.'

'Toni seems in love with you.'

'He acts like a lover, he was acting like a lover all his life. Only to different people. He seduces people so he can manipulate them. At present he needs me on his side so he is seducing me.'

'Maybe he wants to turn a new leaf.'

'I want to kill both of them.'

'Are they worth it?'

'I am worth it. I will never be happy as long as he is alive,' Hana whispers. 'I'd rather die.'

'Happiness sneaks on you when you least expect it. Maybe happiness has nothing to do with beauty, wealth or talents. Maybe we all receive a few moments of happiness to distract us while we keep busy with the miseries of life.'

'I think you need a holiday in Slovenia and I have a deal for you,' announces Toni when Stan comes home.'

'What do you want me to smuggle this time?' laughs Stan.

'News,' says Toni. Seriously, 'I need to know what is happening at home. You don't have to do anything, just listen. You were planning on going anyway. We'll look after things here.'

'Who does Toni think he is? We can pay our own way,' says Stan as we prepare for the trip. It actually comes as a relief to both Stan and myself to be on our own again.

'Perhaps we both really needed a push,' says Stan. I knew he would remember the words.

Emil and Tereza are waiting at the airport. I barely recognise my brother and sister. We wrote and exchanged photos. At least for Christmas. At least a card. They were the children I looked after. Now they are old people. I haven't had time to age yet.

Emil takes us to Hana's home on the outskirts of Ljubljana so we can unload our luggage and freshen up before we meet everybody. Stan and Emil are chatting in front as we travel to Ljubljana. I sit at the back. The silence brings back fragments of memories that touched me. I remember mum's words: Just do whatever you have to do and you will get used to it. You get used to anything. Almost anything. It might be hard at first but it gets easier until it becomes a habit. Even the most unpleasant things become a habit. Don't even think about it, just do it, mum used to say. When you come to the river to swim, jump in and let your body get used to the water. No use thinking about the temperature and whether you can swim. Thinking about it makes you wonder if you can do it or not. I remembered my father often but I hardly ever thought about mum before. She did what had to be done. She was sensible. I am not sensible at all. I cry for the years I spent away from home. What is this thing called home, anyway?Home is where the heart is, they say. Your feet take you where your heart is. Right now my heart listens to the words of my parents. I wipe my eyes.

Useless and romantic, someone once described my dad. Dad was a story spinner but what else could he do being bedridden. I never knew dad apart from his story telling and being bedridden. Dad never explained and never complained about his health or his destiny. He died before I was old enough to ask.

I heard rumours that dad left the seminary when he met mum; so it was mum's fault that dad did not become a priest. Is that why his parents did not like mum? I will never know if my dad was a communist revolutionary, a sinner or a saint. I wish I knew what mum and dad loved in each other. Mum brought dad the sweetest fruit and the best pieces of meat and the crispest salads. He held her hand and kissed her fingers. There was a sacred secret magic between them that made me feel warm and safe. I realise how important my parents were to me. Their words made imprints on the lily white pages of my soul. I wonder if anybody else remembers what I remember. Their words must be written on my soul because they appear in my memory whenever I need them.

'We are given a one way ticket and nobody can turn back the clock,' said dad. 'Mistakes can never be erased but experiences help you grow. Always count your blessings and never your costs.' Dad loved me, the thought suddenly brings tears to my eyes. He loved me in a special way. I looked after his other children. I was sensible like mum. He needed me like he needed mum. Mum and I took care of his family.

'Every story is an unfinished story,' said dad. 'You will add another chapter. You are my next chapter.' Most of dad's stories ended with the prince kissing the princess and then they lived happily ever after. The magic of his stories lingered over us and provided sweet dreams as we fell asleep most nights. I wanted to be the princess and live happily ever after in my castle. But I always knew that Hana was the princess. I don't think we would have survived without dad's dreams. Not long before he died dad read a handwritten story to us. I noticed that he closed his eyes as he read. He must have known the story off by heart. It was like a poem only I didn't know about poetry then and had no imagination. I just loved the sound of dad's telling. And the smell of our togetherness. The fragments of dad's words come back.

'With your eyes closed you can make any wish come true. You can walk on the velvety path of the forest, see the fairies dancing and hear the music in the branches of the trees. In the magic land you can be anything you want to be. Imagination is your greatest treasure. It is your own magic land and it is with you wherever you go, wherever you are. Things around you happen as they do, good and bad, they happen without you and despite of you. When you open your eyes you see fences, walls and barricades but when you close your eyes you can walk on the silky path of your choosing.'

'But magic is not real,' I said in my childish innocence.

'Close your eyes and your magic land will be real,' said dad before he died.

There is magic scattered on the way into my childhood. It seems that every bush on the way home is burning with memories. I look at what I once saw with the eyes and the heart of a child. Perhaps dad's fairies illuminated the path.

Dad never spoke about the injuries he received in the war. He did not like to speak about the war at all. I wish I could ask him what he was fighting for.

When I started school I got a new pair of shoes from the shire. Only three children from my class got new shoes. We also got free lunches. I wondered if we were especially good or especially poor. There were other good hungry children without shoes. The president of the shire told me that my father was a hero of the revolution. Maybe the fathers of other poor children weren't heroes.

Mum was numb with grief when dad died but I helped her by looking after the children. She kept busy but she never fully recovered. After Hana and I got married I think mum wished herself to die to be with dad.

We arrive to Hana's place. Flowering bushes surround the white brick walls of her home. I never really knew Hana. Hana and I changed. You cannot visit the same memories twice. Memories and people change. Maybe dad knew us. Nothing much happened in his life, he had time to close his eyes to see.

We unpack and return to Emil's home where my relations are waiting. I am again a cousin, an aunty, a sister; we are family but it would take me a lifetime to know these people. I have no time to really know them. I came to find out what people are saying about Toni and Hana. We hug because we know that we are a family. My nieces and nephews bring flowers to welcome us; homemade slivovic is offered to settle the dust and kill the germs. The strong spirit makes me cough but I have to swallow it as this is my welcome home drink. They pour another and it brings tears to my eyes; the tears seem appropriate because my relations like seeing me so touched by their welcome. The slivovic and welcome also bring tears to their eyes.

'Here is to Stan and Maria,' says Emil. 'We could always count on our Maria.'

'She was our second mother,' Tereza tells.

I remember my sons; I want them to share the closeness and warmth of the family; I am sorry that I took them away from all the people that would love them and share their lives with them. Stan and I are all the family they know.

'I want to stay here forever,' I say to Stan. 'I want our boys to live here.'

'If it wasn't for Toni we would never leave,' says Stan.

'If it wasn't for Toni we might never return,' I say.

'Our children only know Australia. You can't ask them to start a new life because we changed our mind,' says Stan. He walks for hours along the river with his fishing rod. Maybe he is remembering his childhood and collecting memories that will last for the rest of his life.

'Toni and Hana, Sasha and Freddy are the talk of the town. The media is spying on everyone who is connected to them. No doubt the journalists will want to talk to you if they find out that Toni and Hana are staying with you in Australia. Everybody is only too willing to share the rumours. They are careful when talking to me though, because I am Hana's sister. Sasha is apparently spreading vicious gossip about Toni,' says Tereza.

'What is she saying?' I feel like one of those undercover agents collecting evidence.

'The scandal is like a breath of fresh air, people forget their little lives while they speculate about the big news,' says Tereza.

'What news?'

'They say that Toni escaped because he killed Freddy and that Sasha will follow when she sells the business.'

'Everybody is buying papers in the hope that some new little detail about them will emerge,' says Emil.

'Sasha is running the factory now,' says Stan's niece Diana, who is working in Sasha's office.

'What is she like?' asks Stan.

'Sasha is elegant and smart. She would never do anything that is vulgar or disrespectful or cheap. She is convinced that Toni will leave Hana and marry her.'

'How do you know all that,' I ask.

'I hear things. Everybody knows.'

'Was Toni going to leave Hana?'

'Never. Toni loves his possessions and his family is his most precious possession. His wife and his children are untouchable,' says Stan's brother.

'Did Freddy know about Toni and Sasha,' asks Stan.

'Maybe he did or maybe he didn't. Sasha and Freddy were business partners, polite to each other in the office but lived separate lives,' says Diana.

'Were Sasha and Toni lovers,' I ask Emil.

'Whatever that means,' says Emil. 'They might have had sex but Toni never had any intention of leaving Hana. She was his anchor, his conscience, his icon, the mother of his children. I think Sasha became more and more frustrated and demanding. She believed if she got rid of Freddy,' Toni would marry her.

'When Toni became involved in politics, he began to avoid Sasha. 'He had to present an image of a clean, devoted, family man,' says Tereza.

'I heard them arguing in the office,' tells Diana. 'Sasha demanded that Toni leaves Hana and marry her. He said that he couldn't do this to Freddy. He would kill me if he found me with you, Toni argued. Kill him then, said Sasha.'

'Did they question Toni?'

'He dropped out of politics to avoid his family being smeared by the scandal,' says Tereza.

'Toni knows the local police and the judge and the politicians,' says Emil.

'Have they any clues who killed Freddy?'

'They questioned Robert.'

'Why would Freddy's only son, kill his father,' asks Stan.

'Since Freddy met Veronika, he had no time for his son,' says Emil.

'Veronika is Freddy's girlfriend. She had twins only months before Freddy was murdered,' explains Tereza.

'Freddy never spoke to his son after he learned that Robert was involved in stealing his car. Robert tried to explain that those Iraqi refugees would kill him if he didn't get them the car but Freddy said that he does not care.'

'Sasha reported her gun stolen,' says Tereza. 'She told the police that she placed the gun on her dressing table for self-protection since Freddy's car keys were stolen. 'When I woke up the gun was gone and Freddy was dead, she said.'

'She told the police that Toni supplied the gun,' adds Emil. 'Toni denied ever seeing the gun but he admitted that someone delivered a parcel to him and asked him to give it to Sasha. He did not know what was in it.'

'When police found the gun in the river,' they arrested Robert. Milos came to the police station and testified that he and Robert were watching videos on the night Freddy was murdered,' adds Tereza.

'Toni came to Sasha's office and begged her to keep away from him until the investigation was over,' says Diana.

'What did she say?'

'You bastard, she yelled.'

Toni's friend Adam invites us for dinner to get news about Toni and Hana. Adam is a director of a prestige Bellevue hotel. Stan and I are awed by the grandeur of the hotel's interior and the views over Ljubljana.

'How are my friends going,' says Adam. 'I miss them.'

'They enjoy Australia,' says Stan.

'It is hard to understand why anyone would want to leave this beautiful place but they adore Canberra,' I add.

'It is very quiet here now compared to what it was like,' says Adam. 'Political elite dined and wined and slept with their mistresses in this hotel. If the walls could speak.'

'You should write a book about it.'

'I used to get orders from Belgrade for ballerinas and strip dancers and film stars. Everybody pretended that the actresses and dancers and singers were cultural performers for political functions but they only came on the stage so politicians could choose who they wanted to sleep with. It was done openly and nobody thought anything of it. That's how things were in good communist times. We had to be in good books with politicians. Toni sometimes helped me.'

'He would,' says Stan looking at me. I believe that Stan enjoys Toni's misfortunes.

'Sometimes men wanted younger girls and they invited university students to sing and dance. I wouldn't have dared to whisper about it until Slovenia became independent.'

'Is it still happening,' asks Stan.

'It has gone underground. Men are much more careful and no, it does not happen much. Our politicians are too close to home here.'

'Was Toni sleeping with girls here,' I ask.

'Toni was too busy wheeling and dealing,' laughs Adam. He was also too much in love with Hana.'

'You don't have to protect him. I know everything about Toni and his girls,' I blab. 'I am immediately sorry. I came here to find out what others know.

'I didn't think that there was anyone who knew everything about Toni,' laughs Adam.

'Hana mentioned it,' I say with much humility.

'Toni told us that Freddy was divorcing Sasha to marry Veronika,' Stan changes the subject.

'Oh, vivacious Veronika. You will probably meet her. Everybody likes Veronika,' says Adam.

'Except Sasha, I suppose.'

'Sasha is not worried about Veronika. She found her own saviour in young Milos, the new director of her factory.'

'What is Milos like?'

'Charming,' says Adam with a mysterious smile. 'Clever and charming. He is a dashing bachelor who knows what he wants and how to go about getting it.'

'What does he want?'

'Milos helped Sasha keep young Robert out of jail. He also saved the factory from bankruptcy. He might even push Toni into divorcing Hana,' says Adam.

'Why would he want to do that?'

'Sasha wants it and what Sasha wants she must have.'

'What is in it for Milos?'

'There is always money.'

'Whose money?'

'Sasha and Robert rely on Milos. Excuse me for a moment,' says Adam as he is called to the phone.

'I have no idea what this is all about. People only tell us what they want us to know and think and feel,' I say to Stan. 'We are simply not used to secrecy and intrigue, we never had to deal with this kind of people.'

'Where does Milos come from?' I ask as Adam returns.

'His father, Milos senior, was a big shot in the Yugoslav army. A colonel in KOS, I think. He was a frequent visitor here in the olden days. He was Serb of course.'

'What is KOS?'

'Contra intelligence service.'

'A spy?'

'He was catching spies, I think.'

'Where is he now?'

'There was a big gold affair years ago. Milos' mother Francesca is Slovenian, born in Italy. She often came and talked to me. The rumour had it that people sent her things from Italy through Milos senior. They questioned Francesca and searched their home but they found nothing. Milos had some kind of diplomatic immunity. Eventually an order came from Belgrade to search his office. They found about ten kilos of gold in his locked office desk.'

'Is he in jail?'

'They were transferred to Serbia and we never heard of them again.'

'When did Milos junior reappear?' Asks Stan

'He has been around most of the time, I think.'

'How old is he?' I ask.

'Milos is about ten years younger than Sasha. In his forties, handsome, smart, smooth.'

'Sasha must trust him to let him take over her factory,' I say.

'She is a shrewd operator. Milos has a degree in chemistry and economics and he has connections. He is also very popular with workers.'

'Why didn't she give a job to her son?'

'She wants Robert to go back to uni. He has no qualifications. He never held a proper job.'

'Is Milos married?'

'Nobody is quite sure about his personal life. He seems very close to Robert.'

'I have to pass Toni's message to Sasha,' I say to Stan on our way home.

I am a little nervous as I ring Sasha's office. I heard of Sasha even while still at home but I never spoke to her.

'How nice to hear from you,' says Sasha. 'I don't know if you remember me at all but I heard so much about you from Hana and Toni. Can you drop by my office for a coffee and a chat?'

'It was easy,' I say to Stan.

'She will want you to think so,' says Stan cautiously.

Sasha is coming towards me and my first impression was that she is an ordinary, friendly, middle aged woman. People made her sound formidable but she seems very down to earth sensible. She has clear olive complexion and bright green eyes. Her long fingers play with expensive looking pen. We are both eager to break the ice. I decide that I don't have to hate Sasha.

'Would you see that we are not disturbed,' Sasha says to Diana.

I am delighted to meet Hana's Australian sister, she hugs me. Her voice is warm but it has a school bell clarity.

'Toni and Hana wanted me to say hello,' I smile.

'How are they? I really miss them.'

'Fine, they like Australia.'

Sasha is waiting for more information.

'I really don't understand why they would want to be in Australia at this time of the year. It is very hot there now,' I try to prolong the small talk.

'When are they coming home?'

'Toni said that they are coming soon but they didn't say when exactly.'

'I suppose you know that Toni and Hana are getting a divorce and that Toni and I are to be married.'

I am stunned by Sasha's directness. She is searching my face for tale tell signs of shock and disbelief. Once the mask is off, it is easier to be sincere.

'Nobody told me,' I say.

'Their marriage has been dead for a long time. Toni was waiting until children finished their education. Then came this dreadful business with Freddy.'

'Have they found the murderer?'

'My son Robert was apparently the intended victim but he was away with a friend.'

'Why would anyone want to murder Robert?'

'He got mixed up with the wrong crowd since his father lost interest in him.'

'Why did Freddy lose interest in his son?'

'Freddy got involved with Veronika,' laughs Sasha. 'He could not marry her of course but she became pregnant and had twin daughters just months before Freddy got shot.'

'Why couldn't he marry her?'

'It wouldn't be good for his business. You see, I own the business. Freddy did not know that I was willing to give him the divorce and have him continue in his position as a director. I wanted to tell him so as soon as Toni would say that he is ready to leave Hana.'

There is something cold and calculating in Sasha's words.

'So Robert is in the clear?" I ask.

'Robert wouldn't hurt a fly. He was scared of his father but he loved him. He was crushed when Freddy turned away from him.'

Sasha's green eyes are steady reading my responses.

'You love Toni?'

'We love each other, yes. We are two of a kind, Toni and I, we thrive under pressure. Toni feels protective towards his family but he has nothing in common with Hana. She never had to work so she is not interested in business. She will be looked after. That's what she always wanted. Someone to take care of her. I know that she no longer loves Toni. Not in the same way I do. We have been lovers for years.'

'Did Freddy know?'

'Toni and I provided girls for Freddy to play with. As long as he had enough fresh meat for sex and enough power in the factory, he was happy. What else can a man ask for anyway?'

The way Sasha says fresh meat hurts me. I don't like Sasha any more.

'You think men only care about sex and power,' I try to smile.

'What else is there?'

'You said that Freddy became involved with Veronika.'

'Poor man had midlife crisis. A temporary bout of insanity. It often happens to men before dementia hits them,' Sasha tries to make a joke of it.

'Excuse me,' says a handsome young man entering Sasha's office.

'Meet Hana's sister,' says Sasha. 'Milos is our new director. Would you join us?' Sasha turns to Milos.

'Pleased to meet you,' Milos throws a glance in my direction. 'I am busy at the moment. I just wanted to ask you about that Hungarian account but we can do that over lunch.'

Milos leaves the room. He has no time for an elderly woman who is wasting Sasha's time. I feel that he does not like me but maybe I don't even exist in his conscience. Probably even Hana means nothing to him. Maybe he is not interested in women.

Hana's daughter, Sofija, invites us for drinks on her thirtieth birthday. There is a small crowd of young elegant people mingling and chatting politely. Stan and I definitely don't belong but we make the best of it.

Sofija looks like Toni. Her long bony limbs communicate in elaborate gestures. With her short wisps of hair she looks like an overgrown elf. Words like elegant and sophisticated come to mind.

'Where is the lucky man who will make you an honest woman,' Stan tries to joke.

'Don't start,' says Sofija. 'Mum told me for years not to let any man make me a baby before I finish my studies.'

'Are you still studying,' I ask.

'I finished uni only last year, admits Sofija. Now I am busy studying life.'

'Your body clock is ticking,' I warn.

'I think I will let it tick away. I don't feel the need for the baby right now.'

'I am sure if the right man came along,' says Stan.

'I am not even looking for the right man. I have too much fun being single. I don't want to be tied down just yet.'

'Your parents would love to become grandparents,' I say.

'I'll let Janez look after the succession and the family name,' laughs Sofija looking at her brother who is a handsome image of his mother.

'With his blue eyes and blond hair he would make beautiful bambinos,' laughs Sofija.

'What about it?' says Stan.

'You start with disposable nappies and end up with disposable self-esteem. I am not rich enough yet to invest in Barbie doll industry,' laughs Janez.

'Don't you plan on getting married?' I ask astonished at this new generation.

'Why should I? I like my freedom. I like meeting people. Maybe one day I will want to build a nest but not yet. Life is much too precious to spend it all with one person. Once married, you are stuck.'

'Don't you want someone of your own,' I ask incredulous.

'I want to remember people I like with kindness. People who go through divorce become bitter and never forgive each other for not being in love anymore.'

'Most people never divorce. They make a commitment.'

'I am committed to freedom. You don't own people, you like them, maybe even love them but then you let them go.'

'But the children need daddy and mummy,' I argue.

'Maybe they do and maybe I will marry the woman that has my child but at the moment I am not sure that it is necessary for me to have a child,' says Janez.

'Have you ever been really in love?' I ask.

'I am in love all the time. Since I was a baby I was in love but I don't crave love like some sick addict. People get addicted to love and chocolates and drugs and alcohol and cigarettes. I am not an addictive person,' says Janez.

'You just want to enjoy your little affairs,' says Stan.

'One can have an affair with a bottle of wine or a good meal or a chitchat on the computer,' laughs Janez.

'I don't understand,' says Stan.

'I don't expect you to.'

'Wouldn't you like to have a permanent relationship,' I ask.

'As much as I would like to have an everlasting life. But I don't believe in ever-after or in heaven. What is on offer here and now sounds good enough to me,' laughs Janez.

'We have six grandchildren,' I say to Sofija.

'How boring and predictable,' she smiles. 'I am sorry,' she corrects herself, 'but this is not for me. Different scene. Different continent.'

'You are a dying breed,' laughs Janez. 'Sorry, I don't mean literally.'

'You would like to live forever but you are too lazy to have babies,' says Stan.

'I will have to let my soul slip into someone else's body,' laughs Janez.

'Transcending is in,' smiles Sofija.

'What,' Stan makes a face.

'They believe in some kind of reincarnation,' I guess.

'People like making babies and I am willing to offer them my soul,' teases Janez.

'How do you propose to do that,' I ask.

'The silver thread that keeps my soul in this body will break when my body dies and then my soul will become free to roam the universe.'

'You are dreaming,' says Stan.

'In your dreams the silver thread is only temporarily broken because on waking up you return into your body but when you die your soul is released.'

'In your dreams you get a taste of astral level of living,' helps Sofija.

'You ARE dreaming,' says Stan.

'And who is to say that events of my dreams are less or more important than events in my physical life.'

'What are they on about,' Stan turns too me

'I met Milos in Sasha's office. He is a very handsome man,' I change the subject.

'You like Sasha's new toy boy,' smiles Sofija.

'Is he Sasha's lover.'

'Looks like it. Or Robert's."

'When did Milos come into the picture?'

'I didn't know that he existed until Sasha appointed him as a director.'

'Do you like him?'

'I barely know him. As long as Sasha likes him.'

'Did Toni like him?'

'Dad is a bit jealous of anyone getting too close to Sasha.'

'I think Sasha just wanted to make dad jealous,' says Janez.

'It irks dad because Milos is so much younger and so handsome,' smiles Sofija. 'Anyway why such interest in Milos? '

'Toni and Hana asked me to find out what is happening.'

'Ask Diana,' she is Sasha's personal secretary.

'I don't understand the young generation,' says Stan. 'They are so different but then maybe it is because we lived so far from each other.'

I begin to wonder who is right. Maybe I am not as lucky as I believed. My children are as ordinary as I am. Young people want new toys all the time but as soon as they bring them home they lose interest and push them out of sight and out of mind.

'Normal person wants to have a family,' says Stan. 'It's only natural.'

'Emil's and Tereza's children are married and have babies,' I say.

'There is Diana. Talk to Janez while I have a woman to woman with Diana,' I say to Stan.

'Are Milos and Sasha lovers,' I ask directly.

'Milos brings her flowers but then he brings flowers to other girls. He is very generous.'

'Does he buy you flowers?'

'And other stuff.'

'What stuff?'

'When he travels interstate he brings souvenirs.'

'Isn't Sasha jealous?'

'I think they are just good friends.'

'Has Milos got a girlfriend?'

'I have never seen him with anybody.'

'Do you like him?'

'Everybody likes him.'

'Except Toni.'

'He is jealous.'

'What about Robert?'

'You should ask him.'

Diana is twenty-six and has no boyfriend. Maybe she is hoping to marry Milos. Or Robert. The thought makes me see things differently. I never met Robert. He was born after I left.

'What is Robert like?'

'He is in and out of court. Milos is busy keeping him out of trouble,' offers Diana.

While shopping in Ljubljana I find Milos and Robert sitting in a garden café.

'Small world, I say and sit myself next to them before they could stop me.'

'Robert, you met Hana's sister,' says Milos a little annoyed with my intrusion.

'I saw you with mum but we were never properly introduced, says Robert. His handshake is limp, his voice is high and apologetic. His eyes are darting in all directions like he was afraid. I realise that Robert is vulnerable.

Both men seem uncomfortable and obviously waiting for me to come to my senses and vanish. I know that I am pushy but I came here to push for information.

'Cakes look delicious. What do you recommend,' I turn to Robert.

'I like Black Forest myself but mum goes for vanilla cream slices,' smiles Robert. Cakes seem to delight him. His grey eyes become animated. 'Let me get you both so you can see who is right.'

'If you promise to eat half of each,' I strike a deal. It's easy to like someone who likes cakes. Milos does not order cakes. He excuses himself. He has things to do.

'Tell me about Australia,' says Robert. 'I always wanted to go to Australia.'

'Why?' I become exited.

'I never told anyone about it,' says Robert. 'Not even mum or dad or Milos. It has to be our secret.' The shared secret means an instant intimacy.

'I hope you will came, I say sincerely because we created an instant likeness. 'My boys would love to show you around,' I add the services of my family.

'I actually wanted to stay in Australia. I asked at the Australian Embassy but it isn't that simple.'

'Perhaps you should come for a holiday first to see how you like it.'

'I would like it because it is far from where I am,' says Robert.

'You don't like it here.'

'I wish' ... Robert brushes away an idea.

'I like Black Forest torte best too,' I say. 'What kind of coffee do you drink?'

'Vienna black, long and sweet. It is the only one with real coffee aroma.'

'I must try it. Can I get us two Viennas,' I offer.

'What are your boys doing?' Asks Robert.

I make a brief itinerary of my sons' achievements. I feel slightly uncomfortable boasting about my boys who have families and go to work and pay into the superannuation. My family is following some universal pattern of life. I hope that by boasting about it I will not jinx it. I don't like drama.

'They are very ordinary,' I say. 'Easy to get along. You would like them,' I promise.

I must be insane to invite Sasha's boy into my family. I am glad that he will never come. It isn't that easy. What am I doing here with a drug pusher and smuggler and possibly a murderer? I don't owe Toni and Hana that much. Maybe Hana would not like it. Or Sasha. With his criminal record Robert would never get the visa for Australia. I am safe, thank God.

'How is your coffee, asks Robert.'

'Fine, I like it. It is hard to find a really good coffee in Australia. There is a little continental café next to where I used to work. Embassy ladies meet there. That is the only place that has real continental cakes and coffees. Very expensive but first class. European people appreciate delicacies.'

'I wish there was a way to get to Australia,' Robert still wants to escape.

'We might find you an Australian girl to marry and then you can stay.'

Why am I offering girls I haven't got to a man who is the son of the enemy? A man of a questionable past. I lure him knowing that others will reject him. There is something irresistibly gullible and likeable about Robert.

'What would you like to do in Australia?'

'I don't really know what I want to do with my life. I just need to have a new start.'

'Would you go back to uni,' I ask.

'I started chemistry but I hated it. I would like to study art and literature but there is no money in that.'

'Do you need the money? Couldn't you get some casual work in the factory and go to uni part time.'

'I might do that.'

'Gives you a sense of independence and achievement, said my son when he did the same. He was mowing people's lawns at weekends while he was doing economics at uni. Mowing lawns gives me all the exercise I need and I get paid for it, he said.'

'I think I will have to go away and start my own life,' decides Robert.

Robert is in his late twenties. He is not at all like Sasha.

'Have you seen your baby sisters,' I ask casually. '

'I see them almost every day. They are gorgeous. They are beginning to talk.'

'Parents can't wait for babies to start walking and talking but as soon as they do, they tell them to sit still and be silent,' I repeat the joke.

'Veronika is an excellent mother. She talks to the girls all the time and she calms them down when they get excited. She has the touch for it, or something,' says Robert. 'They are very lucky, my sisters, I mean.'

'Veronika is your age, you must have known her from before.'

'She arrived a few years ago and I met her at dad's funeral.'

'Did dad tell you about your sisters?'

'Mum did. Dad and I didn't get on at the time.'

'What was your dad like?'

'I never thought about it,' says Robert after a short silence. 'What was he like? I don't even know what I am like.'

'We try all our lives to find out what we are like,' I laugh with Robert. 'Like they say, you are one thing to one person and something quite different to another.'

'I don't even know what I am to myself. A friend or an enemy,' he laughs to cover up the shared intimacy.

'Often we are our own worst enemies,' I say and we consider this.

I wouldn't mind Robert coming to Australia. Am I being my own worst enemy? What would I do if Robert actually arrived at our door? He could be the worst influence on my boys but somehow I feel that he could not influence anyone in any way. But then he influenced me to have Black Forest cake and Vienna coffee. Sometimes a weak person has more influence than someone aggressive. Milos is aggressive. I felt that. I would always be on guard with Milos. But Robert is likeable.

'That's what Veronika says. She said that my father was his own worst enemy.'

'Why would she say that?'

'Mum wanted him to quit his job. He wasn't happy but could not decide to give up what he had.'

'Until you are prepared to give up what you have, you can't make a new start.'

'I can see it now,' says Robert.

I don't know what he sees.

'When you put thoughts into words things become clearer,' I say. 'Sometimes we discover who we are when talking to others. I was very lonely in Australia until I found a friend, Paula. She died.

Why am I telling this to a young boy I just met?

'You would like Veronika,' says Robert.

'I am glad you do. She is your family now.'

'I would miss Veronika and the girls if I went to Australia,' says Robert.

'You could come together.'

'I suppose,' says Robert. 'She is doing well in her business.'

'Milos seems capable and helpful,' I say pretending that I know Milos well. 'Where did your mum find such handsome, smart man?'

'Milos and I were friends for years,' says Robert.

'Did he always live in Ljubljana?'

'He comes and goes. He was in Bosnia for a while.'

'What did he do before he become a director of Plastika.'

'He was in export and import,' says Robert. 'I actually worked for him sometimes. After I dropped out of school.'

Robert and I are not close enough yet to ask him what Milos imported and exported.

'What did you do?' I try to sound naive and innocent.

'Driving, delivering and collecting. That sort of thing.'

I want to ask about the keys Robert stole from his father and about Freddy's murder but it is too soon.

'You meet all sorts,' Robert volunteers more information. 'That's when I came across those refugees.'

'What refugees,' I play ignorant.

'Iraqis. They wanted to go to Germany. They said that they knew Milos so I gave them a lift from Macedonia to Ljubljana.'

'How many?' I ask carefully.

'Eight. I barely saw them. They were in the back of the truck with the stuff I delivered for Milos.'

'What did you deliver?'

'Parcels.'

'What happened when you came to Ljubljana?'

'They wanted me to drive to Austria. I parked in front of our house. Dad was away and we needed a rest. They were sleeping in the garage when police arrived and searched the truck. They found drugs under the seat and a parcel of money in the glove box. I knew nothing about it.'

'Did they find the refugees?'

'They must have escaped while police searched the house.'

'Did your father know?'

'No. The Iraqis said that they will kill me if I don't take them to Austria. They said that they paid to be taken to Austria. I don't know who they paid.'

'So you gave them the keys to your father's car?'

'They arrested me on the possession of drugs. Milos paid the bail and got me out. I gave him the key and he gave me back a copy of it to hang in dad's room. Milos sorted the refugees out in the end. Next my father got killed.'

'Any idea who killed your father?'

'No idea,' he says after a few moments. 'Oh, is that the time,' he adds getting up. 'I am late,' he apologises.

'I made a mistake. I became an obvious investigator.

I am in Ljubljana with questions unanswered and time on my hands so I call on Adam again.

'I just had coffee with Milos and Robert,' I say casually.

'Oh,' says Adam. 'Aren't they a bit young for you.'

'Robert told me that they were friends for years.'

'With friends like Milos you don't need enemies,' says Adam.

'Why?'

'I think Milos is behind all the trouble Robert has,' Adam leans towards me. 'Smuggling came to Milos through his mother's milk. The apple doesn't fall far from the tree. I have no proof, of course, but knowing Francesca and Milos'

Adam is an old man now. He likes to bask in the glory of the days when he was a confidant of the Yugoslav hierarchy. He knew the Yugoslav elite intimately.

'Are Milos and Robert smugglers or murderers or lovers?' I laugh to make it sound like a joke.

'Nobody knows exactly. No evidence. Even if there was it wouldn't change things. People with friends in high places can afford to do what they like. Milos' father was transferred to his home in Belgrade when they found a cupboard full of gold in his office. Nothing happened to him.'

'Who do you think killed Freddy?'

'They are pointing a finger at Robert but I know that Robert could never do it. He idolised his father.'

'But he stole the keys of his car.'

'He did what Milos ordered him to do; he was scared.'

'What about Milos?'

'Milos and Robert were together. I don't think we will ever know who did what.'

'Toni is scared.'

'As long as he keeps low and out of the politics he will be alright. Nobody wants anything to come out. He better stay out altogether. Australia seems just far enough.'

'Sasha told me that they are getting married. She won't let him stay in Australia.'

'They are both shrewd operators. Only I happen to believe that Toni does not like shrewd women. He wants to stay with Hana. She is the untainted part of his life. Toni likes to come home and be a loving head of the family. Why should he go home to a wife of his murdered friend?'

I heard that Veronika comes in the morning to organise her hairdressing business so I make a morning appointment. I introduce myself to Veronika and give greetings from Toni and Hana.

'How nice to meet you,' says Veronika with a naturally husky voice. 'Can I offer you a cup of coffee?'

'Perhaps we could go for coffee in town later,' I suggest.

'I like to do Hana's hair. I like Hana,' says Veronika without reservation. She tells the girls what to do while she is away but she is neither pushy nor subservient. She seems guileless and direct.

'Ready,' she turns to me. 'I'd just like to check on the girls and then I am all yours. Would you like to see my twins,' she says.

'I would love to,' I say genuinely.

Veronika's baby sitter is tidying the two bedroom flat on the second floor of the block of flats nearby.

'Freddy bought this flat for me before he was murdered.'

There is warm cosiness in the flat. 'Mind if we have coffee here,' says Veronika. I can let the sitter go and keep an eye on the girls while they are asleep.

'I like that,' I say. I like everything about Veronika. She seems the most open and unafraid person I met at home. There is no anxiety, conspiracy, shame or cunning. We peep at the two pink bundles sleeping peacefully in their cots.

'Freddy was besotted with the twins,' Veronika says simply. I don't want to miss a minute of being with them, he said. He kept bringing tons of toys and clothes and books. I think he searched the world to find something to surprise me with.'

'The nursery looks like a fairyland,' I smile.

'We were going to get married as soon as he got the divorce. His marriage was long finished anyway. It's not like I broke a happy family.'

'Of course.'

'He filed for the divorce a week before he was murdered.'

'What a tragedy. I heard rumours that Robert murdered him,' I say.

'No way. Robert adored his father and he adores his little sisters. Robert is not a baddy some would have you believe. Maybe he is a bit gullible though.'

I like Veronika. Why are some young people so much easier to like? Maybe they still believe that the good will prevail over the evil like it does in the fairy tales. My boys believed in the justice and as students they protested for all sort of courses. They grew out of it now, of course. Old people become wise, cunning, conniving, shrewd and suspicious. They lose their innocence and ideals.

It is so difficult to know the truth. In Australia we take things at their face value. People have no reason to be evasive or careful to hurt someone's feelings. Here more is hidden than revealed. I hear the words, I see the faces but I am only guessing the meaning of it all.

'Here we go,' says Veronika, placing Vienna coffees in front of us. Did Robert learn to like Vienna coffee here or did Veronika learn to make it to please him. I wonder if Veronika knows that I spoke to Robert.

'I hear that Sasha is going to marry Milos,' I lie.

'I believe that Milos has some kind of a hold over Sasha and Robert. I don't like Milos.'

'Robert should get married and start a family,' I say.

'I don't think he is a marrying type,' smiles Veronika.

'Why not?'

'I suppose he needs to find out what he wants, who he is, that sort of thing,' says Veronika.

'I suppose we all do, I concede. Sometimes we rush into things and then regret it.'

'I think I can hear the twins,' says Veronika.

We chirp over the waking toddlers before I excuse myself.

Hana rings as I come home.

'Toni and Hana are coming back,' I rush to tell Stan.

'What happened,' says Stan. 'Why couldn't they wait another couple of weeks?'

'Hana said that they want to spend some time with us here. I can't wait to hear what is happening at home.'

'You wanted to come home to Slovenia now you call Australia home,' says Stan.

'Don't you? Maybe we have no home.'

'We have two. Going home from home.'

Only Hana comes down from the plane. She seems composed but under her serene exterior I sense a raging torrent of emotion.

'Toni has some business to attend in Vienna. He will be here in a couple of days,' says Hana.

'That will give us time to catch up on the news,' says Stan. He takes Hana's suitcases and opens the doors with his elbow.

'You must be tired,' says Stan. 'Would you like to go straight home or stop for a drink?'

'I want to go home,' says Hana.

At home Stan again opens the car door to let Hana out. He hands me the smaller bags and takes the suitcases himself. When he opens the front door he lets Hana in and follows after her. I come last. I am happy that Stan is finally nice to my sister. He barely tolerated Hana in Australia. Even Stan is not immune to Hana's charms. I suppose Stan is the only bull in this paddock now and he feels free to display his charms. The thought makes me smile. I am not jealous, of course, I am not. It would be absurd. I realise that in Hana's presence men simply display their plumage like courting birds.

'Sit down and I will get you a drink,' offers Stan while I bring things in. I notice that Stan is generous with vodka. Toni was generous with vodka. Maybe Stan has a chance to be Toni while Toni is away. He never competed with Toni but now he became Toni.

'Put your feet up and stretch on the couch. It's not easy being cramped on the plane for twenty hours,' says Stan as he smooths the cushions and Hana lifts her feet off the floor.

'I am glad you are still here,' says Hana.

'We love the way you decorated your home,' says Stan. He pours himself a little vodka with orange juice and sits next to Hana. He never drank vodka before.

Stan is actually flirting with my sister. I never knew this flirtatious side of him. My sensible husband can be as charming as Toni. Things are never what they seem.

Maybe I tried to be Hana all my life. Maybe I wanted to inspire men like Hana does. Maybe both Stan and I admired what Toni and Hana had.

'I feel quite homesick already. Tell me what it's like in Australia now,' I say sitting next to Hana.

'Is her bed ready,' Stan turns to me.

'Of course it is ready.'

'What would you like to have for dinner? Maybe you would like to eat out.' My romantic husband, I smile to myself. We always took each other for granted. There was never a cause for jealousy. There isn't now either.

'If you go to the restaurant around the corner they prepare take away meals. You can pick something and bring it home, 'says Hana. I think she wants to get rid of Stan.

'How come you decided to return so suddenly?' I ask Hana when we are alone.

'Sasha rang Toni to come urgently.'

'What does she want?'

'She did not say. At least Toni did not tell me.'

'Are you all right?'

'I don't want to go on like this. It might be better if they married and left me alone. I don't need either of them. I am tired.'

'Toni loves you, everybody says so.'

'I don't love Toni any more. I don't even like myself. I just want to sleep and forget the whole nightmare.'

'You are tired.'

'I am tired of life. I was on a roller coaster for too long and I never knew how to get off it.'

'But you enjoyed the ride.'

'I did at the beginning and then I just went along. Toni lies. Everything he says is a lie, he lies without a reason. He is addicted to lying. If one lie does not impress the listeners enough he will invent another. He is an artist creating fiction. The ordinary, mundane reality does not satisfy him. He says what people want to hear. He needs to be admired and loved by everybody so he lies to everybody. I am sure he lies to Sasha. I can't listen to his lies anymore.'

'Did you tell him that?'

'One way or another he managed to convince me that he is telling the truth. If I don't appear convinced he gets into a rage. Or cries. Real wet tears. He is acting like a romantic lover but it is all an act. I am tired of it. He gave me unbelievable excuses for being away all the time. He begged me to believe him and I did.'

'I suppose nobody is absolutely truthful,' I defend Toni's behaviour.

'Toni should be home after tomorrow but I don't really want him,' says Hana.

'Did you argue?'

'He lied to me, to my children, to Sasha and Freddy and everybody else. Nobody knows where they stand with Toni.'

'Maybe that is the secret of his success.'

'You never lied. We relied on you; you made us feel safe, Hana snuggles into my arms.'

'We admired you,' I smile. 'If we could only go back in time. I think about mum and dad often. I remember dad telling us stories. Close your eyes and you can be anything you want to be, dad used to say. Your magic land comes with you wherever you are.'

'I lived my life with my eyes closed,' smiles Hana as Stan brings in a banquet of food.

'You are a good man,' Hana pats Stan's hand. 'I am glad Maria and you are making each other happy.'

'We do our best,' beams my husband. Hana eats very little.

'I slept and ate on the plane,' she says. 'To me it feels like morning.'

'It will be soon. I better leave you two to chat,' offers Stan and goes to bed.

'We had a wonderful time,' I tell Hana.

'I wish we could swap our lives permanently,' smiles Hana. 'I think I need some fresh air to clear my head.'

Hana has been steadily drinking all evening.

'It's almost midnight. Take a sleeping pill instead to get a good night's sleep.'

'I took several but they don't help.'

'I will come with you.'

'I'll be fine. I need to be on my own. I am used to it,' smiles Hana.

The police wakes us at dawn. They tell us to sit down.

'I have bad news,' says the policeman professionally sombre and respectful.

'It's Hana. She was found dead on the side of the road.'

'How? What happened? When?'

'When did you last see Hana?' Policeman ignores my questions. They came to express sympathies and then investigate the circumstances of her death.

My beautiful sister is dead. Left in the ditch beside the road. Found by a dog. A little boy rushed to the police station terrified. I should not have let her go on her own. She wanted to be on her own.

'We were talking late last night. It was close to midnight when I went to bed. Hana wanted to go for a walk on her own. I went to sleep without checking if she returned.'

I wish I knew where Hana travelled in her thoughts as she walked on the dirt road along the river. A car hit her and the driver did not stop. Her body wasn't moved.

'Where is her husband?'

'He had some business in Vienna,' says Stan. 'He should be back tomorrow. I have a number of a friend David who he is staying with. Hana left it on the bench there.'

We are in shock. Tereza, Emil, Sofija and Janez were notified and they come over to the mortuary to identify Hana's body. Janez tries to contact Toni on his mobile but Toni's phone isn't on. The police try to contact his friend David. I leave a message on David's answering machine for Toni to come immediately. I do not say what happened. By late afternoon Toni arrives and goes straight to the police station.

'I wish I was dead instead of Hana. I will never forgive myself. I should have come with her,' says Toni. He cries openly. Sofija and Janez comfort him. People gather around them.

Our town is on the map again. TV cameras follow us, reporters are asking questions. People look sad and ashamed of their imperfections in the face of death. Everybody is watching everybody else for reactions. Everybody is appalled and bewildered.

Two days later they arrest Toni. Traces of Hana's blood were found under the mudguard of his car. The forensic experts demand Toni's clothes and shoes.

Nobody knows why the police came to check Toni's car.

The rumours are alive and spreading fast. I find from the newspaper that forensic police established that Hana was hit by Toni's car. Her body was thrown on the side of the road. There was a heavy rain after the accident and the road was muddy. The autopsy shows that Hana was drunk. She also took tranquillisers. She probably wandered onto the road.

Sasha and Robert come to the church service for Hana. We don't know when the coroner will release the body for burial.

People watch each other as they express their sympathies.

'I am so sorry,' says Sasha. I liked Hana.

I cannot be rude to Sasha at the church service so I accept her condolences. She invites me for coffee. I have a feeling that she wants something. Perhaps she wants me out of her life. I am determined not to give her anything.

'How long are you staying?' She asks as we sit down in a little café.

'Have you seen Toni?' I reply with the question.

'His friend David is coming from Austria to testify that Toni was with him when Hana died,' says Sasha.

David can prove that Toni did not murder Hana, I rearrange her statement.

'In the good old days they used to stamp your passport every time you crossed the border. It would be so much more simple,' smiles Sasha.

'I am sure they will establish his whereabouts at the time of Hana's death,' I say. In my heart I hope that they did stamp Toni's passport and he is holding the proof of his innocence. I don't want to believe that Toni is a murderer.

'Someone must have told the police about the bloodstains under the mudguard of Toni's car,' I say.

'I am sure the police will clear the mystery,' says Sasha. I visit Toni in jail. He looks like a caged lion, handsome even behind bars.

'You believe me,' he looks straight at me. 'You know that I have nothing to do with the accident.' I look at him for a long time. His hands are on the glass partition reaching for my hands. Something tells me that he is innocent. Maybe I am the biggest fool but I want him to be innocent.

'What were you doing in Austria?' I ask.

'Business.'

'You could prove it,' I say.

'David is going to the police to tell them that we were together.' I am looking for a sign of Toni's guilt.

'Do you think that I killed Hana,' asks Toni looking straight through me.

'I don't,' I say without hesitation. I haven't even thought about it properly. How did I make up my mind about his innocence? I want him to be innocent. Is that the effect Toni has on people?Maybe there is still a minute romantic reminder of the romantic me hidden in my sensible cloak, maybe part of me still loves Toni; maybe even a tiny loving renders you blind; incapable to see the truth. 'He is a habitual liar,' Hana's words ring in the background. He is the most convincing liar. He lies for no reason. If you don't believe one lie he tells you another. He tells people what he thinks they want to hear.

'Did they stamp your passports when you crossed from Austria to Slovenia?'

'They don't do that anymore. It means a lot to me that you believe me,' says Toni.

'You will have to convince the jury and the judge.'

'Sasha got it into her head that I will marry her. I never said that I would.'

'Do you think she killed Freddy?'

'She wanted to get rid of Freddy to spite Veronika; and to force me to marry her.'

'Are you going to marry her?'

'Never.'

The loss of my beautiful sister is like a stone in my chest. I cannot even cry to melt the sadness away. I remember the pain when I lost Paula. Part of me died. Paula and Hana. Both of them shone in my life. The light went out. I am less alive. I hope Toni is innocent.

I go to church more or less regularly, I repeat the appropriate words but I did not talk to God since Paula's funeral. Now I need God; I have to reach Hana and Paula; I wish to reach my father and my mother. If there is an afterlife they will remember me. I will live in their memory. We only live in someone's remembering. Hana made our family special. Paula was my guardian angel in Canberra. Mum taught me to be sensible. Dad gave me the magic land. They made me who I am.

I hope that Toni and David were in Austria when Hana was killed. I have to find David before he goes to the police. He has the key. At the airport I introduce myself to the only man of Toni's age that comes on his own. We sit in the airport cafeteria.

'Was Toni with you when Hana was killed,' I ask. David hesitates.

'Toni had to see Sasha before he went home.'

'He was with Sasha.'

'I only promised to cover up so not to upset Hana. I am not covering up for murder. I have to go to the police now and tell them the truth.' I go to see Toni again.

You lied to me,' I say.

'I was with Sasha on the night Hana died but I don't know who drove my car,' Toni confesses. 'If you don't believe one lie he tells you another,' Hana's words ring in my memory.

'You did not have to lie to me,' I say.

'Sasha gave me an ultimatum.'

'What ultimatum?'

'She rang me in Australia and vowed to testify that I killed Freddy if I didn't come immediately.'

'Did you kill Freddy?'

'How can you ask that?'

'Did you?'

'I had no reason to kill him. He was my best friend.'

'Who did?'

'I am going to find out one way or another. I will clear my name.'

'You could have stayed in Australia.'

'Everything I have is here. In Australia I am nothing. My family is everything to me.'

'What about Sasha?'

'I told her that I love Hana. I would do anything for Sasha but I wasn't prepared to leave Hana.'

'What did Sasha say to that?'

'She is a cunning bitch. I suppose she is much like I am.'

'You must have an idea who killed Freddy and Hana. Could it be Milos?'

'He was with Robert.'

'What about Robert?'

'Robert would lie and cheat but he would not kill. Could it be an accident? Or a suicide. She was drunk. They found tranquillisers in her blood.'

'Someone killed her with your car; she died very conveniently for you and Sasha.'

'I should have been with her. She wasn't thinking straight,' says Toni.

I still cannot believe that Toni killed Hana. He wouldn't do it to his children. 'Everything he says is a lie,' I remember Hana's words. I have no idea what a liar could do.

'All I ever wanted is to make Hana happy. She was a much better person than I am,' says Toni.

One is happy or one is not, mum used to say. You cannot make an unhappy person happy.

'You are the only person that really believes me. You know me.' I see real tears running through Toni's fingers as he covers his face. Is he crying for himself or for Hana? Is Toni crying to convince me that he is telling the truth? 'Real wet tears,' said Hana.

'I am sure your friends will help you prove that you are innocent.'

'I returned a couple of hours after Hana. Sasha and I spent the night drinking and arguing. She is a vindictive person.'

'Do you think Sasha killed Hana?'

'She was with me when Hana was killed.'

'Did she get Milos and Robert to kill Hana?'

'Milos is after Sasha's money. I hate the cunning bastard but he had no reason to kill Hana.'

'Hana had a premonition that something dreadful was going to happen. She was running away from a woman with a stick.'

'I tried to make it up to Hana,' I really did. Maybe I should have never married her. She was too good for me.'

'Who else knew that you were with Sasha?'

'Robert knew. Possibly Milos. I don't think that Robert would cover up for anyone. I don't know if Sasha told anybody else. Robert became a pawn in Milos' schemes.'

'Would Milos frame you to get rid of you?'

'Hana probably recognised the car and wanted to stop it. It makes sense. Whoever was driving for whatever reason simply did not stop. She was thrown off the road and he went on his way. He had no way of knowing that Hana would be on that road. But why my car?'

'The driver of the car must have told the police about the bloodstains. He wanted to frame you.'

'That's it,' we must find out who informed the police,' Toni cheers up. 'It shouldn't be too hard. It must be someone we know. It must have been done on the phone. I have to talk to my lawyer.'

'One way or another the truth will come out.'

'If we could only turn back the clock.' Toni looks at me with tears in his eyes. It would be so easy to comfort him. I place my hands on the cold glass to cover Toni's hands. There is a cold barrier between us, there always was. Just as well we can only touch the glass partition. Toni once saved my life. He once kissed me. I have never experienced anything like that again. The light was turned on and my life became illuminated. Everything had a miraculous glow until I found Hana and Toni kissing under that cherry tree.

For a brief moment Toni and I returned into that moment when we were still so undamaged.

'I am going home. I wish you all the best,' I say. He must not see me cry. I am glad to leave Toni behind. I do not have to agonise whether he is telling the truth. Nothing will bring back my beautiful sister. He is welcome to say whatever he wants. He is not real. A sense of freedom overwhelms me. Toni is nothing to me.

Toni and Hana were the prince and the princess who lived in the magic land happily ever after. I lived in the safety of Hana's shadow. Maybe Stan also lived in Toni's shadow. We were the spectators of their heroics and shared in their glory while we plodded on with our ordinary lives. My father told us that one finds the magic land within himself. Perhaps my magic land is my family in Australia.

I will never know what was going on in Hana's head and heart. She took all her thoughts with her.

'It's time for us to go home,' says Stan.

The whole family come to say goodbye. There is a family likeness, the names are familiar; there is a common language.

The places we created in each other's hearts and homes will be quickly filled with other things. Something old and something new and great empty distances in between.

'Stan is homesick,' I tell my family.

'It will be good to leave all this behind,' I say to Stan.

Our past is here but the only past for our children is in Australia. Stan and I are the only family they have. Deep inside I carried regrets because I deprived my children of their rightful home and family but now I know that home is where you blossom. My children blossomed in Australia. I have no right to take away their home.

I wonder what my children remember. Maybe I should have taken time to get to know the people that touched my children with words and actions. Maybe I should know the secret, sacred places they remember in their silent intimate moments. Maybe I should walk into their magic land. Or maybe I shouldn't. This is their chapter of life, their blossoming. I only provided the nourishment for them to blossom. Everybody only has one chance to experience the magic world of becoming.

I provided the house and the garden where our children may have found whatever the home is meant to be. My blossoming produced fruit to sustain theirs. There must be a familiar corner in my garden where my boys stored their memories for safekeeping; where they left bits of themselves and of their childhood. They carry with them the words that were part of their becoming. I wonder what part of me they carry to pass on to the next chapter of life. Stan and I were a family and a nation for our children. Something old and something new.

Chinese carried the bones of their ancestors so they would not be strangers in the new country. I carry memories. I will tell my grandchildren about my father's magic land. Perhaps they found magic land on the computer.

With your eyes open you see distances and obstacles, dad said, but close your eyes and you become a part of the tapestry of life where every colour and every fragment is equally important.

I visit Hana's grave before we leave. She rests next to my father and mother.

'Hana had everything to live for,' says Tereza.

'The bastard should rot in hell,' says Stan.

Nobody asks which bastard.

'Until we meet amongst angels,' mum had the words inscribed in the stone on dad's grave.

I have to believe that there is another life, another chance to be whatever we are meant to be. Redemption and afterlife is all we need to believe in.

'I am glad we came,' I say to Stan.

'Maybe we would never come if it wasn't for Toni.'

'For the sake of their children I still hope that he is innocent.'

'Don't waste your sympathies on Toni.'

'I think he loved Hana.'

'He had a funny way of showing it.'

'Janez and Sofija believe that Toni is innocent.'

'There is a chance that Sasha and Toni were in the car that killed Hana,' says Stan on the plane. 'Maybe they only intended to tell Hana that they will get married.'

'Perhaps it was an accident.'

'We will never know.'

'The truth finds a way to the surface.'

'I love Australia,' I say as our plane circles over Canberra again. The tranquillity of the Australian Capital Territory feels good after the hustle and bustle of Europe.

'It is great to be home again,' says Stan.

'This is home,' I say as my eyes embrace the city we helped build and change.

'Canberra grew up with us. Can you imagine that this was a sheep paddock when we were born,' says Stan.

Canberra is spread into the hills and valleys around Lake Burley Griffin. The valleys are a perfect basin for this artificial lake so people can choose to have water views from their homes. The hills give people an opportunity to build their homes high up and enjoy the view over the city.

'Canberra was good to us,' I say to Stan as we fasten the seat belts for landing.

'We have everything we need here,' says Stan

'This city is a monument to builders like you.'

'It needed to be built so we built it.'

Wherever you drive in Canberra you are likely to spot a house Stan built. European non-English speaking tradesmen built the city for English speaking public servants employed by the government. When we arrived most Australian married women did not go out to work. Migrant women joined the work force and their children grew up almost unnoticed.

I am sorry Paula is not here to look at my snapshots and hear my tales. I realise that I have nobody to tell about the tragedy of Hana's life. Comedies and tragedies on television are more colourful. It is different at home in Slovenia where everybody is related, connected and familiar; they want to know.

I got used to my solitary life. One really gets used to anything.

Australians are distracted with the Centenary celebration of the Federation right now. One hundred years of Australian nationhood. We look at the road we travelled and the changes we have seen and made.

Much of Australia was built and changed by the young, eager Europeans. The winds of war scattered us all over the world.

'Snowy Mountains Scheme is one such monument to new Australians. Canberra is another,' says Stan.

'We were part of both.'

'I am proud.'

People listen politely as I tell my travel stories. They are only mildly interested in the video we made in memory of our once in a lifetime experience. Our children only took minutes to go through hundreds of snapshots of their relatives and other people who would love to meet them. They barely knew Toni and Hana. They were never touched by Slovenia.

People share world news about terrorism and dangers of new diseases. Wars and threats of wars. Bible groups warn that the end of the world is near.

Tereza writes about events that are still alive in our memory.

The forensic experts checked the car again. They found fresh unknown fingerprints and hair and fibre that did not belong to either Sasha or Toni or Hana. They still did not find the person who drove Toni's car.

Toni rings from America. He and Sasha are travelling around the world.

'Nothing to do with us,' says Stan.

Biographical information about the author, Cilka Zagar

I, Cilka Zagar, was born in Slovenia. I have a Bachelor of Education Degree from Western College of Advanced Education in Perth. I majored in Inter-cultural studies. I also completed the Major in Justice Studies with Edith Cowan University. I worked as a primary school teacher. Most of my work was in special education. I also worked as an Adult education teacher with TAFE. I am a NAATI accredited interpreter.

I have been an Aboriginal liaison officer and have often represented the views of Aborigines and migrants. I write fiction and non-fiction and had books published in English and Slovenian languages.

In 1990 Aboriginal Studies Press published my book *Growing Up Walgett.*

I collected local Aboriginal legends and history which were published by Armidale Catholic Education Office.

In 2000 Magabala published my book *Goodbye Riverbank.*

In 1995 my novel *Barbara* was translated into Slovenian and Mohorjeva Druzba published it in Ljubljana.

My novel *Magdalena and the Black Opals* was translated into Slovenian and published by Mladinska knjiga in Ljubljana in March 2000.

In 2004 I wrote biographies of eleven women from eleven countries which Historical society published under the name *OPALADIES.*

In 2007 Historical society published the biographies of eleven Lightning Ridge miners who came from eleven countries under the title *Opaladdies*.

I published numerous novels, poetry and histories with Print-on-Demand Availability.

I am a regular contributor to Slovenian and English publications.

In 2018 Slovenian Matica published my book of poems *Od tu do tja nikjer doma.*

Review Requested:

If you loved this book, would you please provide a review at Amazon.com and Amazon.co.uk?